Keep You SAFE

MELISSA HILL

HQ

ONE PLACE. MANY STORIES

HQ
An imprint of HarperCollinsPublishers Ltd.
1 London Bridge Street
London SE1 9GF

This edition 2017

1
First published in Great Britain by
HQ, an imprint of HarperCollinsPublishers Ltd. 2017

ISBN HB: 978-0-00-821712-9
TPB: 978-0-00-821714-3

Printed and bound by
CPI Group (UK) Ltd, Croydon, CR0 4YY

With much love and thanks to Sheila Crowley
– a true force of nature.

Chapter 1

The bell rang out and on cue they started to approach all at once, like a stampeding herd.

Standing back to let the first wave pass while shivering in late March wind and cold, I pulled my gloved hands out of my pockets and tugged my woolly hat a bit more firmly down over my ears, tucking my wispy dark hair underneath it. Another blast of wind hit me in the face, turning my cheeks an even brighter shade of pink.

I knew that I could just stay in my car and keep warm while waiting for my five-year-old, Rosie, to emerge from Junior Infants class at Applewood Primary. However, she and I have a ritual of sorts and the typically inclement Irish weather wasn't going to stand in the way of it.

Each and every day after school, I wait for Rosie just outside the school building, a bit down the front path by the main hall. During the more temperate months we walk the half-mile home together to our two-bed cottage in Knockroe, a small satellite town about forty minutes' drive from Dublin.

I have never failed to meet Rosie in our chosen spot since she started school seven months ago. I was determined to never let her exit the class and not have me there – at least until my daughter told me that she wanted to walk home by herself or with friends. I wasn't one of those helicopter parents or anything like that, but, come hell or high water, I would make sure I was there – especially since Rosie was still having nightmares about that one time after preschool.

The day when no one was waiting.

Hard to believe that fateful day was almost two years ago – it still felt like only yesterday. A chill worked its way up my spine – one that this time wasn't triggered by the cold.

In her preschool days, my husband Greg had been the one responsible for picking up Rosie. Working from home as a free-lance software designer, it was he who had more flexibility and usually had the opportunity to step away from the office he kept in the spare bedroom, and head over to the preschool to pick up our daughter. Since I work as a nurse at a clinic in a nearby town, I generally keep more irregular hours.

I had long been thankful that my husband could play such an active role in Rosie's childhood, especially while my own commitments prevented me from being around as much as I would have liked.

My commitments are different these days.

Because there had been one time when Greg couldn't make it to the preschool at the allotted time of 12.45 to pick Rosie up. Not because he didn't want to, had forgotten or neglected to pay attention to the time, but because he had collapsed in our kitchen earlier that morning while making himself a cup of tea.

Sudden Adult Death Syndrome had ended my beloved husband's life in seconds; he likely didn't even realise what was happening.

I wasn't aware that I'd been made a widow when the preschool teacher called me at work that afternoon to say that they couldn't get in touch with Greg at home. That terrible realisation didn't come until later.

Calling our home phone as well as Greg's mobile, trying to figure out what was going on, I remember feeling irritated that Rosie and her teacher had been left waiting. I was annoyed at Greg and wondered where he was, especially since I couldn't get an answer on any phone. So I told my supervisor at the clinic that I needed to head out; pick up my child in Knockroe, drop her home to her dad and would then come back to finish my shift.

It was only after I had sped the short distance there, apologised to the preschool teacher and hustled my daughter back to the house, that I realised my life was forever changed. If I could go back to that moment so I could enter the kitchen first in order to prevent Rosie from finding her father immobile on the floor, I would.

As it was, there was no changing the past, but I would do my damnedest to make sure that I was always there at the end of the school day so that she didn't fear the same thing happening to me. She'd already had a tough enough time of it for a five-and-a-half-year-old.

My daughter was everything to me – all that I had these days.

Rosie's classmates started to appear, refocusing my thoughts and preventing me from once again going down that dark road of introspection as I examined our lives without Greg. Scanning the crowd of Junior Infants, I immediately picked out Rosie's bright green winter hat, shaped like the head of a T. Rex. My little girl had never been the princess type. She adored dinosaurs, wolves, dragons – anything fierce and scary – perhaps even more so since her dad died, and I often wonder if in her own little way she finds comfort in their strength.

'Mum!' she called, waving a hand, as if I hadn't spotted her yet, her dark curls bouncing as she moved, green eyes wide with excitement. She dragged her backpack – dino-themed again – slightly on the ground and I walked forward to grab it. I didn't want to have to shell out for another any time soon. As a single parent, I now did everything I could to avoid unnecessary expenses, especially when we only had my salary to depend on.

Though both in our late-thirties, my late husband and I had been one of the burgeoning number of Irish families who, despite both being gainfully employed, still couldn't quite afford that first step on the housing ladder, and the money we'd been saving to buy a house (minimal at best, as the rental house in Knockroe wasn't cheap) now had to go towards day-to-day household expenses, as well as the creation of a small contingency fund – just in case.

These days, I was a big believer in contingencies.

'Hey, honey,' I answered, closing the distance between us. 'Here, give me that, don't drag it.' Rambunctious by nature, Rosie was hard on shoes and on school belongings, and was growing out of her clothes at a pace that staggered me. She took my hand without breaking stride, and walked determinedly towards our battered old Astra while I trailed in her wake.

'Be careful, don't step in the mud,' I cautioned automatically. 'And why don't you have your boots on? Where are they?' I looked disbelievingly at the flimsy ballet flats she currently sported.

'They're in the bag. I don't need them; sure we're only getting in the car.' She shrugged and not for the first time, I was taken aback by how much like Greg she sounded. Always so easy-going and carefree, while I was the one more inclined to worry.

We reached the car and I opened the door so Rosie could jump in the back seat. 'Buckle up. Car or not, I'd still prefer you to wear your boots in this weather, hon. We don't want you coming down with a cold and your boots are warmer.' I shut the door and headed around to the driver's side. Climbing in, I fished my iPhone out of my pocket and handed it to her. 'Here you go, DJ,' I said pre-emptively, knowing that when Rosie was in the car she liked to take charge of the music, usually opting for the American rock anthems so beloved by her father. 'So what happened in school today?'

I started the car and pulled out of the parking area as the heat blasted, and Rosie summoned up the Eagles' 'Take It Easy' and began telling me about her day. She outlined all that had occurred, from the new letters they were learning to the Brachiosaurus picture she had drawn in art. I hummed words of encouragement until something she said caused a tinge of panic to flutter through my heart.

'And they sent Ellie home after lunch because she's sick.'

'What's wrong with her?' I asked casually. Ellie Madden sat beside Rosie in class. I wasn't a hypochondriac or anything – as a nurse I couldn't be, or I'd drive myself crazy – but I was always keenly aware of my daughter's health, as well as that of her classmates.

I had to be.

'She has chicken pox,' said Rosie dramatically, though she kept her attention firmly focused on my iPhone.

Chicken pox. I quickly felt myself relax, though I felt for poor Ellie and her parents.

Such diseases were a normal rite of passage for school-going kids – especially so soon after the Easter holidays when infection tended to be rampant amongst friends and families meeting up during the break. But chicken pox was something I had dealt with firsthand with Rosie a couple of years before, so at least I didn't have to worry about it. But that didn't mean I was worry free either.

'Ah, I see. I wonder are there many in your class who haven't had it yet.' I tried to think of what other poor kid – and parents – from the school might soon fall victim.

'Ms Connelly asked around after they saw the spots on Ellie's neck. There were only a few: Kevin, Abigail and Clara, I think. I can't get them again, can I?' Rosie peered up from the device then, concern in her eyes, as I turned into our driveway and parked outside the small two-storey house we'd moved into as a family two and a half years ago.

As I got out of the car and helped Rosie gather her things, I shook my head.

'No, you can't,' I confirmed. 'I mean, technically, you can later as an adult but it's called shingles then.' Rosie was a naturally curious type and loved soaking up facts and general knowledge. My more traditional West Cork parents found it strange the way Greg and I had always talked so honestly to her from the get-go, instead of dumbing things down for kids like their generation often did.

'Good,' said Rosie as she walked into the house. 'I *hated* being itchy.'

Though Greg and I had met, worked and lived in Dublin for all of our five-year marriage before Rosie came along, we both hailed from small-town backgrounds, and had hoped that moving to a closer-knit community in a more rural setting would be good for Rosie – particularly when she started school. So when I was offered a nursing position in a recently opened clinic in the larger town of Glencree – five miles away – we decided the quaint little village of Knockroe was the perfect place to put down roots.

While I loved the place, I still felt a bit like an outsider in the community, especially after losing my husband less than a year after moving there. Because I worked in the neighbouring town,

I hadn't got to know many Knockroe locals all that well, save for the other school parents and a few of the neighbours close by. Most of the townspeople, though kind, tended to leave me to my own devices and, shy by nature, this mostly suited me.

Though I'd had no choice but to come out of my shell over the last seven months or so when it came to the school run and other Applewood Primary-related events, like the Christmas pageant, odd fundraiser and occasional birthday party or play date.

After following my daughter inside, I went into the kitchen and deposited her belongings on the counter. I listened to Rosie's footsteps on the stairs as she headed up to her room. While she never admitted it, she routinely avoided going straight to the kitchen when she first entered the house. I had never asked her about it and guessed it was a coping mechanism she had devised for herself after dealing with what she had seen on That Day.

I opened her backpack and pulled out her books, lunchbox, as well as a couple of school notes directed to parents. Yep, there was indeed one about chicken pox asking parents to be vigilant. Much like the one we'd got for head lice before Easter.

The joys of primary school.

But these school-related bugs brought to the forefront another temporarily dormant fear I didn't like to revisit. I hated being reminded of the fact, but here's the truth: Rosie wasn't vaccinated for any such typical childhood illnesses – mumps, measles or the like.

I had found out very quickly that when you made such an admission to health professionals, school authorities, or, worst of all, other parents, you were immediately judged. Written off as irresponsible, foolish and downright stupid.

But in reality I wasn't any of those things – rather Rosie was severely allergic to the gelatin component in almost all live vaccines.

Greg and I had only discovered the issue after she had experienced a horrific cardiorespiratory reaction after her first round of immunisations as a baby. Back then, we were faced with a horrible decision and literally caught between a rock and a hard place.

Our daughter could face a potentially life-threatening situation if she wasn't vaccinated, but was certain to if she was.

Damned if you do, damned if you don't.

So after countless hours of research, much soul-searching and finally on the advice of our GP, we had no choice but to opt Rosie out of the standard childhood vaccination programme and hope against hope that herd immunity would prevail.

This was why I was acutely aware of infectious disease warnings from school; I couldn't afford not to be.

It was my job to keep her safe.

Chapter 2

'Clara Rose and Jake Alan – you'd both better be ready to go!' called Madeleine Cooper as she stood at the bottom of the stairs that led up to her kids' bedrooms.

She hoped the use of their middle names would light a fire under their asses and get them moving. She impatiently looked down at the small gold watch that she wore on her wrist and pursed her lips. Nope; they were going to be late.

Looking once more up the stairs, she raised her voice a few more decibels. 'I'm *serious*. If the two of you aren't down here in the next ten seconds, I'm telling your father. Ten – nine – eight…' Her voice trailed off as five-year-old Clara's bedroom door was first flung open, followed by eight-year-old Jake's a beat later.

Two blond heads rushed onto the landing so fast they almost collided, but continued on racing down the stairs. Madeleine cringed as her son ran his hands across the glass-fronted staircase as he made his way down. A day didn't go by where she didn't have to clean grubby handprints off everything. As her husband Tom routinely argued, the minimalist decor that looked so cool in the interiors magazines wasn't the cleverest idea for a house with children. But Madeleine sure as hell wasn't compromising on comfort over style. Just because you had kids didn't mean they should rule the roost.

'Look, it's not as if this is a new thing,' she chided. 'We *always* go to Granny Cooper's on Monday nights. And we haven't seen her since before the holidays.' The two murmured something apologetic as they rushed through the hallway to fetch their coats and Madeleine turned back towards the kitchen to where Tom sat at the table checking over the kids' homework. 'Are you ready, honey?' she asked. 'Your mother will be wondering where we are.'

'Pure nonsense, all this new-fangled phonics stuff,' he said in a distracted voice, and from that angle Madeleine noticed a couple of new silver streaks in his hair. And the stress lines that had been eased somewhat during their trip to Florida over the Easter break had sadly since returned to her handsome husband's forehead.

The four of them had had such a ball in Clearwater, swimming and kayaking in the gulf, taking endless walks along the powdery sand, and enjoying sunset barbecues on the patio of the beach house they'd rented for their two-week stay.

The frowning man sitting in front of Madeleine now was a million miles from the one laughing and splashing in the water with the kids by day, and strumming Willie Nelson tunes on his guitar as the sun went down over the Gulf of Mexico.

Back to reality.

'What ever happened to just learning the letters instead of pronouncing the sounds?' Tom complained. 'That teacher of Jake's has a lot of nerve too. Look at what she wrote on his maths homework from last week; he actually got points off even though he answered the bloody question correctly. All because he didn't do it with the "new" standards. A load of crap, if you ask me. All these lazy pen-pushers in the Department of Education who know nothing about education making nonsensical new rules that we don't need.'

Madeleine rolled her eyes good-naturedly at yet another diatribe from her husband on why the 'new-fangled' ways of learning were ridiculous – totally different to how *they* did things back in their day. A contrarian by nature, it wasn't unusual for Tom to rail against the status quo, but times moved on and she was sure the teachers knew what they were doing. In truth, Clara was a lot further on in reading than Madeleine had been in her very first year at school. However, it was late and she didn't have time to discuss this just now, especially since she knew what his *next* point would be.

'This is why we should be thinking again about homeschooling them. Because of this palaver. I've told you, Maddie, it's seriously worth looking into—'

'Not now,' she said, cutting her husband off, irritated that he seemed to have forgotten the fact that, like him, she had a job, so where on earth would she get the time?

But her 'job' – a popular blogging channel for mums that was rapidly growing in popularity and reputation – was all too easily overlooked. To Tom, *Mad Mum* was just a frivolous hobby and a means for Madeleine to entertain herself while the kids were at school. How quickly he'd forgotten that she was once a marketing executive at the top of her game, before giving it all up six years ago and in some fit of madness (the blog wasn't just a play on her name) taking early redundancy to be a stay-at-home mother. Madeleine grimaced. She adored Jake and Clara but God knew (as did so many of *Mad Mum*'s fans) that she was never going to be a candidate for Mother of the Year.

Though to be fair, Tom was an amazing dad; brilliant with the kids (way better than she was most of the time) and a wonderful husband. He was senior management in a top Irish bank and related job pressures meant that she'd always borne the majority of the childcare load.

All well and good while the kids were younger, but now that they were both in school, was it really that terrible for Madeleine to want to get some of her own life back?

She supposed she shouldn't blame him too much though; her husband had just become so used to the current family dynamic that he'd forgotten the fact that she needed something other than parenthood to define her. And *Mad Mum* filled that role very well.

Madeleine had originally started the blog as a means of blowing off steam while alone in the house with the kids all day, bemoaning the day-to-day trials of motherhood in a good-natured but deliberately *non*-mumsy way. At work, writing compelling copy for various campaigns had always come naturally to her, so this felt like a natural extension. And by outlining her frustrations and warts 'n' all experiences with her new-found domestic role, it was, she supposed, an attempt to rail against the po-faced and somewhat smug 'how-to' guides for mums already out there, and she sensed an appetite for some down-to-earth straight talking.

Still, she'd been taken aback by the overwhelmingly positive response her witterings had received, and very quickly her visitor numbers and social media following spiked to remarkable heights. Ever the marketeer, she quickly realised that she had, quite by accident, amassed a captive and thus potentially very valuable demographic, one that admired and trusted her.

But it was really only when Clara started play school a couple of years ago, freeing up Madeleine's mornings, that she'd taken steps to turn *Mad Mum* into an actual business.

And while Tom had always been supportive of her endeavours, over the last year or so, she got the sense that he was a little taken aback by the business's increasing drain on her time as she set determinedly about securing advertising and sponsorship. Of course he didn't yet have a true inkling of exactly what those efforts were achieving.

But her beloved would get one hell of a surprise at the meeting they'd scheduled with their accountant next week when he realised Madeleine's 'little' media business might actually end up pulling in something close to his salary soon. Thanks to the blog's burgeoning visitor numbers, avid social media followers, as well as recent TV appearances, her profile was on the rise, and the site had already pulled in some heavy-hitter online advertising partners.

No way was she going to cut the boots from under all that by going back to having the kids at home all day. In truth, Clara starting proper school last year and thus Madeleine getting her life back had been a godsend, and the additional free time the impetus she'd craved to get her business plan into high gear.

'Hon, we don't have time to talk about it now,' she told Tom, glad of an excuse to fob him off. She loved him and they'd always been a great team, but there was no denying that middle age (and no doubt parenthood) was turning her once laid-back and easy-going husband into a grumpy old man. Such a pity that their next family holiday wouldn't be until the summer; though she could help Tom recapture some of that relaxed gulf coast vibe by plying him with the odd margarita now and then, she thought wickedly.

After grabbing her handbag, Madeleine checked her freshly curled and newly lightened tresses in the hallway mirror, and once again tried to hustle her errant family out the door.

Hopefully the 'bouncy do' would hold up well enough for tomorrow's TV appearance. Madeleine had only got the call from the Channel 2 producer immediately after lunch and had just managed to snag a last-minute appointment with her trusty hairdresser before picking Clara up from school. She wanted to look her best for her slot on *Morning Coffee*, a popular lifestyle show featuring an ever-changing panel of female guests chatting about interesting topics of the day.

Tomorrow they would be discussing *Mad Mum*'s latest blog – a controversial piece by Madeleine, which had very quickly gone viral, about why maternity leave was a Very Bad Thing. She smiled, looking forward to the inevitable public outcry and debate, something her profile thrived on.

While most of her posts about motherhood were often deliberately tongue-in-cheek, this was a topic she actually believed in wholeheartedly. If it wasn't for maternity leave, and how it neatly assigned all the earliest and most difficult child-rearing responsibilities onto the hapless mother – setting up a lifelong 'default parent' and allowing Dad to take a less active role – then she and Tom wouldn't be even *having* the homeschooling conversation.

Placing his pen down, her husband conceded. 'All right, maybe we can talk about it later. I'm just sick to the teeth of civil servants telling us how to live our lives, Maddie. I know how *I* learned maths and look at me now? What's wrong with kids learning things the old-fashioned way?'

'I know, I know, it's all so different these days,' she soothed, kissing him on the head. 'But get your ass in gear – we'll be late at your mum's.' Not that Harriet Cooper would mind. Tom's mother was as laid-back as they came and, unlike Madeleine's own late mum (who before she died two years ago was routinely scandalised by the forthright opinions her daughter laid bare in public), was a big supporter of *Mad Mum*.

Tom got up and followed her into the hallway where their children waited, lost in their own conversation.

'Clara, for goodness' sake, stop sniffling and just blow your nose. Go on the two of you, get in the car,' Tom chided them good-naturedly, as he helped Madeleine on with her coat, a sand-coloured cashmere Ralph Lauren number she adored.

Another major benefit to earning her own money again; she could once more afford the beautiful things she'd had to forgo when they were just a single-earner family. She wrapped a colourful silk scarf around her neck and pulled on her leather gloves. She'd picked out a gorgeous DVF top for her TV stint tomorrow, something patterned to try to compensate for the fact that the camera added ten pounds. Which reminded Madeleine to see about maybe arranging weekly group running sessions with some of her friends. Now pushing forty, she knew she needed to try harder to keep herself in tip-top shape.

The couple followed their children out to Tom's BMW, which sat parked in the driveway of their five-bed faux-Georgian house, about half a mile from Knockroe village. Both kids were now loaded in and sitting dutifully in the back seat, already enraptured with the DVD screens on the back of the front seats. She and Tom did attempt to keep in check the amount of screen time they seemed to default to, but there was no denying that the darned things kept them quiet.

Might write a piece about that soon, she thought wickedly, her mind racing. Something irreverent and completely contrary, sure to send the do-gooders into convulsions.

Tom started the engine and backed out of the long pebbled driveway, just as Cara began a heavy fit of sneezing. He made a face. 'Here we go. Did you see that note from school today? About the girl in Clara's class sent home earlier.'

Madeleine was checking her reflection in the mirror and reapplying her lipstick. 'No, I haven't had a chance to go through their bags.' She sighed inwardly. 'Why – is something going round?'

He shrugged. 'Nothing serious. Chicken pox apparently.' He threw an eye back at their sniffling daughter who did look pretty miserable. 'But Clara hasn't had that yet.'

Madeleine knew. 'Well, I suppose we'll just have to cross our fingers,' she said optimistically, for Clara's benefit. Little ears heard everything and she didn't want her daughter worrying unnecessarily. While the pox wasn't too serious, it was uncomfortable all the same, and her heart broke at the notion of her little girl coming out in those nasty sores and, depending on the severity of the dose, perhaps even being bedridden for a few days, poor thing.

Of course, one of the great benefits of working from home was that Madeleine didn't have to call in sick to take care of the children if needs be. It was one of the reasons she'd taken the redundancy package in the first place; Jake been a poorly toddler and she had been exhausted from making excuses for missed meetings and freaking out over work absences for the first two years of his life. The logistics became even more of an issue when Clara was born, so while Madeleine had been dubious as to whether full-time motherhood was really for her, a much-needed respite from all the haring around (as well as the financial package her firm was offering) was ultimately too difficult to ignore.

Still, to her mind, time away from the workplace was always going to be a temporary arrangement – at least until the kids were old enough and she found something else to sustain her creatively and professionally. Thankfully *Mad Mum* filled that role on both counts.

But she worried the family had become a little too comfortable with these domestic arrangements and now her thoughts came full circle and again returned to Tom's argument for homeschooling. Once again, *she'd* be the one having to make the sacrifice and, work commitments aside, why would she want to take on the responsibility of that along with everything else?

She was already overcommitted to not only her business, but also volunteering for various school fundraisers, her book club, Knockroe Tidy Towns and other community endeavours, not to mention that she could be called for a guest slot to any TV or radio station at a moment's notice.

In order to grow her business to the level that Madeleine aspired, profile was important – it made a huge difference, as any marketeer worth their salt would tell you.

Not that her kids' education *wasn't* important of course – it was just nice to be able to pack them both off to school each day and have someone else deal with them for a while.

Madeleine sighed again as she wondered if she was a bad mother for thinking that way, but then chided herself. She knew from day one that she wasn't going to be perfect. It was a bit late now for stressing about it.

She was only vaguely aware that the car had gone silent and that her family's attention was on her. 'I'm sorry? What was that?' she asked, turning to face her husband. She noticed that Tom was frowning.

'Is it true, Mum?' Clara asked, her nose streaming and Madeleine gulped. Damn, the poor dote really was coming down with something. Hopefully it would be a day or two before the worst of it kicked in.

At least until the TV thing is over and done with…

Yep, she was indeed a bad mother. Terrible.

'Is what true, sweetheart?' she replied.

'What Kevin Campbell said; that he's never had chicken pox, and when people get sick at school that it's *our* fault,' her five-and-a-half-year-old said indignantly.

Madeleine gritted her teeth. Number one, Kevin Campbell was a known brat who liked to start trouble, and number two, the kid had no idea what he was talking about. But number three – and more to the point – Kevin Campbell's mother was obviously gossiping about *their* family within hearing distance of her child.

Now she understood why Tom looked so annoyed. He couldn't stand Christine Campbell – not only was she always in everyone's business in Knockroe, trying to tell them how to live their lives and thinking she was so smart with her 'supposed' Diploma in Sociology from UCD, but she was also a notorious shit-stirrer.

And Madeleine knew that Christine especially hated how, with the increased popularity of her blog and subsequent TV appearances, Madeleine's profile and thus her community standing had grown and threatened to supersede Christine's own self-imposed Queen Bee status. Not that she had the slightest iota of interest in celebrity or overthrowing Christine's 'reign' – she was all about expanding *Mad Mum*'s reach.

But it was completely out of order for the woman to make such comments, especially in earshot of her son. Jake and Clara shouldn't be singled out like that. And moreover, her and Tom's parenting decisions didn't need to be questioned – by anyone. It was nobody else's business.

'Ah, don't listen to what Kevin says. He has no idea what he's talking about. Just ignore him.'

'But is it true, Mum?' Jake piped up, interested. 'Would it be our fault if other kids got sick? Because we don't get injections like everyone else?'

'No, it wouldn't be your fault,' Tom said, through gritted teeth. He turned to look at his wife. 'I'm going to phone that Campbell woman and—'

Madeleine quickly laid a calming hand on his arm. 'Don't give her the pleasure,' she interjected wisely. 'You know Christine relishes getting a rise out of people, and she would love nothing more than to debate with us, *again*, on the vaccination thing. Just ignore her.' Christine Campbell and her ilk never failed to get her husband – who was fiercely protective of not only his family, but also his principles – riled up.

She turned round to face her kids. 'Guys, your classmates getting chicken pox is not your fault and never will be. OK?'

To say nothing of the fact that you didn't usually vaccinate for chicken pox anyway. So at least they didn't need to worry on that front, and hand-wringers like Christine Campbell could go stuff it.

Clara and Jake nodded solemnly.

'We're here.' Madeleine smiled, as Tom pulled into the entrance of his mother's home on the other side of the town, and she unsnapped her seat belt, mentally crossing her fingers that Clara's sniffles were just your typical run-of-the-mill perma-cold and nothing more troublesome. At least not anything that would put the kibosh on her plans for tomorrow. 'So stop thinking about whatever nonsense Kevin was spouting,' she reassured her children, 'and focus on wishing poor Ellie get well soon.'

Chapter 3

'**P**ut the kettle on and crank up that coffee-maker, it's *Morning Coffee* time! Our panel today is outspoken *Daily Record* journalist and media commenter Gemma Moore, bestselling author Anita Wright, former Miss Ireland and beauty expert Claudine O'Donnell, and the newcomer to today's gang, mummy blogger Madeleine Cooper, whose no-nonsense and provocative take on motherhood has garnered her a huge following amongst many Irish women, myself included. Madeleine, welcome to the show.'

'Thanks a mill, Louise, it's lovely to be here.'

'So let's dive straight in. Your latest article… it's already racked up hundreds of thousands of hits, has been retweeted a quarter of a million times, and has also been a major focus of discussion in some of the papers, including Gemma's *Daily Record* – in short it has the place abuzz. Needless to say, Madeleine, you've hit a nerve.'

'It would seem so.'

'First, let's just explain to any of our viewers who might not yet have come across your article… Madeleine suggests that maternity leave is – and these are your own words – "a patriarchal construct that *disempowers* women". How on earth did you come to that conclusion?'

'Well, like I said in my piece, Louise, maternity leave, this statutory practice of assigning care of the newborn solely to mothers for the first six months, sets up a lifelong family dynamic, whereby dads get to go off and carry on as normal, while poor sleep-deprived Mammy is at home meeting all of junior's needs.'

'Sleep-deprived, ha! Yes, we can all definitely relate to that bit.' 'But in reality this doesn't just last for six months. Mum becomes the default carer all through life, the child's go-to for everything whether she likes it or not, which means that *she* – not Dad – is always the one forsaking things to meet that responsibility.'

'Anita, I see you shaking your head there. You don't agree with Madeleine?'

'Of course not. Maternity leave isn't just about meeting the child's practical needs; it's scientifically proven that for the first few months parental proximity is essential for bonding and emotional development—'

'But I'm not denying that at all, and actually by using the word *parent* you've hit the nail on the head. My beef is with the idea that it's women who, by nature of the fact that parental leave is a statutory requirement for them only, are automatically expected to take on that role, whether they like it or not. Really, it's akin to state-sponsored servitude.'

'Well! Strong words…'

'Servitude? Come on: a mother taking time off to look after her own child?'

'But it's far from time off, Anita – that's my point. It's a job in itself and a tough one, we all know that. During that time, we're expected to go off, have our kids, hide away at home or at mother-and-baby coffee mornings, lose the baby weight, go back to work, and revert to behaving like normal childless adults again, as if nothing has changed.'

'I definitely hear you there...'

'But everything *has*. And not only that, but when we do rejoin the workforce after the leave period that default carer role persists. What father worries about leaving the office early to take his child to a dental appointment, or is made to feel guilty about taking a day off when junior is ill? It's an automatic double standard that stems directly from the leave period. And I'm sure we can all agree that when men take a more active role in child-rearing, it's all "Aww, isn't he a great dad," whereas for women it's "For God's sake, can't she keep her personal life under control?"'

'Oh yes, we've all heard that one. Claudine?'

'I have to say I do tend to agree with Madeleine on the idea that mothers taking the lion's share of responsibility does set up a default of sorts, but I take issue with the notion that it's servitude, or anything like it. In my case, I loved being at home with my daughter for those first few months. And don't forget, we're natural nurturers, aren't we? So it's perfectly reasonable that we default to the role anyway.'

'Madeleine? Claudine has a point; women are nurturers by nature.'

'Well, some might be but certainly not all. I've written before about how out of my depth I was in the early days – hell, I'm still out of my depth most of the time. Should all mothers, irrespective of their capabilities, be assigned that role for life? And think about the other dynamic this whole thing sets in place – the notion that only Mum knows best, and Dad is a bumbling buffoon who can't even get the basics right. I've heard countless friends tell me that they don't "trust" their own husbands to look after the offspring, and again, it all stems from them being the ones who've done these things from the get-go.'

'So, what's your suggestion for remedying the situation, Madeleine? Surely you're not advocating that both parents return to work and somehow juggle the childcare between them? Because in that case I'm almost certain that's not in the child's best interests—'

'I'm not suggesting anything, Louise, all I am saying is that we need to look closer at what I think is a long-outdated and yes, completely patriarchal construct. Perhaps both parents should decide between them who goes out to work and who stays, but the important thing is that it's not just poor Mammy who's automatically expected to do so. It's not just maternity leave, it's maternity *life*.'

'Gemma? You've been unusually silent this morning. Not maternity leave but maternity life. A headline worthy of your own newspaper if ever I heard one. Your thoughts?'

'Well… my thoughts are that Madeleine here obviously knows a lot about racking up social media hits, but seems to know very little about the real world…'

'Right, let's leave it there. Lots of reaction from our viewers already and we'll read out some of your social media responses and texts next. But in the meantime, grab a biscuit and join us after the break, when our panel will be discussing which of our female politicians tops the polls in the style stakes… See you then.'

As the show signed off, Madeleine took a quick check of her social media and watched the tweets pour in:

@MorningCoffeeShow Madeleine Cooper talking a lot of sense. More please. #refreshing

@MorningCoffeeShow LOVE @MadMumIE! #goMadeleine #maternitylife

@MorningCoffeeShow Think Madeleine Cooper is dead right in what she's saying, and many dads would only love the opportunity to participate in their child's early days – myself included. #niceone

@MorningCoffeeShow More @MadMumIE on your panel please! #loveher

@MorningCoffeeShow Madeleine Cooper is hilarious… not sure Gemma was too keen on her tho! #iflookscouldkill

@MorningCoffeeShow Hadn't heard of this Madeleine Cooper person before this morning's show. 'Maternity Life' is a new one on me, but thought provoking all the same. #madmum

Madeleine Cooper @MadMumIE is a breath of fresh air – so genuine and down-to-earth. Love that mischievous smile.

Anyone see @MadMumIE on #MorningCoffee? Any idea where her lovely colourful top is from? #stylishmum

Maternity Life? @MadMumIE certainly lives up to her name, but no denying she makes for great TV. Gemma Moore on the other hand… #sanctimonious

Chapter 4

It was going to be one of those days. I kneaded my forehead as I stood at the nurses' station at the end of the hallway on the third floor of the clinic. I could already feel a headache brewing behind my eyes – and the fluorescent lighting didn't help.

'You OK, Kate?' asked Shelly, another nurse who worked on the wards with me.

'Ah, just a bit of a sinus headache,' I replied. I had horrible sinus problems that were always exacerbated by changes in the weather. On damp days like these, my head felt like it was about to explode. Nothing to do about it though except pop some Nurofen and get on with things. Certainly couldn't stay at home and rest up – I had bills to pay.

The latest of which, I guessed, was also contributing to the headache. Only that morning, I'd learned that the car insurance on the Astra had almost doubled for this year – simply because it was an older model. And since I didn't have the funds to upgrade, I would have to pay what amounted to a king's ransom just to stay on the road. 'Don't mind me.' I smiled, changing the subject. 'I'd better check on Mrs Smyth in 304. She was complaining earlier about her back hurting – I'm worried that she's been in that bed so long she might start getting bedsores.'

Shelly smiled and patted me on the shoulder. 'You take it easy for a minute, I'll do it.' She headed off down the hallway, her shoes squeaking, and I was unaccountably grateful for great colleagues and a healthy work environment.

It would have been so easy (and perhaps even sensible) after Greg's death for me and Rosie to pack up our lives and move back to my hometown in West Cork. But despite my parents' insistence, I couldn't do it – not least because in a largely rural area it would be nigh on impossible to pick up a part-time nursing position that would allow me to work around Rosie's school times, but also because I wanted to retain *some* sense of day-to-day normality for my daughter.

Despite being newcomers, our little family had slowly but surely begun to make a life in Knockroe – Rosie had made friends in preschool who would also be attending Applewood, and I didn't want to wrench every last piece of joy and stability from her life.

Granted a rented house wasn't the best situation long-term, but our landlord – a former Knockroe native who now lived in the city – was fair about the rent and quick to respond to any main-tenance issues. My colleagues and superiors at Glencree Clinic had also been invaluably sympathetic and helpful immediately after Greg's death, so even though sometimes it might have been helpful to have family close by, all in all, the balance was tipped in favour of staying put.

And as Rosie had come on in leaps and bounds since she started school, and was almost back to the sunny, good-natured child she'd been before her father's demise, I figured I'd made the right decision.

The Easter holidays were a case in point, where we'd had the loveliest time together during the break, and my daughter was the happiest I'd seen her in an age. We'd gone hiking in the woods, taken a trip to the zoo and spent one very memorable day at a dinosaur expo in the RDS, which, of course, was right up her street.

I smiled then, remembering Rosie's eyes immediately light up at the sight of the dino exhibits area; life-sized renderings of all her favourite prehistoric beasts. She'd been rapt with excitement at the displays, and giggled uproariously when a mechanical Dilophosaurus flashed his frills and sprayed us both with water as we passed by.

We'd spent a full hour brushing sand and uncovering 'lost bones' in the archaeological dig, and I listened gobsmacked as my five-year-old argued robustly with one of the attendants about how the latest *Jurassic Park* movie had got so many details wrong about a monster I'd never even heard of, let alone could pronounce its name. Though the tickets for the exhibit had been costly, my daughter's shining eyes and bouncy gait that day, and even for the rest of that week, meant it had been worth every penny.

I truly had my little girl back.

And now, as the worst seemed finally behind us, I was determined that we should have lots more enjoyable mother/daughter days to look forward to and, depending on finances, maybe even think about taking a real holiday next summer or the one after.

I checked the clock then and realised it was getting close to the end of my duty shift at two. It was nice to be finished early afternoon, but it wasn't as if I didn't have other 'duties' of sorts to attend to.

I took Rosie swimming on Wednesdays, and on Thursday

nights she had ballet practice. So I knew that I would spend those evenings talking sequins and writing frighteningly big cheques alongside the other Knockroe mothers while my daughter practised her Grand Pliés.

Not that I minded, really (apart from the big cheques of course). It was about the only 'girlie' pursuit that Rosie enjoyed – and she was far more graceful than I had ever been at her age. It was just challenging having to play double duty all the time. Greg always used to make sure dinner was on the table no matter what time I got home, and I missed those days. I missed him.

Quickly moving through a final checklist for rounds, I waved goodbye to Shelly as she emerged from Mrs Smyth's room.

'We're all grand here,' she said, giving me a thumbs-up. 'Try to take it easy tonight with that sinus thing, and see you tomorrow.'

It only took fifteen minutes to drive from Glencree to pick Rosie up from school. Parking outside Applewood, I left the car running and headed for the gate. Sure enough, my daughter soon pranced over – wearing her boots today, good girl. I gathered her into a quick hug and then hustled her to the car. Buckling her in to her booster seat, I kissed one of her pink cheeks. 'You're going to match your ballet tutu if you get any rosier.' I smiled. 'So what's up, buttercup? How'd today go?'

A world-weary sigh. 'Clara Cooper went home sick this time. After big break. She was coughing and sneezing all morning, and when we were sitting together for reading time, I told her that she had spots on her neck – here.' Rosie paused, pointing to an area just below her neck at the top of her chest. 'I said that she'd better go tell Ms Connelly because of Ellie and the chicken pox. Kevin started making fun of her then. He can be so mean.'

I nodded in sympathy. 'You did the right thing, and take no

notice of Kevin. Even if Clara shouldn't really be at school if she's sick,' I added, mostly to myself.

Clara Cooper, daughter of the town's mini-celebrity Madeleine Cooper, and her popular blog or forum or whatever they called it. A self-confessed 'Mad Mum' according to the humorous articles and photographs she posted. Though I couldn't call myself an avid follower, I'd caught a couple of her TV appearances and radio slots and liked her no-nonsense, slightly mad-cap approach to motherhood. Her philosophy was that women shouldn't be too hard on themselves by taking it all so seriously and overthinking every aspect. And while I admired the sentiment, I guess it's easier to apply such a motto when you have a partner with whom to share the load.

Though I didn't know the woman particularly well, I liked Madeleine; she was one of the people in the community who'd reached out to me in the immediate aftermath of Greg's death, not just to offer condolence but genuine assistance. Where so many others seemed uncomfortable around me – afraid even – Madeleine had even given me her phone number and urged me to call her for a gossip, cry, anything at all, and I appreciated that.

Still, I'm sure the teachers at Applewood didn't appreciate her sending her child to school with a contagious illness, especially when she worked from home. It was one thing to be laissez-faire; quite another altogether to be wilfully careless.

Then I thought of something I'd heard in the background at work this morning, a promo on breakfast TV about a later show on the same channel… Madeleine Cooper had been mentioned as one of today's panellists on *Morning Coffee*.

Now I got it. Clara's poorly form and that morning's impending live TV appearance must have put poor Madeleine in a bind, and I felt lousy for assuming that just because she didn't physically clock in for work somewhere didn't mean she wouldn't have the same parenting balls to juggle as the rest of us.

'Yep, poor Clara had an awful cough, and her face looked hot. She really shouldn't have come to school at all, I think,' Rosie added sagely.

I looked at my five-and-a-half-year-old, marvelling at how wise she was for her age. Again, she reminded me of Greg in that regard. He was always so finely tuned in to everything that was happening around him and very little fazed him.

'Yep. Sounds like she might have caught the pox all right.' I sent some goodwill little Clara Cooper's way and hoped it was a mild enough dose.

*

The next few days seemed to fly by in a blur.

On Thursday afternoon, I hustled Rosie home from school, sat with her through homework while also simultaneously preparing a lamb tagine recipe that I had come across on Pinterest the other night. I could put it on and it would be ready for us by the time we got back from ballet later.

She hadn't eaten much of that day's lunch and had also refused a snack before we left, so would surely be starving later.

Now, I pointed her in the direction of her room so she could get ready for class.

'Make sure you bring a cardie for your arms, sweetheart. It's always chilly in the studio,' I called up after her.

Looking around the kitchen, I grabbed my chequebook and iPad and threw them both in the way-too-big handbag I carried with me everywhere. Child-free women used bags like this as accessories, while those with kids knew that there was no way to get through the day without a surplus of supplies within arm's reach. I idly remembered Madeleine Cooper posting something about this one time, except she presented it in a far more humorous and creative way than I ever could.

Moments later, Rosie was ready and we were off. I was feeling in good spirits; I simply loved the days where my organisation skills paid off and I didn't have to run from one commitment to the next like a frantic lunatic. Sometimes I was really on top of my game.

Sometimes.

Upon entering the ballet studio a little way outside town, Rosie and I were met with a flurry of activity. My daughter was pulled in the direction of the practice area by her friends, and I was shuttled to a waiting area where mothers, and the odd father, watched their whirling dervish daughters through glass.

'Kate – over here!'

I turned towards the sound of a familiar voice and saw the frizzy red hair of Lucy Murphy: unofficial mayor of Knockroe (by way of the fact that everyone knew her) and one of the few friends I'd made locally. We'd met when our daughters attended the same preschool.

Lucy was a stay-at-home mum and a couple of years my senior. Her husband Dennis worked in insurance in Dublin and she had two daughters, Stephanie and Laura. Laura was a few months older than Rosie and a year ahead of her at school while Stephanie was a couple of years older again.

'Hi, Lucy,' I said, greeting her warmly.

'Great to see you, love,' she said, coming in for a small hug before she got straight down to business. 'I'm collecting donations for the recital costumes.' (Of course she was.) 'Though I fear for Jennifer, let me tell you, her first choice on the outfits was just way too revealing. Can you imagine? They're five-year-olds!'

I nodded and murmured my agreement. Jennifer was one of the instructors at the dance studio, and her taste in recital gear was a bit more… liberal than most. While I tended to side with Lucy as it related to what my daughter was going to wear when she strutted her stuff on the stage in front of friends and neighbours, I also knew that I didn't have to offer any complaint. Lucy would simply handle it for the rest of us and everything would get sorted accordingly. It must be wonderful to be that confident and capable.

I took a seat on the bench along the wall for the parents as Lucy buzzed off, happily barking orders at parents and children alike.

Some people tended to be put off by her bluster, and I realised that it was easy to feel that way. I myself had felt a bit over-whelmed when I first met her a couple of years back. A bit like a hurricane – she comes in really strong, churns everything up, and then mellows out. However, over time, she has become one of my biggest advocates and friends. When Greg passed away, she really helped me keep it together and I don't know what I would have done without her.

Lucy organised my house when I was in too much of a fog to do anything, kept the receiving line of sympathisers moving, made sure both Rosie and I were fed, did my washing, helped me with pretty much everything day in and day out.

In the immediate aftermath, my parents had of course come up to stay, but they're in their late sixties and in poor health, and were themselves too wracked with grief to be of any real help. And while I had others – work colleagues and old friends from Dublin – around at the time willing to do what they could, Lucy was the drill sergeant we all needed.

Now, I watched through the glass observation window as Rosie's class started. This was really the first time this week I had been able to just sit and breathe, I realised.

I reached into my bag, grabbed an elastic and pulled my tousled shoulder-length hair up off my shoulders, tying it into a makeshift bun at the nape of my neck. It was starting to get greasy and I really needed a shower but there'd been no time. Later hopefully, when Rosie had gone to bed. She usually went up about eight, and while Greg and I used to relish the few hours together before our own bedtime, now the silence made his absence even more pronounced. So I tended to keep myself busy by cooking, reading or going online and wasting time on Pinterest and the like.

Inside the studio, my daughter was standing in fifth position as normal, but something she was doing caught my eye.

She put her hand up and scratched her back, right along her shoulder blade. I grimaced; she must have grabbed the wrong cardie by accident earlier. That purple one she had on was an itchy wool, and now she was paying the price.

'Is anyone sitting here?'

I looked up to see Christine Campbell, a tall woman with a slightly aloof air about her. Her son Kevin was in Rosie's class and, by all accounts (including Rosie's), a bit of a troublemaker, constantly causing grief for the teachers. Typical boy stuff, really. She also had a daughter Suzanne, who was older and in a more senior ballet class.

I didn't see Christine often, but our daughters' class times sometimes overlapped. She and Lucy knew each other well, though personality-wise they seemed to me to be chalk and cheese.

'No, go ahead.' I moved my oversized bag and placed it on the floor at the same time that Lucy rejoined us and sat back down.

All at once, I felt like I was smack bang in the middle of a gossip sandwich as the two women tried their utmost to outdo each other for local 'news'.

The topics were wide ranging and flung about rapidly – Christine conveyed her annoyance about a neighbour who had illegally constructed a shed against a boundary wall and how she was going to talk to her solicitor cousin about it, while Lucy condemned a hapless mother who'd promised she would volunteer at the Applewood PTA, but had not turned up to a meeting. I grimaced, making a mental note to be sure to keep any volunteer commitments.

But since I myself was short on scandal, I searched my brain for something to contribute to the conversation.

'I heard poor Clara Cooper went home early from school with chickenpox the other day,' I offered. 'Is Kevin OK so far?' I added, knowing that Christine's son was one of the kids in Rosie's class who hadn't had it yet. I glanced towards the dance studio and frowned. My daughter was still scratching.

'I know. I was the one who picked Clara up,' Lucy commented. 'Madeleine rang me first thing that morning – Clara woke up a bit poorly, but Madeleine was due at Channel 2 for a TV thing and had to send her in. She asked if I'd do the honours in case she got any worse.'

'Typical,' Christine harrumphed, her horn-rimmed glasses falling down her nose. 'Getting someone else to do her dirty work. Mad Mum is right. And I'm sure it's only a matter of time till my poor Kevin gets it.' She pushed the glasses back up and rolled her eyes. 'Doesn't surprise me that Clara did either. You know what the bloody Coopers are like.'

I bit my lip guiltily, having forgotten that Lucy and Clara's mum were also close, and had grown up together in Knockroe. And I especially regretted bringing up the subject in front of

Christine. Lucy had once confided that Madeleine's rapidly growing celeb status was a sore point as far as Christine was concerned, and I hadn't intended to open that particular can of worms.

I started to reply, but Lucy beat me to it. 'Ah leave it, Christine. To be fair, you don't usually vaccinate for chicken pox anyway.'

At this, my ears pricked up. 'What do you mean?' I asked, turning to her. 'What's that got to do with the Coopers?'

Rosie's allergy or the fact that she couldn't be immunised wasn't common knowledge amongst the school community, mostly because of the inevitable negative reaction it provoked amongst parents. And I didn't want my daughter to be singled out in any way because of reasons she (or I) couldn't control. So when before Easter the school secretary had sent out Health Service permission forms for the MMR booster to be carried out in the school, I had quietly marked an X in the 'Decline' box and forgotten all about it.

But now I couldn't help but wonder if perhaps the Coopers and I had something in common.

'But Madeleine and Tom don't *believe* in vaccination full stop,' Christine said bitterly. 'Complete nonsense. Not to mention irresponsible.'

My mouth went dry. So while I'd had no choice but to opt out of the standard vaccination programme, it seemed the Coopers had wilfully declined.

'Don't believe in… you mean the Cooper children haven't had shots – for anything?' I asked, feeling more than a little unnerved.

This was what Greg and I had worried most about – the idea that so-called 'herd immunity' wasn't guaranteed to protect Rosie so long as there were parents who chose not to participate. Yet I couldn't condemn the Coopers for anything when I didn't know the reasons. For all I knew, their children might also have some kind of autoimmune condition or other valid reason not to go along with protocol.

'Yep. Apparently they don't trust the HSE and the pharmaceutical companies, even though all that controversy over the MMR jabs was written off yonks ago.' Christine rolled her eyes. 'Give me a break. They're just lucky this time that chicken pox is fairly harmless.'

This time.

I swallowed hard, not sure what to make of this.

'Well, I hope Kevin avoids it anyway. Nasty, scratchy dose,' I mumbled sympathetically. 'But not too hard on the kids if it's mild enough.'

Lucy had gone unusually quiet and, sensing she was uncomfortable with the discussion, I decided to change the subject. 'Oh look, they're starting,' I said, turning back to the ballet class and feeling bad for bringing all this up in the first place.

But Christine wouldn't be diverted. 'A bit poorly my ass. Kevin was saying that Clara was coughing the day before that too,' she said. 'What kind of mother sends a sick child to school so she can go off to flatter her own ego? And *what* kind of parents take their kids out of class for an extra week over Easter so they can go and sun themselves in Florida?'

I remembered Rosie saying something about Clara being absent the first few days back after the break, but hadn't realised it was because she was still on holiday. Must be nice to be able to fly off somewhere warm and sunny for so long. I could only dream.

'Ah, Christine, it's not as if the kids missed that much for the few extra days they were away,' said Lucy. 'And in fairness to Madeleine the other morning, she really didn't think there was anything to worry about…'

'Oh save it, that's no excuse. A blind man could see that the child was coming down with something, though of course maybe those Prada sunglasses her mother likes to wear messed up her eyesight...'

'Christine, seriously,' Lucy reproached, 'there's no need for that. I know Madeleine. If she honestly felt that Clara was ill, she would have cancelled the TV thing, end of story. As it was, the little dote just had the sniffles and a bit of a temperature when I went to pick her up.'

'Well, Kevin said he spotted a cluster of spots on her neck. And if a five-year-old can see it, I don't understand how the child's own *mother*—'

'That could just be heat rash from the temperature,' I said matter-of-factly. 'Pox don't cluster.'

'Thank you, Nurse,' Lucy chuckled, evidently hoping to lighten the mood. 'In any case, Christine, Maddie was distraught and full of apologies when she got back from Dublin,' she insisted. 'She couldn't have known.'

As Christine muttered something unintelligible, a thought started rattling around in my head. It was what I had just said: that chicken pox didn't cluster.

They don't, I reminded myself. There were just individual sores when the rash popped up.

I nodded, affirming my own train of thought. Christine's son was probably just being a typical five-year-old boy. Making everything seem more dramatic and exaggerated than it actually was.

Returning my attention to the studio where Rosie practised, I smiled with appreciation as she pirouetted gracefully. She did a slight bow in front of her teacher and classmates and then returned to the barre.

Whereupon once again, almost absent-mindedly, my daughter raised her arm and scratched her back.

Chapter 5

Rosie turned over in bed and pulled the covers up over her head. Shoving her face into the pillow, she tried her hardest to stifle the sound of her cough. She rolled over onto her back, then sniffled and pulled her leg up to her chest, so she could scratch her knee.

She didn't feel well.

And she was *very* itchy.

Rosie had noticed when she got home from ballet and started undressing to put her pyjamas on that she had some little red dots on her arms. And there were a few on her chest, too. She was sure that if she turned on the light and looked at her knee, she would probably find some spots there too.

But her mum said that you couldn't get chicken pox twice.

Rosie felt worry build in her chest. She really didn't want chicken pox again. It had been miserable the last time. She couldn't stand the thought of being cooped up in bed, not being allowed to play with her friends or her dinosaurs, and having to take long, warm baths just to try to ease the itch that came with those yucky blisters.

She shuddered, thinking about it.

Maybe she was just tired. That had to be it. It had been a long week and maybe she was just feeling a bit worried because her friend Ellie wasn't well and then Clara had gone home sick the other day too.

Kevin hadn't looked like he was sick though – and he said he'd never had chicken pox before – so how could *she* get them twice?

She swallowed hard and took a deep breath, trying to calm herself. That was what Mum had told her to do any time she was feeling overwhelmed. Of course, she had told her that because of what she had seen with her dad, but Rosie supposed that trick could be used in this situation as well.

Taking one, two, three deep breaths, she closed her eyes in the darkness and willed herself to go to sleep. In the morning, everything would be fine. She would feel better.

But then her eyes sprang open as it felt like something had bitten her on the back. She cranked her arm around awkwardly to shove her hand up the back of her pyjama top to reach the area. Once the itch was scratched, she ran her fingers over her skin and felt a few flat bumps. There were more of them all over her too, she just knew it.

Breathing hard again, she whispered to herself like her mum told her to do when she needed to calm herself down. 'You're fine, just go to sleep. Everything is OK. You don't have chicken pox. Everyone knows kids can't get them twice.'

Debating on whether or not to get up and tell her mum about this, she decided against it. Mum worried about things. And Rosie knew she'd be even more worried if she had to take time off work to take care of her, when there was no need.

She was a big girl now.

'Just go to sleep,' she told herself quietly in the darkness, trying to count sheep like her dad had once told her. But that had never worked, so instead Rosie decided to try counting the names of all the different dinosaurs she knew – especially all the new ones she'd learned from the exhibition she'd been to over Easter. And after tossing and turning for an hour or more, she finally fell asleep, achieving a fitful slumber.

Several hours later she woke, realising that she had kicked all of her covers off. She felt hot and cold at the same time and her pyjamas felt wet and her skin clammy. She was covered in sweat!

At once, the problem of the previous night came rushing back to her and Rosie realised that she didn't feel better – at *all*. Instead she felt much, much worse.

'No, no, no,' she said, feeling a fresh wave of panic. She was so warm – she had to have a fever, like that time she'd had a bad flu and her mum had explained all about how fever was the body's way of getting rid of bad germs.

Bad germs like chicken pox?

And as much as she wanted to jump out of bed to look at herself in the mirror to confirm that the spots were still there, she just couldn't. She felt exhausted.

Rosie wanted her mum, but when she opened her mouth to call out, she found she could barely manage a squeak.

'Mum…' she croaked. When she didn't hear any footsteps on the stairs, she tried again, this time a bit louder. Her mum had to hear her – mums just knew, somehow, when their kids needed them. Particularly her mum.

Sure enough, a moment later, Rosie heard, 'Coming, honey,' and she felt some of her panic subside.

Mum would make this OK, she thought. *In just a second, Mum would tell her that everything was fine – that this was just a flu and she would be right as rain in no time.*

*

On Friday morning, I pushed the button on the Nespresso coffee-maker Greg had bought the year he died, and waited for my morning dose of caffeine to be dispensed.

Looking quickly at the clock on the microwave, I guessed that I needed to get Rosie up this morning. Usually she was very good about getting herself out of bed and ready for school. No worries, still plenty of time, I told myself as I grabbed my coffee cup and took a tentative first sip, savouring the warmth.

Then, picking up my phone to check for any messages from work, I heard a small whine coming from upstairs.

Rosie was calling for me, and something about her voice wasn't right.

Immediately, my brain defaulted to panic mode, as it did so often.

How would I shuffle my day around if she needed to stay at home because she wasn't feeling well? Trying to summon just how many days of annual leave from work I had left, I called out back to her.

In fairness, I'd been lucky – Rosie hadn't missed a single day since starting school last September. Quite the feat considering most of her classmates seemed to have perma-sniffles, and I chalked it down to my insistence on her eating Vitamin C-rich fruit and veg as well as a regular multi-vitamin for us both to heighten our immune system – especially given my own exposure to various bugs at the hospital.

But it was impossible to fight everything all of the time.

I placed my coffee cup on the counter and raced upstairs, mentally reorganising my day as I opened my daughter's bedroom door to make the inevitable diagnosis: *Yup, you're staying home today.* My thoughts drifted to Madeleine Cooper who had evidently faced that self-same scenario earlier in the week.

But nothing could have prepared me for what I actually saw when I entered Rosie's room.

My little girl lay uncovered, her dark hair limp and damp and sticking to the sides of her face. Her skin was flushed and her pyjamas had patches of wet here and there, as if she had been sweating throughout the night.

And on the surface of her skin that wasn't covered by clothes there were spots. Lots and lots of small red spots on her face, her neck, her hands, even her feet.

My mouth dropped open in shock, and my mind automatically jumped to the thought: *Of* course *she had to be the kid who gets chicken pox twice.*

But then my professional training sprang into action and cautioned me against being too hasty with my diagnosis. I saw Rosie looking at me, studying me, and a small crease appeared on her forehead, while her expression changed from worry to fear and finally… panic.

I quickly tried to rearrange the look on my face, willing myself to appear calm and in control.

When I was feeling anything but.

'Mummy, I don't feel well,' she whimpered.

I picked up my pace, closing the distance to her bed. I sank to my knees and reached out, placing my hand on her forehead.

She was burning up.

'Do I have chicken pox again?' she asked weakly. 'How could I have it again?'

'Shush, honey, I don't know. Let me take a look at you,' I said, trying to keep the tremor out of my voice as I peered at the spots on her skin. 'Let me unbutton your top, sweetheart, I want to see your chest.'

Rosie allowed me to unbutton her pyjama shirt while my fingers trembled. Somehow I just knew what I was going to find next.

Her chest was covered with a rash. Small, red clusters. Everywhere.

My mouth was suddenly dry and I licked my lips, willing myself to say something to comfort my daughter.

'I'm so itchy, Mummy. And so hot.' She was still watching me closely, and then she coughed violently, spittle lining the corners of her mouth.

My mind raced as I placed a hand on her forehead again and my heart pounded with fear. 'I know, sweetheart, I'm sorry. I'll take you to the doctor. We'll get you sorted.'

The rash, the clusters. *This is different*, the nurse inside me protested. *This isn't chicken pox. Chicken pox don't cluster. And they aren't flat either. This was something different...*

And with a sudden terrifying realisation, I knew. But I couldn't allow myself to even *think* the word.

No, it simply wasn't possible. Where would Rosie have picked it up? It was chicken pox that was going around the school. Not...

Unless...

My thoughts turned then to the other sick child, Clara Cooper. Who, according to Christine, wasn't vaccinated against serious childhood illnesses.

Just like Rosie.

Clara – who had been sent home from school three days ago with suspected chicken pox.

Except she hadn't. This wasn't chicken pox.

This was out and out measles.

Chapter 6

'It's OK, petal, we're going to make you feel better,' Madeleine soothed as she hovered over Clara's bed.

On Tuesday morning, while in make-up at the TV station, her worst fears had been realised with a text from the school principal confirming that Clara was indeed sick. Talk about timing…

She'd given her some Paracetamol after all the coughing and sneezing the night before hoping to nip whatever it was in the bud, but noticed at breakfast that her youngest was still a bit off. But she really couldn't keep her at home that day, she had the TV thing to do, and Tom had already left for work hours earlier…

So Madeleine had very quickly weighed up the odds and decided that she'd chance sending Clara to school, and would rush straight back once she'd done her thing at the studio. It was a gamble but what choice did she have? She couldn't cancel *Morning Coffee* at the last minute; the show aired at eleven and she needed to leave right after the school drop-off.

Chances were Clara would be grand – kids were always up and down with these things and usually rallied well – but just in case Clara felt worse, she could mitigate the risk by asking Lucy to do her a turn. No point (or indeed time) in getting her husband to trek all the way home from Dublin, and she couldn't ask her mother-in-law for a dig-out either, because Harriet didn't have a car.

Ever the trooper, Madeleine's friend immediately agreed to collect Clara just after eleven and stay with her at their house until she got back. 'It's no bother. Knock 'em dead and Clara will only love being able to watch you on TV.'

The two had been friends for ever – Lucy's eldest was the same age as Jake so she and Madeleine had shared the whole Newborn Mania thing – and routinely helped each other out when it came to their offspring, often alternating school runs and sports practice drop-offs. Her friend was also decidedly non-judgemental about Madeleine's columns, something that was rare enough in Knockroe. Many of the other women in her circle (in particular Christine Campbell) had already been a bit suspicious and defensive about how Madeleine had mostly kept to herself when Jake was born – very quickly dropping out of local mother/baby groups, and unwilling to get into discussions about the trials of sleepless nights or feeding routines, or engage in the seemingly endless debate between breast and bottle.

At the time, she felt it was hard enough getting to grips with the huge changes a newborn wrought without overanalysing every last aspect. Their own parents' generation didn't have that luxury, and for the most part just took things as they came, which suited Madeleine down to the ground. She hated how motherhood was so damn competitive and judgemental. She'd heard about that aspect from other friends before, of course, but nothing could have prepared her for just how damaging and destructive it could be to insecure newbies. 'There is no "right way",' Madeleine's mother used to tell her, when in the very early days with Jake she fell into the trap of worrying and comparing herself to other women who seemed so sure about what they were doing. 'Same as marriage, you just take it one day at a time. But the most important thing of all, pet, is to enjoy it.'

It was the best piece of parenting advice Madeleine had ever received. Thankfully, Tom too held little truck with outsiders interfering or undermining, and agreed that the two of them should trust their instincts for what they did know, and just research anything they didn't.

Some days were great, others absolute shit, but from then on Madeleine refused to put pressure on herself to make everything 'perfect' or 'normal'. Like her mother said, to a baby every experience was their perfect and their normal, so no sense tying yourself up in knots about it.

Lucy was of a similar mind in some aspects, but was also much better than she at finding common ground with others who didn't share the same philosophy. Whereas Madeleine's own failure to do so had driven her to find solidarity with like-minded mums online via her blog, rather than suffer her more judgemental local counterparts who refused to admit that motherhood could be anything other than unicorns and rainbows.

Though she admitted she'd got things *badly* wrong with Clara this week and, worse, hadn't she known deep down that her daughter was coming down with something – especially when they'd heard a dose was doing the rounds?

She probably should have kept her at home – and on any other day would have – but if she'd cancelled at the last minute the *Morning Coffee* producers would likely never invite her back.

As it was, the team were delighted with the reaction to her appearance on the panel, and had already asked her back for another stint. It could only lead to bigger and better things as the show's viewers were exactly her target audience and, following the slot, *Mad Mum*'s blog and social media engagement had sky-rocketed. Good all round, apart from the fact that that journalist, Gemma Moore, seemed to have taken an immediate dislike to her, which she couldn't understand. Everyone knew how these things worked and surely Gemma realised that Madeleine was purposely hamming it up for entertainment?

In any case, based on the social media response, it had worked.

So while she still felt terrible for sending Clara to school when her daughter truly was ill, all in all Madeleine stood by her decision to bite the bullet and take things as they came. Tom had agreed with her, which made her feel somewhat better at least.

'Don't be so hard on yourself – sure, for all we knew, Clara was just coming down with yet another bout of the sniffles,' her husband reassured, kissing her on the forehead, when Madeleine had remonstrated with herself for the decision.

There was no denying the various iterations of coughs and colds had indeed seemed endless since the kids started school, and in fairness their youngest was strong as an ox most of the time...

Clara coughed violently then, and Madeleine stroked her little girl's hair, feeling guiltier still. She truly hadn't believed there was anything to worry about, and even now, a few days on, there was no sign of any telltale sores.

But if her daughter did in fact have chicken pox, there was nothing to do now but wait it out and let the thing take its course. Heartbreaking to see her little girl so ill though, she thought, softly caressing Clara's cheek. At least she only had one sick child to concentrate on – Jake had had the dose before, so Madeleine sent him to school the next morning without the worry at least that she would get another recriminating phone call...

At that moment, her mobile phone sounded from where she had placed it on Clara's dresser, and a sudden surge of panic rushed through her. Hell, what if she'd just jinxed herself and her son *was* in fact now down with something too?

But when she looked at the caller ID, she felt herself calm down. It was Lucy. Likely calling to get the scoop on Clara. She was a good friend and, after picking her daughter up from school on Tuesday, had gone out of her way to reassure a panicky Madeleine that all was in hand. 'No need to break any speed limits on your way back. Take your time – she's fine.'

'How's Clara doing?' her friend demanded now, before Madeleine could even issue a greeting. Taken aback at her tone – it wasn't like Lucy to be so short – she looked again at her daughter who seemed to be dozing off.

'She's fine, thank goodness – you know yourself, you've been through it with Steph. Poor thing will be itchy and miserable for the next few days but—'

Lucy cut her off. 'Have you talked to anyone from the school since?'

Madeleine furrowed her brow. What did that have to do with anything? Everyone knew the thing was going around, hadn't they got that note on Monday...

'Well, I obviously phoned to tell them that Clara wouldn't be in for the rest of the week, that the poor little thing had caught the blasted pox and—'

'Oh God, you really don't know, do you?'

What the hell? Madeleine thought, irritated. Why all the drama for crying out loud? Was there a reason why Lucy wouldn't let her finish a sentence? It was actually starting to sound like she was phoning for a gossip and Madeleine didn't have any time or inclination for gossip. Just then, Clara was her only concern. 'Well, I kind of have my hands full here. I don't know what else is going on at the school and, to tell you the truth, I don't particularly care—'

'Maddie,' interjected Lucy harshly, 'I don't think Clara has chicken pox.'

Her eyes widened in disbelief. 'What are you talking about? *Of course* she has chicken pox. Ellie got it first, and now Clara has it. Her temperature's subsided and granted there's not many sores showing up yet, but all we can do now is let it take its—'

Again, her friend cut her off. 'Madeleine, let me finish. I just got off the phone with Kate O'Hara. Rosie is sick too.'

'Ah, poor thing.' Madeleine felt sorry for Kate, who was a single mother and would be seriously put out by having to miss work to look after little Rosie. And as she expressed as much to Lucy, she could almost sense her friend shaking her head on the other end of the line.

'No, you see, Rosie already had chicken pox a couple of years ago. And before you say it, no, she isn't one of those kids who gets it twice either. Please, Madeleine, quick, just tell me what Clara's chest looks like – is there a rash?'

Madeleine felt confused, but did as she was told. With the phone pressed to her ear, she looked at her sleeping child – thankfully Clara had found some peace in slumber – and pulled down the bedclothes a little.

Then she whispered quietly into the phone. 'I don't know. Like I said there isn't much of a pox outbreak yet, but now that you say it, just under her neck there is a kind of rash, I suppose, little bumps clustered together. Pretty much what you would expect with—'

'Madeleine, you have to get Clara to a doctor, fast. And get Jake out of school too. I'm serious.' Lucy sounded almost frantic on the phone and her normally mild-mannered friend's panic made Madeleine's mind race. But her heart almost dropped into her stomach with her friend's next words. 'I don't think that Clara has chicken pox, sweetheart, but she could have measles. Rosie definitely has – Kate recognised the difference right away. You know she's a nurse. But, anyway, it's not common knowledge yet, at least I don't think it is, the way that people know... well... the way people know about Jake and Clara. But it seems Rosie isn't vaccinated either. She has some allergy that prevents it and—'

Feeling like her head was spinning, Madeleine looked down at her daughter and tried her hardest to recall what Jake had been like when he'd had measles, but it was a good six years ago and she really didn't remember. It had been a mild dose, so hadn't really stuck in her mind, other than the fact that the doctor had berated her for not vaccinating her eighteen-month-old against it in the first place...

And now it seemed Clara had picked it up. But where?

Suddenly, Madeleine's mind drifted back to their holiday in Clearwater over the Easter break. There'd been something in the news at the time – she'd hardly paid attention to it amidst all the activities – about some kind of outbreak in one of the Orlando theme parks?

And little over a week ago the Coopers had shared an eight-hour flight home from that very location, with countless other Irish families who'd spent Easter in the theme parks...

'Oh my goodness,' Madeleine gasped, as the full realisation of what might be happening hit her.

The countless hours and days she and Tom had spent researching measles when Jake was a baby, trying to decide whether or not they could realistically avoid the MMR vaccination.

First and foremost, they'd been hugely uncomfortable about the vaccine's link to autism, and while the original research paper suggesting the connection had long been discredited, it was very difficult to ignore the multitude of real-life anecdotal experiences

that were so prevalent. The very idea of their happy, thriving, bab-
bling Jake regressing to a withdrawn, unresponsive state within
days – perhaps hours – of receiving the vaccination was enough
to break Madeleine's heart, and it certainly gave her pause.

While Tom had been raised a free-thinker and found it easy to
rail against the establishment, she hailed from a more traditional
Catholic background, used to trusting and going along with
generally accepted advice and thinking.

Initially, Madeleine couldn't credit that the government and
health boards would realistically offer something that could harm,
rather than protect, children. That was before she started to read
through the reams of research on the vaccine and its potentially
harmful ingredients, as well as the troubling suggestion of collu-
sion and lobbying from the pharmaceutical companies.

But it was the worrying realisation that worldwide governments' and health officials' ultimate priority was not the health of
an individual child but 'herd immunity' that truly concerned her.
She'd spent hours upon hours reading up on both sides of what
was a very heated and controversial argument, but, ultimately,
the whole decision came down to her baby son's safety.

'Suppose we don't give him the vaccination,' she'd said to
Tom, when Jake's first MMR shot was imminent and they were
by then seriously wavering about going along with protocol, 'and
he catches something terrible? I don't think I could ever forgive
myself—'

'Could you forgive yourself if we *do* vaccinate and it triggers
something potentially worse?' he'd argued, and Madeleine's heart
constricted. 'It's a huge leap of faith, Maddie,' he went on, but
by then she no longer needed persuading. The health board's
concerns might be for the safety of the population at large; but,
as parents, theirs *had* to be for their son.

And once you understood something like that, once you'd come to a realisation that rocked the very foundations of your beliefs, you couldn't go back. Their family knew that all too well.

'Look, it's not as if measles is the end of the world either,' her husband concluded. 'I had it when I was a kid and, yes, it was nasty, but I recovered fine.'

Madeleine's brother Paul had also seen off mumps as a child, and she herself had gone through a mild bout of measles when she was ten.

So they figured, even if the worst came to the worst...

But then poor Jake went and picked the disease up only a few months later anyway, while they were still hand-wringing over the whole thing.

Admittedly, it was at first terrifying to discover that their help-less little one-year-old had contracted something serious, but she and Tom had managed it and, thank goodness, all had been OK.

So when the time came to vaccinate Clara, they truly didn't even think twice. What were the chances of her contracting measles too? And, if she did, wouldn't they just deal with it again?

Despite repeated protests from their GP, urging them to recon-sider, Madeleine and Tom eventually concluded – based on both their research and experience – that avoiding the vaccine was the lesser of two evils. It was a risk, but a calculated one.

Or so they'd thought.

Rosie isn't vaccinated either...

But now, like a blow to the solar plexus, the big difference in this situation hit Madeleine full force. Jake had been young enough to contain and to prevent infecting others, but Clara was in school. With lots of other children. And, given that their daughter had contracted the disease by nature of the fact that she was unvaccinated, it was obvious she'd now passed it on, and even worse, to someone who, according to Lucy, didn't have the vaccination option.

This was a scenario that Madeleine and Tom hadn't run the odds on.

Realising that she had left Lucy in silence on the line, she whispered, 'And Ellie Madden too?' Christ, had she passed it on to the entire Junior Infants class, the whole school even? Oh God…

'No, apparently Ellie actually does have chicken pox – that's already confirmed. But, Maddie, get Clara to a doctor straight away. And you have to get Jake out of school too, once it's in your house, he's likely still infectious, even though…' To her credit, Madeleine was grateful to Lucy for not making a big deal of their refusal to vaccinate. Goodness knows she and Tom had faced considerable ire from various quarters before about it.

'I talked to the principal at Applewood,' her friend went on. 'Kate made them aware right away, and they're hoping to keep this quiet for the moment. It's a good thing it's nearly the weekend as they don't want a full-blown panic, but they need to identify who is the highest risk – anyone with autoimmune issues or anything like that. There are very few others there who aren't already immunised, thank goodness, but…'

Lucy's voice trailed off and right then Madeleine felt deeply ashamed that her family – her choice – had visited this on the school.

'You know, kids that aren't protected can still be helped, Madeleine. I looked it up and if you do vaccinate within seventy-two hours of a suspected outbreak, infection can still be prevented. So I just thought that maybe it's not too late for Clara…'

Despite herself, she felt defensive. 'Lucy, I'm sorry but I can't talk about it now,' she said wearily. 'That's between me and Tom. It's a family decision.'

And she knew exactly what her husband would have to say on the matter. *No way.*

'Sorry, Maddie,' Lucy replied quietly. 'I just thought... sorry.'

Madeleine took a deep breath. She knew her friend was only trying to help. 'No need to apologise. It's just a shock... and I'm trying to get a grip on what I should do.' In truth, she was still a bit floored that this had happened, but at the same time she needed to get her ass in gear... she'd have to call Tom at work and the GP of course, as well as haul Jake out of school and a million other things...

A cold shiver ran its way up Madeleine's spine as she looked back at her feverish daughter and suddenly a new realisation set in – one that carried with it a whole new level of worry. Measles... Clara really was ill too – a lot more feverish and uncomfortable than Jake had been.

Maybe it would be more serious this time.

The odds were small, but they were still odds: measles could be fatal.

For all these years, she and Tom had played them, and now that horrible realisation, albeit distant and buried, rose once again to the fore.

Oh God... what have we done...

Madeleine swallowed hard, and her thoughts instantly turned to Kate O'Hara, who was in the same situation as her at that moment. Well, almost the same. After all she had Tom to share the burden, whereas poor Kate was on her own.

'Is Rosie OK?' she asked, trembling. 'Should I call her mother?'

Lucy was circumspect. 'I'm not sure that's the best idea just at the minute. Like you, she has a lot on her plate now.

Maybe you should just focus on Clara for the moment,' her friend advised.

Madeleine nodded. In truth, the idea of talking to Kate just then was horrifying, especially if she too suspected Clara was the carrier.

Lucy was probably right and she knew Kate much better than Madeleine did. In fairness, she hardly knew Rosie's mum at all, having only minimal contact with her at the school or related activities, and of course that time when the poor thing lost her husband.

But, more to the point, what could Madeleine possibly do for Kate's daughter now other than apologise?

Deciding she'd spent more than enough time wallowing, she said goodbye to Lucy before springing into action and trying to get a handle on this thing.

First, she called Tom's work, but, failing to rouse him anywhere in the building, Ruth his secretary promised she'd get him to call his wife straight back. No response from his mobile either, so Madeleine immediately phoned their GP's surgery, quickly outlining the situation to the receptionist.

'Measles? Are you sure, Madeleine?' Rachel Kennedy, another mother with a much older child at Applewood asked. 'Isn't Clara immunised against that?'

Swallowing her mortification, she explained to Rachel that no, neither of her children had received the MMR jab.

'I... I had... no idea. I'll have to get Dr Barrett to call you back about a house call then.' Rachel's disapproval was so thick Madeleine could actually feel it down the line. Her voice dripped with scorn. 'Obviously you can't bring a highly contagious child to the surgery.'

Obviously.

'I understand that. Thanks, Rachel.'

After hanging up the phone, Madeleine moved once again to her daughter's bedside and choked back a sob at Clara's now undeniably rash-ridden feverish body; the full implications of her and Tom's decision now well and truly coming home to roost.

Chapter 7

I felt ready to tear out my hair as I paced the floor at Glencree Clinic. My personal and professional lives had once again merged in the worst way.

Yet I hadn't worked, at least here, for days.

I'd spent the weekend at home with Rosie when I was more certain of my diagnosis and she displayed all of the classic measles symptoms. Of course, I had consulted with a GP too, but ultimately for measles – much like chicken pox – you had to let it run its course. It's a virus and can't be treated with antibiotics.

On Friday morning when I called in to work and stayed at home with Rosie, I worked to control her fever, tried to keep her comfortable, all the while wondering how on earth this had happened, and hoping against hope that my tough cookie survivor would have the strength to battle it out.

This was the outcome Greg and I most worried about back when her allergy was first diagnosed and we had to make a call on the MMR vaccine.

'If she catches something, we'll just have to deal with it,' my husband advised, typically implacable. 'It's unlikely though – herd

immunity for measles is very high in this country. And anyway
what choice do we have?'

None whatsoever I knew, realising now that Greg's faith in
so-called herd immunity had clearly been misplaced. Measles
might be rare these days, but it was still possible.

And for my poor Rosie just now, terrifyingly real.

At least I knew my own chances of getting sick were slim. As
a healthcare professional I was vaccinated as a matter of course
against most standard infectious diseases. Still, as any parent
knows, those first few hours dealing with a coughing child and
a germ-filled house is enough to drive you crazy.

But I'd thought we were getting through it OK – or rather
Rosie was – until tonight.

Lucy had come over earlier in the evening to help me out and
confirmed that yes, little Clara Cooper had indeed also gone down
with it, but according to Madeleine seemed to have improved
over the weekend.

I started to think positive; maybe Rosie was close to being out
of the woods too? But then, almost out of nowhere, her early fever
returned. And spiked. Seriously spiked, over 104 degrees. Almost
in tandem, my heart dropped the other direction.

I knew the danger zone all too well and my daughter was in it.

Lucy and I hustled to get her undressed and into a cold bath,
but still, we couldn't get her fever down. I've dealt with a lot of
stressful medical situations, but it's completely different when it's
your child, your own flesh and blood.

While I was trying my damnedest not to panic, in truth I was
very scared. But even though I was scared, I'm not an idiot. And
when Rosie had a febrile seizure, right there in the bath, I knew
that this was very serious. Fighting the infection was consuming
her and I needed to get her to hospital – fast.

Unlike the good hour it would take to reach one of the Dublin hospitals, Glencree was only fifteen minutes down the road, and my workplace was well enough equipped for paediatric emergencies. Notwithstanding the fact that I implicitly trusted my colleagues to do their best for my little girl.

Lucy and I got Rosie wrapped up and into the car, but the poor thing was in a bad way, shivering and burning up at the same time. I swallowed the lump in my throat, trying to remain strong, hoping and praying that it was just one seizure and that it wouldn't happen again.

But then it did – right as we were flying down the road in Lucy's Jeep, only minutes away from my workplace. I held on to my daughter in the back seat – to hell with the seat belt – trying to get her to turn on her side safely so she wouldn't choke on her own tongue.

All the while screaming inside and praying to God not to do this to me again.

Please don't take my daughter away too…

When Lucy squealed to a stop in front of the clinic's entrance, I had to do everything in my power not to jump out of the car and start screaming for assistance. Thankfully, Lucy had no compunction about doing just that on my behalf.

Minutes later, my still-thrashing daughter was strapped to a stretcher and hustled indoors. I recognised several of the staff and nurses and knew one or two of the paramedics on shift, at least by name.

They would help Rosie, I reassured myself. They had the equipment and resources to control her fever – much more so than what I could do at home. I allowed myself to feel just the tiniest bit of relief and reminded myself that while febrile seizures were scary, they were mostly harmless; a natural result of the body's high temperature when fighting illness. On a practical level, I knew all this but it still didn't make it any less scary.

Rosie was in good hands in Glencree, it was the best place for her just then. I had to trust the very talented people around me. I had no choice.

A little later, they were indeed able to stabilise her and bring her temperature down just a little.

I literally pounced on Dr Jackson, the on-call paediatrician who just then was coming my way. I knew her a little, but personal decorum goes out the window when you're frantic for your child.

'How is she? Will she be OK?' I babbled, my heart in my mouth at the sight of the doctor's worryingly expressionless face.

'Kate…' she began, using *that* tone, one I'd heard uttered by hospital staff countless times (hell, I'd used it myself) when bracing themselves to give people news that wasn't good.

Oh God… Terrified, I waited for the doctor's next words to come out of her mouth, bracing myself for the worst.

'It's looking like Rosie has pneumonia,' Dr Jackson told me gravely, and I gasped with horror.

Pneumonia…

My God, how had I missed it? I should have had my little girl seen to long before now… what kind of idiot was I? I was supposed to be an RN for goodness' sake… I had a goddamn Masters degree and still I didn't realise my own child had pneumonia…

The doctor put a gentle hand on my arm. 'As a precaution, probably best if we transfer her to Dublin where they can keep an eye on her,' she said, referring to the national children's hospital in the city. We've given her antibiotics and are now trying to get her hydrated and in better shape for the ambulance journey, but it's going to take a little time.' She smiled gently. 'Kate, I know what you're thinking and, please, try not to be too hard on yourself – sometimes it's hard to tell with these things…'

'I just can't believe I didn't even consider it…' Especially when pneumonia was one of the most common complications with measles. I burst into tears, and allowed Lucy to lead me to a nearby chair, whereupon she let me cry on her shoulder exhausting myself even further.

Dr Jackson lightly patted my shoulder, and advised that I would be able to reunite with Rosie when they'd finished prepping her for the transfer, while once again reassuring me that I couldn't have known.

But of course I could; I'm her mother, aren't I? The one who's supposed to protect her from harm and keep this kind of stuff from happening in the first place.

Fat lot of good I was at that, I thought sniffing.

I stood up and began pacing, wearing a path in the linoleum floor as I waited to see my daughter.

'Come on, Kate, try to relax,' Lucy said as she fought back a yawn. It was now three o'clock in the morning. I had already told her repeatedly that she should go home to her own family, but she'd insisted on staying. 'Rosie's in good hands   think positive.'

I shook my head. 'No, if I sit down, I'll drive myself crazy thinking.'

About how this was all my fault. How I should have known. Why had I waited *three whole days* before getting her seen to, assuming she could just fight this on her own?

Right then, a nurse entered the general waiting area and gave me a gentle smile. It was enough to make me want to run over and hug her, yet I still couldn't be sure if it meant…

'Rosie's sleeping now, and we have her on an antibiotic drip.

The ambulance should be ready soon, and you're free to go back in and sit with her while we wait.'

Almost sick with relief, I thanked the nurse and looked quickly at Lucy, who offered to head back to the house to bring me some toiletries and clothes – things I hadn't had the time or the foresight to grab when we hightailed it over here hours ago.

I nodded my assent and she asked me if there was anything I needed specifically, but my mind was blank. I didn't care what she brought me frankly, because I couldn't recall a thing that I needed as much as I wanted to be by my little girl's side. Hold her close, keep her safe.

Like I thought I'd been doing up to now.

On entering Rosie's hospital room, I was immediately struck by how big the bed was and how small and fragile she was. My heart felt like it was breaking.

My God; she's only five years old...

She was so pale and she had monitors and machines all around her, tracking every heartbeat, every breath. I walked slowly to the side of the bed and sat down, taking Rosie's little hand in mine and murmuring, 'Mummy's here, buttercup. It's going to be OK.'

But was it? a small voice in my mind asked. Again, my brain instinctively tried to go clinical on me – it was ready to spout off the measles statistics that I had been trying not to think about since I first spotted that telltale rash. I tried to tell it to shut up.

It's just pneumonia – the antibiotics will sort it, it will be OK.

I worked my hardest to take Lucy's advice and try to think positive, but my mind was too busy lecturing me that there were no guarantees from one minute to the next.

I understood that lesson better than most.

Chapter 8

The following week, Madeleine felt herself breathe a sigh of relief and offered up the quietest of thankful prayers as the GP took another look into Clara's mouth and nodded.

Her rash still looked angry and sore, but her fever had all but disappeared, thank goodness. Some colour had returned to her cheeks, and today – a week since first displaying any signs of illness – Madeleine's five-year-old was looking much more like herself.

Dr Barrett stood up and took a final glance down at Clara. 'It looks like you are on the mend, princess,' he said with a smile. 'You're a very lucky girl.' His smile disappeared as he looked at Madeleine. 'As are you,' he added in a grave tone.

She kissed her daughter's forehead, tears of relief pricking at the corners of her eyes, but her attention was returned to Dr Barrett when he cleared his throat and motioned with a sharp jerk of his head that he wanted to speak with her – privately.

She turned to leave the room and dutifully followed in his wake.

'When will Tom be home?' Dr Barrett enquired. In his sixties, the Knockroe doctor had been on first name terms with Madeleine's family for years, and had been her GP since she was a child. She secretly wondered when he was going to retire. Tom said that Frank Barrett would retire at his funeral. He was probably right.

'Not until later. He had to get back to work. He was here for the first few days, of course, but when it looked like she was out of the woods, he went back yesterday.'

Tom had been wonderful at keeping poor Clara's spirits up, especially when one day he'd arrived home with, of all things, a blow-up kayak and a huge cuddly dolphin, promising their little girl that once she was all better, he'd take her out on the water like they did in Florida. This had raised a much needed smile from her rash-covered face, and even a few giggles when Tom and Jake proceeded to re-enact on the floor of her bedroom the loveliest moment of their trip; a memorable day out on the gulf when a family of blue dolphins had appeared and proceeded to jump up and down alongside their kayak, delighting them all, especially Clara.

'He only has so much annual leave left unfortunately, and we have holidays booked for the summer,' Madeleine babbled to the doctor, which earned her a stern harrumph. 'I'm sorry, you're right – that shouldn't matter at a time like this.'

Especially when it had been a holiday that had got them into all this trouble in the first place.

'You're right, she must have picked it up on the flight back from Florida,' Tom had agreed, when the doctor first came to examine Clara, echoing Madeleine's early assessment.

On the GP's advice, her husband had been in touch with the health board to report the incident and put them on alert for potential contamination amongst other passengers.

'The timeline does sound right,' the doctor concluded. 'You got back, when – Saturday week? So she would have been exposed about ten days prior to showing any symptoms. Unfortunately, further exposing her classmates at Applewood in the ensuing time,' he'd added pointedly, and, thinking of little Rosie O'Hara, Madeleine winced.

Now Dr Barrett turned to face her as they reached the living room. 'I don't know if you and Tom are really cognisant of just how lucky your family is – how lucky *Clara* is. Especially when you already dodged a bullet with Jake.' He narrowed his eyes at her from behind his spectacles and ran a hand through his full head of shockingly white hair. Madeleine sensed a lecture. She wished Tom was here – especially as she guessed what was coming next. It was so hard having to defend their position over and over – mortifyingly difficult actually, given what they'd just been through. Her husband was much better than she at arguing the reasons behind their decision not to vaccinate Clara, and Tom had for the most part taken this recent misfortune in his stride.

'We just need to wait things out, Maddie. She'll be fine. We've been through this before,' he reassured, when, after Clara's diagnosis, Madeleine had castigated herself for their failures. But Tom had once again proceeded to reiterate the reasons why they had decided against the jabs in the first place, outlined their full decision-making process when Jake was a baby and arrived at the same conclusion. 'We said the risk was one we weren't willing to take, and now it's time for us to stand by that,' he'd repeated gently, while Madeleine thought it was all fine and well to make such decisions without having to face the fallout of the reality: namely a sick child who was feverish and uncomfortable.

But, in truth, Clara did seem to be fighting it well, and now, thank goodness, looked to be in the clear.

'I need to encourage you again,' Frank Barrett reiterated. 'When Clara is fully recovered, go and get your children protected against the rest of all these godforsaken illnesses medicine conquered years ago. I'm serious, Madeleine.' She put up a hand, trying to appease him, but he continued. 'No, as your doctor, it is my job to say this. You know, there are a lot of GPs in this country who wouldn't even allow your kids near their surgery. The only reason I haven't had that policy with you is because I have known your family for ever. But I have to put my foot down now. Do you know just how bad this could have been? Do you have any idea? I'm receiving complaints from parents all over Knockroe and beyond. Madeleine, they don't want their kids around yours – especially not at school.'

'Please, Frank,' said Madeleine, trying to keep her voice from quivering. 'You know this is something that Tom and I have always felt very strongly about—'

'Bah!' Dr Barrett bellowed, throwing up his hands in frustration. 'Nonsense. Conspiracy theories against the pharmaceutical companies. For heaven's sakes, Madeleine, you know those autism studies were debunked years ago. I thought you were smarter than that; I *know* you are. All vaccines have ever done is eradicate serious illness. Do you know how many people in Third World hellholes would love to have access to something as simple as the freely distributed preventative medicine we take for granted? Do you know how many lives it would save?'

The doctor sighed heavily and dropped onto the sofa, seemingly exhausted. He looked at one of the plush throw pillows that he had disturbed from its artful arrangement and appeared thoughtful.

Madeleine could sense him softening somehow – like his rant had run out of steam. She didn't know what to say to him. She understood his point of view, of course she did. But they'd been through this time and time again when the kids were younger.

'Do you want a glass of water? A cup of tea, maybe?' she asked kindly. He had done so much for her family over the last week, and she understood his stress.

Dr Barrett shrugged. 'Tea would be great. Thank you.'

Madeleine retreated to the kitchen, vaguely aware this was one room of the house that had yet to be completely rescued from neglect when Clara was in the throes of her illness. And, as if the house wasn't bad enough, after the last week, Madeleine knew that she too badly needed taking in hand. She put a hand up and ran it through her hair, now flat and straggly, and she guessed her unmade-up face looked haggard, and a million miles from her bubbly blonde TV persona.

Washing her hands, she swallowed the compulsive urge to automatically grab the bleach and begin scrubbing things down right there and then – to try and restore order. Instead she put the kettle on and brought it to a boil. She pulled a teapot down from the cabinet as she eyed the wine glasses that were housed right above it.

What I wouldn't give for one of you bad boys just now, she thought ruefully. Alas, it was barely noon and she wasn't one of those people. Not yet at least.

Though her Mad Mum alter-ego would probably advise her to go right ahead.

Allowing the tea to steep, Madeleine closed her eyes and thought about what Dr Barrett had said. He was right, of course. She knew that they had been lucky in that it hadn't been anything more serious. Clara was on the mend.

They'd got through it, dodged another bullet. Everything was going to be OK.

She nodded as if to reassure herself of this as she placed the teapot and cups on a silver tea tray that had belonged to her mother. She knew it was a bit old-fashioned, but there was also something about it that was just so nicely ceremonial. She had always loved it and took it out every chance she could. Though Tom had kept the basics stocked up, unfortunately there were no biscuits or anything else to offer the doctor, and a trip to the supermarket was long overdue. She sighed. The last week had well and truly been utter chaos, but at least things were looking up now.

She walked back into the living room and set the tray on their walnut coffee table, taking extra care not to scratch the finish. Pouring a cup of tea, Madeleine looked at the doctor and asked, 'Sugar?'

Dr Barrett shook his head. 'Just milk will do. Thank you.'

The doctor took a hesitant sip and closed his eyes briefly, as if allowing himself a brief respite as the warmth of the liquid spread through his body. Suddenly, he reopened his eyes and placed his cup and saucer on the coffee table. Something about his demeanour had changed once again, as if it was time to get back to business.

'You know that little Rosie O'Hara is in hospital?'

Madeleine looked down at her milky tea and nodded solemnly. 'I know, I heard.' Lucy had filled her in on the news – that on Monday she had gone with Kate to the local clinic because Rosie's fever had suddenly spiked. And that the little girl had soon after been transferred to Dublin.

Returning her eyes to meet Dr Barrett's, she had the uncanny feeling that he was studying her. Gauging her reaction. Of course he'd given her that lecture before too – about social responsibility and their contribution (or lack thereof) to herd immunity.

But how could you realistically proceed with something you

truly felt was unsafe? Especially when there was no law against not vaccinating.

'She's in a critical condition, Madeleine. I don't know if you know *that*. She has pneumonia, and some swelling in her brain apparently. She's not going to have an easy road of it. Not like Clara.'

Madeleine's throat went dry. Why was he telling her this? To make her feel guilty? Trying to blame her outright for Rosie's condition? As if she didn't feel bad enough.

Thanks to Lucy, she was all too aware that her daughter was being blamed by other Knockroe parents – and the school – for infecting Rosie. She didn't need to be made to feel guilty about that from the family doctor as well.

Madeleine placed her cup and saucer on the tray and stood up. She appreciated the house call that Dr Barrett had made, but now it was time for him to go. She had more than enough to do around the house and she still had Clara to attend to.

And this whole conversation was making her feel really uncomfortable.

'I've already sent Kate our best wishes. I know what she's going through, after all.' Madeleine intended her words to sound soft, but as they fell from her lips she realised there was more of an edge to them than she'd intended.

But she just couldn't face any more guilt, any more regret. This, taken with the stress and worry about Clara over the last week, was getting on top of her. What was done was done and there was nothing Madeleine could do about it now. She couldn't go back and change things or stop Clara from contracting the disease. The time for such decision-making was years ago, long gone. And at that time, she and Tom had made the decision that felt right, that was the best one for their family. She couldn't think about the impact of that choice on other people just now. It was all too overwhelming.

Madeleine just wanted the doctor to leave so she could deal with this on her own, away from stern glares and accusing tones. Though if this was what her doctor – a close acquaintance – was saying, she wondered what strangers or indeed other locals would say when they heard about Rosie's hospital admission.

Dr Barrett clearly picked up on the mood. 'Well, I suppose that I should be going,' he said, standing up. 'Let me know if there is any change with Clara. Otherwise, I think she is indeed on the mend. But again you and Tom should think about what I said about the other jabs. It's still not too late.'

He focused a keen eye on Madeleine then and she felt as if all of her thoughts, doubts, and worries were on display. Incredibly, despite her relief that Clara was on the mend, this visit had actually made her feel worse; had sent her entire world out of whack.

It was truly awful that little Rosie was in hospital; there was no question about that. She felt for Kate and she was desperately sorry that Clara's infection had played some part in that. It wasn't her daughter's fault though; these things were always a risk, and nobody had any control over how another child might fight infection.

And, more to the point, wasn't it common knowledge that Rosie was unvaccinated too?

In any case, Clara was going to be OK, that was the main thing.

It was the only thing that Madeleine should be thinking about just then.

Chapter 9

I felt my eyes grow heavy as I sat in the recliner that had been placed in the corner of Rosie's hospital room. However, as soon as I got close to sleep, some beep or boop would be emitted from the machines surrounding my little girl's bed, and I would spring awake, my heart thumping.

I was exhausted. I hadn't truly slept in days, and felt at times both over-fuelled by adrenaline and as lethargic as if I had been trying to run underwater. This must be what torture by sleep deprivation felt like. I would honestly sell my soul to the highest bidder if it meant that I would get more than an hour of sleep at a time.

Of course, it wasn't as if I didn't have people around me telling me to take care of myself. Lucy, Rosie's paediatrician Dr Ryan, various shift nurses – they all told me I needed to sleep, and I knew they were right. I understood that I needed to focus on myself too, but I found it impossible. The stress alone was making my body rigid with anxiety. No matter if I wanted to rest, I felt constantly on. My mind still raced with worry and the never-ending chorus of 'what if?'

Until Rosie started to show signs of any improvement, my life was at a standstill.

After fixing my hair into a more comfortable top knot, I got up from where I sat and walked to her bedside, dropping to a kneel. Her eyes were closed and she was sleeping. They had her on a respirator at the moment because she was having problems breathing due to the pneumonia. I would have given anything to remove the machines and tubes that seemed to engulf her. I wanted her to be awake so I could talk to her and reassure her that she would be OK, but I knew that sleep was good for her and it was what she needed.

Resting my head against the rail of the hospital bed, I felt myself starting to nod off again until I heard someone come into the room.

'Kate?' It was Frances, a friendly nurse I'd come to know in the six days we'd been here.

She checked on my little girl's condition, but from her chart I already knew there was little to report. They'd taken blood tests on admission to the hospital which had confirmed pneumonia. As it was, we just had to wait for the antibiotics to do their job.

Wait. It seemed like all I'd been doing this past week.

To my surprise, the nurse took a seat alongside me. 'How are you?' she asked, touching my arm. 'You know you really should try to—'

'I know. But sleep isn't easy…'

'I understand. It's a horrible time, but rest assured we're doing all we can. Measles, it can be such a nasty business when it takes this course. But, to be honest, it's a long time since I've come across an outbreak in this hospital.'

She paused for a moment and then leaned forward in her chair, clasping her hands in front of her. 'I heard that the other little girl from Rosie's school has since recovered?'

'Apparently so.'

'And there haven't been any other cases in the school or in the town apart from Rosie?'

'No, I don't think so. Not that I know of anyway. Thank goodness.'

Appearing thoughtful, Frances seemed to be studying me. 'I understand the reason why Rosie isn't vaccinated. And I know it was a hard choice that you and your late husband had to make. But do you happen to know why the other little girl wasn't?'

'I really don't know the family all that well...' I answered. My head felt foggy.

'No idea if it's a political position? Something religious perhaps?'

She seemed to be just making idle conversation, but something about her tone of voice made me perk up. I tried to climb through the swamp of grey matter in my head.

'Why do you ask? And what does it matter?'

But the nurse didn't have time to answer my question, because at that moment Lucy entered the waiting room with Christine Campbell in tow.

Handing over my recent post as well as some other bits and pieces I needed from the house (my iPad and charger, one of Rosie's favourite dinosaurs, a random book that had been on my bedside table), Lucy took a seat beside me. Christine sat on my other side as I introduced Frances.

'Christine was really anxious about Rosie,' Lucy supplied when I looked curiously at our new visitor. It was nice of Christine to come, and surprising too when I didn't know her especially well.

But that was one of the positives about living in a small community.

'Oh you're all from the same town?' Frances smiled. 'I was just asking Kate about that other little girl with measles. Do you know her too?' she enquired pleasantly.

I shifted uncomfortably. Given that Clara was almost certainly the cause of Rosie's current trials, I didn't like to think about the Coopers all that much. While I was happy that little Clara had recovered, I couldn't deny that I felt a little... jealous too. That they were the ones with all the luck and resources, as well as having each other to lean on when things were hard. While I had nothing and no one.

Apart from Lucy of course, who had once again been wonderful. My mother had tried to make arrangements to travel up from Cork, but my dad was poorly with sciatica and, as she didn't drive, she was relying on a lift from a generous neighbour.

Part of me was almost glad she hadn't yet managed it. At least I could stay here at the hospital and focus all of my attention on Rosie, without having to think about hosting my mother too, who suffered from her nerves and, God help her, wasn't the best in a crisis.

But while I was reticent to discuss the Coopers, Christine was practically jumping in her seat waiting for her turn to speak. 'Yes, we do know the family,' she said, her tone barely concealing her disapproval as she pushed her glasses back to the top of her nose.

'Unusual that she wasn't vaccinated either, isn't it?' Frances said conversationally. 'Unlucky too, I suppose.'

'Nothing at all to do with luck,' added Christine with narrowed eyes. 'It's because the girl's parents – the father in particular – are a pair of sanctimonious lunatics. Tom is one of those conspiracy theory types,' she added bitterly.

I shot Lucy a look. I was grateful for Christine's visit, but my daughter's bedside wasn't the place for gossip, or airing personal grievances.

In turn, my friend apologised with her eyes.

'Christine, like me, the Coopers have just experienced a very scary time, except *un*like me, they've managed to come out of it OK. Whatever the reasons for their choices, it's their business. I'm just glad their little girl is better. That's all that matters.'

Lucy spoke up. 'Yes, and also Madeleine has been so concerned about Rosie. She asks about her all the time. The mother and I are friends,' she added, for Frances' benefit.

'Please understand, I'm not trying to gossip,' the nurse went on. 'I was just wondering about their reasons, maybe there's a good reason—'

'Nope. Absolutely not. They knew exactly what they were doing in not vaccinating. And they took the risk anyway. Put all of our children in danger.'

'Christine, please...' Lucy looked mortified.

'I see,' the nurse murmured softly.

'And, Kate, you know my cousin is a solicitor? Well, we were discussing the situation about the Coopers over lunch the other day... and he tells me there is a school of thought that suggests if you decide not to vaccinate your child, and another gets seriously ill like Rosie has, you could potentially be held liable.'

I shook my head; was Christine seriously suggesting that *I* was the one responsible for Rosie's plight? 'Are you saying I'm to blame for this?' I gasped, a bit hysterically.

I looked to Lucy for help, but she wore an expression I couldn't read. Was it confusion? Or concern? Why couldn't I follow this conversation?

Jesus, I needed to sleep.

But Christine's dark eyes were bright and she was shaking her head.

'No, Kate, she's not suggesting at all that you're responsible,' Frances put in. 'But I think what your friend *is* suggesting is that the other parents could be. They failed to vaccinate their child. That same child contracted a preventable illness, passing it on to Rosie who's since become very ill.'

'What does it matter who's responsible?' I cried. 'Please,' I implored Lucy. 'I can't deal with this. I… I'm not able for visitors just now. My daughter needs me.'

The nurse stood up. 'Kate is right. Perhaps this isn't the best time…'

I felt myself start to relax just a bit, but Christine wasn't finished. 'But you have to think about this, Kate. I mean, I'm not trying to force your hand or talk you into anything you are uncomfortable with, I just want you to think about it. There was a deliberate choice made. You couldn't vaccinate Rosie without risking her life. The Coopers weren't faced with that decision – they just decided not to bother. And don't forget Madeleine sent Clara to school that morning, knowing she was unwell. This was what my cousin found interesting. Think about it. She doesn't protect her kids from infectious diseases and then she sends her feverish daughter to school. She *deliberately* put ours at risk.'

'No,' I said, shaking my head. 'It was just unfortunate, just one of those things. And it's a risk I had to take every day too knowing Rosie isn't protected. It's just as much my fault as anyone else's.'

'How can you not see it?' Christine persisted. Lucy put a hand on her arm, trying to quieten her.

'Because nobody does that!' I cried, outraged at the very suggestion. 'No parent would *ever* intend such a thing.'

But amidst my protests, the alternative scenario sparked a thought in me.

If Madeleine Cooper, knowing Clara was ill, *hadn't* sent her daughter to school that morning, wouldn't Rosie have avoided getting measles?

And wouldn't my little girl now be at home making up fearsome scenarios for her dinosaurs, instead of lying in a hospital bed, fighting for breath?

Chapter 10

MAD MUM MUSINGS
Parents Not Allowed

I see a woman hovering under a seven-foot play frame, arms aloft like a wedding guest waiting to catch the bridal bouquet. But then she turns and I see, not anticipation, but outright terror on her face.

'Oh my God, she's going to break her neck,' she gasps, horrified. 'Anyone know who her mother is?'

The kid apparently in such grave peril is mine – except she's been climbing that play frame since she was four. When I tell the woman this, she stares at me, eyes wide with recrimination, and I realise that, yikes: this mama bear's a helicopter.

A species of parent that is all too common in our favourite playground.

I love taking my six- and eight-year-old kids to the playground for many reasons: first and foremost so they can play and muck about – with other kids or by themselves – as well as learn to negotiate the world on their own terms.

They run around, laugh, climb play frames and make friends – all the usual things kids do at parks and playgrounds – while I sit on a bench at a safe distance, chat to other parents or (gasp!) idly scroll through my phone.

For my two, it's a space that remains free from everyday restrictions (within reasonable limits). I don't stand over them or interfere and it seems this, at least to the helicopters, makes me not just a Mad Mum but a Very Bad one, perhaps even worthy of social services intervention.

Because helicopters come to the playground to be Alert At All Times, hovering endlessly over their charges – coaxing up the ladder and down the slide, bouncing gently on the seesaw, swinging endlessly on the swing.

I know not every parent is the same, and there's no denying that it can be hard to just let kids at it, especially if it's your and Junior's first time in the place, and you see everyone else hand-holding. And if you don't, it immediately makes you look like you don't give a shit.

I'm also sure no one ever thinks he or she is a helicopter parent, and it goes without saying that everyone is just trying to do right by their child.

But does more worry equal more love?

For my part, I'm inclined to be free range because I remember my own childhood and how my parents didn't have the time, let alone the desire, to watch every misstep or foresee every potential problem.

Don't child-proof the world, is my motto. World-proof the child. (Thankfully my husband agrees with me.)

And every time someone else is horrified that he or I let our brood try something potentially 'too dangerous for their age', I wave concern aside with the assertion that aren't they better off learning now – before it's too late – to respect the danger of what they are doing and negotiate it safely?

I want them to try things they thought they couldn't do, fail, try again and repeat until they are successful. Isn't this a necessary life skill in itself?

Psychological studies also show that children benefit from, if not actual danger, the feeling of danger and related sensations that result from activities like climbing up to get a bird's-eye view, playing with dangerous tools, or exploring on their own.

With that in mind, I recently read an article about a playground in New York that embraces an interesting philosophy: parents (helicopters or otherwise) are not allowed.

After the adults sign a waiver, their kids are let loose on a small field full of all kinds of detritus; tyres, a plastic water cooler, pieces of wood in all sorts of sizes and shapes, thrown out household equipment etc., where they do what kids have done for ever: have fun and figure out how to make and break things.

Given all the stuff lying around for them to play with, it's inevitable that some of them will occasionally get dirty and scuffed up and scratched.

In fact, that's pretty much the point.

So parents, maybe try to switch off those whirring fret-motors at the playground, come back down to earth once in a while and even consider sitting with some of us feckless miscreants for a minute or two?

It'll work wonders for your nerves and you never know, you and your kids might just have some fun...

Clara Cooper couldn't wait to get back to school.

She felt herself nearly shaking with excitement as her mother pulled up in front of Applewood Primary. Clara just wanted things to get back to normal; she was eager to go to drama class again and see her friends and, as much as she would only admit it secretly to herself, she even missed having to do homework. She felt desperate to feel like a normal kid, instead of a sick one who had to be quarantined from her life and everyone in it.

'All set, honey?' her mum asked with a smile.

Clara was about to reply when her stupid brother interrupted her.

'Why would anyone be excited to go back to school?' he sneered. 'I'd rather be at home watching TV.'

Sometimes Jake could be an idiot. He just didn't get it – but Clara wasn't going to let him ruin her mood.

'Yeah, I'm ready, Mum. I'm really excited, actually.'

'That's my girl,' said her mum. 'At least I know which one of you is the smart one,' she teased. 'Do you want me to walk you in? Or...'

But Clara was already shaking her head. Jake had flung open the door of the car and jumped from the vehicle as soon as it came to a stop. He threw up a hand in salute and shouted, 'Bye, Mum,' as he ran towards his friends, who were gathered at the classroom doors.

Clara wanted to follow his lead. After a couple of weeks of being sick and coddled around the clock (not that she hadn't liked that – she had felt terrible after all), she was now ready to spread her wings and be independent.

'I'm fine, I just want to go see my friends. Is that OK?' she asked politely.

Her mother grinned. 'Of course! Now, just wait a minute though. Let me get a picture of you – I want to put it on Facebook. So many people have been asking about you and I want to show them just how well you look and how excited you are. Speaking of which, Auntie Fiona is picking you up later. Now that you're better, Cam and Brian are staying with us for the afternoon, and she's going to bring you all back to our house.'

'Great.' Clara forced a smile, but in truth she wasn't too keen on her cousins coming to visit. Brian was OK, but Cam was just so moody and nasty to everyone. She didn't know why his mum and dad didn't warn him to be kind and show manners like hers insisted she and Jake always did. But, she supposed, some kids were just like that.

Her mum held up her iPhone and snapped a picture, nodding in approval. 'Perfect. Now you go and have a lovely day. Dad and I are proud of you, sweetheart – you're such a trooper.'

Clara waved goodbye and hopped from the car. Taking a deep breath, she felt like skipping, but tried to play it cool, scanning the outside of the school for her friends. Spotting some other girls from her class, she strode with purpose in their direction.

As she walked, her thoughts briefly turned to Rosie. She felt a small burst of worry enter her chest. Clara knew that her classmate was still in the hospital – at least that's what she had heard her mum say. She was a bit worried about Rosie.

They weren't best friends or anything, but she still really liked her. Rosie was fun, not at all girly and she loved playing dinosaurs with the boys. Clara liked dinosaurs too but her best friends Rachel and Megan didn't really, so it was nice to have another girl who enjoyed playing with them too.

And she also felt a bit bad for Rosie because her dad died. Clara really couldn't imagine what that must be like, but guessed it must be a terrible thing. She couldn't imagine losing her own dad. And now poor Rosie was in the hospital – she had become much sicker with measles than Clara.

That was something else she couldn't imagine because she had felt like she was going to die while she had them. What must it be like to feel even worse?

Furrowing her brow, Clara decided that she would keep Rosie in her thoughts, but that she wouldn't let her worries ruin her first day back. Picking up her pace, she felt her spirits buoy once again, especially as she heard the squeals of delight from Rachel and Megan. She ran the final steps to her friends and they all cried out in excitement.

However, the girls' obvious excitement at being reunited attracted the attention of another classmate they usually tried to avoid.

Kevin Campbell.

The young boy approached the three girls with a scowl on this face. He was flanked on either side by two of his other friends – older boys who liked to be nasty.

Great, more meanies.

'Who said *you* could come back to school?' he sneered. 'Are you trying to get everyone else sick now?'

Clara turned to look directly at Kevin. She hated having to talk to him, but she knew from experience that ignoring him just made him worse. So she faced him down, like her mum and dad had taught her.

'Principal Connelly talked to my doctor and my parents. Everyone said I was ready to come back. Just go away. It's none of your business anyway,' she said, trying to keep her voice steady. She felt Megan stand reassuringly close alongside her.

But this answer didn't satisfy Kevin.

'It is my business. I don't want to get sick because of *you*. I don't want my friends to catch your rotten diseases. You know, I heard that Rosie could die. Do you know that if that happens, it will be your fault, Clara? I wonder how old you have to be to go to jail? They might not lock you up for killing her, but they will definitely lock your parents up – and then you and Jake will be put up for adoption or something.' His friends laughed loudly, which merely served to egg Kevin on. 'Probably be better that way anyway. My mum says that your parents are stupid and crazy. So it's good if they do get locked up. I mean, murderers should go to jail – especially ones who kill kids.'

Clara felt a lump grow in her throat. Her mum had told her that Rosie getting sick hadn't been her fault. But now she wasn't so sure. What if Rosie *did* die? She willed herself not to cry, but still a tear leaked from her eye.

Of course, Kevin saw it. 'Are you going to cry, Clara?' he guffawed. 'Well, you probably should. If I were you, I would feel terrible for killing one of my friends.'

'Shut up, Kevin,' yelled Rachel, trying to intervene on behalf of her friend. 'Clara hasn't killed anyone and Rosie isn't going to die. Just shut up. You don't know anything.'

She and Megan began pulling her away in the direction of the classroom. Clara allowed herself to be led – anything to get away.

But regardless of the distance they put between her and the bullies, Kevin's words still echoed in Clara's brain.

If Rosie died, *would* it be her fault?

Chapter 11

I was spending most of my days and nights at the hospital, and today Lucy arrived around midday and insisted that I get some space between me and the chair beside Rosie's bed, for my own mental and physical health.

Yesterday, the medical team had removed Rosie's ventilator and were confident that the antibiotics were working well in treating the pneumonia.

So all I could do now was wait.

The poor thing was still very weak, and barely alert most of the time (though a dinosaur balloon the Coopers of all people had sent had raised a smile), but according to Dr Ryan, she finally seemed to be heading out of the danger zone.

Which was the only reason I was even considering Lucy's suggestion.

She had assured me that she wouldn't leave Rosie's side until I returned, and while I initially refused, I realised after a quick look in a mirror that I really did need to take myself in hand, enough to pop back to Knockroe to collect a few things from the house, and wash my hair at least.

'I left you some bath oil – that lovely new Jo Malone scent. Go and unwind for a bit, have a snooze, eat a pint of Ben & Jerry's, or whatever, just get out of here for the day, OK?' she had urged.

And, despite myself, I knew she was right, which was why, having kissed my little girl goodbye, I found myself pulling into my driveway for the first time in what felt like days, weeks... I wasn't even sure of the timeline any more.

I did know that it was about a week and a half since Rosie had been put on the ventilator, and all the while I was at the hospital, Lucy had been running my house as well as her own. I told her just now before I departed that I really appreciated her; she was everything I needed in a wife. That made us both laugh, and for that brief moment it felt good to just feel something akin to normal.

Now, after dragging my exhausted body into the house, I felt myself exhale just the tiniest bit when I stepped into the kitchen. Everything looked so calm and... normal. This week's post had been brought in, there were some fresh flowers in a vase on the counter. Anyone walking into this house would have no indication of the chaos the occupants had been living through over the last two weeks.

Though, to be fair, even when my life *wasn't* falling to pieces, my kitchen never looked like this.

'Bless you, Lucy,' I whispered, so as not to break the near-perfect peaceful silence that enveloped me.

I dropped a bag full of dirty clothes near the washing machine and proceeded to the sink to put a kettle on for a pot of tea. I pulled out a tin of loose mint tea that I reserved for moments when I needed to truly unwind and spooned three teaspoons into the pot. As I waited for the water to boil, I headed upstairs to the bathroom and drew the warm bath that Lucy had encouraged me to take, pouring in a generous amount of that delicious oil.

I rubbed my shoulders trying to ease some of the tension out of my body and nodded to myself. *Yes, I needed this.*

A moment later, the kettle sounded and I returned to the kitchen, poured the boiling hot water into the teapot and, allowing it time to steep, turned my attention to the kitchen island.

Pulling the piles of post closer, I saw that Lucy had handily created two stacks – one that obviously comprised less urgent bills and official documentation that she hadn't brought to the hospital and another made up of cards and various other bits and pieces. I debated for a moment as to which pile I should tackle. Though the cards would surely be heartening, the realist in me made me opt for the bills. I was never one to shy away from the bad stuff – might as well tackle it head-on. That's what Greg used to say about facing unpleasant situations.

Grimacing to myself, I noted the irony. My whole life these days was about tackling things head-on.

I found the pile to be exactly what I expected. A load of payment demands: electricity, gas, TV – a couple overdue because I hadn't spent any time focusing on the day-to-day administrative affairs of my life lately. Quickly growing tired of seeing the amounts grow into a bigger and bigger total sum, I tried to keep my thoughts from overwhelming me as I also started to panic over the fact that it had been almost three weeks since I'd done a day's work. Which reminded me – I needed to return that call from my supervisor at Glencree, no doubt wanting to discuss my situation and when I might be able to return to my duties at the clinic.

It scared me that I wasn't currently in a position to answer that question, and wasn't sure when I would be.

But no, now wasn't the time to think about it, I argued with myself. Lucy was right, today was for de-stressing, not adding another burden to my already teetering worry-pile.

In the other group of letters, there were indeed lots of Get Well Soon cards for Rosie, as well as notes of support for me from other Applewood parents, and I was reminded again of how wonderfully supportive this community was in times of need, and how quick everyone in Knockroe had been to rally round me both now and after Greg's death, irrespective of how well or little they knew me personally.

Christine Campbell was a case in point, who, along with Lucy, was constantly and very kindly asking if she could help, or if I needed anything while Rosie remained in Dublin. Although I still hadn't quite forgiven her for that suggestion at the hospital before that the Coopers might be directly to blame for our current misfortune, I was touched by her generosity.

At the time, I'd very quickly put an end to that conversation. 'There wasn't an accident, or a faulty product or something – there isn't anyone to blame,' I'd argued, horrified by the suggestion. 'This is just about kids getting sick.'

However, Christine's reply echoed in my head occasionally. 'No, it's about personal responsibility, or lack thereof,' she had insisted. 'Madeleine sent her sick child to school knowing Clara wasn't vaccinated against *any* serious illnesses. And, unlike you, she and Tom *chose* that situation. Really, you should talk to my cousin…'

But I honestly couldn't wrap my head around Christine's insistence. And I had told her, the nurse and especially Lucy – since she was friends with both me and the Coopers – exactly that.

It was uncomfortable to even think about. In fact, it felt almost… tacky. How could I even think about casting blame on anyone for this, let alone take another family to court? One from that very same community that had so readily taken me and Rosie to their hearts. It wasn't even worth thinking about, and once again I urged my brain to just… stop.

Relaxation, relaxation...

Grabbing my phone (just in case there was any change at the hospital), and my teacup, I headed for the stairs, determined once and for all to switch my mind off and submerge myself in a tub full of sweet-scented bubbles.

I sighed with pleasure as I lowered myself into the warm tub and felt my muscles immediately unwind as I submerged my body completely.

What I wouldn't give at that moment for Greg to be sharing the water with me, rubbing out the knots that had over the last two years made themselves a permanent home along my shoulder blades. Though, in all honesty, I didn't even need a massage as badly as I did a simple hug from someone who wasn't a friend or a child. I could barely remember what it felt like to be touched by a man in a physical way.

'The things you take for granted...' I whispered, recalling all of the times that I had been too busy for a quick hug goodbye from Greg in the morning, or all those other moments at the end of a busy day I had fallen asleep without kissing him.

Swallowing hard, I knew from experience that I needed a distraction in order to avoid walking down the road of self-pity. So, sitting up a bit, I reached across to the lid of the toilet where I had laid my phone on top of a towel. Social media always provided a welcome respite from obsessive thinking. There was something inherently relaxing about mindlessly scrolling through other people's lives.

Reading through my own page alerts and checking my messages, I found many many notes of encouragement and brief 'thinking of you' posts that had come in over the last while from old friends in Dublin and Cork, as well as other Knockroe locals I didn't even know. I'd called my mother and pleaded with her not to worry about travelling all the way up here; that I had everything under control.

In truth I didn't need the hassle.

Several people had tagged me in images that contained inspirational and uplifting quotes, and I went through and acknowledged what they'd posted so they'd know I'd seen them. Others had tagged me in a short local online news piece that had mentioned a recent but minimal ('minimal' ha!) measles outbreak in the area, quoting the usual facts and figures. I ignored those; I didn't need the internet to tell *me* about measles.

As I continued to read through the newsfeed detailing other people's day-to-day activities and happy photographs, I allowed myself to find a comfortable lull where I simply glimpsed at other people's comings and goings. There was something inherently hypnotic about scrolling through multiple unrelated stories of everyday life and, for the first time in what felt like an age, I started to feel myself relax at last.

Until I saw it.

Clara Cooper's beaming (rash-free) face staring back at me as she apparently returned to school this morning for the first time in almost three weeks. Though Madeleine Cooper and I weren't connected socially, Lucy's activity had popped up on the sidebar and I'd spotted that she'd liked something on Madeleine's profile.

Rosie's classmate looked so vibrant, so *well* and so utterly opposite to my frail little girl, still so weak and frighteningly lifeless in her hospital bed, surrounded by seemingly endless bleeping machines.

And, before I could help myself, I threw my phone across the floor and burst into tears.

Chapter 12

Madeleine sat at her desk in front of her laptop – she was working diligently through *Mad Mum*'s social media replies and messages while she waited for Jake and Clara and her in-laws' kids to come home from school.

Earlier that morning, she'd slotted in a hairdressing appointment to get her roots done after the school run, had applied a luxurious Crème de la Mer face mask to give her skin a boost, and had stopped off at the café for a quick latte and chat with Lucy.

And after a couple of weeks sporting comfy leisurewear while tending to Clara, today she was a wearing a wonderfully soft baby blue cashmere top and her favourite skinny jeans. In short, Madeleine felt back to herself.

As she mentioned to Clara earlier, Tom's sister Fiona was dropping Jake, Clara and her own two boys home in exchange for Madeleine keeping an eye on them until dinnertime, while her sister-in-law went to a dentist appointment. While having multiple kids in the house was chaotic at the best of times, Fiona's oldest, Cameron, was especially tricky to look after. Still, it was only for a couple of hours: she could manage them for that long couldn't she?

A direct message notification pinged just then, and Madeleine flipped from one site to another. Yet another follower had left a thumbs-up and comment on her new piece about parents in the playground.

You're so right! Sometimes my kids can't get near the slides with all those blasted Helicopters (LOL) hovering around. Headwreckers...

Madeleine acknowledged the comment before turning her attention back to the task at hand.

She was so relieved to once again be back to a routine. Clara had returned to school; work was up to date – everything was back to normal.

Well, almost.

She couldn't help but think of Kate O'Hara. Madeleine wondered if she should make another call to Rosie's mum. She had never heard back that first time, back when Clara too was sick, and she knew from Lucy that Kate had her hands full tending to her daughter.

Of course she'd sent flowers (and a dinosaur balloon) to the hospital and had even suggested a potential visit, which Lucy had very quickly shut down. 'It's really not the best idea at the moment, Maddie. Things are still delicate. Perhaps better wait till Rosie's out of hospital and in the clear?'

And even though nothing had been said out loud, she still felt dreadful about the possibility that their family could be responsible for visiting the infection on little Rosie, though obviously nobody was to blame for how the poor thing reacted. Pneumonia – horrific...

Oh blast it, she'd try her again. The last thing Madeleine

wanted was for the woman to think she didn't fully appreciate Clara's part in what had happened, or worse, that she and Tom didn't care. She reached for her phone and scrolled through her contacts. She had saved Kate's number from before and, finding it, she pressed the button to connect the call.

Almost straight away, as if the phone was out of coverage or switched off, she heard a voicemail notification. Then briefly considering that perhaps you weren't allowed to use mobile phones in the hospital area Rosie was in, she bit her lip and, taking a nervous deep breath, spoke into the handset.

'Hi, Kate, Madeleine Cooper here again. Hope you got my message from before, but again I just wanted to check in and see how everything is. Needless to say, I know what you are going through – so scary. I heard that Rosie is still unwell and... I just wanted to wish her – and you – all the best. I hope she liked her dinosaur balloon? Also...' Madeleine paused for a bit. 'I also wanted to let you know that I really do feel terrible about all of this, we all do – Clara getting sick and then Rosie... Anyway, just to say that I've been thinking about you both every day. And if there is anything I can do – anything at all – please don't hesitate to ask. Anyway, I'm rambling now... But really, Kate, do keep in touch if you can. Bye.'

Madeleine ended the call at the same moment that she heard a mess of children enter her house. Closing her eyes briefly, and sending good vibes in Kate and Rosie's direction, she saved that day's work on her computer and jumped to her feet.

'I'm running late so I'll just drop and go, OK?' Fiona, her sister-in-law, called out from the hallway downstairs. 'Great to see Clara looking so well. Talk to you later.'

'No problem, Fi, they're in safe hands!' Madeleine called back, heading down the stairs.

'I doubt that, but what choice do I have?' Tom's sister joked, brown eyes sparkling with amusement as she rushed out the door. 'Needs must.' Then she popped her head of dark curls back in the door. 'You didn't forget the cupcakes, did you?'

'I didn't,' Madeleine reassured her, smiling. 'Blue icing and chocolate sprinkles, I remember.'

'Great. I should be back before dinner so the snack should keep them going till then. See ya!'

In the hallway, Jake and his six-year-old cousin Brian were already in the middle of a noisy dispute over what group of comic book superheroes, Marvel's *Avengers* or DC's *Suicide Squad*, would prevail in a fight. The other brother, Cameron, who was a few months older than Jake, quietly stood watching the exchange, but, as always, her eight-year-old nephew was the quietest one of the bunch.

Except, Madeleine realised suddenly, he wasn't – not today. Instead, Clara was the one who seemed withdrawn and sullen. She seemed unmistakably downcast as she took off her coat and dumped her schoolbag on a nearby chair.

Madeleine's first thought was, *Oh shit, we sent her back to school too soon.*

But, in all honesty, Madeleine was ready to get life back on course, and she knew Clara was too. She'd been getting cabin fever from sitting at home bored-out-of-her-mind. There were only so many books your mum could read to you, or episodes of *Paw Patrol* you could watch before the novelty started to wear off…

Though at least Madeleine had managed to get a good blog post out of it. Still, the response to that had been nothing compared to the stir her most recent column about parents in the playgrounds had caused.

Thanks to that, she was once again scheduled not only for a slot on tomorrow's *Morning Coffee*, but also had multiple requests for radio and newspaper interviews wanting her to expand further on the post.

So the timing seemed great; her daughter had got the all clear from Dr Barrett the week previous, the school principal was satisfied she was no longer infectious, and Clara herself was desperate to reunite with her school pals.

But looking at her daughter now, Madeleine wondered if she'd once again misjudged things.

Mumbling a brief greeting at the boys, she went over and put a protective hand on Clara's forehead, tentatively anticipating a fever. But no, her daughter was cool as the proverbial cucumber. Madeleine furrowed her brow. What was going on then?

'Hey, honey. You OK?'

Clara looked up at her mother solemnly and shrugged. 'I'm a bit tired. I want to go up to my room for a while.' With that, she pushed past the rest of the group and trudged upstairs.

Madeleine watched, feeling confused. It was as if a completely different child had returned home from the one she had dropped off at school that morning. That little girl had been eager and excited to go back to school; she had been full of beans. Whereas this version of Clara resembled a deflated balloon.

She shook her head and returned her attention to the three boys. Jake and Brian were gradually getting louder and louder in their banter, and she noted that Cameron had started to wear an agitated look.

She moved quickly to head things off at the pass. 'All right, you two, settle down. You all have homework to do, so get cracking on that and I'll go get you a drink and some snacks. Cameron, come and help me?'

The older boy dutifully followed his aunt into the kitchen while the others continued to loiter.

'So how was your day, sweetheart?' she asked him, as she prepared drinks for the kids. Saying nothing, Cameron shrugged and kept his gaze focused on the kitchen cabinets as she kept chattering. 'I've been busy today. With Clara going back to school I was able to get some work done, and I just finished editing something new before you all came home.' Madeleine knew that, much like her kids, her nephew didn't really know anything – or care – about her work but, regardless, she kept talking. 'I put a nice picture of Clara up online now that she's better. It's great that she's well again, isn't it?'

She pulled out a box of cupcakes she'd picked up at the café earlier and put them on the counter next to where Cameron sat, then turned towards the coffee-maker where she inserted a pod and pressed the start button for a cuppa for herself.

'Here you go – blue with chocolate sprinkles.' Winking, she turned around and leaned against the counter, crossing her arms and enjoying the sight of her nephew happily engaged with his cake. Luckily, she and her sister-in-law were of the same mind when it came to sugar: a treat now and then never did anyone any harm; in fact, some studies suggested that the more parents tried to restrict them, the more kids wanted them.

Which, when you thought about it, was true of just about everything.

'Nice, isn't it? I bought a blue one for Clara too. I'm hoping it'll cheer her up. She seemed a bit down in the dumps just now.'

Madeleine wasn't expecting any feedback on that particular comment or indeed any of her ramblings, but suddenly her nephew spoke.

'She is sad,' Cameron said simply and she was surprised,

because he really wasn't one for chatter, and also because he didn't usually have much to do with his cousin by way of the fact that they attended different schools.

'Do you know why?'

There was a long pause as Cameron seemed to be contemplating his aunt's words. His eyes flickered to her face briefly before once again looking away.

'A mean kid. At school. She told Jake in the car that he said you might be going to jail.'

Madeleine furrowed her brow. Cameron was difficult to make sense of at the best of times but... 'What kid? And what do you mean? Why would I go to jail?'

'You and Uncle Tom, Jake said. For getting kids sick.'

Now she understood. Madeleine turned back to the counter to collect her coffee but mostly to ensure that Cameron didn't see the sharp change in her facial expression.

She felt her blood pressure rising – he had given her just the right amount of information for her to get the gist of exactly what had been said to Clara.

And, if she was a betting woman, Madeleine would put money on who had said it.

Christine bloody Campbell's kid, Kevin.

Turning back to Cameron, she fixed a smile on her face and then walked over to where he sat. 'OK, sweetheart, when you're finished, wash your hands and then go on into the dining room. It sounds like Brian and Jake are already in there, and you all need to do your homework. I am just going to check on Clara for a second and then I'll be back down to help you. OK?'

Climbing the stairs in search of Clara, she thought of her newly recovered daughter being taunted by a loudmouth brat on the poor thing's first day back at school. Now that she knew what was wrong, she needed to quell her daughter's fears. She and Tom had done their utmost to teach the kids to always stand up for themselves, but her daughter having to listen to such crap while she was still vulnerable from her illness was not on.

On entering her room, she found Clara lying quietly on her bed.

'Hey, Cam told me that you had a bit of a tough time today. Why don't you tell me about it?' Clara snuggled up to her the moment she sat down on her bed. 'Did someone say something mean to you?'

She nodded and buried her face in her mother's chest. Then Madeleine heard her stifle a sob and it broke her heart. 'Are you and Daddy going to go to jail because Rosie and me got sick?' she mumbled, turning her head to once again look up at her mother.

Madeleine worked her hardest to keep her expression composed.

'No, honey, we're not. That's absolute nonsense. Now why don't you tell me exactly what happened and I'll do my best to make it all better, I promise.'

Even if it meant calling up Christine Campbell to give her a piece of her mind, Madeleine decided, gritting her teeth resolutely. Though she knew that the woman would only relish the drama.

In any case, she thought, softly caressing her daughter's hair, this nonsense needed to stop.

Chapter 13

'You've got to be joking...' I growled, as I turned the key in the ignition of the Astra for the fourth time. In return, I received the exact same response that I did the first three attempts. Nothing.

Even with my limited knowledge of cars and how they worked, I had a sense that this wasn't a case of me needing a simple jump-start, but a brand new battery or worse.

'Bloody hell, this is all I need,' I muttered, fighting the desire to punch the steering wheel. So much for a stress-free afternoon.

That photograph of Clara Cooper I'd seen had very quickly put an end to my intentions of a chilled-out bath and, when I'd got out of the water, I was relieved to find that at least my phone was still working, even though I'd shattered the protective glass. Add the cost (and hassle) of a replacement to my never-ending list of expenses and I was just about ready to throw back my head and scream.

And now this. The useless piece of junk on which I'd recently shelled out a small fortune to keep on the road, and which was the necessary lifeline between me and the hospital, had gone and died a death.

Honest to God, how much more was I supposed to take?

I flung open the driver's door, got out of the car and wrenched my handbag out behind me, thinking about my options or lack thereof. I needed to get back to my daughter, and since my vehicle now seemed useless...

Extracting my newly cracked phone from my handbag as I walked back into the house, I made a quick call to arrange a callout from the local mechanic, and then maybe I could see about taking a taxi.

But the fare for the twenty-odd miles to the hospital in Dublin would be extortionate, probably enough to clear me out for the rest of the month. To say nothing of how I could possibly afford the return journey.

'Dammit!' I cried, dropping my phone on the kitchen table and plopping myself down in a chair. Why did everything have to be so *hard*? Couldn't the luck gods even glance – never mind smile – at me for just *one* day?

I had really been teetering on the brink lately, especially when they'd put Rosie on the ventilator. For her sake, I knew I had to stay strong and get through it, but now it felt as if every day seemed to present a new roadblock. I had never felt more defeated in my whole life.

If only a light at the end of the tunnel would present itself, I thought. *Just the tiniest ray of hope, that's all I need, I swear.*

At that moment, a knock sounded at the door and I raised my head, following the sound. Looking down at the time on my phone, I realised only a few minutes had passed since I called for the mechanic.

'Well, that was fast,' I muttered, as I walked out to answer the knock. Perhaps luck was smiling on me after all. Even if it was just in the form of a speedy mechanic.

But when I opened the door, I didn't find a guy with a tow-truck on the doorstep ready to assist. Instead, Christine Campbell's smiling face greeted me.

'I was driving past and was surprised to see your car,' she said by way of a hello. 'I didn't think you *ever* left the hospital. How's Rosie today? Is she off the ventilator?'

I opened the door wide and granted her entry. 'Yesterday, yes. Lucy insisted I come home for a few hours while she's stable. But my car seems to be protesting – it obviously doesn't want to go back.' I filled her in on the fact that I was waiting for a tow while also trying to figure out how to get back to Dublin without the use of just my own two legs.

'Maybe it's good that I was passing then. I can give you a lift up, of course.'

I exhaled. 'I can't tell you how much I would appreciate that.'

Within the next few minutes, the mechanic duly arrived and made preparations to tow my old banger to his workshop in the town, while I braced myself to receive news of how much I owed to get it running again.

Though what was another bill at this point, I thought ruefully, as I left my phone number for him to reach me.

As if on cue, my phone rang just as I was getting into Christine's bright yellow Beetle and, immediately recognising the number, I grimaced. Work.

'I'm sorry but I need to take this,' I told her, creating some distance for privacy. 'I'll just be a sec.'

Christine looked curious but nodded without further comment. Good – I didn't want to have to explain myself to her just then.

I already knew I'd have enough explaining to do to my employer.

'Hello, Jennifer.' I rubbed my neck readying myself for the discussion that was to come. 'I'm sorry I didn't get a chance to call you back…'

'Don't worry, I completely understand and I can only imagine. How is… everything?'

'I'm still not really sure, truth be told. She's improving a little but very slowly…'

I waited for Jennifer to continue, knowing that this was work-related and not a social call. A respectful beat passed between us, and then she began. 'Look, I really am sorry to have to put work stuff on you now – I know you have a lot on your plate at the moment. But do you think that we can chat?'

'Of course.' I knew that I would have to address my absentee-ism from Glencree at some point. Obviously that time was now.

I had used up my five days' compassionate leave, as well as all of my remaining paid holiday time about a week ago. A couple of my co-workers at the clinic, sweethearts that they are, had pooled together and offered to exchange some of their own paid leave to help with Rosie's cause. It was something that I never in my wildest dreams expected – nor wanted to accept – but the gesture was so lovely it had moved me to tears, and I would go to the ends of the earth to make it up to them. But now I guessed that all my paid options, statutory or otherwise, had well and truly dried up, which was why Jennifer was making the call.

'Like I said, Kate, I hate to have to raise it at a time like this—'

'But you're obliged to. I know.' I wiped my mouth with the back of my hand. 'And I'm assuming I've well and truly blown through my all holidays by now?'

Jennifer sighed. 'Sadly, yes. So the next step – as I'm sure you're already aware yourself – is your Parental Leave entitle-ment. From a HR point of view, Kate, it's my duty to outline that you are entitled to eighteen weeks' unpaid leave to tend to your daughter. That basically means you are guaranteed the ability to return to your position at the end of that term under the same pay and conditions. However, if you need longer than the statutory eighteen weeks, the Health Services Executive is not required to guarantee your position or conditions, and reserves the right to fill your position if you choose not to return at the end of the period. Needless to say, I'm only mentioning this if the worst comes to the worst which I'm sure...'

She trailed off then, obviously uncomfortable, and I nodded, swallowing the lump in my throat. I was familiar with the Parental Leave Act, basically a form of carer's leave. It's the same statutory protection that afforded me to take maternity leave after I had Rosie and return to my post at the same rate of pay. While I was grateful for its existence, I seriously hoped that I wouldn't need even another week, let alone eighteen, but until the doctors gave Rosie the all-clear I had no way of knowing when I could return. It was a fair proposal, and a welcome one in terms of a weight off my mind regarding work obligations – aside from the fact that during that time I wouldn't be earning a cent.

'Thanks for clarifying, Jennifer. I appreciate it and yes, hopefully I won't need to take the full period.'

'No problem, take as much time as you need. I'll post out the paperwork today for you to sign too. No rush – get it back to me whenever you can. And, needless to say, we're all thinking of you and Rosie and hope she's on the mend soon.'

'Me too. Thanks, Jennifer,' I said, appreciating her words, but already I was doing the calculations in my head.

Eighteen weeks – almost five months with no money coming in. I thought about the car, the rent on the house and my rapidly growing pile of bills – all taken against my conversely declining bank balance...

And once again I wanted to lie down and cry.

'What's wrong? Do I have something on my face?' I asked, sitting back into Christine's car.

She said nothing, but as we drove off I had the distinct sensation that I was being sized up somehow. There was something about her that was inherently cat-like – especially when she peered down at you through those glasses, and I wondered if she was now regarding me like the proverbial canary.

'Actually, I was just wondering if you had given any more thought to what we talked about at the hospital before. About the Coopers?'

I swallowed hard. That simply wasn't going to happen. Regardless of the fact that I seriously doubted the Coopers had any kind of legal case to answer that kind of thing just wasn't me. And notwithstanding that, how would blame and recriminations help my daughter in any way?

Christine was still waiting for an answer.

'Honestly? I think the very idea is ludicrous.' She opened her mouth to argue, but I held up a hand and continued, stopping her. 'I know what you are going to say, and, yes, maybe if Clara hadn't contracted measles or Madeleine hadn't sent her to school while she was infectious, Rosie and I wouldn't be in this situation. But these things happen – bad luck happens. And the very idea of going after a fellow parent, a fellow neighbour for recompense… it's the last thing I'd consider. It's not the kind of thing I'd ever even *think* about. So while I know you're mad at the Coopers, and I appreciate your reasoning, I really would prefer not to discuss it any more.'

In my brief time dealing with Christine, I'd discovered that one of the best ways to get her to stop talking about any topic was to say that you agreed with her.

And I hadn't this time.

'It's not just my reasoning though. I've spoken to Declan – my cousin – about it again since, and the more he thinks about it, the more he feels it's a clear-cut case of wilful negligence. I'm sorry, Kate, but I think you aren't fully considering the extent of what this has done to you, and to Rosie. Obviously you're not working at the moment, I'm guessing the rent on the house isn't cheap, and now with the car breaking down too… I'm sure the bills are piling up.'

Christine easily rattled off all the very issues I'd just been worrying about, as if she'd been privy to my thoughts. Or had she in fact been eavesdropping on my call from Jennifer?

I wanted to argue her point and opened my mouth briefly to counter, but then realised I couldn't. Yes, my financial situation looked pretty bleak at the moment. But I did have a little savings (originally set aside for a birthday weekend away for Rosie) to at least cover the rent for this month and the next. I could keep going for that long surely?

Rosie would be on the mend soon and I'd be back to work in no time. And say what you want about the Irish healthcare system, but it was a huge relief to know that at least I didn't have to worry about the cost of Rosie's medical care. Mercifully, the state would cover that.

'That might be so,' I admitted, 'but I certainly don't need handouts if that's what you're suggesting. People were kind enough when Greg died and I'm not going to be the town tragic case who's always looking for charity. Whatever happens – well, I'll just have to work it out.'

My stomach churned though when I realised just how naïve and simplistic that sounded. How was it going to work out? How exactly? And what would happen if, God forbid, poor Rosie *didn't* get better soon?

The very thought broke me, and the dam of emotion that I'd been holding back these last couple of weeks while trying to keep it together for my daughter's sake, burst with a vengeance.

I put my head in my hands.

'Oh God, Christine, I'm so afraid.' The admission, out loud, startled me. Up until then, I had only admitted it to myself in the hospital when no one else was around – which often felt like all the time.

I sat back in my seat and stared out the windscreen as she drove. 'You're right; every time I pick up the post, there are more bills – electricity, insurance, and now the car. And it's just... I wish I could see a positive end in sight for Rosie, but, in truth, I have no idea if or when she'll be home. Please understand I appreciate you and Lucy and everything that you guys do, and have done for me since I moved here, but I have never in my life felt more alone.'

Christine reached across and took my hand in hers, and I appreciated this small dose of human contact. When she spoke again, her voice had softened.

'It's OK to be scared, Kate. It is. I can't imagine the way you feel. I would be devastated if anything happened to my three.' She squeezed my hand. 'But you also can't allow yourself to be taken advantage of.'

Her tone was still soft, but there was resolve behind her words. And I felt something stir within myself. Was that what was happening to me? Had I been made into a victim? Was I completely subject to the whims of the universe throwing whatever shit it wanted to at me?

'Is that what you think?' I asked quietly. Christine's question now made me wonder how other people were actually viewing me. Usually I didn't care. But this was different. Was that all people thought I was? A hapless victim?

Christine considered my query and I could tell she was weighing up the right words to use. She took a careful breath and said, 'I think that other people's actions – or inactions rather – have impacted your and certainly your family's life, for the negative. And I believe that those same people don't understand the enormous damage their reckless decisions have caused…'

She let her words trail off, and I once again considered all that had happened. Two children, both unvaccinated. One for health reasons, the other by choice. Two sick little girls. One who'd recovered, seemingly effortlessly. Another still fighting pneumonia in the hospital.

And then there was me. I'd been forced to essentially give up work, had a mountain of bills the size of Everest to pay, and was only weeks away from being penniless. Even my shitty car – my only form of transport to my sick daughter twenty miles away – wouldn't play ball for me.

None of this would have happened if Rosie hadn't gotten sick, would it?

My mind suddenly flashed to that photo of Clara I'd seen on Madeleine Cooper's social media earlier. Thanks to the fact that her daughter had sailed through her illness, there was a woman who was back to normal and had the *time* to put up pictures and write chatty posts online.

Whereas I barely had the energy to brush my teeth…

I suddenly felt like screaming and pulling my hair out. The stir of such emotion in me made my heart pump furiously and it felt as though it was the first time in weeks that particular organ had beaten with determination.

And Christine seemed to sense the change.

'Please, let me introduce you to my cousin, Kate,' she said, her eyes steady on me. 'I really think Declan might be—'

But the remainder of her words were cut off by the urgent ringing of my phone, and my heart sank to the depths of my stomach when I realised it was Lucy from the hospital.

It dropped to my feet when I heard her tone. 'Kate, sweetheart,' my friend said, and though she tried her best to hide it, I sensed panic dripping from every word, 'Rosie's had an episode and the doctors are with her now. You really need to get back.'

Chapter 14

*Everyone still good for tomorrow night at Julie's? Been a bit too
busy to read the book, but I am definitely on for the vino! M xx*

Madeleine smiled as she sent a quick group text to the members
of her monthly book club. The group was due to meet at another
member's house the following evening, and while events of the
last few weeks meant that she would have to forgo discussion of
this month's title, she was very much looking forward to kicking
back with a (very large) glass and a gossip.

'Come on guys, time to go!' she called upstairs to the kids,
once again having to rush them out for a long overdue trip to
their grandmother's house.

Tom wouldn't be coming to Harriet's with them this time,
as he was putting in extra hours at work to try make up for
the time off he'd taken when Clara was ill. Madeleine was fine
with that; she certainly didn't want to have to miss out on their
usual two weeks in Portugal this summer because of dried-up
annual leave.

She was just checking if the kids had correctly secured themselves into the back seat of her little Audi speedster (Jake in

particular was a demon for not clicking the belt in properly) when her phone beeped with a reply from Julie Wells, host of tomorrow night's book club.

Probably best to leave it this time, Madeleine. Talk soon.

Madeleine frowned. Weird – was Julie really holding it against her that she hadn't read this month's selection? Especially when the book was usually just an excuse to get together for a glass and a gossip. There were always one or two members who made an attempt at a discussion if the title in question was particularly good or controversial, but most of the time the aim of the club was forgotten within the first half-hour, and the remainder of the evening spent catching up and having a laugh.

And Madeleine badly needed a laugh; it felt like she'd been cooped up for ever when Clara was ill, and since her daughter's recovery she'd been mostly underwater trying to catch up on work. She wanted to glam up a bit in nice clothes and heels and spend the night having a good old gossip.

You sure? I really don't mind coming along anyway. I can just stay quiet in the corner for the discussion part (difficult I know!) and then join in for the fun bit afterwards.

The reply came back almost immediately.

Honestly, it's not a good idea. Maybe next time.

Sitting into the driver's seat, Madeleine frowned. Was it just her or did Julie's reply seem... curt?

Who'd have thought reading the book every time was such a

big deal? And it wasn't like her club buddy to be so rigid about the rules either.

It was one of the reasons Madeleine enjoyed the group meetings so much actually – the gang was a bunch of Knockroe locals, some of whom she'd grown up with, others fellow parents she'd got to know since the kids started school, and a great mix of both working and stay-at-home mums and a couple of singletons. All of whom supported her blog and had in fact urged Madeleine to expand the business when both of her children would be at school. So why this po-faced response?

Then the thought struck her as she drove towards her mother-in-law's house. Had she perhaps hit a nerve with that more recent article, the one about the playgrounds?

She supposed a couple of the women at the club could be miffed about the whole 'helicopter parent' thing, and there was always the risk of people assuming Madeleine was writing about them whenever she mentioned real-life instances. But there was no question she thought about any of her friends in that way, and the last thing she'd ever do was use her blog to poke fun at any real person.

She sighed. The downside of *Mad Mum*'s more controversial slant...

Madeleine really hoped this wasn't the cause of her friend's ire, but maybe she'd phone Julie when she and the kids got back from Harriet's later.

Just in case.

*

'I'm just so glad that this ordeal is behind you, sweetheart.' Madeleine smiled as Clara's grandmother pulled her in close and embraced her in a hug.

Her youngest was still a bit despondent and tired after her ordeal at school today, but, all in all, she had recovered well and seemed excited by her first social outing in weeks. Not the most adventurous jaunt admittedly, but Madeleine was happy to see some colour in her daughter's cheeks as she embraced her grandmother.

'And you must be feeling considerably better, too,' said Harriet, glancing at Madeleine. It wasn't a question. 'Of course you are. What parent wouldn't be counting their lucky stars? Measles, my goodness.'

Madeleine nodded and gave a small smile, tucking a strand of blonde hair behind her ear. She had always gotten along very well with her mother-in-law, but now felt a little uncomfortable. Harriet knew all about what had happened recently – and of course that Clara and Jake had never been vaccinated – but she was never sure how her mother-in-law felt about it.

Madeleine's own mother thought she was an idiot for declining to vaccinate the kids, and when Jake had come down with measles, had wasted no time in telling her so.

Then again, Harriet had raised a free-thinker like Tom, and of course had been through it all with Fiona's kids too, so perhaps she wasn't quite as critical of their choice as so many others.

'Too much conflicting information,' Tom had eventually concluded back then when they'd gone over the arguments for and against for the umpteenth time. 'Not to mention way too many get-out clauses from the pharma companies. And as for the government...' he spat disdainfully, '... only interested in maintaining herd immunity, and couldn't give a hoot about individuals.'

And while it wasn't quite so easy for Madeleine to believe that last part about the government not caring, based on research she tended to agree with him on the other points. Even now, it didn't seem like a week went by without some related controversy in the news about other vaccinations, like the troubling side-effects from the HPV jab in young girls, and the horrible instances of narcolepsy in some children following swine flu shots.

'And how is the other little girl?' Harriet asked now, as she pulled back Clara's hair and began plaiting it in a French braid.

'Still in the hospital, I'm afraid,' offered Madeleine quietly. 'I actually tried to call Kate – the mother – earlier to see how things were.' She really wished she'd had the opportunity to talk to Rosie's mum personally rather than hide behind voicemail, because she truly didn't want Kate to think that she didn't care or was indifferent to their plight. She had just come out of a similar trauma, and she couldn't even imagine what it would be like if Clara was the one who'd ended up in the hospital.

'And her prognosis?' Harriet pushed, and by her tone Madeleine guessed her mother-in-law had something on her mind. Much like her son, she was very forthcoming with her opinions and while usually Madeleine appreciated that in a person, she wasn't in the mood for disapproval or recrimination of the kind she'd already got from Frank Barrett.

'Getting better I believe,' she said non-committally, though she couldn't be sure whether or not this was true. She just didn't want to go down this rabbit hole with Harriet now.

Luckily, a sound from upstairs where Jake was playing temporarily diverted the other woman's attention.

'Sweetheart, why don't you go see what your brother is up to?' Clara's grandmother urged her gently. 'And if it's just boring boy stuff, come back down and we'll figure out something fun to do.'

Uh oh, there was a lecture coming for sure...

Clara duly headed in the direction of the noise, allowing Harriet to sit back on the sofa and run a hand through her cropped ash-blonde hair as she regarded her daughter-in-law.

'You do know, dear, that the outbreak has been mentioned in the local news... aren't you worried – given your profile – about people making the connection?'

Madeleine shrugged, surprised. 'Even if they did, I don't see why it would be an issue, Harriet. I mean, even if a connection is made to Clara, it's not like I'm trying to hide something. Tom and I have always been upfront about our preferences. Not everyone agrees with our stance – I know that – but at the end of the day we have nothing to hide. Besides, it's hardly a "measles outbreak", only two kids have been affected and one is already better.'

Harriet cocked her head and raised her eyebrows. 'You really think people aren't talking? Only yesterday I heard somebody in the shop downtown discussing it.'

'Talking about what?'

'About the fact that it seems Clara passed a highly infectious – preventable – disease onto a vulnerable classmate. People don't look too kindly on those who go against conventional medical wisdom, as I'm sure you know – especially educated, intelligent people.'

Madeleine was somewhat stung; firstly, by the idea that people in Knockroe had been talking, but particularly at the thinly veiled insult to her and Tom's intelligence. She'd thought that Harriet of all people should understand the root of their reasoning.

'That's not to say that I agree with these people, Madeleine,' her mother-in-law added, which mollified her somewhat, 'but you must admit, it's not a good situation. And my advice to you – as someone who is occasionally, and it seems increasingly, in the public eye – is you would do well not to court any controversy.'

Madeleine couldn't think of a reply to this and, after a beat, in which the two women sat in awkward silence, Harriet continued. 'My point is that it might be best for you to lay low for a while, dear, perhaps not be so quick to move on and forget? Of course I appreciate now that Clara is better – thank goodness – you want to put the whole frightening episode behind you and get on with your life, but the other little girl is still in hospital and people tend to have awfully... strong opinions about these things. If I were you, I might think about how I would respond if a wider audience – the general public, I mean – makes the connection and perhaps wants to proffer *their* opinions.'

Madeleine thought about it. She understood where Harriet was coming from, but it wasn't as if she used the blog or any other media she was involved in to foist her opinions on anyone else. *Mad Mum* was only ever intended as a light-hearted, jokey take on motherhood, and a million miles away from a serious forum about the pros and cons of childhood vaccination. She'd started it for that very reason, as a foil to the more prevalent How to Be a Perfect Mum brigade.

And what were the chances of her audience making such a connection in any case? No, Harriet was just playing devil's advocate after overhearing the obligatory gossip and mutterings of a small town like Knockroe.

Her mother-in-law was simply making a mountain out of a molehill, Madeleine was sure of it.

Once little Rosie O'Hara got out of hospital, the whole thing would be forgotten about in no time.

Chapter 15

'Look, I'm not saying that people shouldn't keep an eye out, what I am saying is that for their sake, as well as your own, kids don't need to be mollycoddled.'

'But how is helping them up and down a slide mollycoddling exactly? And perhaps those parents who "hover" over their kids, as you like to put it, aren't necessarily trying to keep them safe, but actually want to spend time with them, play with them.'

'Sure, and there's absolutely nothing wrong with that...'

'Then why are you ridiculing them? Making fun of people for actually wanting to spend quality time with their kids, when chances are they've been out working hard all week and may have barely seen them from the start of one day to the next. But, of course, you don't have consider those things, Madeleine, because you're at home all day—'

'OK, guys, let's not turn this into a working versus stay-at-home parent situation...'

'Honestly, Gemma, I think you're taking that piece way too seriously. My point was not that parents shouldn't play with their kids – that helicopter stuff was completely tongue-in-cheek as I'm sure most of our viewers can appreciate. But the crux of the article is that for kids, playgrounds have become joyless and safety oriented to the point of boredom. They want to explore, they need to get a bit scraped and cut up now and again… it helps with their development. It reminds me of this discussion I had with one of my friends recently about jelly head – have you ever heard of jelly head?'

'No, but perhaps some of our *Morning Coffee* viewers have…'

'Well, just in case, it's this little soft spot on a baby's head that acts as protection for their skulls—'

'The fontanelle.'

'Yes that's it, thanks, Anita – I knew there was some fancy medical name for it.'

'Leave it to our author panellist to find the right word.'

'Haha, exactly. Anyway… it fuses up at around eighteen months, I think, but my point is that it's there for a reason – to safeguard the brain. When they're at crawling stage, babies need to be hardy, they fall over, crash into things, sometimes even get dropped by their parents…'

'Now that's a guilty look if ever I saw one – Madeleine Cooper, are you telling us that you might have dropped one of your own children at some point?'

'Um, guilty as charged, Louise, like many parents watching this morning, I'm sure! But it certainly didn't do Jake any harm, not that I know of anyway. I suppose my point is, kids are hardy by nature, so there's really no need for parents to drive themselves nuts worrying. And then of course there was this other time when Clara had just started to crawl… I laid her down on the bed, took my eye off her for a split second and when I turned back hadn't she rolled off it…'

*

I sat in the hallway of the hospital, numbed by what had happened the night before.

I'd honestly thought that finding Greg dead on the kitchen floor two years ago would be the worst thing I'd ever have to endure.

But I was wrong.

Last night, watching the medical team crowd round my convulsing daughter, Rosie's little body wracked in seizures as they worked to stabilise her... the memory of that horrific visual prompted even more tears, when I honestly thought I could cry no more.

Lucy's face when I finally arrived back at the hospital with Christine, telling me that they'd rushed Rosie to ICU following a sudden onset of multiple seizures. They'd put her on a cocktail of anti-convulsant drugs and back on the ventilator, but it didn't look good...

Since day one, I had been struggling not to think about the official stats on childhood measles and its complications:

One out of twenty kids comes down with pneumonia.

One out of every thousand will develop encephalitis.

Encephalitis can leave a child deaf or with an intellectual disability.

For every one thousand children who get measles, one or two will die.

Die.

A one in one thousand chance. That was the type of odds my little girl was dealing with just then.

I stifled a sob, at the same time wanting to curse someone, something. I was so angry with myself, yes. But I was also terrified. Terrified that I would lose her – my little Rosie – the only thing I had left.

'Kate, you have to think pos—' Lucy began, trying to soothe me as she rushed along the corridor with me, trying to keep up.

'Please don't tell me that just now!' I raged, tears filling my eyes afresh. 'I'm scared to death and trying not to rip off my own skin. I've never felt so helpless.'

No, that wasn't quite true. I'd also felt completely that way two years before when I'd found my daughter screaming in the kitchen right after she discovered her dad's lifeless body. That was a pretty helpless moment too.

My heart lurched for Greg too. If there was ever a moment I needed him, it was then. But of course that wasn't possible.

I reached the ICU then, frantically searching for Dr Ryan, unable to believe that something like this could happen the minute I'd left her side.

Why *had* I left her side? To take a fucking *bubble bath*…

I thought my brain was literally going to explode while I waited, watching with horror as I noticed the body language and facial expressions of the medical team gathered around her. I knew that look.

Oh please God, no…

I can't even remember being taken out of the room, Lucy's arm around my shoulders, my body wracked with sobs and my brain pounding with sorrow and despair.

Kids are hardy… there's really no need for parents to drive themselves nuts worrying…

To go through all that, I thought, looking down at my hands to see my knuckles whitening, to spend all of last night watching my little girl fight valiantly for her barely lived life while I could do nothing but stand there, helpless…

She's only five years old…

To go through all that – a night of utter torture and despair

– and now have to hear *that woman* on TV, jabbering about how kids *should* be put in danger, that it didn't do them any harm…

A loud sob escaped from my mouth, and I stared unseeingly up at the TV, fresh hatred burning through my veins.

How dare she? I raged, furiously wiping my eyes. How dare Madeleine Cooper say such a thing, when it was her bad decisions – her downright irresponsible choices – that had put me and Rosie through hell these last few weeks?

How *dare* she?

I'd heard those stupid voicemails, pathetic attempts at an apology and faux concern by sending balloons, when the truth was the silly bitch couldn't care less. That woman and her family had simply picked up and got on with their lives, as if what had befallen Rosie was absolutely nothing.

And now here she was on national TV, dressed up to the nines with her perfect make-up and bouncy blonde curls, being paraded as some kind of parenting expert…

I felt sick to the core. Now I was long past crying, and still too numb for grief. The only emotion I felt just then was… rage.

Rage at Madeleine Cooper for visiting this misery on me, just when I'd started to pick up the pieces of my and Rosie's life after Greg's death. Rage at the woman for adding insult to injury by taunting me in my darkest hour.

'*I believe that those same people don't understand the enormous damage their reckless decisions have caused…*'

Christine was right: the Coopers *should* be held responsible for this, and be made to face the true cost of their recklessness.

My shoulders shuddered and spontaneously collapsed with another bout of tears.

Because my poor little Rosie was the one who'd ended up paying for it.

Chapter 16

ditzy123: Did anyone see Madeleine Cooper on the TV this morning? Isn't she brilliant – so easy-going. I LOL'd when she said that she'd dropped her kid as a baby – I mean, who hasn't? Though not sure I'd admit it on national TV…

shazzababe: I did see her and yeah, she's great. I've actually been following her blog for a while – really funny and down to earth. It helped me a lot in the early days with babs TBH, as she really tells it like it is, and doesn't bang on about how you're 'supposed' to do this, that and the other. She looks amazing too – I loved the dress she was wearing. Just goes to prove what she was saying before that being a mum doesn't mean you have to forgo style. She's fab!

booklover9: Madeleine is great craic. I read her blog too and follow her on Facebook and it's like having a natter with a great friend. Telly needs more people like her, not like that sourpuss Gemma Moore. I don't think she likes Mad Mum at all, ha!

ditzy123: She was a bit harsh on her earlier, wasn't she? Though no better woman than Madeleine to take it – I'd say she doesn't let anyone walk over her. Interesting to watch though, I thought Gemma was going to explode. And I think Madeleine enjoys goading her. And yah, I loved her dress too! I'd say it's expensive although in her blog she often mentions normal person's stuff from the high street. She's the biz…

Madeleine smiled as she read through the social media reaction to her latest appearance on *Morning Coffee*. She guessed some of her comments – in particular the admission of dropping poor Jake – would be provocative, but had tried her best to keep it all light-hearted, and was glad to see that her tone had hit the mark.

She was also somewhat relieved to see that she wasn't the only one who seemed to think Gemma Moore had it in for her. She'd been quite taken aback when the journalist had taken such a combative stance towards the *Parents Not Allowed* blog post. Perhaps the helicopter thing had hit a nerve?

Oh well, there was nothing Madeleine could do about that; once her followers and the general public seemed to have taken the post and the sentiment behind it in the spirit in which it was intended that was all that mattered.

But thinking of Jake… Madeleine took out her phone and brought up the number for the mum of one of Jake's school friends.

'Hello, Carol? How are you doing, sweetheart? It's Madeleine here,' she said pleasantly, when the other woman picked up.

'Madeleine, hi.'

'Listen, I'm just checking in to see about a play date with Nathan. Long overdue, I know, and Jake has been bugging me about it for ages, but things have been busy lately and of course with poor Clara being sick… So anyway, would this Thursday suit? I can pick Nate up after school if you like?'

'Actually, I'm not really sure that's a good idea, Madeleine…'

'Well, would Friday be any better?'

'I actually meant that I'm not keen on the play date in general. Not after the whole… episode with Clara.'

'You mean the measles? But she's well over that now and long past being infectious. In fact, she went back to school last week.'

'It's not that. It's just… I'm sorry, Madeleine, but, to be frank, I'm uncomfortable with the fact that Jake isn't vaccinated. I didn't know.'

'But Jake had measles years ago – he's fine.'

'He's still not vaccinated though.'

'I don't understand. Like I said, he can't get it again and in any case I'm assuming Nathan *is* vaccinated. So what's the problem – exactly?'

'The problem is that I don't want to take any chances, not after what happened to little Rosie O'Hara.'

'Oh…'

'I'm sorry, Madeleine. Obviously the choices you make for your children are your own business, but I can't run the risk of—'

'I see.'

'Especially when it seems that poor Rosie took a turn for the worse over the weekend. Last I heard she was in a coma, so you understand…'

Madeleine wasn't sure if she'd hung up on Carol McDaid without even saying goodbye but it didn't matter. *A coma…* what on earth?

She dialled Lucy's number as fast as she could, forgetting in her haste that she could just hit her friend's name in her saved contacts, but she was so eager to talk to her, so desperate to find out what had happened.

Mercifully, her friend answered on the second ring. 'Lucy, I just spoke to Carol McDaid, who said something about little Rosie taking a bad turn at the hospital. What's going on?'

Her friend sounded shaken. 'That's right, I'm afraid. I was there when it happened. The poor thing started going into convulsions, and got so serious she nearly had to be resuscitated. Poor Kate had gone home for a rest at the time...'

Oh my God. Poor, poor Kate. 'So how is she now? What's happening? Carol said she was in a coma... Is there anything I can do, does Kate need—?'

Her friend exhaled hard. 'Well, the poor thing is in a state understandably, and worried sick about what's going to happen next. They've diagnosed Rosie with viral encephalitis. She still hasn't fully recovered from the pneumonia, so, at the moment, she's on a ventilator and some drugs to try to bring down the swelling on her brain and stop the convulsions but it's very touch and go...' She paused, sounding shaken. 'It was horrific, Madeleine; I really thought she was going to die and poor Kate did too. The doctors had to induce the coma to try to prevent serious damage to her brain apparently... I'm not sure, I haven't spoken properly to Kate since Friday. But it's a horrible situation and naturally she's all over the place.'

'I don't believe it. All this from measles? A coma?'

'Well, from the encephalitis really. The doctor said it's an extension of the virus which attacks brain tissue. But it seems everything stemmed from the original infection, yes...'

Her words trailed off and there followed a prolonged silence during which Madeleine was sure she could feel reprobation coming down the line.

'What can I do? How can I help? I tried to phone Kate but she's not picking up and—'

'Madeleine, there's nothing you can do, nothing any of us

can do – not now anyway. But I'm sorry to say this and really hate doing so, but you really, *really* shouldn't have sent Clara to school that day.'

Madeleine wanted to cry with guilt. While she already felt bad enough and had since been on the receiving end of a few different forms of recrimination, now hearing it from her best friend, her closest ally… was like a shot to the heart.

But how could she even think about defending herself when a little girl was fighting for her life?

'I know, but… but I couldn't have known, Lucc. I had no idea that something like this would happen, and Clara got through it fine…'

'I'm sorry, I shouldn't have said that, but I'm upset too, for Rosie – and for Kate. Honestly my heart was breaking to see her being dragged out of ICU while they tried to stabilise Rosie. It's horrific… such a nightmare for any parent. And of course I know that you never meant any harm. But, Maddie, you must also know people aren't happy and already they're starting to point the finger.'

Madeleine knew that much; she'd experienced it just now with Carol McDaid. Tom's mother had also mentioned similar murmurings the other night, but at the time Madeleine had brushed Harriet's concerns away

And thinking back on her correspondence with Julie Wells the other day about the book club: *Probably best to leave it…*

She'd been too stupid at the time to realise the other woman was giving her the brush-off.

Oh God, what have I done…?

She could fix this, Madeleine decided. She would talk to Kate, do whatever it took, ensure that Rosie got the best possible care. She didn't know if the O'Haras had health insurance but it didn't matter, Tom would know who to talk to at the hospital, or if not, he'd get in touch with someone who would.

'Where is Kate now?' she asked Lucy.

'At the hospital I'd imagine. Although no, she did say something about getting her car back this morning. It broke down the other day – that's why she wasn't back at the hospital when Rosie's convulsions started. To be honest, I'm kind of glad she wasn't. Truly, Maddie, I'm not quite right myself after it. After staying in ICU all night with her, I went straight home and hugged the life out of my own two. That kind of terror, no parent should ever have to go through it.'

Madeleine bit her lip. 'The poor thing. So you think she might be at home now? Or in town at least?'

'I think so. But, sweetheart, I really don't think—'

For the second time that day and possibly in her entire life, Madeleine hung up the phone without saying goodbye.

She jumped straight in the Audi and was on the other side of Knockroe within minutes, speeding on the windy country roads the whole way. Sod it, this wasn't the time for stupid rules and regulations, not if she wanted to catch Rosie's mum before she travelled back to the hospital.

She was only a few yards from the entrance to Kate's driveway, when she spied a yellow Beetle pass by on the other side; Christine Campbell's unmistakably recognisable Volkswagen. And she couldn't be sure, but she could have sworn Kate O'Hara was sitting in the passenger side.

Did Christine know Kate, and if so how?

Madeleine wasn't sure why, but all at once she felt a heavy, leaden knot form in the pit of her stomach.

Chapter 17

Christine chattered away while I was only half listening.

She kept saying: 'You're doing the right thing, seriously. And Declan is brilliant. He'll be *perfect* for this, believe me.'

In the wake of my nightmarish weekend, Christine had jumped all over my split-second concession to her idea of seeking redress from the Coopers. But my initial urge for revenge on Friday morning in the wake of Rosie's trauma was by now already fading, and doubt was creeping in.

Which is why Christine was determined to have me pay a visit to her cousin at his office first thing this morning, before dropping me off at Nolan's garage to pick up my car. She wasn't going to give me any time to talk myself out of this.

And I started to wonder as I sat quietly in the car, if this was Christine's cross to bear or mine?

Thankfully (I think) I didn't have too much time to ponder that line of enquiry because before I knew it we were pulling into a small row of offices in Glencree.

Christine's cousin worked in the same town as I did? The way she'd talked about him, I'd assumed he was with some big-shot Dublin solicitor's practice.

And I wasn't sure if this made me feel more worried, or at ease.

'OK, Kate. Here we are,' she cooed, as if she was trying to wake a baby out of a peaceful slumber. I looked at her with cautious eyes, and realised my stomach felt tied in knots. Was I really going to do this?

'I thought you said you didn't make an appointment. What if your cousin isn't here this morning? Or busy or something?' I secretly hoped that maybe the guy had decided to go off on holiday. To the moon, even.

Christine waved this objection away as she climbed out of the car. 'He'll have time for us. Don't worry about that.'

I grimaced. I wasn't worried – it was actually just a secret hope. I had a feeling that I already had taken this too far.

Getting out of the car, I glanced around, feeling as if I was doing something wrong or dirty even. What if someone from Knockroe, or work, saw me going into a solicitor's office? It wouldn't take a genius to put two and two together and come up with a conclusion.

Somebody's getting sued.

And word travelled fast in these parts, where everyone seemed to know everyone, even in neighbouring towns.

I pulled my jacket up around my neck as if trying to fold into myself. My hand fished around in my bag for a pair of sunglasses and, when I found them, I pushed them on my face without hesitation.

'Are you coming?' Christine called to me. It was then that I realised that I had been glued to one spot – my feet felt like they were encased in lead. I wondered if my expression was giving away my hesitation. Did I look like a deer caught in the headlights?

'Right. Yes. Coming,' I mumbled in response, as I willed myself forward, one foot at a time. My heart was racing.

Calm down. You haven't committed to anything. You are just here to talk. Explore options. That's all. Just an introduction and a quick chat with Christine's cousin and then she'll take you back to the hospital to Rosie.

Thinking of my daughter and picturing her little face swallowed up by the ventilator mask finally gave me the same sense of resolution I'd felt after that horrific night in ICU, and I felt my breathing begin to even itself out as I followed Christine along the row of businesses dotting the small cul-de-sac in which we were parked.

Rosie. You're here because of Rosie. This is all for Rosie.

Ahead of me, I saw Christine throw open a door of one of the offices and disappear inside. She didn't even wait for me to follow her.

A beat later, I pulled the same door open and made my way through the entrance. But I heard Christine already engaged in conversation with a man, who was answering her with contemplative muttering. I noticed right away he had a nice voice. It was the same steady type of timbre that George Clooney had, comforting – a voice you could trust.

I wondered how successful this guy was in a courtroom with a voice like that. Pretty good, I'd be willing to bet. But then I remembered that it was barristers, not solicitors, who argued in the court system in Ireland, so the point was moot.

'Kate. I'd like you to meet my cousin Declan.' Christine smiled.

Declan turned and offered his hand and I immediately felt blindsided. For some reason, I'd assumed her solicitor cousin would be older; a grey or balding fifty-something in dusty old tweeds.

'Hello, Kate, lovely to meet you. I'm Declan Roe.'

But this guy looked to be a couple of years younger than both of us. He had nice teeth, a dimpled chin, chiselled cheekbones, luscious dark hair and uncomfortably arresting blue eyes.

In fact, he was a dead ringer for the guy who played Superman in the movie Rosie and I had watched over Easter and, as I went to shake his hand, I wondered if a small part of my mind was stupidly projecting.

Declan's polite smile faded just a little bit then. Probably because I was staring at him the same way people stared at monkeys in a zoo. Or maybe *I* was the monkey in this situation. All I know is that I needed to start talking, or else the guy was going to think that his cousin had suggested a complete basket case for a client.

Which of course I was, but in a different way.

'Hello.' Clearing my throat, I straightened my shoulders and made a conscious effort to compose myself and act like a normal human being.

'So,' he said, without further preamble. 'I believe there's a legal matter you wanted to have a chat about?' He glanced between the two of us as if to confirm, and I was surprised to notice some hesitation in his tone and body language.

I thought Christine said her cousin was champing at the bit to talk to me about a potential action against the Coopers? So why did he look uncomfortable?

All at once, I realised that she'd used her powers of persuasion on us both and Declan was as unsure about this as I was.

It was a relief to be honest. If Christine's cousin had agreed to talk to me out of mere courtesy, hopefully he would be quick to explain the folly of even attempting to mount any action on Rosie's behalf, and outline the various reasons from a legal point of view as to why such a case would not hold.

At least that might get Christine off my back.

Chapter 18

I was right. The moment I sat down across from Declan's desk, Christine started talking.

And continued talking. About how adamant the Coopers had always been about not vaccinating their kids, how irresponsible they were for taking them out of school to go on holiday, how Madeleine had always looked down on the other mums in Knockroe, believing herself to be superior and now with her new-found TV fame was lording it over everyone even more…

I don't think I'd realised until then just how deep the negativity Christine seemed to harbour towards the Coopers –or Madeleine, at least – was, and I couldn't help but wonder if all this truly was about helping me.

My discomfort must have started to become apparent, because Declan looked at me earnestly from across the table and then spoke to his cousin. 'Christine, would you mind going out front for a bit so I can talk alone with Kate?'

At first, she looked put out to be excluded from something that she needed to be involved in. But, truth be told, she was making me feel really overwhelmed, and I needed some distance from her.

Especially if I was ever going to make a logical, well-informed decision about this situation.

Declan obviously sensed this. 'I'll need to talk with her about some issues that are privileged,' he added simply.

I appreciated the angle, and Christine fell for it, though of course no contract or agreement had been signed or even mentioned. So there was nothing that fell under client privilege. However, I was happy to let him run with the ruse if it meant I got a few moments' headspace.

'Oh, right, of course,' she mumbled. 'I'll just wait out in reception. Take your time, Kate.'

She got up from where she sat and exited the room, delicately closing the door behind her, leaving me alone with Declan.

'So,' he said, with a twinkle in his eye. 'My cousin can be a bit... much.'

I smiled, relaxing a little. It felt good, and I hadn't realised just how tense I'd been since all of this had happened. It felt like for ever since smiling had come naturally to me.

'Christine explained a little about the situation with your daughter. How is she?'

I know he was only being polite, but he sounded so unexpectedly concerned that I was a little taken aback. And became once again overcome with emotion as I thought of my little girl.

'We don't really know yet to be honest. I'm not sure what Christine has told you but...'

'Tell you what, Kate, why don't you tell me everything how you see it. I'll be honest with you; I don't actually know any of the specifics, other than what's been filtered through Christine. And I think we both know she's not exactly impartial.' He smiled, once again putting me at ease. 'And just in case she's given you the impression that we've been discussing you at length behind your back, that isn't the case either. She suggested something "theoretically" to me over lunch with the family one Sunday and I gave her a broad-stroke legal opinion without knowing any particulars. Then she phones me yesterday telling me she wants to bring you in today. To be truthful, I'm probably just as overwhelmed as you are.'

'Oh.' His honesty and candour disarmed me and I felt a little better about the fact that Christine had not been completely forthcoming with either of us.

Then Declan opened a legal pad and picked up a pen. As he did so, it struck me how huge his hands were, and how it seemed like he'd be more at ease outdoors on a farm than in a tiny one-windowed office. Then again Christine had mentioned that this was a family firm, so perhaps he'd followed in his father's footsteps?

'I have to be honest too. I'm not entirely sure what I am doing here at all,' I admitted. 'I don't want to waste anyone's time. And this… kind of thing isn't really my style.'

Declan nodded as he considered what I had just said. 'Have you discussed this with your husband?' I saw him glance briefly at my left hand to my wedding ring. Evidently the fact that I was a widow didn't come up when Christine was giving her cousin the rundown on my situation over dinner.

I cleared my throat. 'I'm a widow. My husband passed away almost two years ago.'

I felt suddenly and inexplicably guilty then, and tried to figure out why. Was it because I was verbalising my relationship status to another man for the first time in an age? Or was it because I knew the very idea of legal action was something Greg would never have approved of if he were still here – in fact he would have been horrified.

My face must have shown my discomfort because Declan cleared his throat and said, 'I'm sorry. I didn't know.'

'You couldn't have known if Christine didn't mention it. I suppose that's one of the reasons she wants me to consider this. I'm kind of up shit creek at the moment. I'm on unpaid leave, have a mountain of bills to pay and have no idea how bad my daughter's condition will get.'

With that – the mere act of verbalising the reality of the direction my life had taken – my voice broke and, much to my utter horror, I burst into tears.

'Oh God, I'm so sorry.' I sniffed, feeling like an idiot for breaking down in front of a complete stranger. Talk about time and place…

But once more Declan seemed to know exactly the right thing to say.

'Tell you what,' he said, when I'd once again managed to compose myself, 'why don't you start from the very beginning, and tell me everything…'

*

When I'd finished, I watched as Declan tapped his pen on the pad of yellow paper in which he had been taking notes.

'I'm so sorry, Kate, it sounds like you've had a truly horrific time of it. How's your little girl now? What's the prognosis?'

I looked away. 'That's the issue. We don't actually know – not until her brain activity has stabilised and they can assess any damage. In the early hours of Friday morning they induced the coma to stop the convulsions, and she's been under for three days now. They're monitoring her in the meantime, but until they start weaning her off the coma drugs or she comes out of it herself, they don't know whether the seizures will return. If they do, or she stays under too long, there might be… brain damage.' I put a hand over my mouth almost involuntarily, as if to stop those horrifically distressing words falling from my lips.

'Jesus.' Declan seemed to shudder. 'That's awful, I'm so sorry. Again I can't even imagine what you've gone through – what you're still going through. All this from measles…'

'I know. And now I've started to question myself all over again about the allergy and whether we should have just bitten the bullet and given her the MMR vaccination when she was a baby. The choice back then was weighing up the certainty of a dangerous reaction taken against the risk of contracting measles. But now I'm thinking at least maybe we could have handled the reaction, whereas brain damage…'

This was what had been killing me in the days since Friday. Rosie could have been protected – by me and Greg, way back when. But as Dr Ryan had reassured me at the hospital, nobody could ever have guessed how Rosie would react to measles, or envision her developing a serious complication like encephalitis on top of pneumonia.

But still I couldn't help but feel that *anything* would have been better than this.

I breathed out, hoping to get back on track. 'So, that's where we are. Even in the very best case scenario, Rosie will require extreme levels of care, and might be in hospital for months. I'm a single income earner, currently out of work unpaid. Once the statutory period runs out, I don't know what I'll do, but in the meantime I have bills to pay and a very sick daughter to attend to. I suppose I just feel …' I shifted uncomfortably '… and in particular your cousin feels, that all of this could have been prevented had the other party not sent her infectious child to school.'

There, I'd said it. I'd uttered the words out loud. I'd blamed someone other than myself for what had happened to Rosie. I thought it would feel liberating, but instead it felt... wrong.

Declan exhaled deeply. 'Well. It's a tricky one. An action like this would be based primarily on negligence.' He tapped his pen on the edge of the legal pad. 'And to succeed in a negligence claim, the plaintiff, in this case you on behalf of your daughter, would need to establish various proofs. One is that the defendant – the other parent – owed the plaintiff a duty of care. Another is that the defendant breached that duty of care, that the plaintiff sustained injuries and or losses – which you've just outlined – and, finally, that the defendant's negligence was the proximate cause of the plaintiff's injuries and losses.'

I nodded, trying to take it all in.

'Point one is a matter of law to be decided by a judge,' he went on. 'The relevant concepts that would be taken into consideration would be those of reasonable foreseeability and what solicitors know as "the neighbour principle".' He exhaled and sat forward in his chair. 'The concept of the neighbour principle is defined as, and I quote, "those to whom a duty of care might be expected to be owed, would be those so closely and directly affected by their actions that they ought reasonably to have them in consideration when directing their mind to the acts or omissions that are being called in to question".' He looked at me. 'It's legal speak so all a bit gobbledegook, I know. But do you follow?'

I nodded. He was basically saying that if you were aware that something you did might affect someone vulnerable, you needed to take that into account before you did that thing that would affect them.

'In your situation, Kate, you would have to establish that the other parents knew or ought reasonably to have known that their failure to vaccinate would cause a risk to other children. Ultimately, if a duty of care was held to exist, then the remainder of the case would turn on the facts. For example, knowingly sending a child to school whilst in an infectious state clinically could ground the proposition that this was unreasonable behaviour.'

Declan turned the pen in his huge hands as he continued to outline his reasoning.

'But if a judge decides that no duty of care is owed, then the case fails at that first hurdle. To my mind, if a duty of care is owed, then the other facts are arguable – in the legal world it's described as a *prima facie* – an arguable case to be made on behalf of you, the plaintiff. And I'll be honest with you, Kate, if what you're saying is true and the sequence of events happened exactly as you described and, more importantly, you have a witness, your friend Lucy, willing to testify that yes, Mrs Cooper knowingly and intentionally sent her child to school aware that she was infectious, then it seems to me that there *is* a wilful negligence issue at play here. What we need to ascertain is – and perhaps this is for a judge to decide – did Mrs Cooper fully assess the potential outcome of her actions or, in this scenario, inaction? And does negligence in this situation extend to – not just sending a sick child to school – but failing to vaccinate the child at all?'

My eyes flickered upwards, surprised. 'So you *do* think the Coopers might have a case to answer?' This surprised me; I'd assumed once Declan heard everything that he'd laugh me out of the office.

But no, he was taking this seriously. Very seriously.

'The law is a strange thing, Kate. Everything is open to argument and interpretation. And while of course there's lots more to tease out in this situation, for the moment, I suggest you go home and think about the implications of actually going ahead with something like this. I'm guessing that you're not here exactly of your own volition.'

'Well no, as you say your cousin can be… persuasive, but I was so angry the other night when Rosie almost died. And Madeleine… the other mum…' I trailed off, not wanting to tell him that seeing Clara's mother on TV blathering happily about child safety or lack thereof had set me off. 'When Christine told me that you were prepared to talk to me, I decided I might as well at least have the conversation. To get her off my back if nothing else,' I added lightly.

But Declan seemed to think it was all perfectly normal and straightforward. 'Well, from a legal point of view, I'm already envisioning how such a case could be framed. Naturally, I need to examine precedent, and carry out some further investigation of my own, but if you're asking if there's something there then I'd have to answer yes – on the civil side, certainly, as of course there's nothing criminal here. But, Kate, if you were considering this as a quick-fix answer to your financial problems, I should warn you, civil cases can take years to come before the courts.'

It's not just that, I thought, remembering how arrogant and cavalier Madeleine Cooper had come across on that TV show.

Based on what Declan was saying now, the woman had recklessly put not only Rosie, but the whole school – maybe even the entire community – in danger. What if Clara had come into contact with an unvaccinated newborn, or any other vulnerable people? And who's to say that she hadn't?

I'd thought about it long and hard since Friday, and kept coming back to the same conclusion: Madeleine Cooper needed a wake-up call.

She needed to know that you don't get to make a career out of being irresponsible, and that the choices you made had serious consequences, affected other people's lives.

'It's also worth considering that situations like this can be hard, especially in small towns,' Declan went on. 'Any action that pits neighbour against neighbour is likely to spark a variety of opinions – including some negative ones. Would you be prepared for something like that?'

I gulped. Of course, this was one of the initial reasons I'd been so reluctant to pursue anything like this at all.

'I know what you're saying, and honestly I'm still so taken aback that you think there might actually be something there that I haven't even thought about the possible ramifications, bad or otherwise.'

But now it seemed I would have to. Should I seriously consider this, consider taking the Coopers to court for what they'd visited on Rosie?

The old me would have immediately said no way. But something had changed in me in the early hours of Friday morning, I knew that. Seeing my daughter come so close to death had altered me in ways I couldn't quite explain.

I'd almost lost Rosie then, and by some miracle that hadn't happened, not that night anyway.

But the problem was – and this was something I wasn't yet able to process – as things stood, I still didn't know if I was going to lose her anyway.

And there was no way I would allow Madeleine Cooper to get away with that.

Declan sat quietly in his chair, watching me, as if he knew I was coming to a decision of sorts.

'Like I said, I really think that you should go off and think seriously about this. And, in the meantime, I believe I should also do my due diligence. I never want to lead any client, or potential client, down the wrong path. As far as I'm concerned, Kate, this is a two-way street. You have to be comfortable with me, but I also have to be comfortable with you. Sound fair?'

I nodded. There was something inherently reassuring about this approach, as if a partnership of sorts was being proposed.

And, for the first time in weeks, I began to feel a little more in control.

'And while you do consider everything and really think about the angles, is there anyone else who can give you a hand – with the day-to-day stuff?' he enquired. He was obviously referring to my situation, my home life and whether I had anyone – besides Lucy or Christine – to lean on. It was an honest question – and a simple one to answer really – but it hit me like a truck.

No, there wasn't anyone like that. My husband was dead, I had no siblings, my parents were elderly and had a life of their own some three hundred kilometres away. Notwithstanding the fact that I was almost forty years old and I couldn't – *wouldn't* – expect anyone else to upend their lives just to help me out.

I crossed my hands on the polished oak table and stared at them. These hands had been doing everything on their own for the last two years. Because they had to.

I straightened my shoulders and looked Declan right in the eye. 'I'm not a victim,' I said simply.

I wasn't sure if that answered his question. But it certainly answered the one that had been bumping around my own head lately.

Declan's arresting eyes studied my face. His gaze was intent, steady. 'I wouldn't have thought for a second that you were.'

Chapter 19

Realising that the sun was setting in Glencree and his office was growing dark, Declan reached forward and flipped on the lamp perched on his desk corner. He quickly pulled back the sleeve of his shirt to check the time and then rubbed his eyes tiredly.

Ever since Kate O'Hara had left his office that morning, he had immersed himself in searching for precedent on cases similar to what had been presented to him.

This could be a monster project – emotionally, legally, politically even. It had all of the touch points of something that could be big – precedent-setting, in fact. The kind of case he'd dreamed about when he was a student.

But instead of the ground-breaking law-changing civil work that had been Declan's passion, he'd been stuck on conveyancing, land registry technicalities and the endless right-of-way issues that so many Irish people relished fighting over. Granted that had always been the bread and butter of his father's practice and it paid the bills, so Declan couldn't complain, but for once he longed to work on something that really got the synapses firing.

Kate O'Hara's situation could be it.

'Knock, knock,' came a voice from the doorway, his sister

Alison – a twenty-one-year-old UCD law student in her final year, who helped out now and again to bulk up her experience. 'Why are you still here this late of an evening?'

Declan pulled his gaze away from his computer screen and turned to face her. 'Just doing a bit of research. That's all.'

'On what?' Alison asked, entering the room. Her brow was furrowed; she was obviously trying to figure out what pressing boundary dispute he would be working so late on.

'It's a case, a potential one. Hey, remember when you were in the States last year and that MMR vaccination trial was going on?'

'The one where the dad took the mother to court for not vaccinating? Of course. Why do you ask?' Her eyes widened with interest. 'Something similar on the cards here? Wow.'

'Kind of, but not the same. Christine brought in a woman from Knockroe today. Her daughter wasn't vaccinated and now she's in a coma. Measles.'

'What? Why wasn't the poor thing vaccinated?' Alison asked, making a distasteful face. She reached into her pocket and extracted a rubber band in order to pull her jet-black hair up into a messy ponytail. 'Don't tell me, the dad's the anti-vaxxer.'

'No, that's not it. Seems her daughter couldn't be vaccinated when she was a baby due to allergies. But another girl got sick and passed the disease on to Kate's daughter at school, and it seems the other family are the anti-vaxxers.'

Alison pursed her lips in disapproval. 'Unbelievable. What is wrong with people? You know, I've always said it was only a matter of time until something like this happened. But wow, Declan, sounds like an amazing case! Can I help – please? I would give my right arm to—'

Declan put his hands on the desk and tapped his fingers as if playing an invisible drum. 'It's not even a case yet, though I do think there's something there. Apparently, the other mother knowingly sent the kid to school while infectious – not that she intended any harm I'm sure but—'

'Wilful negligence. But how can we prove that she did so—'

'Alison, hold your horses. *We're* not proving – or indeed trying – anything. The mother, Kate, was here purely on an exploratory mission. To be honest, I don't think the possibility of legal action had even entered her mind until Christine got in her ear…'

'Good old cuz. If there's a tile loose on the path, you can bet Christine will find someone to stumble over it.'

'Stop it, she's not that bad. But, for once, I'm thinking she might be right with this one. Kate's daughter almost died, and she still might. And when you think it could have been prevented…'

'Jesus, this is why I hate these freakin' hippy conspiracy theorists. You know me, I'm all about personal liberty, but honestly they should all be rounded up and forced to take a needle themselves. Grr.'

Declan had to smile. 'Don't hold back on saying what you really think, Allie. One thing's for sure though, with something like this, there are bound to be some very strong opinions on either side.'

'It'll be amazing! Parents up and down the country will be going nuts over it. The media'll be salivating, the Health Service will be hand-wringing and the internet will probably explode! Oh, Declan, you have to do it.'

He sighed deeply and ran his hands through his hair. Glancing out the window, he said, 'It's not that. I wouldn't be looking at this as a way of raising my profile. It's something else. I don't know how to describe it…' He swallowed hard. Declan especially didn't want to try to explain this to his sister. 'It's the mother, Kate.' He looked down as he said the name and then glanced up to meet Alison's eyes. She was giving him a warning look. 'No, it's not like that.'

He knew that she was thinking in the most basic of interpretations: that Declan was attracted to Kate. Not that Kate was unattractive, but the woman was going through unimaginable suffering.

'Obviously she's really vulnerable at the moment, but there's something else too. She's tough. And honestly, she's been dealt a shit hand.' He recounted to Alison all about Kate's husband, her job situation, the whole nine yards. 'I want to help her. And for some reason I sort of feel… responsible… for helping her get out of this. She said earlier that she wasn't a victim, and I believe her. I just wonder how many times you can get kicked when you're down before that spirit becomes broken. What's more, she didn't come in here guns blazing and looking for immediate recompense the way that most people do when they feel they've been wronged. If anything, she's sceptical and hesitant about the process. And I do feel that she – and certainly her daughter – truly have been wronged in this situation. And I want her to feel that she has someone in her corner. If this is what she wants to do, that is.'

Declan sat back in his chair and cupped his chin in his hand, trying to decide if there was more to say. He was struggling to find the words.

Alison raised her eyebrows. 'I'd forgotten about your Knight in Shining Armour complex.'

He waved off her words. 'No, it's not like that. I really do feel that this is definitely a case worth exploring. It sounds like Kate's heading for a tough future, assuming her daughter comes out of this even halfway OK. And based on what I learned about her this morning…' he paused a little, realising he was speaking his thoughts aloud at this point, '…I think she's going to need an outlet – a distraction of sorts – something to work towards to help her get through it. I could be wrong, but she just strikes me as that kind of person.'

Alison shook her head. 'You know, Dec, Dad always said you weren't suited to law and, for once, I think he was right. Too much of a bleedin' heart.'

Chapter 20

Madeleine honestly could not believe it.

She twirled a finger through one of her curls as she listened delightedly on the other end of the phone line. The woman's name was Joanne, and she was an editor for one of the big UK book publishers with offices in Ireland. And she (along with everyone else in the company apparently) wanted to publish *Mad Mum*'s articles in book form.

'We're all just really big fans of *Mad Mum* and we would absolutely love it if you would consider publishing all your blog posts together in one collection with us.'

Madeleine forced herself to breathe. She was so excited she thought she was going to fall down. 'Wow,' she replied. 'That is... that is just incredible. I'm a little taken aback to be honest. This isn't a joke or something?'

Joanne laughed. 'No, Madeleine, this is absolutely on the level. One of our publicity managers has been following your blog since she was on maternity leave last year, and she was talking about you all the time when she came back. Of course, we've seen a couple of your appearances on *Morning Coffee*, which, as I'm sure you know, have had a phenomenal response. We also think you've hit a bit of a zeitgeist with your funny, down-to-earth approach to motherhood – women are sick of being lectured to – and we want to introduce your writing to a whole new audience. Which we know we can do in book format. Mother's Day of next year would be an ideal time to publish with the obvious gift element, but, to be honest, I think it's the kind of thing that would do well at any time of the year.'

Madeleine was seriously flabbergasted. She'd known that visitor numbers to her blog had spiralled upwards following her recent TV slots, but she'd had no idea that her errant ramblings would attract the attention of a top publishing house. It would be amazing to see all of her blog posts and articles together in one tome, let alone see what the kudos of publishing a book would do to her overall profile.

'So what do you think?' Joanne continued. 'Naturally, you'll want some time to think it over. And of course have your agent look over the offer. Do you have someone representing you at the moment, and if not would you like me to make any introductions?'

Crikey. Now an agent was being suggested too. This really couldn't have gone any better. All those hours slogging over pieces she had no idea would ever end up being read, let alone cultivate a following like the one she had now. And eventually growing that audience enough to attract offers from businesses. And now, it seemed, publishers.

She relished the thought of a top publicist bringing her name up at an editorial meeting because they, of all people, happened to love her blog.

She wanted to punch the air like a teenager. A really excited teenager. But instead, she took a deep breath and cleared her throat so as to come across like the serious businesswoman she was. 'That would be brilliant, Joanne, thank you. This does sound like a very interesting opportunity for *Mad Mum*. And I look forward to reviewing all the details.'

'Absolutely,' agreed Joanne. 'And just so you know, I dropped my daughter on the head once too.' She chuckled. 'I think every mother has at one time or another, but none of us were prepared to admit it until now. I'll have the offer couriered over to your home today as well as a list of contacts for some great Irish agents we work with.'

As she hung up the phone, Madeleine felt like dancing. This was unbelievable!

Her entire day – her entire *future* even – had changed just like that.

*

I scrawled my signature on the line that Declan indicated and then pulled my hand back, as if I had just been burned. I noticed how messy my writing was – usually my cursive script was much more precise and orderly. This looked like it had been written by someone else entirely.

Perhaps it had.

'You all right?' Declan asked me with a questioning look on his face and I nodded without making a sound.

'So what's next?'

He pulled the papers back to the side of the desk where he sat. He stacked everything neatly together then pressed a button on the very complicated-looking phone positioned nearby.

'Alison, I have the signed plenary summons. Can you come and get it?' He turned his attention back to me. 'Now, we file it at the courts. I'll get a registered letter out to the Coopers outlining the action, which they'll have by the end of the week. At the absolute latest.'

I swallowed hard. I couldn't believe I was really doing this, but I was.

Declan and I had talked again at length after our first meeting, whereupon I reiterated that I didn't care so much about victory, or even getting as far as any court, so much as I wanted to send the Coopers a message.

Thankfully, he seemed happy to go along with that, rather than suggest any sort of gung-ho approach. Right from the beginning Declan Roe had struck me as the kind of guy who would be happy to be in my corner whatever I decided, and I appreciated that.

Unlike his cousin who I think was secretly hoping I would march down Knockroe Main Street with a megaphone announcing that I planned to take the Coopers for everything they had.

But this wasn't about money.

'OK, then we'll go through the usual legal motions to start the process and take it from there.'

I spent all my days and nights at the hospital now, while the doctors monitored Rosie's brain activity, waiting for her to show even the slightest sign of improvement.

But she didn't. And with each passing day, I became more and more despondent, knowing that the longer she stayed under, the greater the chance she would suffer permanent brain damage. But there was nothing else the medical team could do.

If this didn't work and the seizures returned, the doctors were out of options.

As was Rosie.

I think if there had been even the slightest change for the better in her condition since that awful episode, I wouldn't be in Declan's office now.

But I was, because there hadn't.

Now, I supposed all I could do was wait for the Coopers to get the letter detailing my suit, or as Declan referred to it in legal terms, the plenary summons, and see how they reacted.

Don't get me wrong, I didn't feel good about this. But I knew I *needed* to do it – had to do something to hit back at the wave of misery and misfortune I'd been drowning in.

I was tired of bad things 'just happening' to me.

It was time to fight back.

Chapter 21

'This is complete and utter *bullshit*!'

Tom Cooper was way past the point of being angry. He was irate. He was incensed. He was ready to explode.

Shaking the letter that had arrived at their house by registered post the previous morning, he raised his voice even louder and yelled, 'I'm fighting this. The whole way, and I'm countersuing that b— that *woman*. There's no way she is pinning the blame on us for this. No way in HELL.'

He slammed the offending piece of paper on their family solicitor Matt Townsend's desk, and looked to those assembled around the office including Madeleine – as if to say, *Go ahead, I dare you to disagree with me.*

Madeleine still felt sick to her stomach. The high that she had been riding since learning of her publishing deal had evaporated the moment she'd opened the letter.

At first she'd thought that there had been some sort of mistake. A clerical error or administrative oversight of sorts. It was only when she'd scanned the words on the paper, that she realised this was actually happening…

Kate O'Hara was issuing legal proceedings against their family, looking to hold them accountable for little Rosie's condition.

She'd phoned Tom at once, but he'd immediately dismissed the very idea.

'Complete nonsense. How can we possibly be blamed for the other girl's illness, just because Clara wasn't vaccinated?'

'It's not just that, though,' Madeleine whispered, outlining how the main thrust of the complaint was that they – *she* – had sent Clara to school knowing she was ill.

And then Tom lost it completely. She could scarcely remember a time when she had seen her husband so angry. 'What? But how were you supposed to know she had measles? No, she's not getting away with this. I'll call Matt immediately and get this sorted. And we'll talk about it later. But whatever you do,' he added gently then, 'do not blame yourself for this, Maddie. You did nothing wrong. *We* did nothing wrong.'

In the meantime, Madeleine suggested simply phoning Kate and talking this through with her. She was sure that once she (finally) got Rosie's mum on the phone or sat down with her over coffee, everything could be straightened out.

Did Kate truly feel Clara was to blame for this, or was she just looking to lash out because her daughter was still unwell?

But Tom argued vociferously against this. He insisted that Madeleine shouldn't talk to anyone – not even Lucy – because her best friend was also close to Kate.

Madeleine disagreed. There was no way she was shutting her friends out over this. Especially since there was no way she and Tom even had a case to answer, she was sure of it.

But now, sitting in their long-time family solicitor's office in Dublin, Madeleine didn't feel so sure this was going to go away, at least not easily or quietly. Tom kept talking about a countersuit and going after Kate for slander and defamation.

Oh God, it was just a huge mess.

Madeleine had never had a panic attack before, but she was pretty sure that she might be close to experiencing one for the very first time. Her head was swimming and she was struggling to formulate or verbalise a sentence, let alone get a word in edgeways.

'What should we do? How do we fight this?' demanded Tom. 'This woman is not going to get away with this. Dragging us into some bullshit civil claim because she can't take care of her own daughter. Well, if she thinks she's having financial problems now and thinks that *we're* going to be the answer to her prayers, she's got another think coming. I'm going to drag her over the coals so hard she's not going to know—'

'Tom!' Yes, he was trying to protect their family and she loved him for that, but just now he was totally out of control. Madeleine wasn't just concerned about his level of rhetoric, but the fact that his face was so red she worried he might have a heart attack. She opened her mouth to continue, but their solicitor beat her to the punch.

'Please,' said Matt calmly from the other side of his desk, pulling the letter out of Tom's reach. 'Sit down for a minute. Let's talk about this.'

Madeleine swallowed hard but felt the smallest amount of tension ease from her stomach when her husband duly obeyed the request. Maybe their solicitor could achieve what she had so far failed to do and keep him in check. She was also confident that Matt would be able to diffuse this situation, change Tom's mind about a countersuit, and propose some sort of rational action for solving all of this.

Allowing herself to hope, she turned her furrowed brow to the man who had done so much for them as a family. Matt had advised them on many legal situations over the years (albeit, none like this), had helped them buy investment property, set up a trust for both of their kids, drawn up their will – he had been a true confidant, and Madeleine respected his opinion and advice.

She was sure that he wouldn't steer them wrong.

Matt steepled his fingers on the polished cherry-wood surface in front of him, and leaned forward to meet the gaze of his clients on the other side of the desk. For the first time, Madeleine noticed the grey around his temples too. How long had he been their solicitor? Fifteen years, maybe? He and Tom had been to university together and her husband had known him long before they were married. In any case, she trusted his advice would be sound.

'All right, Tom, I know you're upset. It's never a nice feeling to be issued with something like this. Especially after everything your own family has been through lately, what with Clara's illness and everything.' Momentarily breaking from his monologue, he turned to Madeleine. 'How is she by the way? All better now?'

Madeleine's mouth was dry, but she managed to get the words out with a nod of her head. 'Yes. Right as rain now, thanks. She's back in school.'

'All right so. Next steps. We have to file a response to this first off. And to do that we need to set forth some reasons why you should not be held liable for the plaintiff's damages. This will help us form the basis of a motion to dismiss.'

These were the kind of words Madeleine wanted to hear, and it made her spirits temporarily buoy.

'Yes. That's perfect. That's what we need. For it to be dismissed.' Out of the corner of her eye, she saw Tom open his mouth and get ready to speak, but, worried he'd only work himself up again, she cut him off. 'How does that happen? We can just talk to Kate and get this sorted out, yes?'

Matt smiled sadly. 'I'm afraid that is a bit too simplistic,

Madeleine, I'm sorry. And I would recommend keeping all correspondence about this between myself and the other solicitor. Of course, Ms O'Hara can voluntarily withdraw proceedings, but oftentimes a Motion to Dismiss is granted by the courts when a settlement is reached, there is a lack of jurisdiction, or there is a failure to prove duty of care. In this case, she has jurisdiction. So, we could easily get this taken care of if we settle. Or, if the factual allegations of the complaint are in fact untrue. We are really going to have to talk all of this through.'

Madeleine nodded, considering this new information. 'But can't I simply go and talk to her? That would be so much easier and frankly—'

'Dammit, Madeleine, you aren't talking to her! OK? Can we establish that? You've done enough talking,' Tom suddenly bellowed, catching his wife – and indeed Matt – completely off guard.

She felt her face flush red with embarrassment. Yes, he was stressed but Tom *never* spoke to her like that in public; and he certainly didn't do so in the privacy of their own home. However, she couldn't address his unacceptable behaviour in that instant because he was already pushing his next topic of enquiry to Matt. 'For the record, we aren't settling. There isn't a chance in hell of that, OK? So she can either dismiss this, or, I swear to God, I will fight this bitch every step of the way.'

'Tom!' Madeleine yelled, once again shocked at her husband's completely uncharacteristic aggression. But he ignored her. 'And that's not all. If that woman thinks she's going to have *my* family fund her single mother lifestyle, she can piss up a river.'

Madeleine's mouth dropped open. Now she was so appalled she felt sick. 'Oh my God, what is *wrong* with you?' She looked at their solicitor who seemed relatively nonplussed by the exchange. 'She lost her husband, Matt. Kate is a widow. He died, unexpectedly, but for some reason Tom makes it sound like she's some sort of leech.'

She knew plenty of single mothers. Nothing made them different from her. Not at all, except for the fact that they were a million times stronger for taking on parenthood all by themselves. Whereas at least she had support. Or she thought she did, Madeleine clarified, glaring at her irate husband. 'And now her daughter is in a coma. For God's sake, Tom, have some compassion.'

But, if anything, Tom was only getting more emotional and incensed with every passing second. He seemed oblivious to the room, and his mortified, angry wife.

'We've broken no laws. There is no law against non-vaccination in this country. How dare she? Of course I'm sorry that her daughter is sick but that's nothing to do with us, nor is it our fault she didn't vaccinate her own kid. Why is this woman knocking on our door for this? I mean it. She is *not* going to drag my family's name through the mud with this accusation and downright character attack. I have a career to think about. I have a reputation and business interests. No one is going to make some sort of example out of us. Our kids are entitled to a positive future without somebody thinking they can take it all away from them. No way is she getting away with this, Matt. We're fighting it, and what's more we want a countersuit. We *want* to sue her. We want to sue her ass off, so she thinks twice the next time she decides to do something like this...'

At that point Matt interjected with some advice about what they needed to do from a legal perspective if a countersuit truly was Tom's choice. Madeleine felt her vision narrow and heard a strange ringing in her ears, even as she continued to witness the exchange between the two men, or, more to the point, Tom's diatribe about the threat to their family's character and personal liberties.

But at the mention of the character attack, Madeleine started to think about her own rapidly growing public profile. She thought about all that she had accomplished in the last year or so. It was this realisation that really frightened her.

This lawsuit – especially if it got as far as the courts – could be highly public and very divisive. She thought about what her mother-in-law had pointed out before, about public opinion and what a hot-button topic vaccination could be. What would people say when word got out? Would they feel the same way as Kate did, and blame Madeleine for visiting the measles virus onto her daughter? What would they think of her?

She had spent long enough on the internet to know how vicious and unforgiving anything to do with harm to a child could be. If these proceedings went ahead, would people fall on her family's side, or Kate's?

And if they didn't and she and Tom were castigated for their stance on vaccination, would Madeleine and her family very quickly become social pariahs?

Chapter 22

Later that week, I sat next to Rosie's bed.

She was as silent as ever. The only sounds that came from her were electronic ones, the various beeps and boops that showed her vitals and expressed that she was still of this world.

I, however, was not silent. I made it a point every day to sit close by and talk to her, stroke her beautiful curls and discuss what was happening, how much I loved her and how I missed her. How very much I wished she would get better. I had to believe that she could hear me – I needed to feel close to her. Especially now, when I felt so scared about what was happening outside the hospital walls.

'I'm only doing this for you, honey,' I said, wondering if I was really talking to my daughter or myself. 'And if you woke up this minute and showed any sign that everything was going to be OK, I would stop the action immediately. I would.'

Brushing a curl of my daughter's hair back from her forehead, I let out a heavy sigh. If anything I felt more exhausted now than I had in the weeks before. I knew that much of it was based on stress. Pretty soon, if not already, all of Knockroe town, perhaps even Glencree, would hear what was going on. And while I was sure I would have supporters like Christine who believed I was doing the right thing, I also knew that there were going to be critics too. My thoughts turned immediately to Lucy, one of Madeleine Cooper's closest and oldest friends. Whose side she would be on?

I had to pray it would be mine, because if this got to court, I needed Lucy to testify that Madeleine had indeed sent Clara to school knowing she was ill.

I had yet to broach the subject with her and I knew it would be a very hard thing to ask.

I didn't get to ponder that line of thought too much though, because suddenly I realised I wasn't alone. There was a soft knock at the door and I looked up with surprise to see that it was Declan. I was expecting contact from him about next steps soon, but I certainly hadn't expected him to show up *here*.

And he must have read it on my face. 'I'm sorry, I hope I'm not being too forward popping in unannounced. It's just, I've had some thoughts, and I wanted to save you from having to leave Rosie's side for any of this stuff. I also figured I'd try to meet the medical team while I'm here. But I appreciate that I'm intruding, I should go...' He started to edge towards the door, and I motioned for him to stop.

'No, really. It's fine. I was just... talking to her.' I nodded towards the bed. This would be the first time Declan 'met' Rosie, and I couldn't shake a sense of weirdness about this situation. This was awkward – and I knew that he must feel it too. He had to.

'May I say hello to her?' he asked softly.

The tense knot that had found a permanent home in my shoulders seemed to disappear and I felt myself offering a grateful smile. Far from being awkward or uncomfortable, Declan was treating this like a normal situation, and he wasn't making those clucking noises of concern and sympathy that so many others did.

'Of course. I'm sure she'd like that.' I was telling the truth. Rosie was an old soul, and she hated when adults tried to talk around her or over her, simply because she was a kid. She liked to be involved in conversations, no matter if the participants were old or young.

I turned back to the bed. 'Sweetheart, I want to introduce you to someone. This is Declan Roe. He's going to be helping me with some things.' I didn't expect a response, of course, but since this was about her, I felt it appropriate for Rosie to 'know' the man who was representing her… *our*… interests.

Declan walked to the other side of the bed and sat down in a chair without invitation. He met my gaze and somehow gave me a look that conveyed immediate comfort, as if willing me to believe everything would be OK.

I don't know why I thought that. He just had that type of presence.

'It's very nice to meet you, Rosie. I wish it was under better circumstances,' he said, returning his attention to my little girl. 'I want to let you know that I am going to do everything in my power to help you and your mum. She's really worried about you. Everyone is.' He sounded so unexpectedly tender – this complete stranger talking to my daughter like he truly cared about her – that I felt a lump in my throat. 'But I am going to try to help. Because I think your mum would like someone to help her while you're in here, and that's me. I'm going to help take care of your mum for you until you're again ready to take over.'

With that, I felt my eyes well up with tears. I sniffed, trying to hold them back, but then a huge wave of emotion overcame me and I lost it. Seriously, lost it.

Declan's head shot up and he looked startled. He obviously wasn't expecting to hear me sobbing. Immediately, he stood and rushed around to my side of the bed. He crouched down next to me and put a supportive arm around my shoulder.

'Hey… I'm so sorry,' he said gently. 'If I said or did something wrong, I'm sorry. Really, I didn't mean to.'

He thinks he's done something wrong…

I snorted an ugly laugh in the midst of my crying. My unkempt hair was stuck to the side of my face, and I was pretty sure there was snot coming out of my nose. I was the definition of a mess.

'No. You didn't say anything wrong. Please,' I stuttered. 'It's just… this is stupid, and please don't take it the wrong way, but I suppose it's been a while since somebody's done that – been in my corner, I mean. Don't get me wrong, I have my friends, Lucy and Christine of course who've been wonderful. And I know you meant help in a professional sense. It's just that… Oh, I'm rambling. I'm sorry. It's just that hearing you say that you've got my back, I feel for the first time that maybe there's some fight left in me after all…'

It was like the legal action was something to aim for, a light at the end of a very dark tunnel that I had been stumbling around in for so long. I was no longer a victim.

Declan offered a small smile. 'That's good. That's how you should feel. And, for what it's worth, I meant every word, Kate. I'm going to think of every angle with this thing.'

I sniffled, wondering what I must look like at that moment.

'Do you need a tissue?' he asked, eyes twinkling.

I felt myself flush and a semi-hysterical giggle escaped my mouth. 'Right. You really do think of every angle. Yes, please. A tissue would be great.'

He stood and crossed to a table upon which a box of Kleenex

was perched. Bringing the entire box back, he offered it to me and grinned. 'You might need more than one.'

I laughed, a real one this time. It was probably one of the first genuine laughs I had had in weeks, months even.

'Now, if you wouldn't mind, once you've finished blowing your nose, do you think I could possibly speak to Rosie's doctor? It's time to get this show on the road.'

*

Madeleine winced as she listened to Tom banging around in the kitchen. She had no idea what he was doing and, frankly, she wished that she could take the kids and head to Harriet's or Fiona's for the night, but she was well aware of how that would look. Not to mention that she wouldn't dream of disrupting their home life.

Her own was disrupted enough.

She and her husband had barely spoken since they had gotten home from their solicitor's office. She thought that some of his fury would wear off, but, if anything, the situation had got worse. It seemed that the longer he had to stew, the more upset Tom became.

And it was obvious, despite his early reassurances, that he was now beginning to blame her for much of what had happened. 'Why didn't you keep her home from school that day when you knew she wasn't well?' he'd muttered on the car journey home. 'Did you really have to do that stupid TV interview?'

'Do you think I would have ever *dreamed* of sending her anywhere if I truly thought she had measles?' Madeleine shot back, stung. 'You had a choice yourself, Tom – you were the very one who pointed out that we couldn't have known. She's your daughter too and you could have just as easily made the decision to keep her home.'

'I know that. But, for God's sake, Maddie, you're the one who's supposed to be—'

'Supposed to be what? The twenty-four-hour on-call parent? You were at the accountant's meeting last month, you heard the pre-tax profit figures for my stupid little hobby. And have you already conveniently forgotten what happened only last week with the book deal? You know that my business is no longer just some kitchen-table thing, Tom, and Clara is your daughter too. You basically made the same call, but the difference is, you're not beating yourself up about it.'

Now, Madeleine recalled the look that Rebecca Kelly, one of the other Applewood mothers, had given her outside the school that very morning, as Clara and Jake jumped out of the car. She had been just about to call out a hello but then decided not to – due to the outright disdain she'd seen written all over the woman's face.

Had word already gotten out about Kate's lawsuit? Surely not.

Then her thoughts drifted to Lucy. Madeleine had been keeping a distance from her friend these last few days. Firstly, because she needed a little space to process her own thoughts about the lawsuit, and, secondly, because she couldn't be sure whose side Lucy was actually on. She must have been the one who'd told Kate or Christine Campbell that she had intentionally sent a feverish Clara to school.

She recalled too how her friend had played down her early sug- gestions about contacting Kate or visiting her daughter, protesting that it wasn't the best time. Had Lucy known all along that Rosie's mum was intending to take a case against her and Tom?

Madeleine was well aware that Tom certainly felt an amount of prejudice against Lucy at the moment. Primarily because she knew that he knew she was not only Madeleine's friend, but also a close confidante of Kate's.

But would her friend truly land her in it like that? Madeleine didn't think so. Lucy wasn't the type to stir up trouble. More likely it was Christine who had been in Kate's ear – especially when it seemed Kate's solicitor was Christine's younger cousin. Madeleine didn't know the guy personally, given that the family weren't from town, but surely the cousin wasn't so stupid as to waste the court's time by issuing nonsensical lawsuits.

And maybe Rebecca's reaction that morning had nothing at all to do with Rosie's situation, maybe the woman was just having a bad day.

In fact, it was very likely Madeleine's own mind was playing tricks on her at the moment because she was extra sensitive. No, Lucy would never betray her like that, she was sure of it, and right now she had to trust the people who were close to her, not push them away.

She opened her laptop and logged into her blog with a relieved sigh. Here at least was a space where she felt more in control, and where the stresses and strains of the outside world didn't seem to penetrate.

Given the fallout with the summons, it had been several days since she had updated anything on *Mad Mum*'s blog or social media, and she felt guilty about that.

As expected, her notifications and messages were through the roof and, for once, she felt happy to throw herself into the effort of attending to them all and immersing herself in her audience.

Madeleine was again so grateful that, as always, she had this outlet to blow off steam and just… lose herself in the mundane.

Thank goodness for the internet.

Chapter 23

Emotional distress. Discriminatory treatment. Loss of enjoyment. Recklessness. Those were just the general damages. Then there were the special damages. Medical costs. Lost income. Out-of-pocket expenses. Defamation.

Defamation! My mouth dropped in shock and I looked at Declan. It was barely a week since he'd issued the summons and subsequently the official claim's bill, but already the Coopers had hit back. 'Defamation: are you joking me? Loss of enjoyment: seriously?' I exclaimed. I shook the paper I was holding so hard I felt it crinkle and crackle in my grip. I was seeing red, that's how angry I was.

Declan leaned across his desk and gently took the offending document out of my hand. In their counterclaim, the Coopers had essentially copied every single item in our original Statement of Claim document and then thrown other – seemingly frivolous – claims in for good measure.

How dare they? It was ridiculous. And downright insulting too.

I'm not sure what reaction I expected exactly, but I certainly didn't anticipate this. Christine was right all along; Tom and

Madeleine Cooper were unapologetic, arrogant and completely deluded!

The nerve of them…

'I don't think we want to rip that up,' Declan said, laying the document on his desk and smoothing it.

'But, Declan,' I said, 'they have essentially made a mockery of our claim. We also mention pain and suffering, emotional distress, loss of income, and out-of-pocket expenses. All of that is correct and reasonable, considering. We didn't go overboard, or be frivolous and I feel like this is just throwing those valid concerns right back in my face.'

Not only that, but they had, according to Declan, put me 'On Proof'. Most of the legal terms in relation to this went over my head, but he explained that basically Madeleine Cooper and her husband were denying that they were responsible for passing on the infection via Clara, and putting the onus on us to prove it.

'Kate, try not to take it so personally. I told you that a counterclaim was a possibility and, honestly, I'm not in the least surprised by this. I know it can feel very personal and shocking, but really this is probably just the defendants' solicitor throwing his weight around.'

I huffed indignantly. 'But it comes across just so bloody… pompous!' I growled, folding my arms against my chest defensively. 'Lost income? For real? Madeleine works from home and I doubt that Tom was forced to take parental leave because he couldn't work while Clara was sick.' I felt myself getting worked up into even more of a lather. Me and Rosie were the injured parties here!

And instead of apologising or offering to help like any decent person would do, the Coopers had simply turned around and told us – *me* – to prove it.

All of this was borderline surreal.

Declan held up his hands. 'Of course I agree with you, but – and I'm just playing devil's advocate here – if the husband had to take up any of his annual leave for instance…'

'But I wasn't the one who sent my highly contagious daughter to school! And why was Madeleine leaving me apologetic messages or sending presents to the hospital if they seriously thought this was all *my* fault?'

Suddenly, I felt the energy drain from my body. What the hell had I been thinking? The Coopers had not only called my proverbial bluff, they had now completely upped the ante by countersuing *me*. I'd got a reaction from them all right, just not the one I'd hoped for, or expected.

Thinking about that alone made me feel ready to launch into a violent rage. How could *any* of this be considered my fault?

'Kate,' said Declan calmly. 'Look at me. Please.'

Trying to breathe deeply, I looked up and met my solicitor's gaze.

'I need you to understand that this is a very normal and all too common legal response. I would have honestly been shocked if the other solicitor *hadn't* taken this course of action – though, to be fair, the defamation thing was a bit of a surprise.' He allowed a small reassuring smile to find its way onto his face.

I swallowed hard. 'You aren't just trying to make me feel better?'

He shook his head earnestly. 'No. I'm not. I wouldn't do that to you, I told you that before. We're in this together. All we have here is the Coopers' solicitor acting in their clients' best interest. None of it means anything until we get into the nitty-gritty of the actual particulars. Does that make sense?'

I shrugged. Honestly, none of this made sense any more.

'All of this is nothing more than legal posturing, believe me. We are going to reply to this and I'll apply to get this counterclaim thrown out, which I'm sure any judge will do without blinking. By issuing a response like this, what their solicitor is doing is entering an appearance, which basically means that he's replying on the Coopers' behalf and entering a defence – an intent to defend our claims bill. The judge will look at both claims, assess in particular the duty of care issue and assess whether or not it stands. If he decides that it does, from there on it's all guns blazing. We'll then start the process of compiling evidence and recording witness information – basically building our case. Does that make sense?'

I nodded softly, but the truth was I was completely bamboozled.

'Of course, there is always the chance that they could be trying to call our bluff too. There could even come a point where the Coopers may decide to mediate and settle before we even get to court.'

'And what happens if they don't?'

'If the judge agrees on the duty of care claim,' Declan said confidently, 'then we'll have our day in court.'

He said this as if it was all so simple and straightforward.

'So what next?'

'I'm already on it,' he answered, automatically infusing in me a confidence I didn't feel. 'Alison's preparing all the documentation for the Motion to Dismiss hearing – we should have a date on that in a few weeks – and we are working on the authorisations for all of the medical records so we can establish the timelines. From the wording of the Coopers' counterclaim, they're putting us "on proof", basically putting the onus on us to prove that Clara infected her.'

I shook my head. 'But Clara must have. She got sick first. No question.'

'True. But what they are implying is that Rosie could have just as easily caught the disease from anyone.'

I thought back to those first few days when everything happened just before our lives had been upended. Clara had been sent home from school one day, and Rosie had woken up feverish three days later.

It was a tight timeline but it *was* a timeline.

To say nothing of the fact that the Coopers had just taken a flight from a destination that had recently suffered a measles outbreak. Whereas where had Rosie been over Easter? At home in Knockroe, with me.

And unlike Clara, I thought, my mouth hardening into a thin line at yet another example of the Coopers' blatant disregard for the rules, my daughter had returned to school when term resumed, unlike Clara who was off enjoying herself in Florida, taking home a souvenir to her schoolmates that could still yet prove to be fatally dangerous.

I checked my watch, realising I was wasting too much time seething at the Coopers when I should be at my daughter's bedside. 'I'd better go,' I told Declan, standing up suddenly. 'I need to be at the hospital.'

He looked at me speculatively. 'You sure you're still OK with all of this, Kate? Like I said before, we can pull back at any time.'

'No,' I replied firmly. 'Do what you have to.'

While admittedly I'd had a huge case of the jitters and major second thoughts once I'd given Declan the go-ahead to issue the summons, now I was glad I hadn't just lain down like a meek doe and accepted my and indeed Rosie's fate.

But now – with a response like that from the Coopers?

Bring it on.

Chapter 24

A week later, I was surprised I didn't get pulled over as I raced to the hospital; I was honestly driving that fast. And I suppose I should also be thankful that I didn't cause an accident either, as I was surely the absolute epitome of a dangerous driver – texting and speeding, all while feeling a mixture of optimism and panic. And my car wasn't the only thing going Mach 10; my mind was racing too.

The hospital had phoned first thing; Rosie had shown some signs of waking up.

Rushing out of the house, I'd sent a harried text to Declan, telling him that I wouldn't be able to make this morning's planned meeting at his office as I'd been called to the hospital.

He sent an immediate reply, wishing Rosie well and asking if there was anything he could do, and I felt grateful that he hadn't pressed by looking for more details.

Because I couldn't give him any. I had no idea what this meant. It was surely good news that she'd awakened of her own accord, but here was the important question: would the coma spell have done the trick in letting her brain heal and stopping the seizures?

After screeching into the hospital car park, I found the first available spot. I sprang from the driver's seat and broke into a run, heading straight for the entrance.

The hospital doors opened automatically for me and, within seconds, I was punching the button for the lift, willing it to open, a myriad thoughts rushing through my brain – most of them incomplete and abbreviated.

Would my little girl be OK? Could this nightmare be close to being over? My heart hammered in my chest and I realised the only thing I wanted was to see Rosie open her eyes, and say my name. It felt like so long since that had happened. Something so simple would make me the happiest woman on earth.

Finally, the lift doors opened in front of me and I punched in the floor I needed. Waiting for them to close, I looked up as if I could see through the floors and into Rosie's room. When the lift finally arrived at the relevant floor, I burst out and tried to tell myself not to run. The nurse in me said it wasn't safe.

But no matter, my feet wouldn't listen to my admonishing and off I went like a Derby champion straight out of the gates.

And, finally, I was at Rosie's room.

Dr Ryan was in there with some of the medical team. They all stood over Rosie's bed, closely monitoring the machines and her charts. I could feel the sweat trickle down my back. I had to see my little girl. Was she awake? Was she fully conscious?

Sensing my presence, Dr Ryan turned around and met my gaze. I widened my eyes expectantly, hoping she would nod, smile or give me some indication that everything was OK. However, stoic as always, she retained her maddening sense of mystique and motioned for me to approach the bed.

I felt like I was walking underwater, everything was moving in such slow motion. As I neared the bed, I heard the sounds from the machines, the same sounds that I had been hearing for weeks.

As Rosie's small body came into view, my heart soared when I realised her little eyelids were twitching and fluttering, as if she was struggling to rouse herself from a deep sleep and wanted nothing more than to return to the dreamland in which she'd been residing.

Suddenly, I broke from my fog and rushed to her side, practically pushing one of the nurses out of the way. Dropping to my knees, I hovered over her small body, breathing in her scent. 'Rosie? Sweetheart? It's Mum. Wake up, honey, I miss you,' I cooed. 'Please wake up, it's OK.'

'Kate,' Dr Ryan said gently. 'Just give her time. It's happening.' Her voice was barely above a whisper, but I felt the promise of her words lie heavy on my being.

'How much longer?' I pleaded, not looking up from my daughter's face. 'When will she…'

But I didn't finish my sentence, because at that moment Rosie's eyes stopped fluttering, and opened completely. Her beautiful green eyes stared ahead, blank. I saw her pupils dilate and she blinked four times in rapid succession, as if trying to focus on something, anything, after spending time in black nothingness.

I let out a small cry of delight and my own eyes filled with tears. 'Honey? It's me, Mum. Rosie?' I urged, and I could hear the begging in my voice. I was dying for her to respond but the nurse in me once again warned me to settle down, give her time. The poor little thing had been through hell and back these last few weeks, and of course she needed time to orient herself, figure out what was going on around her. She was trying to make sense of where she was and what had happened since she had last been awake.

Stroking her hair and taking a deep breath, I wiped away a tear that had made its way down my cheek. Dr Ryan was already springing into action and, in my peripheral vision, I saw her checking my daughter's vitals, looking at readings from the various monitors, doing all the things she was supposed to be doing.

But I couldn't focus on anything except Rosie. At that moment – like always – she was the centre of my world.

Her eyes fluttered once again and momentarily closed and, in that moment, my heart sprang fully into my throat and I had to resist the urge to cry out, *No, come back! Don't leave again!* But my panic subsided when her eyes opened again and she turned her head towards me ever so slightly.

At this, Dr Ryan leaned in closer to the bed and turned Rosie's head to face her own. She took out a penlight and shone it into her eyes.

'Good girl, Rosie, good girl.' The doctor then pulled back the sheet and lifted one of Rosie's feet into her hands, quickly dragging her fingernail against the sole, causing her to flinch in response. 'That's good.' Next, the paediatrician quickly snapped her fingers close to Rosie's left ear, and I was ecstatic to see her turn away ever so slightly from the sound.

Then, it was as if a light dawned behind Rosie's eyes for the first time since she had opened them; she drew in a sharp breath and whispered hoarsely, 'Mama?'

I felt a burst of emotion rush through my chest at those words. 'Yes,' I laughed tearfully, relief flooding through me at hearing the words I'd been waiting so long for. 'Yes, sweetheart, Mummy's here.' My voice was thick with tears as I gently cradled her head, turning it slowly to face me. 'I'm here and I've missed you so much.'

I began covering her face in kisses, all the while crying with relief.

'Kate?' Dr Ryan said gently then. 'I know this is a very

emotional and important time for you, but we need to examine her fully now, OK?'

I pulled back a little from Rosie, but my hands protested, continuing to touch my precious little girl's face, hair, arms, hands. It was as if I broke contact, Rosie might fall back into the abyss.

'Of course. Of course, I'm sorry, I don't mean to be in the way, it's just—'

Dr Ryan smiled kindly. 'Of course and you don't have to explain. We're happy she's awake too. And you can be close to her again in a little while. We just need to check her out fully, OK?'

I kissed Rosie's forehead one more time and then one of the nurses helped me to my feet. Dr Ryan and the team took their positions around the bed, and I moved to the corner of the room so I wouldn't be in the way, all the while keeping a watchful eye on my daughter.

Just as I did so, a text buzzed from Declan, hoping that everything was OK and, in a burst of joyful enthusiasm, I decided to call and tell him the good news.

Right then, I was so ecstatic I wanted to tell the whole world that my beautiful little girl was awake and had called my name.

After taking a final glance back at the bed, I headed for the hallway for some privacy and stood just outside the open door.

'Ah, this is really fantastic news, Kate,' Declan enthused, sounding equally delighted. 'I'm so happy for you, and for Rosie.'

'It probably means that we can drop the case of course,' I said, a smile creeping to my face as I realised how silly and pointless all of that felt now. 'Now that she's OK, we can forget the whole thing and just move on.'

'Well, yes of course, whatever you prefer,' he replied quietly. 'You could drop the case. But I would encourage you not to do anything rash at the moment, and especially without considering all of the angles first. Rosie might be awake, but we do need to make sure her health prospects are, in fact, OK.'

I scowled, annoyed that he was so quick to rain on my parade. 'She's going to be fine, Declan, OK?' I whispered sharply. 'I know it. She's awake now and she spoke to me. Everything is going to go back to normal.' I felt annoyed, insulted even by the suggestion that Rosie being awake didn't mean that all of my problems were going to go away when right then I felt like I'd just won the lottery.

But the very idea sent me crashing back down to reality. Was he right?

'Kate, I understand, honestly. All I'm saying is that it's probably wise that you don't make any rash decisions at the moment, or do anything about dropping the suit until we know more, OK?'

I paused, trying to assess his intentions. But then remembering that he had been my and Rosie's advocate throughout all of this so far, and that perhaps I was being a bit unfair, phoning him while my emotions were running high, I sighed. 'I'm sorry, Declan. I didn't mean to snap like that. I'm just… This is all so overwhelming. It's what I have been waiting for ever since the night I almost lost her, and, well, I was just thinking that finally this nightmare might be on the way to being over. If Rosie is OK, then I'll be able to go back to work. She can go back to school and we can… well, we can get our lives back and move on. And you know that I'm already in two minds about this thing.'

Declan murmured softly that yes, he understood. 'But you should also consider that your troubles might not magically go away with Rosie regaining consciousness. We have our date for the counterclaim hearing now, so we still need to deal with that much at least.'

'I know.' Now I felt like an idiot for assuming that I could just make everything go away. Things – legal things – were already in place, stuff that I'd instigated by taking this stupid action in the first place. I stole a glance back into Rosie's room, wondering what was taking so long. The team were still moving around her bed, taking notes and consulting.

'In any case, Kate,' Declan said encouragingly, 'whatever you want to do, I'm with you all the way. It's entirely up to you.'

'Thank you. I suppose like I told you that first day, it feels like my life has been off-kilter for a very long time.' Of course Declan didn't need to know any of this, but I felt the need to explain my thinking. 'Since Greg died obviously. But before this happened at least I'd been coping. I had a routine; me and Rosie had a routine. I dropped her off at school in the mornings, worked around her school hours, helped her with her homework, took her swimming and to ballet lessons. We watched TV together in the evenings and read books at night, and at weekends we went to the playground and chatted with neighbours...' I swallowed hard. 'I miss that. I want... I *need* things to go back to normal.' A tear escaped from my right eye and I brushed it quickly away. 'But, most of all, I didn't have all this *anger*...' By then I was no longer sure if I was talking to Declan or myself.

But before he could reply, Dr Ryan's voice rang out from behind me.

'Kate? I don't want to alarm you, but we need to take Rosie down for an MRI.'

I almost dropped the phone. 'Why? What's going on? What's happened?'

'Kate,' said Dr Ryan evenly, 'we just need to take an MRI. She's not responding to certain stimuli, and I think it's best we do this straight away.'

I was already nodding in agreement and moving towards my daughter. 'Of course, of course, whatever you need to do. Please,'

I responded, anguish palpable in my voice as again I felt myself sweating through my shirt.

But yet I didn't understand my anxiety. An MRI was surely routine? Normal procedure for someone who'd been through what Rosie had.

For all of the medical knowledge I happened to possess in my brain, for the life of me I didn't know. I didn't know much about neurology, and I wished desperately that I could simply absorb Dr Ryan's experience through osmosis.

I would give anything to know in that moment if everything was going to be OK, or if, God forbid, this was the start of yet another nightmare.

Chapter 25

'What do you think is taking so long?' I whispered to Declan, who, overhearing the doctor's words while still on the line, had immediately rushed to the hospital to offer me some support, and I guessed to figure out next steps based on how things turned out.

Now he sat beside me in silence just outside the imaging room. He turned with a look on his face that suggested he hadn't really heard what I'd said. 'Sorry, what? I was miles away.'

His concern for Rosie was touching and I felt grateful that he was here. He had become a good friend and such a close ally in the last few weeks, and oddly it felt right to have him here now.

I offered him a tired smile. 'I said I wondered what was taking so long.' I knew he didn't have the answers, but it felt somewhat comforting to have someone else to speculate with. If only to break up the tension I was feeling.

But then, as if answering my prayers, the imaging room door opened and Rosie was pushed out on a gurney. Dr Ryan followed behind and nodded to me when she saw me.

'We can go back up to Rosie's room now and get her comfortable. The results should be ready shortly.'

I jumped to attention with Declan right behind me. 'Doctor,

please, what do you think? Is everything going to be all right? Is she OK?'

The look on Dr Ryan's face confirmed my worst fears.

'Kate, the MRI will tell us more. But my worry is that during the worst of the seizures, Rosie suffered a hypoxic brain injury. Essentially, her brain experienced a partial lack of oxygen.'

I was already shaking my head. Her words couldn't be true. 'But when she woke up... she said "Mama"... she was looking around... she was there. She knew me, she was with me. I could feel it.'

I felt Declan move closer behind me. I wondered if he was preparing himself to catch me when I crumpled to the floor. Surely that must be coming. My legs felt like they were made of jelly. He reached out and put a steadying arm on my elbow.

'Kate, I know this is scary. But Rosie is still in the very best of hands, OK? We are going to do everything we can to take care of your daughter, I promise.' Dr Ryan turned her attention to a nurse who seemed to be studying me intently. 'Breda? Let's get Kate back to Rosie's room and maybe we can give her something to help her calm down.'

'I don't want drugs,' I snapped, suddenly defensive.

Dr Ryan looked into my eyes. 'You are very pale right now, Kate. And we are all worried about you too.'

Declan placed an arm around my shoulders. 'It's OK, Kate. Let's go back upstairs with Rosie. I think it's best if you sit down and try to take it easy until we know something for sure. Come with me.'

I allowed myself to slump into him – I let him support me as he led me back to Rosie's room. Maybe he was right, and Dr Ryan too. I needed to calm down.

I needed to breathe.

*

Back in Rosie's room, I held my little girl's hand and watched her. Every now and then she would look in my direction; otherwise, she seemed intent on staring at inanimate objects, like a chair across the room, the blank television screen, a cup of water that rested on a table next to her bed. Dr Ryan told me this was normal – she was probably trying to recover her sense of self and focus her eyes.

The doctor also told me it was likely that Rosie was experiencing a 'fog' of sorts. She still had a lot of drugs in her system.

I kept all of this in my mind, but devoted my energy on the fact that she had indeed muttered 'Mama' before. That was a positive, and it wasn't common for someone with brain damage.

'You know on television, when someone wakes up from a coma, they are always perfect,' I mused. 'Smiling and happy, as if nothing happened.' It wasn't a question, or even a declarative statement. Just a simple ironic observation. 'Reality is a bitch.'

Declan sat next to me. His gaze too was on Rosie.

'But she's awake, Kate. She's awake. She wasn't this morning, and now she is.'

I turned to look at him, and he met my eyes. He was correct, of course. I should be thankful. That thought alone brought me to tears. 'You're right,' I admitted. 'You're right.'

I squeezed Rosie's hand. She turned her head ever so slightly in my direction and I waited for something more, but nothing came. Taking a deep breath, I worked to encourage myself just to be happy about that. That her eyes were open. That she seemed to know my voice, was aware that I was there.

Hearing light footsteps enter the room, I looked up to find Dr Ryan approaching the bed with a man in tow. She introduced him – Dr Franklin. He was from the neurology department, and the pair had been reviewing Rosie's MRI. It seemed they had news.

'Should we go somewhere else?' I asked, suddenly concerned about what Rosie would hear and what she might think if they were delivering bad news about her condition.

Dr Ryan smiled kindly. 'There isn't any reason to go somewhere else unless you would be more comfortable.'

In all honestly, I just wanted to be by my daughter's side. So I told them it was fine to stay put. 'So, what did the scans reveal?' I asked, steeling myself for the worst news.

Dr Ryan turned to Dr Franklin and communicated something with her eyes. Then, she turned back to me. 'Kate, I realise that this has been a challenge since day one—'

I put up a hand to stop her. 'Really, I can handle this. Please don't sugar-coat things for me, tell it to me straight. This isn't the first time I have been through a living hell.' I swallowed hard. There was no reason right now to be anything but brutally honest – and I knew that this wasn't the first time that Dr Ryan had to deliver tough news either.

The neurologist cleared his throat. 'Well, Ms O'Hara, it appears that Rosie's brain was denied some oxygen during her seizures, which in turn caused some brain cells to die. This usually only takes a few minutes. Ultimately, when the brain is denied oxygen, there is a disruption of the transmission of electrochemical impulses, which impacts the production and activity of neurotransmitters. These regulate many cognitive, physiological and emotional processes. So while Dr Ryan's original concern about Rosie having experienced a hypoxic brain injury is true, her brain wasn't completely denied of oxygen, so that's a positive.'

I nodded, trying to digest his words. 'So what does that all mean, now that she's conscious? Can we correct the damage that has occurred?'

I knew a little about closed head injuries and brain injuries. Just a little. I knew that you could work towards recovery, but it was hard, and a very long process. And there were no guarantees. I remembered several cases throughout my career: some brain-injured patients had been working to regain their full faculties for years.

Dr Ryan took a deep breath, but Dr Franklin stepped in again.

'Unfortunately, it's hard to predict at this early stage. It simply comes down to a waiting game to see what functions Rosie recovers and what progress she makes.'

I ran my hands through my hair and considered this. 'But we at least know that she's responding, talking even?'

Nodding his head in agreement, the neurologist said, 'Yes. That's part of it. But this is about more than simple cognitive functions like speech or vision. We also have to consider that Rosie may suffer some... physical disability.'

This caused me to swallow hard. 'Meaning?'

'Meaning that she might not gain full function of her arms and legs and may even experience spastic movement or rigidity. Additionally, because of the correlation between cognitive function and coordination or learned movements, she may well have forgotten everyday tasks, like tying her shoes or how to brush her teeth.'

In that moment, I had a burst of memory of Greg and me teaching Rosie how to tie her shoes, only a few short years ago. She had learned to do that once; I knew I could help her learn how to do it again. I was determined to be positive.

'So just relearning some skills. I understand.' I nodded thoughtfully. That didn't sound so bad. My girl was a tough cookie; I knew she could handle that much.

Dr Ryan, however, was looking at me hesitantly. 'Kate, we need to stress, it might not be that simple.' I started to speak, to assure her I understood. This might not be simple, but we would deal with it. We would *get through it*. She and I had survived so much already.

But I was quieted from offering further commentary when I heard the physician's next words.

'Until we know the full extent of Rosie's injuries and have the chance to monitor any potential progress she makes from here on, I need you to understand that there is a strong possibility that Rosie will have special needs. She may never recover all of her cognitive function, she might not be able to walk again, and it's highly likely she will need specialist care. This is the reality, and I'm sorry that it's not better news. Our rehabilitation team here at the hospital will work with you through everything and address issues as they occur. You have to be ready to look at this from many perspectives – medical, emotional, financial...'

I was listening to every word, but I found myself hung up on the phrase 'special needs'. I tried to picture Rosie in a wheelchair, needing assistance with simple things, like feeding herself and walking. Somehow I couldn't picture it, and I suddenly also couldn't picture my future. How would I *ever* return to work? And specialist care... where was the money for all this going to come from? What was going to happen to us?

I had been so foolish, thinking that if she would just wake up life could get back to normal. If Rosie opened her eyes, then bam! Everything would be OK.

I squeezed my little girl's hand again. I pleaded with her to give me something, anything, that showed she – my tough cookie five-year-old – was still there. That she was present with me, ready to fight with me.

What I was rewarded with was the smallest twitch of her fingers. It could have been anything, but I was going to take it as a good sign.

I looked at Declan then. His gaze was sympathetic, but there was something else in there too. And, suddenly, he offered me his hand. His grasp was firm communicating something: *I will help you.*

And, right then, I knew I had to push on. I had to be strong.

This thing wasn't over – not by a long shot.

Chapter 26

Four weeks later, Judge Patrick Dowling peered over the top of his spectacles and considered the two solicitors currently taking up space in his courtroom.

'All right, what's next?' he bellowed to his clerk and Declan gulped.

He had no idea how today was going to go down, but he hoped against hope that the High Court judge was in a good mood. Today was the first major hurdle in Kate's case and, given everything that was happening to her right now, he was determined that it would herald some good news for a change.

'A Motion to Dismiss in the matter of *O'Hara* v. *Cooper*, and same in the counterclaim of *Cooper* v. *O'Hara*,' answered the clerk blandly.

The judge rifled through the two motions that sat in front of him and read through the details of the original claim and the reasons behind the requests for dismissal.

'Approach the bench,' he ordered without looking up. 'In the matter of *O'Hara* v. *Cooper*, what is your reason for requesting dismissal?' He turned his attention to Matt Townsend, and Declan noticed him flicking his eyes ever so quickly to where the defendants' solicitor sat.

'My clients request dismissal because this case is frivolous and unfounded,' answered Townsend in an even voice. 'It cannot be proven that the defendants' daughter is the reason that the plaintiff's child became sick. And my client can hardly be held responsible for what the plaintiff has experienced since this unfortunate situation happened.'

Dowling snorted as if he had found something funny. 'Interesting point, especially considering your clients have decided to file a counterclaim against the plaintiff listing the very same elements.' He looked again at the man sitting at the defendants' table and was pleased to see his face flush.

At this, Declan felt himself exhale a little. Seemed like the judge wasn't all that enamoured of the Coopers' pleas.

Townsend opened his mouth to speak, and offer a defence of the counterclaim but Dowling had moved on. He clearly believed his observation did not require a response.

'Mr Roe,' the judge addressed Declan then. 'You're the plaintiff's solicitor?'

'I am, Judge. And I would request that the original claim proceed, unless the defendants would prefer to settle. We would also request for the counterclaim to be dismissed and the duty of care *prima facie* to be upheld.'

'Where is your client today?'

'With all due respect, I didn't believe it was necessary for Ms O'Hara to be present in court today. She is a single parent and has opted to stay with her daughter, who remains seriously ill in hospital.' Declan kept a neutral expression on his face, even as he heard Tom Cooper shift in his seat nearby.

'How long has she been in the hospital, Counsellor?' enquired the judge.

'Judge, what does that have to do with today's motion?' interrupted Townsend.

Judge Dowling turned a frosty glare towards the defence table. 'I believe I am the one who asks questions in my courtroom, Mr Townsend. I'll remind you to speak when you are spoken to.'

There was more rustling from where his client sat. Tom Cooper clearly was not pleased.

'Mr Roe?' pressed the judge.

'A little over eight weeks,' Declan replied.

'I see. And according to the Claims Bill, your client is currently on parental leave?'

'Yes, Judge. She has used all paid time off that was available to her, but is now on unpaid leave. Because her daughter has suffered considerable complications directly resulting from the measles virus, it's unlikely that my client will be able to return to work at the end of the allotted eighteen weeks. Furthermore, my client's daughter requires special needs rehabilitative care. In the meantime, my client's out-of-pocket expenses directly relating to her condition have been extensive, especially while also dealing with loss of income.'

Judge Dowling considered this information. 'And why was this child not vaccinated against the disease, Mr Roe?'

Declan recounted the medical reasons why Rosie could not be vaccinated. The judge then turned his attention to the defence.

'Same question for you, Mr Townsend.'

Matt Townsend cleared his throat and locked eyes with the judge. 'My clients have chosen not to vaccinate their children for personal reasons.' He didn't elaborate, which caused the judge to raise his eyebrows.

'I'm waiting to hear these personal reasons, Counsellor.'

For a moment, there was complete silence in the courtroom, and all eyes turned expectantly to Townsend.

'Judge, my clients did not immunise their children because they distrust the vaccine and believe it may put their children in danger. My clients believe—'

But the judge cut him off. 'Oh yes, I am well aware of the conspiracy theories surrounding the MMR vaccine. However, if I remember correctly, those claims have been repeatedly disproven. And the physician, a Dr Wakefield, I believe, who originally made the claim is no longer allowed to practise medicine, is that not correct?' He didn't wait for an answer. 'So, tell me again why your clients' child had not been vaccinated?'

Townsend cleared his throat. 'It is not a legal requirement under Irish law to vaccinate a child,' he said plainly. 'My clients' reasoning for such is no less valid than the plaintiff's reason for not doing so.'

Declan began to speak then, but Dowling again showed he was in charge. 'Yet the plaintiff's counsel has explained that Mrs O'Hara's reasoning is based on a life-threatening allergy, and the mere fact that said plaintiff is a medical professional means that she must have an appreciation for science.'

Declan had to work hard not to smile. This really was not going well for Townsend, or Cooper for that matter.

'Judge, I would encourage you to also understand that both children displayed symptoms within days of each other. There is no way to prove which child passed the infection to whom,' pleaded Townsend.

Judge Dowling narrowed his eyes at the lawyer. 'But it is my understanding that your clients apparently sent their daughter to school aware that she was infectious.'

'Yes, but—'

'And given that the child in question was not vaccinated as per the HSE's recommended schedule, I would be inclined to agree that a duty of care was indeed owed, not just to the plaintiff, but to the community in general.'

'Judge—'

'Which is also wholly pertinent to the defence's counterclaim, making it, in my view, seem especially frivolous given your client alleges loss of income, medical expenses, even loss of enjoyment – all arising from the fact that they themselves chose not to protect their own child.'

'Judge, one of my clients did have to take time off of work and he and his family went through considerable distress and worry as their daughter suffered, and obviously the sickness interrupted their lives.'

'All of which could have likely been avoided had your client followed HSE vaccination protocol, could it not?'

With that, Judge Dowling turned his attention back to the paperwork in front of him. He made a considerable show of turning each page while looking at the corresponding solicitor. Finally, he spoke, but by then Declan was all but certain he was about to be delivered a win. Willing himself not to be too presumptuous, he tried to keep his expression composed but still couldn't fight his inward delight that they'd got over hurdle one.

'Mr Townsend, I am quite frankly appalled that you agreed to file such a counterclaim given your client's own failure to act in this situation. You are correct; it is not a legal obligation for Irish citizens to vaccinate their children, but, as I see it, if they do not then they must be expected to bear the cost of that risk, and thus owe a reasonable duty of care to the community at large.

'With that, I hereby deny the defence's Motion to Dismiss *O'Hara* v. *Cooper*. And I furthermore grant the plaintiff's Motion to Dismiss *Cooper* v. *O'Hara*. The original Statement of Claim is valid and I find the issues mentioned therein legally sound. This case may progress unless the defence would like to propose settlement at this time.'

It was a statement, but also a question. However, Matt Townsend was still reeling from the early loss he had just been delivered and it caused him to wait a beat too long for Dowling's standards.

'Mr Townsend? I'm talking to you.'

He blanched. 'Sorry, Judge. No, my client does not wish to propose settlement at this time.'

'Very well. I suggest, Mr Townsend, you put a bit more thought into how you are going to present your defence in future, as your counterclaim was not only frivolous but hastily thought out and sloppy. Thank you.' He handed the legal filings over to his clerk. 'Counsellors. You're dismissed.'

Declan nodded dutifully at the judge and gathered his briefcase.

As he left the courtroom, he couldn't help but smile at his little victory, and thanked his lucky stars that the other solicitor had been arrogant enough to play directly into his hands by issuing that counterclaim.

No judge was ever going to allow a party who'd declined vaccination by choice to make such claim. He'd hoped from the outset that this would pave the way for the judge to allow the duty of care *prima facie* and he'd done just that.

This was the kind of legal manoeuvring he'd always been so excited about at university, Declan recalled, a spring in his step as he went outside to call Kate.

Finally, he was getting to flex some muscle and practise the kind of law he'd always dreamed of.

And, in the process, help someone who truly deserved it.

Chapter 27

'Lucy, will you hold on for just a sec?' Madeleine said, answering her mobile to her friend. 'I'm actually just on the other line with Tom.'

'Of course. I completely understand. No problem. It's just so… horrible. Is… there anything I can do to help you?'

Madeleine tisked. 'Not unless you can figure out a way to get this whole mess thrown out by a judge who doesn't hate our solicitor.' She picked up the landline and addressed her husband, bidding him goodbye. 'Talk to you later, sweetheart, we'll figure something out, OK?'

After hanging up on Tom, she resumed Lucy's call, and uttered a loud sigh. 'What a day. Honestly—'

'What did you mean about the judge?' her friend replied, confused. 'What else is going on? I mean, from the way you sounded I figured you knew what I was calling about…'

'What do you mean?' Madeleine interrupted, her heart speeding up a little. 'I was talking about the court hearing this morning. The judge upheld Kate O'Hara's claim. But hold on a second, you couldn't possibly have known that. So what were you calling about?' Concern inched into her voice then, as she wondered what fresh hell was about to be unleashed on them now. It was bad enough that the judge was upholding Kate's claim, which, incredibly, meant that this thing truly was headed for court. What could possibly be worse than that?

Lucy sighed heavily. 'Just… just turn on your television, sweet-heart. Turn it to Channel 2.'

'What? Why?' She muttered under her breath a little as she looked around for the remote control, and finally finding it, she turned on the TV.

The lunchtime news was on and Madeleine couldn't quite believe the headline she was seeing scroll across the bottom of the family TV, or the words that were coming out of her *Morning Coffee* co-panellist's mouth.

Gemma Moore was informing the newsreader and lunch-time viewership that 'popular blogger and self-proclaimed Mad Mum, Madeleine Cooper, is at the heart of a controversial legal action – sure to spark a lively debate over Cooper's stance as an anti-vaccination proponent – that has this very morning culminated in a crushing blow from a High Court judge.'

The journalist was live in a TV studio, calmly discussing Madeleine's private family business with the newsreader! She knew that Gemma Moore had a reputation for having no limits, but just then the *Daily Record* journalist clearly had Madeleine set firmly in her cross hairs.

'The lawsuit, which outlines negligence, personal injury and a host of other claims, was filed by Kate O'Hara, a single mother facing the ongoing serious illness of her daughter Rosie, as a result of encephalitis directly caused by measles. Both children were not protected by the HSE-recommended MMR vaccination, and while they were the only two children at the school affected by this dangerous disease, it appeared that Clara Cooper was sent to school by her parents while infectious, which formed the basis for O'Hara's wilful negligence claim…'

Madeleine felt like she had been hit by a train.

But how could you not feel that way when the carefully constructed persona and platform you had spent so much time building came crumbling down all around you?

'… so this morning's High Court ruling suggests that this small community could soon be thrust directly into a savage anti-vaccination debate. The question remains: who really is responsible when children are not vaccinated? Is this a frivolous lawsuit on behalf of Ms O'Hara? Or can the Cooper family truly be held accountable for little Rosie O'Hara's condition?'

'Why is she doing this?' Madeleine's voice shook. 'Why would anyone…'

'I don't know and I'm so sorry. Can I do anything?' Lucy asked quietly.

Madeleine had almost forgotten her friend was on the other end of the line.

'I don't… I just… No. I'm sorry, I need to go. Talk to you later.' And before Lucy could respond, she hung up the phone and continued to listen to Gemma Moore's almost gleeful report on the legal action, her corresponding just-published article in the *Daily Record*, as well as all the background on Madeleine's celebrity blogger status, recent *Morning Coffee* appearances and often controversial take on parenthood.

She cringed as the woman repeatedly rattled off the name and website address of the *Mad Mum* blog, just in case the public might need more information.

Or a target more like, she thought, terrified.

Her vision blurred. She felt dizzy and light-headed. Her whole world was crumbling, and she had no idea what she was going to do.

Her laptop pinged from the kitchen table and Madeleine moved back to it, her hands shaking as immediately, in the wake of the bulletin, she watched comments pop up on her website, blog and various social media channels – almost all at the same time.

Horrible, hurtful, personal comments. She was being openly mocked.

@MomsForHealth: What a joke. One thing for @MadMum to talk about not taking motherhood seriously, quite another to be downright irresponsible! Vaccinate your kids for gods' sake! #measlescourtcase

This had already been shared a couple of hundred times.

@Journalie: Breaking: Irish Mummy blogger @MadMum in hot water for her #antivaxx status. #MadMum or #BadMum–your thoughts?

Then all of the follow-up commentary as the entire internet seemed to pile on with relish.

All of a sudden, everyone had an opinion on her and her family. Some expressed a hope that she and Tom 'lost everything' in the court case. Others even bleated for social services to take away their kids…

As Madeleine scrolled through the rapidly increasing traffic, which had both her own name and that of her blog trending almost instantly nationwide, her panic levels rose in accordance.

Mercifully, she saw that were at least one or two people defending her in the midst of the melee, but they were few and far between. Complete strangers trying to talk reason, while others expressed outright hatred.

@MumtoCharlie Give her a break, we don't know the full details yet. Maybe there's a reason her kids didn't get vaccinated. Could be allergic or vulnerable? #trolls #innocentuntilprovenguilty

@MforMum: Thinking of Kate O'Hara and poor little Rosie. Shame on you @MadMum. #Irresponsible #JusticeforRosie #vaccineswork

Her mother-in-law had been right to warn her, Madeleine realised now, the full horror of it all overtaking her. The public loved to express an opinion – never more so than on the internet – and right now, the full force of those primarily negative opinions was headed directly her way.

These people didn't even know her. They had no idea what was going on with this situation – outside of what Gemma Moore had told them that is.

Gemma Moore.

She was behind all of this. Yes, she and the other woman had locked horns a little on the panel show, but for Madeleine at least it had been harmless banter, just for the cameras. What had she done to seriously deserve all this?

'Oh my God. What do I do?' she whispered into the silence of her kitchen.

She thought about deleting some of the comments beneath her blog and on Facebook (unlike Twitter, at least she could get rid of those) but then hesitated, knowing full well what internet trolls did when they thought they were being 'silenced'.

They just got louder.

Her head spun as she tried to think through her options. It was true that people had short attention spans, and she supposed she could just ignore this. However, she was also smart enough to realise that to remain silent was probably the worst thing that she could do.

Damage control...

She bit her lip, realising the other further-reaching implications of all this too. She could only imagine what was being said around Knockroe, by people who actually knew her and Kate.

She had to address this. Being upfront and honest about what had happened was the right choice. It had always been her modus operandi both on- and off-line, and that wasn't going to change now.

Madeleine pulled up her word processor and began to type a fresh blog post – one that she hoped would go viral just as quickly as Gemma's news story.

She wasn't a villain and this was all being blown way out of proportion. Madeleine was sure people would understand once they heard her side of the story. She would explain everything and let the world know that she wasn't a bad person, or an irresponsible mother.

With luck, Kate would hear about it and read it too, and finally she might be able to reach Rosie's mum in a way she hadn't been able to so for thus far.

She'd let Tom do things his way and, based on what had happened that morning, it had proven to be the wrong move.

Madeleine would make this right. She had to.

Chapter 28

THE *DAILY RECORD* – WEEKEND OPINION

Should childhood vaccination programmes be compulsory?

A recent study released by the American Medical Journal found that uptake of childhood vaccinations has steadily declined over the last decade. In some American states the coverage is now below 85%, leading some government officials to push for mandatory vaccination of all schoolchildren.

This move is being viewed by some as an attack on human rights, while others are applauding the decision. There are no official figures available in relation to the uptake in Ireland. We spoke to leading paediatrician Dr Marcus Geraghty about his views on the future of the Irish vaccination programmes.

'The main worry is the uptake figures. If the number of people availing of the vaccinations falls below 90% the whole programme is at risk,' he said.

'Nobody likes the term "herd immunity", we don't like to think of our kids as cattle. The reality is that if you have a large number of unvaccinated children, outbreaks become more common and prolonged. You end up with a situation where very young babies who haven't yet had their shots end up infected, and so the programme fails.'

When asked if he felt children's vaccinations should be mandatory he said:

'That is a very difficult question to answer. I think education of parents is key. We have to ask why are some people deciding against vaccination? I think the emergence of often false information via the internet has a lot to do with it. Parents have come to me and said they have read about vaccinations causing autism and a myriad other complications. These anecdotal stories are unsubstantiated and they cause undue stress to parents in much the same way as my self-diagnosing the cause of a headache using Google. Invariably it will tell me I have everything from cancer to a brain tumour.

'The reality is that for many years these vaccinations have saved children from serious diseases that have been proven clinically and medically to cause suffering and death. We put warm clothes on our kids in winter so they don't catch colds, we apply sunscreen to stop them getting sunburn and melanomas. We make them wear helmets on their bikes and scooters. If you have it in your power to protect, you should do so. Should vaccinations be mandatory? No.

'Should people vaccinate their children? Absolutely yes.'

We then quizzed Dr Geraghty about the medical reviews – namely that of Dr Andrew Wakefield – that had drawn links between autism and the MMR vaccination, to which he replied:

'I've read the review you're referring to. It has been totally debunked and indeed retracted by the author. Unfortunately, it's caused some serious doubts amongst parents that we need to address, and again it goes back to the education issue.'

Finally, we asked Dr Geraghty about the recent high-profile legal action pertinent to the vaccination debate and currently pending in the Irish courts.

'I will not comment on individual cases as it would be unfair and reckless. I do hope however that the little girl involved makes a fast

and full recovery. I'd also hope that it enables parents to see the real
and present dangers of the very diseases we are trying to eradicate.'

So what's your view? Should the decision be taken out of parents'
hands? Or should it remain an individual choice?

Poll: Should childhood vaccinations be mandatory in Ireland?
   O Yes
   O No
   O I don't know

Comments:
Hunny Bunny: Of course they should be compulsory. I'm anti-Nanny
State, but we can't let the tinfoil-hat-wearing conspiracy theorists put
our kids at risk.

Sallymander replied: I tip my tinfoil hat to you, Hunny. The last
government that rolled out compulsory injections were the Nazis and
we all know that didn't end well.

Bally replied: Your gas, Sally. Not.

5LeafClover replied: It's 'you're gas'.

Cherylturf: Jeez, how did we get from vaccination to two types of
Nazis; real ones and grammar ones? I voted yes. I couldn't live with
myself if anything happened to mine because of a decision I'd made
based on internet rumour.

BillyBray replied: Cheryl, could you live with yourself if one of yours
developed complications because of a vaccination? Google HPV side
effects and educate yourself.

Cherylturf replied: Billy, thanks for your concern for my education. I never said I thought vaccinations were 100% safe, but I also happen to know these diseases, including cervical cancer, are no barrel of laughs. **PS. I fear for you if you think being able to type something into a search engine is 'educating yourself'.**

Papajim: Can't believe how much like sheep people are! Seriously, let the government and Health Service take full responsibility for me and my family? People do realise these people kill as many as they save every year. If mandatory vaccination happens you'll find me at the airport with my family.

J Adams replied: Papajim, can you post a link to where I can read about all these doctors killing their patients? Also being a responsible citizen and parent is not sheepish behaviour, it's what grown-ups do everyday. Don't let the door hit you on the way out.

Debs415: I do feel sorry for the parents of kids with health issues that prevent them being immunised. A girl in my daughter's school has some blood disorder meaning she can't have the jabs, yet there are serious complications for her if she catches measles or chicken pox like that girl in the news at the moment. She depends on the diligence of other parents not sending their kids in sick. There are a few mothers in that school that value their girls' brunches and morning coffees more than staying at home with their sick children. It's a Catch 22 really, but I think mandatory jabs might be the way to go. Far more people will be harmed than be affected by side effects if these diseases are not kept in check, IMO.

Johnny B replied: Do you trust the government and big pharma companies though? When you sign consent to have your child vaccinated you are also indemnifying the pharma companies – why? The answer is because their product comes with risks attached. What happens if these vaccines are mandatory? Do me and my family have the right to go after these multi-billion euro industries if something goes wrong, even though we'd no say in the matter? I very much doubt it. This alone is reason for giving people the right to choose, otherwise it's a slippery slope.

DollyDo: There should be a mandatory course teaching cop-on for people with kids. The amount of loopers not getting their kids vaccinated like that idiot Mummy Blogger on the telly is mind boggling! Do people want to go back to medieval times when vast swathes of the population were wiped out by the very diseases that modern medicine has all but eradicated? Until these know-it-all conspiracy theory gobshites came along. Here we have people turning their noses up at expensive to produce, yet freely available vaccinations that prevent dangerous diseases. A little knowledge in the wrong hands is truly a dangerous thing.

RubyD replied: +1 DollyDo. The mother of one of my daughter's school friends made a big fuss about the MMR booster shots. Keeping her girl out of school that day in case someone would sneak a jab into her kid's arm. The same one won't even allow the kid a treat like the rest of the class on Fridays, and sends us all texts not to allow her daughter sweets or other junk food when she's over for play dates. She seems to think sugar is the enemy, but allows her kids out into the world with no protection from things far worse than a packet of Haribos...

Chapter 29

Madeleine took a deep breath as, later the following week, she sat in the make-up chair at the Channel 2 studio, complying when the make-up artist instructed her to shut her eyes so she could apply eye shadow.

This morning was another attempt at rebuilding her reputation and saving face, but Madeleine had expressly checked with the producer about the other panel guests (namely Gemma Moore) on today's *Morning Coffee* show before agreeing to go on.

While she was surprised that they'd asked her back given the flood of negative sentiment surrounding her just now, she was grateful for the opportunity to face the public, even though she'd been forbidden from uttering a single word about the case, never mind try to defend herself.

'I'm really not happy about this, Maddie,' her husband warned, when she'd told him she planned to face the music and hold her head high by carrying on as normal, rather than cowering in a corner, hiding away from what was being said about her.

Grimacing afresh at the media storm and public outcry that was still raging, she tried to think positive and remind herself that

Tom was just as frustrated as she was about this entire situation. He was angry at everything, not at her particularly.

At least not much, said a little voice in her head. He was still reeling over that blog post she had published on the day of the first news report, but following a speedy warning phone call from Matt Townsend, almost immediately had to take down.

In her own words, Madeleine had essentially pled her case – she had done her best to be sincere and tell the public the truth. But their solicitor had warned her about practically handing Kate and her legal team a victory, and told her not to worry about what the public thought.

Her husband had readily agreed. 'Who gives a rat's ass about what your "followers" think at a time like this? Not when our entire live savings and everything we've both worked for are in jeopardy.'

The words had stung but they had been said out of anger and frustration, and, admittedly, Madeleine hadn't thought about it that way.

Perhaps worst of all, the blog hadn't made the least bit of a difference, and if anything had stoked the fire of public dissent. Try as she might, Madeleine didn't know what the solution was.

However, even if she wanted to further ponder the weight of her worries, it wouldn't have been possible, because her thoughts were just then interrupted by an all too familiar voice.

And the feeling of unease that she had been holding in her stomach ever since the story broke lurched forward and plummeted, like she had just gone over the biggest drop on a roller coaster.

'Hiya!' called the voice. 'Yes, *great* week. You?' There was a bout of laughter and then the voice got closer. 'I'm actually doing *Coffee* today so I'd better get in to make-up and then I'll catch up with you in the green room, OK?'

Madeleine's eyes flew open, which earned her a tut from the make-up person. Mumbling her apologies, she flicked her eyes to the vacant chair next to hers before closing them again, wishing it would make her invisible.

No, this can't be happening to me – I can't be sharing the panel with Gemma Moore. She groaned, in complete disbelief. But how? The producer had expressly denied that her nemesis Gemma would be on today.

Had he lied? Was the studio hoping for a ratings winner with some kind of stand-off? But that wasn't what this show was all about, it was a chatty, light-hearted lifestyle slot, not an episode of *Jerry Springer*.

But then why…

'Morning, Marcie,' Gemma greeted, situating herself in the chair next to Madeleine. 'I know I'm not on the rota for this morning, but Conor called me for a last minute fill-in and—'

Her voice dramatically fell silent, and Madeleine willed herself to play it cool. Clearly, the journalist had also spotted who was sitting next to her.

'Madeleine,' she said simply. It was not a question, and Gemma's voice had taken on an imperturbable edge, as if she too had been duped and was unaware that the two would be sharing the panel this morning.

Madeleine secretly wondered what she had done to this woman – by all accounts a complete stranger – to make her so obviously dislike her. Why else would the journalist, with her sniping article and subsequent TV news appearance, be trying to ruin her reputation?

Regardless, she did her best to swallow the panic she felt. She was no coward and she had dealt with bitches like this before. Not to mention every small town committee and parent–teacher association had someone similar. Gemma Moore would soon understand that Madeleine wasn't someone who was going to be walked all over.

No way.

The journalist broke away from Madeleine's cool gaze and sat back in her chair. A second make-up artist approached then and threw a cape around Gemma's shoulders to prevent any product from getting on her clothes.

Madeleine willed her own attendant to hurry up and put the finishing touches to her face so she could extract herself from this uncomfortable situation. She might have worn a cool façade, but her stomach felt suddenly nauseous.

A beat of silence passed.

'Terribly tragic about that little girl, Rosie. Special needs I hear, just horrible really. So much suffering that could have been prevented.' Gemma paused to let that sink in. 'Do you have any idea when you will be going to court?' she asked sweetly.

This overt attack, as well as the blatant challenge, made Madeleine see red. She felt a tidal wave of sharp responses rush to escape her mouth, but, in that instant, she also remembered what her solicitor (and indeed her husband) had warned her.

'Do not discuss the case with anyone – especially people with loose lips. And don't be tricked into having loose lips yourself either.'

That was the understatement of the year, Madeleine thought. Here she was, sitting next to a woman who had looser lips (and a bigger megaphone) than anyone.

Thankfully, at that moment, the make-up lady indicated that she was finished, and removed the paper collar around Madeleine's neck.

'I'm due in studio,' said Madeleine as she rose from her chair.

'Nothing to say?' shot back Gemma with raised eyebrows. 'That'd be a first.'

She walked away, barely glancing back as she left the journalist in her wake.

It was only after she'd exited make-up and been escorted through to the studio that Madeleine's hands stopped shaking.

Chapter 30

'Tom, please understand, there was nothing I could do. She had me trapped. And it was live TV…' Madeleine pleaded, as she sat on the couch at home with clasped hands against the skirt of her favourite Kate Spade shirt dress.

She felt like a petulant child who had misbehaved at school and, unfortunately, her husband was treating her like one, too. And she wasn't sure she'd ever be able to wear that dress again, at least not without being reminded of this morning's abject mortification.

Across the room, Tom paced back and forth, continually running his hands through his hair. Usually possessing a calm exterior, these days he looked positively unglued. His shirt was untucked from his pants, his tie was loose and his face an unattractive shade of tomato. And there was a hell of a lot more grey in his hair.

'I just got off the phone with Matt; he's furious. What in the hell – I mean – how did this… ?'

Madeleine looked at the floor and then returned her gaze to her husband. She was mortified and ashamed that she might have messed things up for them – again. But there was no way for her to have prevented what had happened on the show that morning.

Because of Gemma Moore, she had been made to defend herself – and her decision not to vaccinate her children – on live TV.

She had been in the middle of a run-of-the-mill segment as planned, talking about things to do with kids during the upcoming summer holidays. It had all been so normal and decidedly innocuous: amusing ways to keep the kids entertained before resorting to iPads or other electronics.

And then, when she'd finished her piece, Gemma had wasted no time in having her say.

'Some great ideas there, Madeleine,' she had chirped in pleasantly, with glittering eyes. 'Of course we all know how much thought you put into being a mum, raising your kids, looking out for them...'

Her voice trailed off and sensing an ambush, Madeleine was hesitant to respond. Despite the fact that Louise, the main presenter, would surely intervene if anything got nasty, she had never felt more on her guard.

Not to mention the mere fact that she was being watched by an audience across the nation made her cheeks flush and she wondered what that looked like on the other side of the camera.

Gemma smiled slightly. 'Hmm. Interesting. Really, it is.'

Madeleine opened her mouth to speak, to try to head off a potential issue with something – anything really – but Gemma beat her to it.

'Considering Madeleine's parenting choices are actually embroiled in hugely controversial legal proceedings at the moment.' The journalist let her words hang in the air as she met Madeleine's gaze. Feeling herself freeze in place, she suddenly realised just how hot the studio lights were. She shifted her gaze uncomfortably to the producers, one of whom was shaking her head at Gemma vociferously.

'Now, Gemma, I'm not sure if—' Louise cut in.

'I was just wondering how Madeleine was,' she persisted all innocence. 'It must be a terrible time.'

Now the woman was actually pretending to be concerned, all the while putting her on the spot about the case – live on the air!

But reminding herself she was a professional and she could handle this, Madeleine opened her mouth to speak. 'As you said yourself, Gemma, this is an ongoing legal situation and I'm afraid I'm not at liberty to discuss it.'

'It's provoked a lot of public discussion though, hasn't it? Lots of people are angry about you and your husband's anti-vaccination stance, and how it has affected another family.'

Madeleine knew she really was caught between a rock and a hard place now. She couldn't discuss the case, but she couldn't appear unsympathetic either, not when the eyes of the nation were upon her. And what had she got to lose, given that right from the get-go everyone was so eager to paint her as the villain?

Stuttering a little, she spoke again. 'Absolutely. And it goes without saying that my thoughts and prayers are with little Rosie and her mum—'

Louise interjected quickly then, her eyes widening at this wholly unanticipated turn in what up to then had been a typically light-hearted panel discussion. 'Yes, I'm sure we're all very sympathetic to the little girl, but I really don't think this is the right place to—'

'I would think your thoughts and prayers should be with her, Madeleine, given that she's still very ill and facing disability due to your irresponsible decision-making,' Gemma persisted, ignoring the presenter.

Madeleine glanced at the ground and felt her head start to spin. 'That's not it,' she replied, spluttering a little, all the while trying to remain calm and collected.

She couldn't mess this up – for more reasons than one. Discussing the case in anything other than general terms would be disastrous legally, but if she said nothing, she would be ruined personally. 'That was a family choice, a personal choice. My husband and I have always had our reasons and—'

Gemma snorted. 'Conspiracy theories, you mean,' she muttered.

'But such theories must be a consideration for any parent, mustn't they?' Louise jumped in gamely, obviously trying to deflect attention away from specifics and speak in more general terms. 'There's been multiple controversies surrounding vaccines that we've discussed numerous times on this very programme. Like the widely reported side-effects of the HPV vaccine and narcolepsy from the swine flu...'

Madeleine took a breath, grateful that Louise had stepped in not just to protect her honour, but more likely head off the likelihood of another lawsuit aimed at the station.

Mercifully, Gemma seemed to take the bait and chattered at length about the proven life-saving abilities of vaccines, and how the so-called Big Bad pharmaceutical companies had eradicated so many diseases and saved lives. She was obviously satisfied to have made her point and got what she wanted in skewering Madeleine live on air and was now carrying on as if nothing at all had happened.

Madeleine, for her part, had said little throughout the remainder of the conversation and indeed the rest of the segment, and while she'd tried to smile and participate in a follow-up discussion about the benefits of coffee over tea, by the end of the show she felt hollowed out and drained.

So much so that she barely heard the producer's profuse apologies, or Gemma Moore's cheery goodbye when they all left the studio.

And, after all that, she had to face Tom's disappointment too.

'What were you thinking? Didn't Matt tell you not to discuss things publicly? Didn't he tell to keep your mouth closed?' he bellowed, making Madeleine flinch.

'Tom, please, don't yell at me. Gemma Moore ambushed me. Completely trapped me! What was I supposed to do?'

Her husband looked incredulous. 'Pull your mic out and walk off the set! That's what I would have done.'

She shook her head. 'From a PR point of view that would have been a disaster. Gemma behaved like a bully and I was right to stand my ground. I think the public will—'

'For the love of God, Madeleine, who cares what the public thinks? When will you get it into your head that this is not some marketing campaign, this is *our life*! And God only knows what could come out if someone really decides to dig their heels in – personal, private family things that need to remain that way.'

She knew what he meant, and even though it had been so difficult on many occasions not to just get it over with and bare her soul about their experience, she had gone out of her way to ensure that she kept the focus away from the personal. 'I know that, of course I know that, but Tom for the last week our family has been vilified! Surely we're entitled to defend ourselves—'

'We are paying *solicitors* to defend us. We are trusting legal professionals with putting together a logical and well-thought-out case to protect our interests. But in the meantime, you persist in taking to the internet and going on live television at every opportunity and basically tearing every part of our strategy to complete shit!' He threw his hands up in the air in exasperation. 'Madeleine – this media thing – it has to stop,' he said softly. 'I don't want you anywhere near a radio or TV studio from now on. Agreed?'

Madeleine had been studying the floor, but now her head flew up. 'But I can't. I've been offered a publishing contract, and my profile is obviously a huge part of that. I can't break it.'

'Seriously, what are they going to do? Sue you? Well, bring it on. What's another lawsuit at this point? And, you said it yourself, since this whole thing came out, people have essentially vilified us, ridiculed you, complete strangers on the internet reducing you to tears. Don't think I haven't seen what's being written and what it must be doing to you...'

Seeing fresh tears form in his wife's eyes now, Tom went to her and bent down on one knee. 'Honey, I'm sorry – I shouldn't have shouted like that earlier. And OK, maybe before now I did discount how important all of this stuff is to you. But don't you think our future as a family is more important to protect just now? And why *would* you want to make yourself a target and risk being put on the spot again by some shit-stirring journo who obviously has some sort of vendetta against you... *us*. Hasn't this family been through enough already with all this... this goddamn vaccination thing?'

Madeleine felt tears begin to fall down her cheeks. He was right. They'd already been put through the ringer enough in the past. And now, people were being openly horrible: making fun of her, being vicious towards her *and* her family.

She had already seen a few internet jokes that had done the rounds recently – images of her wearing a tinfoil hat and looking conspiracy-theory crazy.

Tom was right. It was over. She was no longer *Mad Mum*, she was now Stone-crazy Mum. People were laughing at her, criticising her, vilifying her, and the alter-ego moniker that had once been such a good idea was now the butt of a terrible, unfunny joke.

'We're going to get through this, honey,' said Tom softly, pulling her close. 'But for now, we need to circle the wagons and put on a united front. And we have to trust our solicitors. No more public stuff, OK?'

'OK.' Moving into his embrace, Madeleine silently agreed to his request. Tom was right: he, Jake and Clara – all her family – were the most important thing just now.

And she couldn't run the risk of losing them too.

MUMMYBOARDS.IE

Forum > Health Matters > NEW TOPIC> Mad Mum Vaccination Case?

SallyQ: Anyone see Madeleine Cooper on Morning Coffee this morning? What did you think about Gemma Moore confronting her straight out about being responsible for that little girl's illness? I had a bit of a debate with another mum at the school gate about it earlier. Can you seriously be held accountable for not choosing to get your kids vaccinated? Her reckoning was that the likes of Madeleine Cooper and 'those hippy types' who don't vaccinate put everybody else's kids at risk and should even have their own taken off them for neglect! WTF – last time I checked this was a democracy? Seriously, I'm not a Cooper fangirl, but she does talk sense a lot of the time. Watching that this morning and reading some of the stuff in the paper lately she is being seriously demonised for making a choice for her kids in good faith. Don't think it's fair.

Llllly1: Didn't see the show but most people I've spoken to about that case are either black or white about it. Many parents who got the health board letter about vaccinations went along with it without a second thought and I can't understand how anybody wouldn't even question it.

When I got the call to get the MMR for my DD I struggled with it for weeks. I'd heard the rumours about links to autism. I looked at my happy, smiling baby and knew I couldn't live with myself if I went along with it and she developed problems. But, in the end, I went ahead after speaking with my GP. Ultimately there are leaps of faith involved with every decision we make for our kids. I feel sorry for all parties involved with that case though.

Wexican7: Sorry, but I have to say I feel no sympathy for Madeleine Cooper. As far as I'm concerned it is reckless endangerment. Hope the courts come down hard on her and set an example to other would-be conspiracy theorists and scaremongers.

RainbowK: Wow, that's a bit harsh. Vaccinations are voluntary, how can somebody be prosecuted for making a decision not to vaccinate if it was their right to choose?

Wexican7: Fair point, maybe that's why vaccinations need to be compulsory; that way everybody knows where they stand.

GoodyGumDrops: This whole thing scares the life out of me tbh. When the time came for us to get the MMR for our first, we just went along with it – ignorance was bliss. We are due to get my youngest done next week, and with all the hullabaloo surrounding this case and some of the stuff being posted online it feels a bit like playing Russian roulette. My friend's son actually developed autism a couple of years back; she swears she watched him change after getting his shots. To see her struggle day in, day out breaks my heart and has me torn asunder about whether to get my DD done at all…

CorkGal: Girls, I think some perspective is needed here: there are no proven links between the MMR vaccine and autism. The initial signs of autism materialise in the same age group that the first round of MMR shots are given to – this does NOT mean that one causes the other. Yes, there is a leap of faith involved, but that goes hand in hand with being a parent. How many cases of medical misadventure do we hear in the news? Kids and mothers developing all manner of complications because of misdiagnosis or malpractice in maternity hospitals. Does this mean that we should give birth at home because hospitals are dangerous?

DebbieD: +1 CorkGal. I think that case against Madeleine Cooper should be thrown out. It's a parent's prerogative to make a decision on what they feel is best for their family, and leaving people open to prosccution for making those decisions opens a huge can of worms IMO.

Moodyblue: Guys, I think a lot of people here, OP included, are missing the point. Madeleine Cooper is NOT being prosecuted for refusing the MMR vaccination. She is being pursued because she refused the shots, and then did not give due care and atten-tion when her daughter displayed symptoms of a disease. This caused another vulnerable child to become very ill and develop potentially life-altering complications. Basically, it's a duty of care issue stemming from the vaccination issue, not the vaccination stance itself.

Bonny123: Nail on the head Moodyblue. I think this whole case is going to force the government and Health Service to revisit the entire childhood vaccination programme. There needs to be 100% clarity as to the obligations of parents. They also need to invest in a study to investigate and hopefully dispel these links/rumours that are making parents opt out of the programme. Saying there is nothing to fear is one thing; showing definitively that there is nothing to fear is another.

Chapter 31

The weather was unseasonably cold for June, and I pulled my jacket up around my shoulders and placed a tentative hand on my face, ensuring my sunglasses hadn't slipped down my nose.

It wasn't so much my choice of protection against the elements, but rather against the stares I was sure to attract at the supermarket. Every housewife and their sister in the area did their grocery shopping here. And since it was a weekday afternoon, it was practically a given that I was going to run into someone I knew.

Entering the store, I grabbed the first empty trolley I saw and began navigating it towards the vegetable section, then reached into my pocket for my phone so I could access my shopping list.

It felt like I hadn't been grocery shopping in weeks and, indeed, it had probably been longer than that. But I needed to stock up.

I looked around at the shiny, colourful displays of goodness, comparing it to the 'food' I had been surviving on up to now – hospital fare wasn't exactly fine cuisine. Coupled with the fact that I rarely paid attention to what I was putting in my mouth these days, this annoying, but altogether necessary sojourn was probably good for my future health.

Something Declan had in fact pointed out to me the evening

before, when he'd called over to the house to update me on progress with the case.

He had been brilliant since that night at the hospital when Rosie woke up, and since then had been instrumental in helping me get my head around some of the more practical implications of Rosie's future, while I tried to deal with the emotional side. There was no doubt that while he was first and foremost my solicitor, and remained utterly professional at all times in that regard, Declan Roe was also gradually becoming a much-needed friend.

When I went to make him the obligatory cup of tea last night I had discovered, much to my mortification, that there was no milk, and indeed the only things in my fridge were mouldy cheese, dried-up condiments and wine.

'Kate, you do know that a person cannot survive on wine and mould alone.' Declan's tone might have been playful, but his concern was serious. And there was a look in his eye that I couldn't quite place. Was it worry? Concern even?

I tried to lighten the mood by arguing that maybe I had a bit of French in my ancestry – but his chiding made me realise that I needed to start paying attention to the day-to-day necessities in life, especially for when Rosie came home.

Now that her infection had cleared and she was pretty much over the worst, the next step was for her to start rehabilitation. Depending on her progress, I hoped she'd do well enough that the doctors would agree to let her come home. Though I knew she and I both had a very long road ahead, I longed for that day.

'You're right,' I had told Declan as I took a sip of a Pinot Noir I had been saving for a special occasion (a weeknight meeting with my solicitor was as good as it got these days). 'First thing tomorrow, I will go grocery shopping.'

And so here I was.

However, as I started to roam the aisles, I worked my hardest to ignore the pointed stare of a woman from Knockroe whose name I couldn't recall, but who I recognised as the mother of a girl in Rosie's dance class. I wondered if my hesitation to engage in the nuances of community living had less and less to do with my daughter's condition, and more to do with the fact that I had become increasingly nervous about showing my face in public.

Not that anyone had ever said anything and, while I knew there were many in the community who supported me, I also knew there were plenty of people talking about me behind my back. And I didn't have to employ too much imagination to know what they were saying.

Goodness knows I'd encountered enough of that online.

I grimaced as I placed a plastic bottle of orange juice in my trolley, the thought reminding me that as bad as I might have had it with the odd accusation of my being 'a money-grabber' or 'out for blood', Madeleine Cooper was definitely getting the worst of it.

The other day, Declan had pulled up a clip of Gemma Moore's recent TV ambush of her on *Morning Coffee*. I don't know what the journalist had against her, but one thing was for sure, I certainly didn't want her in my camp either.

And while I was utterly bewildered as to why Madeleine would go on national TV given the huge public reaction in relation to our case, I couldn't help but feel a bit sorry for her after watching that segment, and, even worse, when I read some of the hateful things people were saying about her online.

Yes, I too was angry at her, but obviously I had never set out for this horrible public shaming.

Declan insisted that I couldn't blame myself for things like that and that Madeleine's already public profile taken with such a controversial topic had automatically made her a very easy target. I knew he was only trying to make me feel better, but it wasn't working.

None of this would have happened if I hadn't taken the case.

But then none of it would have happened if Madeleine had just kept her daughter home from school either...

Unwilling to think about it, I gripped the handle on the trolley tightly and continued pushing it forward. Glancing down at my hands, I realised my knuckles were white and urged myself to relax, to calm down.

As I took a few deep breaths in the bread aisle, I pictured my daughter's face and tried to think positive. Fingers crossed, the worst was over: she was on the road to recovery and would be coming home soon. Not that it would solve all of our problems – if anything it would be just the beginning. But it was something to be thankful for, whatever way you looked at it.

And once Rosie finally came home and was back settled under her own roof with me taking care of her, all the other challenges that lay ahead might not seem so insurmountable.

'Kate? Is that you?' called a voice from behind me and I immediately felt myself tense up again. Dammit, of course I was going to run into someone.

Turning around, I was glad to discover that it was just Christine. Thank goodness. 'Hey,' I said wearily, as she pushed her trolley up next to mine.

'You OK? You're white as a sheet. How's Rosie? All still on track for her to start rehab?'

Say what you liked about Christine, but she'd remained a great friend and confidante throughout, and had kept up to date with all that was going on with Rosie even after introducing me to Declan.

Unlike Lucy who, since I'd taken the case against Madeleine, had shied away a little. She was obviously upset with me for doing so and, while I was dismayed that I seemed to have lost my one true friend in Knockroe, I could completely understand that her loyalties were torn. The problem was that I really needed her to testify when and if this case got to trial. Declan had said that our side was still strong without her, but if we could introduce incontrovertible proof that Madeleine was fully aware Clara was ill when she sent her to school, it would make a decision so much easier for the judge.

She'd said she'd pop in to the hospital to see Rosie this week though and, despite her misgivings about me, I knew she still cared deeply about my daughter.

I smiled tightly at Christine. 'Ah, just feeling a bit hesitant about coming here.'

'To the supermarket?' she replied, incredulous. 'Why on earth would you be worried about coming here?'

'Exactly for this reason – running into someone I know.'

'Wow. Thanks,' she quipped sarcastically. 'Glad I rank so highly on your list.'

Chuckling, I swatted her away and offered a small smile as we began walking together down the aisle. 'You know what I mean. And don't take it personally. Things are just…' I struggled to find the right word. 'I suppose awkward is a good word to use. I feel a bit awkward at the moment, with all this stuff that's coming out in public.'

Christine's brow furrowed and she leaned into me, placing a free arm around my shoulders. 'How are things going? I talked to Declan, but I couldn't get anything out of him.'

I smiled softly. 'Well, I should hope so.' Shaking my head, I decided to give her a short and to-the-point overview of what was happening. 'Things are progressing as they're supposed to – at least that's what Declan says. We're just waiting on a trial date now. But

I suppose it's just with all the public attention this is getting… well, it sort of makes these outings uncomfortable.'

Grimacing, Christine asked, 'Well, obviously our *friend* is getting a lot of flack, but people aren't hounding you or anything, are they?'

Obviously she knew about Madeleine's fall from grace, not that she seemed overly concerned.

'I've had one or two calls from the papers looking for comment. But I haven't spoken to anyone. And I don't plan to. This might be news fodder to some people, but it's also my life.'

Christine nodded thoughtfully. 'That journalist Gemma Moore certainly seems to have it in for Madeleine, doesn't she?' Her voice took on an all too familiar gossipy and conspiratorial tone and I didn't like it.

I stopped walking and turned to her. 'Please, don't be that way. I'm sure Madeleine is having a terrible time and nobody needs to add to it.'

Suitably admonished, she muttered a quiet 'sorry' and I began moving again, keeping pace next to Christine while snatching a loaf of bread off a shelf.

A moment later, we rounded the corner at the end of the aisle and I was met with a blast of cold air from the frozen food section. 'In any case, I wish the media would just stay out of it. It's merely whipping up an already difficult situation and—'

However, I discovered that I couldn't finish my sentence, because at that particular moment I locked eyes with the one person I had not considered running into today.

Fifteen feet away from where I stood was Madeleine Cooper. She'd been in the process of plucking a litre of milk off the shelf, and in the seconds that had passed since she realised my presence, the look on her face had gone from one of shock and surprise to horror, embarrassment and finally anger.

Breaking my gaze, she tossed the milk into her trolley and turned violently away, rushing back up the aisle quickly. It was obvious she wanted to get as far away from me as possible.

Or had been warned to do so.

I heard Christine gasp and, in that moment, I pushed my trolley to the side. 'Madeleine, please, wait.' I had no idea what I was doing or even *thinking*, but I knew I had to talk to her.

Christine called out after me, a warning in her tone, but I had no idea what she was saying, so focused was I on catching up to my so-called nemesis. But, for some reason, seeing her there, looking haggard almost, hair messy and face unmade up, dressed down in jeans and an old sweatshirt, completely devoid of her usual bubbly glamour, had made me feel ashamed.

'Hold on, please. I need to talk to you.' But even if provided the opportunity, I had no idea what I was going to say.

Then, suddenly, she turned back to face me.

'What…' she whispered, her voice barely audible, her face painted with unbridled strain. 'What could you possibly want, Kate? What on earth could we have to talk about now? I tried, you know I did, I tried and tried. Wanted to tell you how desperately sorry I felt about Rosie and how I'd do anything to help. But you didn't want to talk me then, didn't take the time to listen to what I had to say. And now it seems, there is nothing *to* say.'

I had stopped my pursuit and now stood lamely in the middle of the supermarket aisle. 'Madeleine, I just need—'

'Need what?' she whispered. 'I'm so sorry that this happened to your daughter but what else do I have that you need to take from me, Kate? How many more ways can you think of to punish me?'

I felt like I had been slapped. The force of her words made me take a step back and put my hand over my heart, I could feel it pounding so loudly in my chest.

'I'm so...' What – sorry? In that moment I was. I wished desperately that I could go back and undo the legal action, because I didn't know if I would ever be able to forget the look on Madeleine's face just then.

'I don't need to hear anything from you, Kate, and I'm not talking to you either. If you have something to say, then you can obviously do so in court. I'm finished playing this out in public.'

Chapter 32

A little while later, Madeleine entered her front door, her heart almost as heavy as the grocery bags she carried.

To her surprise, Tom rushed out to the hallway from the kitchen, a spring in his step, and incredibly, a smile on his face. They'd had so little to smile about lately that she was truly taken aback by his demeanour. Her heart softened on cue; this whole thing had really taken its toll on her husband. Though, thankfully, things had become a little less stressful since they'd decided to circle the wagons and Madeleine had gone quiet on the media front.

But she was never sure when the next blow would strike or where it would come from.

Though judging by the ecstatic expression on Tom's face, whatever was going on must be positive for a change. But while her husband might be happy about something now, she knew she was definitely going to ruin his mood when she told him about her run-in with Kate at the shops.

'Great news, Maddie,' he said, with palpable excitement. 'I just got an email that could be huge for our defence. Seriously huge.' He took several of the bags she had been struggling with out of her arms and onto the counter.

Waiting for him to elaborate, Madeleine smiled encouragingly.

'So do you remember me telling you about that doctor from the States, a neurologist I contacted a couple of weeks back? Dr Pitt?'

She searched her memory for the conversation that Tom was referencing. She couldn't really remember anything like that, but in truth she might not have been listening as hard as she should have been. After all, she had been pretty distracted lately.

But she didn't want to admit that to Tom. 'I think so,' she replied.

'Well, I just received an email from him. I contacted him through his website and told him all about our case. About why we were being sued.'

Tom briefly provided Madeleine with the doctor's bio as she began unloading the shopping bags. Pitt was a ranking member of the California Medical Review Board. Apparently there had been some disapproving mutterings in the US because of his sometimes controversial stance on vaccines, but nothing had ever come of it.

'The guy is perfect, Madeleine. He came out and admitted publicly that the presence of viruses did mean that ultimately some people would get sick and die, but that the human body also had ways of countering these attackers – which has been happening for hundreds and thousands of years before the introduction of vaccines. He believes that there is a new reality that needs to be faced – children should not be injected with unnatural, man-made chemicals – and the pharma companies only promote these "medicines" in order to line their own pockets.'

Madeleine nodded, wondering why this was such a big deal. They'd basically come to the same conclusion themselves years ago. It was hardly news and she had no idea why he was so excited about it. There were pro- and anti-vaccine proponents all over the place, and on the internet especially.

But her husband was still smiling like it was Christmas morning and he had just received a new Lexus tied with a big red bow. She looked blankly at him, urging him to continue. 'And? How does this help us?'

'Because he's agreed to act as an expert witness for us.' Tom cheered. Madeleine really wouldn't have been surprised if her husband had started dancing a jig on the kitchen floor.

'That is promising,' she agreed. She was well aware that Matt Townsend had been having a hard time securing bona fide medical professionals to defend their position on vaccination in building their case for the trial, and it sounded like Dr Pitt was exactly what they needed.

'Madeleine, here is a guy who regularly contributes to respected medical journals. He was recently published in the *North American Journal of Paediatrics*. This is absolutely *huge*. No one is going to be able to call him a quack or some kind of conspiracy theorist. He's still a practising neurologist too, but he has developed this other line around his work. This is seriously the best thing that could have happened for us.'

Feeling her heart lose some of its heaviness, Madeleine moved a few steps forward and put her arms around Tom's neck. 'And you did this all by yourself? Tracked him down I mean?' She had been married to him long enough to know that her husband loved to feel like a hero in situations such as this.

Puffing out his chest ever so slightly, Tom looked at her as he pulled her close. 'Indeed I did. In fact, he was quite indignant about what we had been through and what we were being accused of, so much so that he even agreed to provide his expert testimony at a reduced rate.'

Madeleine thought about it, but decided not to ask just what that rate was. She didn't want to ruin the mood. It was the first time she and Tom had anything to be happy about in weeks. Turning back to the kitchen counter, Madeleine continued putting away groceries. She reached into a bag and, spying the litre of milk she had been holding when she ran into Kate earlier, she debated briefly whether to tell Tom about the encounter.

But she decided against it. Her husband would have a stroke if she admitted she'd been in the same room as Kate O'Hara, let alone spoken to her. She was intrigued though that Kate had seemed embarrassed, apologetic even, when all this time she had assumed the other woman hated her.

But even if Kate had wanted to talk to her, apologise even, Madeleine realised sadly, they both knew that it was much too late for that.

Chapter 33

Declan was sitting on Kate's front step when her Astra chugged into the driveway.

He'd expected to find her at home this morning – he knew she was heading to the hospital after lunch – and he had some papers that he needed her to sign.

But as he rang the doorbell it had dawned on him – maybe she had in fact taken his advice and gone grocery shopping? His suspicions were confirmed when he rang her mobile and she told him that she would be back shortly.

Now, getting up, he walked to the driver's side as Kate pulled to a stop. Even through the tint of the glass he could see that she looked drawn, shaken even.

He was immediately concerned and wondered if something else (something terrible?) had happened with Rosie. Hell, how much more could one woman take?

Trying to put on a smile and keep the worry off his face, he opened the door for her, struck again by how fragile she looked, and how tired.

She had definitely lost some weight since he first met her back in April, and her clothes had now started to hang on her limply.

He knew that she was unaccountably stressed about all that was to come, and now he had the overwhelming desire to pull her close, give her a hug, and insist that she eat a big meal.

Not for the first time, Declan wished he could snap his fingers and make all of this go away, so that Kate's life (and Rosie's) could return to normal.

And then he had the guilty thought that if that were possible, he would never have met her.

Momentarily shaken by the flood of confusion he was feeling, Declan found himself relieved when Kate spoke, interrupting his internal dialogue.

'Hey there,' she said with a weary voice, 'I could have come to the office – I was just in Glencree. You didn't have to come all the way over here; I'm sure you're busy.'

'Well, you happen to be a very important client,' he said, teasing her a bit, which earned him a small smile. He hoped that his tone might lighten the mood. 'Here, let me help you with the groceries,' he offered, heading to the back of the Astra. 'And good on you for taking my suggestion.' He loaded up his arms with bags and refused Kate's help. 'No worries. You go ahead and unlock the door. I think I'd need to have my man card revoked if I couldn't carry a few measly bags from the car.'

Pleased to hear her chuckle, he followed her dutifully into the house. Kate went about opening doors through to the kitchen and Declan hoisted the bags, placing them somewhat clumsily on the countertop.

She started rifling through the shopping, and then suddenly paused. 'Declan, I have to tell you something.'

He had been about to help her empty out some of the shopping, but stopped to meet her gaze. Something in her tone indicated that she was about to give him some bad news.

'I ran into Madeleine Cooper,' she blurted. 'And I tried to talk to her.'

Declan felt his stomach drop ever so slightly. So far, there had been no major missteps with this case on their side. No embarrassments, no talking out of turn, no public faux pas. Unlike the Coopers who had been at the helm of many.

However, he vowed to remain level headed, and simply asked Kate to tell him what had happened. When she'd finished, he nodded thoughtfully.

OK, so it wasn't the best thing to have happened, but it wasn't the end of the world either. Kate was seriously beating herself up about the situation though, and he didn't want her being hard on herself. There was no point.

'Did anyone happen to see the exchange?' Granted there was no gag rule when it came to plaintiffs and defendants talking to each other in public, it was just something he wouldn't necessarily recommend in the midst of pending proceedings.

Kate nodded. 'Just Christine.'

Declan looked perplexed. 'My cousin?'

'One and the same.'

Sighing heavily, he couldn't resist a smirk. 'Is there ever a situation that Christine *isn't* involved in?'

Kate chuckled, but there was something a bit hysterical about her laughter, and Declan chalked it up to feeling overextended and worn out.

All of sudden then, her stomach released a loud gurgle, causing them both to stop and look at each other – only to resume their laughter a moment later.

'All right, seriously, Kate, you need to eat. Your stomach is begging for some attention.' He poked through the remainder of the one bags on the counter and seemed to decide on a course of action.

After removing several items, he pointed to his client. 'Now, you just sit. Leave this to me.'

'What do you think you're doing?' she asked, amazement in her voice as she watched him remove his suit jacket and begin rolling up the sleeves on his shirt. He reached up around his neck to loosen his tie and then eagerly rubbed his hands together.

'It's not what I think I'm doing, Kate. It's what I am doing. I'm cooking you lunch – a proper meal – and I'm going to sit here and watch you eat all of it. OK?'

She grabbed a stool at the countertop and crossed her hands in front of herself dutifully. 'I assume I'm being billed for this?' she asked sweetly.

Declan, who had since located where Kate stored her pots and pans, turned back to her with a twinkle in his eye. 'Jokes. She's making jokes now,' he said. 'Very funny, Ms O'Hara.' He put a saucepan on the hob and then began opening up more cabinets.

He saw her cast a quick glance over what ingredients he had arranged on the counter. 'I'm assuming you are making spaghetti, which means you are going to have to eat it with me, because no one only makes a single serving of spaghetti. And if you are looking for the chopping board, move two cabinets down. Towards the back.'

Following her instructions, he mouthed a silent 'thank you'. 'My own kitchen isn't quite as complex,' he admitted.

'Well, you are a bachelor, don't forget.' Kate smiled, relaxing a little.

As Declan made himself comfortable in her kitchen, he had a brief worry that this felt a bit too comfortable, too casual. Were they overstepping some kind of boundary here? Or did this sort of amicable relationship just naturally happen when two people spent a lot of time together in an emotionally charged situation?

He pushed the thought from his head as Kate headed to the cabinet where she kept the glasses, which was right where he was working. 'Sorry, I just need to reach up to that shelf,' she said, pointing to the cabinet in question.

'Oh, right,' he acknowledged a bit awkwardly, as he tried to step back from where he had been cutting vegetables for a salad. He moved enough so Kate could wedge her way in, and the small corner space forced their two bodies together.

'Um, sorry,' she said quickly as her arm brushed Declan's. 'The one awkward area of this kitchen,' she gave by way of an explanation. 'Greg and I always said that if we'd designed this room, we would never have put in an island. Too cramped.' She tried to ignore the fact that her face had turned bright red.

Declan smiled. 'How long had you been married when you moved here?' A flash of something crossed her face then and he added, 'I'm sorry, it's none of my business. You don't have to—'

'No, really, it's fine,' answered Kate. 'I can talk about it. And it's good for me to talk about it. It's my life, it happened. Really, it's OK and I'm OK. We were married for five years when we moved here. Times were great and for that, I'm thankful. Maybe my marriage didn't last as long as I thought it would, but there were definitely way more good memories than bad.' She wore a smile and this time Declan was pleased to see that it reached her eyes. 'What about you? Been down that road yourself?'

He chuckled. 'No. I came close though. I was engaged to a girl from Dublin a few years ago. But it didn't work out.' He hoped his voice didn't sound bitter. He'd been heartbroken at the time, but he definitely didn't wish his ex-fiancée any ill will.

'So what happened?' she asked. He turned to face her and as he met her gaze he realised she was blushing. 'It's just... you know so much about me.' She smiled nervously and was it just him or had something definitely shifted between them today?

Declan tried to fight the growing worry that he might be crossing a boundary here. 'Well, there isn't much to tell,' he said honestly. 'She pretty much decided that small-town life wasn't what she wanted. And that wasn't good, considering I'm a small-town kind of guy.'

Kate rolled her eyes playfully. 'Yet the small-town guy can cook. Where did you learn that?'

Turning back to the hob in an effort to finish with the food, Declan replied, 'My mother is a great cook. Interestingly, her skills passed on to me, but not to Alison. God love her, she wouldn't even know what this room is used for. Now, voilá, lunch is served. Eat up.'

The pair dug into their pasta and fell into a comfortable line of banter. Declan had broken bread with many clients in the past, but he had to admit that none of his business lunches or dinners ever felt this comfortable.

It was friendly. And he liked how easily their conversation seemed to flow. For the first time ever, they weren't talking about Rosie's case. They were simply two ordinary people discussing their day-to-day lives. It gave him a better picture of who Kate was when she wasn't wrapped in stress, worry and sadness.

And he couldn't deny that he liked it.

'That, Mr Roe, was absolutely delicious,' complimented Kate as she swallowed her last bite of pasta. 'Oh my goodness, I'm so full I think I'm about to fall asleep after it.'

Chuckling, he replied, 'I'm not going to fall for that – you're cleaning up.'

'And I will – right after I get back from the hospital.'

'Aww hell, now you've got me feeling guilty. Go on away, woman, and I'll look after this. You look after Rosie. I can let myself out after.' Then realising this might have sounded too familiar, he added, 'If that's OK?'

'Of course it is. And… thank you. I can't remember the last time I had such a nice meal. And I definitely can't remember the last time anyone cooked for me…'

The pair looked at each other then as the words hung in the air. Something had definitely shifted.

'I… I'd better go,' Kate said, looking terrified.

'Of course. But first, let me give you those papers I wanted you to sign. They're in the car. You can take them with you and I'll get them back whenever.' He swallowed hard and forced himself to not seem weird. Kate was his client. She was going through a hard time. They had talked – ventured a bit too far into the personal maybe, but it was all OK.

'Great. Will do.'

Kate collected her things and Declan headed out front with her to his Volvo to get the documents.

'Take care and say hello to Rosie for me,' he said, handing them to her. 'We'll have to celebrate properly when she comes home.'

Kate smiled then, tears in her eyes, and, almost without thinking, Declan closed the space between the two of them and gave her a hug.

He felt her arms go around him, squeezing him softly as she returned the contact.

'Thank you,' she said quietly, emotion thick in her voice, before breaking the embrace and getting into the car.

Declan watched her leave, his mind suddenly a maelstrom of thoughts he hadn't the first clue how to process.

Chapter 34

Sitting at her laptop with the intention of checking her email, Madeleine was trying her utmost to avoid being distracted by the latest barrage of hateful comments and messages on her social media page:

'If that little girl dies – it's all your fault. How stupid can people be! Vaccinate your damn kids!'

'You nut job! What kind of conspiracy theorist whacko are you?'

'I wish your kids could be taken from you. Jesus, you have some nerve going on TV and acting like some kind of parenting expert. FRAUD! I hope you lose your shirt in COURT! And lose some weight too, fat-ass.'

'Stay strong, Madeleine! A parent knows what's right for their children and what isn't. Don't let the haters get you down!'

'I completely agree with you and your husband, Madeleine. No parent should be forced by the government, doctors or anyone else

to poison their children with chemicals. That other little girl getting sick isn't your fault. Justice will prevail.'

'I love your blog, Madeleine. When will you write again? After the week I've had I need a laugh. Also, can you let me know where you got that nice shirt dress you were wearing on **Morning Coffee** *the last time you were on? Was it Kate Spade? I love her stuff too.'*

Worried that she might break down and cry, she switched quickly to her email program, hoping for better news.

But what she saw there made her feel even worse.

Dear Madeleine,

I hope you are very well. I wanted to let you know that due to unforeseen circumstances, namely the recent media controversy surrounding your blog, we feel it might be best to postpone publication of the Mad Mum *collection for the moment. I'm sure you agree that the current atmosphere is not ideal for propelling the book to the sales heights it deserves. We will of course be happy to re-examine the situation at a later date, perhaps when your legal situation is resolved?*

With all good wishes,
Joanne O'Rourke,
Senior Publisher, Little Blue Books

Exhaling heavily, Madeleine closed her laptop. When would all of this stop? The endless barrage of criticism and outrage about her and Tom's decision-making, their parenting choices and now, ominously, she noted amongst the latest batch of hate mail, her appearance?

She was not a vain woman but surely there wasn't a person alive who enjoyed being referred to as 'fat-ass'.

Whatever about being called fat, the disappointing – but not unexpected – news about her publishing deal going south was a much bigger dent to her professional ego.

But from a business perspective, of course it was a no-brainer for the book to be put on ice, and also no major surprise, given the huge reversal of public, and indeed commercial, support for *Mad Mum* since news of the lawsuit broke. Since then, all but two of her online advertisers had pulled the plug and she guessed it was only a matter of time before the others did as soon as their current contracts expired.

All the hard work and effort she'd put into building her brand and turning it into a successful business was now rapidly going down the toilet.

And all because people didn't agree with her stance on a controversial topic.

The way people – her own neighbours even – were talking, you'd think Madeleine had actually gone round to Kate O'Hara's house and physically injected Rosie with the measles virus.

It was all such a huge disaster and Madeleine had no idea how to get out of it. And of course in reality this was just the beginning. What would it be like when they actually got to court?

She stood up and absent-mindedly checked her appearance in preparation for a quick coffee with Lucy before they went to pick up the kids from school. But she didn't need a stranger on the internet to tell her she looked like shit. Her hair fell limply around her face and her roots badly needed doing, but she was too afraid to go near her own hairdresser's or any salon these days, what with all the tongue-wagging and finger-pointing from every quarter. And worse, Madeleine no longer knew who – if indeed anyone – was on her side.

Except Lucy of course. A chat with her good friend was a long overdue and much needed diversion. She was brilliant for putting things in perspective, and ever since the story first broke had been at the ready on the other end of the phone with a kind word and a cheery story or two to help Madeleine keep her mind off it all and raise her spirits when some of the online stuff got too nasty.

And while Tom was still unhappy with Lucy for the part she'd played in unwittingly giving Kate O'Hara the ammunition she needed to claim negligence, Madeleine knew that her friend hadn't meant for any of this to happen, and would never in a million years do anything to let her down.

But when she reached Molly's Café in the centre of Knockroe, and took one look at Lucy's face as her friend waited nursing a latte at their usual table, she immediately knew something was wrong. And worse, she wouldn't meet her eyes.

'What's going on?' Madeleine asked, wondering what fresh hell the universe was about to unleash on her now.

Lucy wrapped her hands around the cup in front of her. 'I wanted to tell you in person and… I might as well just come right out and say it, but, Maddie, I've agreed to testify. On Kate's side.'

Madeleine felt all the air leave her lungs. 'What? But why? Why would you do that, Luce? You know that I didn't mean any harm that morning, and you agreed with me that it wasn't right for Kate to be doing this. Why then would you turn around and stab me in the back?'

'That's not it. Please understand, Madeleine, it's nothing per-sonal—'

'But of course it is! You, my friend – possibly the only

remaining friend I have left – are going to stand up in court and tell people that I purposely sent Clara to school knowing she was ill. We already know that it doesn't seem to matter whether I meant any malice or not; the very idea that I knew she was sick seems reason enough to make me a monster. Why then would you add fuel to the fire?'

There were tears in Lucy's eyes now. 'I don't have a choice, sweetheart. I saw Rosie yesterday and it almost broke my heart. She's not... good.'

Madeleine collapsed into the seat across from her, stunned. She honestly didn't think things could get any worse and suddenly they had and then some. 'How bad is it? Is she still in the hospital? Will she ever be OK again?'

'She's due to start rehab soon and they're not yet sure when she'll be ready to go home. But it'll be a long road for her, that much *is* for sure.' Lucy sniffed. Then she reached for Madeleine's hand across the table. 'Look, for what it's worth, I know Kate was in two minds all along about proceeding with the case. But now, with this, I realise she doesn't have a choice. And she needs me.'

'Needs you to prove that I'm at fault. That I caused all this.' Madeleine's brain swam with the horror of it all. To think that she could be held responsible for causing serious brain damage to a little girl. It didn't matter that it was indirect or otherwise. This was the reality. Kate O'Hara's reality was of course a million times worse, but that didn't stop Madeleine from feeling nauseous about it all the same.

'I was wondering...' Lucy began then and, at the tone of her voice, Madeleine turned her attention back to her friend, who sounded like she had something else on her mind. 'I was wondering if... well, this is hard to say and please don't take it the wrong way, but is there any possibility at all of you and Tom maybe agreeing to settle all this? Before it gets to court I mean.'

Madeleine thought of her husband and how angry all of this had made him. How he'd vowed to protect his rights, would fight to the death to defend their family's choices. There was no way Tom would back down from any of this.

Of course Madeleine would do so in a heartbeat, especially with what had happened to Rosie in the aftermath, but Tom? No way.

By now, it had well and truly become personal. He'd been apoplectic from day one at the very idea of Kate using their anti-vaccination stance to accuse Clara of infecting Rosie, and since the public began to row in too, and on Madeleine personally, his outrage seemed to grow more with each passing day. For Tom, it was a direct attack on not just their personal liberty but also their family, and her husband would defend both to the ends of the earth.

She could ask again but…

'I seriously doubt it, Lucy,' she told her friend despondently. 'Tom's already so furious with Kate and with the media for piling on over the vaccination thing. As far as he's concerned, we haven't broken any laws and have no case to answer.'

Though Madeleine wondered, now given that Lucy had agreed to provide Kate with the necessary testimony to support her supposed negligence, did those words still hold true?

Chapter 35

I sat by Rosie's bed at the hospital, a lot of thoughts going through my head, the majority of them confusing. But what else was new?

The other day's encounter with Madeleine was still on my mind. I knew I should have kept my mouth shut and not tried to speak with her, but what really bothered me was what had happened with Declan that same day.

OK, I know that nothing *did* happen, not technically speaking. But it still felt like some kind of line had been crossed when he made me lunch. There was no denying we'd become closer because of the case, and I suppose by nature of the fact that he had gone through everything with me when Rosie woke up at the hospital, but on that particular day – particularly when he hugged me – it felt as if there was more to it.

Now, sitting next to Rosie, holding her little hand that fitted limply in mine, I tried to wrap my head around everything. I knew I would have to see him again, and soon.

Should I just pretend like nothing had happened? Or maybe I should clear the air? Thinking of the delicious pasta dish he'd made, my stomach gurgled urgently and I realised I was ravenous, having only had enough time to grab a banana before heading off for this morning's consultation in the hospital with Rosie's physical therapist.

I looked at my watch. It was still early enough, almost eleven, and the hospital café should still be serving breakfast. I'd be here all day so I should go down and grab a bite. I'd be no good to Rosie when she came home if I ended up ill myself.

'Hey, hon,' I said quietly to my daughter. 'Just going to grab a quick bite, OK? I'll be back in a jiffy.'

She smiled, her green eyes twinkling in that achingly familiar way, and made an attempt to mumble my name as I kissed her on the forehead.

As I made my way downstairs to the café, I realised my feet were on autopilot. I had quite literally walked this hallway thousands of times, but since my little girl had shown signs of improvement there was no doubt my footsteps felt a little lighter.

Making my way down to the ground floor, I said hello to some staff faces I'd come to know throughout the endless days and hours I'd spent here. I entered the dining area and found myself relatively alone and it took me no time to order a bowl of cereal, and a bagel with jam. I was craving carbs at that point, and wanted the immediate burst of energy they would provide.

As I paid for my order, I also grabbed a newspaper and asked the lady at the register to charge me for that as well.

Settling at an empty table near a bank of windows, I took a bite of my bagel, opened my copy of the *Daily Record* and started leafing through the sections. In the last while, I'd barely kept up with what was happening in the world, but now that Rosie was out of immediate danger, I felt like I should make some sort of an effort to keep up.

But all too soon something caught me eye – a headline.
Redefining Legal Privilege?

There was something about the words that made my stomach feel uneasy. I grabbed the paper and unfolded it, so I could see the picture that sat just under the article's title. And then I did a double take. No, actually a triple take. I couldn't believe my eyes.

And I didn't think I wanted to either.

It was a photograph of Declan and me from the other day, locked in an embrace outside my car. A feeling of utter violation – not to mention embarrassment – rushed through me. I quickly pulled my eyes from the story and looked around at the cafeteria, sure people were staring at me.

But I was wrong. No one was looking. There wasn't anyone paying attention to me. That feeling was all in my head.

That was beside the point, however. People would see this. My friends would see this, maybe even my parents, Rosie's teachers and her friends' parents would see it. Madeleine and Tom Cooper would see this – their legal team too. And perhaps worst of all, Declan would see it.

That alone would open up an awkward can of worms that I had hoped to simply avoid or pretend was non-existent.

Scanning through the article, thankfully I found very little personal information. Just a summary of who we were – mostly who I was. And a blow-by-blow account of my legal action against the Coopers. But then, some blatantly salacious questions about Declan's professional ethics which maddened me, followed by some faint speculation about me as a person. The newspaper article's words seemed to paint me as some sort of opportunist. And there were quotes from 'unnamed' local sources. People who accused me of 'courting sympathy' after my husband's death and now trying to do the same thing once again with this latest tragedy...

By the time I finished reading, I was seeing red. And I had

completely lost my appetite. I pushed the food tray away from me, pulled the paper closer and quickly ran an eye through the article once again. It was all just so... hateful. I couldn't help but speculate on who the unnamed sources were and I was equally curious to know where the damn photographer had been hiding.

Dealing with this lawsuit was one thing. But I hadn't been prepared for outright character assassination. Why did they have to invade my privacy, allude to the idea that something unethical was going on between me and my solicitor?

I grabbed my phone out of my pocket, scrolled through my contacts and found Declan's number. I figured that if anyone should make him aware of this new development, it ought to be me. I pressed the name and waited for him to pick up.

The phone only rang once before his voice sounded on the other end of the line. 'Kate?' he began, worry thick in his tone. 'Is everything OK? Is Rosie OK?'

My heart gave a small, inadvertent flutter at the concern in his voice. He was so good to us.

'No, I mean yes.' I placed my hand on my forehead. 'Sorry. What I mean is yes, Rosie is OK. But no, everything else is not.'

There was silence on the other end. Declan cleared his throat. 'OK, does this have to do with the other day? About the hug... I'm really sorry if I—'

Oh God, so he thought something was off too. I groaned inwardly, realising that there was no way that we couldn't discuss this now.

'Well,' I said, feeling resigned. 'Kind of. Do you get the papers – the *Daily Record* in particular?' I hoped against hope that it was only the one paper which had run the story.

I heard some shuffling on the other end of the line. 'I haven't got round to reading anything yet but no I don't get the *Record* – bit of a rag if you ask me. Kate, what's going on?'

Rubbing my temples, I answered simply, 'Go online then, to the *Record* website and search for my name.'

More shuffling as Declan did as I requested. And then: silence.

'Are you still there?' I asked him quietly, mortified, like I had walked out of the toilets with a line of paper stuck to the bottom of my foot.

When he spoke his voice was even. I had no idea if he was upset, disgusted or ready to punch a wall. 'Stupid bastards...'

Up until now, most of the media nonsense had existed on the periphery of my life, and suddenly it was moving front and centre. Exactly what I didn't need. Everything was already daunting enough, let alone having to now worry about journalists and cameras following me (or God forbid Rosie?) around, and putting me on high alert about how I might be judged by people I didn't know, as well as those I did.

Guiltily, I thought of Madeleine Cooper. This was new for me, but she had already been dealing with such scrutiny for weeks on end. If this was how it felt, who could blame her for her reaction at the supermarket?

'I'm so sorry, Declan. This is very embarrassing.'

'Stop. None of this is your fault. I suppose we should have anticipated something like this would happen sooner or later.'

'But how can they be so... callous? Rosie is still in hospital for crying out loud.'

'They don't care; they just want to stoke the fires. Madeleine Cooper's gone quiet lately; she hasn't posted anything since that blog post a few weeks back, and definitely not since that TV appearance. So if they can't bait her...'

'Now it's my turn.'

'Probably. So be on your guard. Don't talk to anyone, the hospital staff, good friends even. You just never know...'

The idea of one of Rosie's carers betraying us like that seemed inconceivable, as did any of my friends. But how did I know? People were so easily seduced by the media, and the potential to play their part in any drama was irresistible to some, I knew. Christine Campbell was a case in point. But surely Declan's own cousin wouldn't dream of...

'Anyway, forget about that,' he said then, shrugging off the suggestion that he and I might be anything more than friends, as if it was nonsense. Which of course it was. 'I was going to phone you this morning anyway. I just got word from the High Court.' He paused. 'We have a trial date.'

Chapter 36

Irish Times News – Court Report

On a crisp autumn evening, a small crowd begins to form outside High Court buildings in central Dublin.

There is a mix of people present; some holding signs offering their support of or displeasure with the involved parties, others paying devoted attention to the media crews getting set up in front of the building.

The electricity in the air mirrors that of a carnival.

And while the crowd isn't large – at least not yet – the same cannot be said about the multiple news outlets on site. A mixture of local Irish broadcasters as well as CNN, Sky News, ABC and even representatives from the Huffington Post are all present in anticipation as O'Hara v. Cooper, or as the international media has dubbed it Vaccination on Trial, makes it to the courtroom.

In the months leading up to this day, ever since poor Rosie O'Hara contracted measles and developed subsequent complications that impacted the rest of her life, the attention on the O'Hara v. Cooper case has grown from being a regional interest piece alone to that of an international controversy.

And the debate grows ever more heated.

The peanut gallery continues to debate the issue. Some believe that it would be wise for Kate O'Hara to drop the case. Here is a single mother – a widow – now faced with the reality of a special needs child, all because of another parent's wilful negligence and, more importantly, their voluntary decision not to vaccinate their children. No, concerned health commentators agree, Ms O'Hara should press on with the issue. It is her right.

Others believe Kate O'Hara is being ridiculous. It isn't the Coopers' fault that her daughter became so ill. And haven't they been through enough too? Their own daughter was infected and they themselves have been dragged relentlessly through the coals of public opinion. This is just a shameless money grab on behalf of Kate O'Hara. Frankly, the woman should be ashamed of herself for trying to capitalise on her daughter's condition.

But the hysteria surrounding this case, doesn't start or end with just the lawsuit. The public has also been scrutinising every aspect of both families' lives. What kind of house does Madeleine Cooper live in compared to Kate O'Hara? What is the Coopers' marriage like? Are their kids good students, or are they troublemakers? Isn't Madeleine Cooper a self-confessed bad mother? When did Kate O'Hara's husband pass away? And what exactly is going on with her and her solicitor?

Speculation abounds, and it appears that everyone has an opinion on who is right and who is wrong. Online, Madeleine Cooper's blog's traffic spikes to immense heights, and she sees a drastic increase to her social media following. Moreover, a Facebook page has been launched in Rosie O'Hara's honour – Justice for Rosie – and today alone it has attracted over 10,000 followers.

Passionate anti-vaccination proponents focus on helping the Coopers with their ever mounting legal bills, while, on the other side,

Kate O'Hara's loyal following of concerned and outraged parents pitch in to help her cope with day-to-day living expenses. However, while the funds continue to grow, neither family has claimed any of the money.

The online debate for and against vaccination continues to rage. The Health Service appeals for calm, and, following increased public concerns re the MMR vaccination and a corresponding decline in uptake rates, the Health Minister is believed to have put pressure on the courts system to expedite the O'Hara v. Cooper trial date in the interest of public safety.

Suddenly, a black car pulls up slowly in front of the court buildings.

When the crowd realise that Kate O'Mara and Declan Roe have arrived, a chorus of cheers (and even a few boos) echoes around the concrete plaza. Looking pale as she takes in the commotion, Kate O'Hara turns worried eyes towards her solicitor, who says something in response, as he pats her back. She then allows her arm to be taken by his young female assistant. The trio rush through the throng of people and into the courthouse without muttering a word.

Further excitement then ripples through the crowd as another black car pulls up. This time, Madeleine and Tom Cooper emerge, along with their children and legal team. They walk briskly towards the doors of the court building, following the same path as the plaintiffs moments before.

The only difference is that Mrs Cooper mouths a silent 'thank you' as she catches the eye of an anti-vaxx supporter – a woman who yells, 'It's your choice, Madeleine! Defend your choice!'

After that, Madeleine Cooper grasps her children's hands tighter and forges on, entering the bowels of the building.

As Madeleine walked into the courtroom, she felt as if every fibre of her being was on high alert. She had been shocked by what had waited for them outside.

While of course she knew (all too well) that this trial would attract plenty of interest, she hadn't expected so much media, nor had she been prepared for the crowd of onlookers, and the signs. Looking down at Clara and Jake, she hoped that they had been too overcome with sensory overload to actually read or understand the nasty messages on some of the signs people had been holding. Some had been mean, offensive and downright vulgar – and she knew they had made a mistake in bringing the children with them.

But right from the get-go, Matt Townsend and the legal team had suggested that Clara and Jake should accompany them at the trial. Tom had agreed, though Madeleine was horrified – even when Matt had explained his reasoning to her. 'It will humanise you as parents.'

'Humanise us? We *are* humans! Ordinary people, this is absolutely ridiculous!' she had argued. But the men had insisted it was the best move. Bringing the kids illustrated their close dynamic as a family. It could… *would*… show their bond.

But Madeleine didn't agree.

Especially now as she walked into the expansive courtroom and worked to get her bearings. She recalled her initial reaction to the idea; it felt sleazy. Like she was using her own children as some sort of prop – pawns even. Her stomach churned at the thought. It was like those women on reality shows, soap operas, or in movies who towed their children along to divorce hearings, trying to get more money out of their soon-to-be ex-spouses. Today it looked like she and Tom were the ones working every angle to keep their money from Kate O'Hara.

'This is all wrong,' she muttered under her breath.

'What did you say, Mum?' asked Jake, looking up at her. He was doing his best to wrangle free from holding her hand, but she grasped it tighter because she had just spotted Kate who was already seated on the other side.

Conferring with her solicitor, the pair had their heads pressed close together. Sensing another set of eyes on her, Kate suddenly turned and met Madeleine's gaze. Neither woman's expression changed; they simply seemed to study each other for a brief moment before Kate turned back to Declan Roe.

Madeleine followed Tom's lead down the aisle of the room. She settled the children in the bench behind the defendants' table, both sorted with an iPad chock full of games (sound turned off) and took her seat next to her husband. No doubt the public would see this as yet more proof of her failings as a parent, but the reality was all this would be deathly boring for Jake and Clara and it wasn't as if they could read with all the background chatter. Sod it, after months upon months of endless recrimination, there was little else they could say about her now.

She didn't look in Kate's direction again.

'Mum?' asked Clara from behind her. 'Mum? Can I sit up there?'

Turning to meet her daughter's eyes, Madeleine realised that the courtroom was already practically full with onlookers and media. Glancing briefly to her left, she saw Christine Campbell sitting in the bench behind Kate and Declan, eyes locked on her. Madeleine tried her hardest to keep a neutral expression and ignore the look of judgement that woman seemed to wear permanently when it came to her family. She no longer wondered what she thought and definitely didn't care. The mere fact that Kate's solicitor was Christine's cousin was enough. She didn't need a red pen to connect the dots.

'Honey, no, you have to sit back there. What did I tell you before?' she answered kindly. 'There isn't enough room at this table for you, and me and Dad have to sit up here.'

Clara's brow furrowed as she seemed to digest this, and then she threw an interested glance in Kate's direction. 'Is that Rosie's mum?'

Moistening her lips, Madeleine replied, 'Yes, that's Rosie's mum.' She hoped her voice, and Clara's, were low enough. She didn't want Kate to overhear.

'Is Rosie going to be here too?' her daughter asked hopefully.

Madeleine took a deep breath. She wasn't sure that Clara really understood everything that was going on today. She and Tom had explained to both of the kids that there was an argument of sorts happening because of the fact that both she and Rosie had measles, but she also knew that the intricacies involving such a matter were beyond their comprehension.

Hell, the whole thing was still beyond Madeleine's comprehension and she guessed her daughter was wondering if her classmate was going to be there in the hope of her scoring a playmate in order to break up what would surely be monotonous grown-up stuff.

Wishing again that she hadn't been duped into bringing the kids, Madeleine answered, 'No, honey, Rosie won't be here.' She didn't elaborate any further.

But little Rosie O'Hara was in no condition to be here in the courtroom. Madeleine was relieved when she'd heard late last year that Rosie had finally been discharged from hospital. But she also knew that the little girl was receiving ongoing care and that Kate needed the help of a rehabilitation nurse at home.

It was a horrific situation and she felt so sorry for what had happened, but were she and Tom really and truly responsible for all that? She still didn't think so, but thankfully she hadn't been in Kate's situation so she had no idea how she would feel.

There but for the grace of God…

In any case, Madeleine couldn't help but imagine what the presence of a disabled six-year-old in a wheelchair would do to the judge – and their case.

Hopefully Kate's solicitor had some class and wasn't planning on taking a page out of the Matt Townsend legal playbook.

'Pity,' said Clara, digesting this information and taking a glance around at the other people on the nearby benches. 'Are there going to be any other kids here?'

Madeleine started to shake her head in the negative when Jake interrupted. 'Mum, when is this going to start? How long is this going to take?'

She looked across at Tom and Matt, who were in deep conversation with Patrick McGuinness, the barrister who would be representing their side in court throughout the trial. Her husband seemed completely unaware of what they would be dealing with having the kids present, and she felt annoyed afresh. Right, it was supposed to 'humanise' them – except for the fact that Jake and Clara were going to be bored, fidgety and wishing that they were anywhere but here.

And if they started playing up, how was Madeleine supposed to deal with them effectively without making a show of herself? Especially when all eyes would be on her, and the reason she and Tom were here in the first place was because of their apparently monstrous parental skills…

Smiling tightly, she did her best to keep an easy expression on her face. 'It should be starting shortly, OK, hon?' Jake rolled his eyes. 'And I'll make you a deal. If you can get through this morning, and just play on your iPad and be quiet, we can go to the toy shop later, and you can pick anything you want.'

Jake's eyes glittered. 'Anything?' He was waiting for her to put a monetary stipulation on the deal.

'Up to twenty euro.'

'Fifty,' said Jake.

Madeleine quickly rubbed her right temple. She could feel a headache blossoming behind her eye. Negotiating with her son was like negotiating with a terrorist.

'OK, thirty,' she countered and, despite herself, her mind automatically jumped to her now-defunct *Mad Mum* blog. Back in the day, this would have been perfect fodder for a column. *How to Keep your Kids Quiet in Court*.

But she thought sadly, those days were long gone.

'Deal.' Jake gave her a thumbs-up.

'Good. Now hush.' She looked over her shoulder. The bailiff had just entered the room, which meant that the judge would be close behind. She placed a finger over her lips and met the eyes of both her children, urging them to busy themselves with their electronics. Then, she turned back to face the front of the courtroom. The bailiff cleared his throat and Madeleine felt herself do the same.

Eighteen months of drama, heartbreak, soul-searching and legal preparation had led to this moment.

The trial was beginning.

Chapter 37

Throughout that first morning, as my and the Coopers' barristers outlined the circumstances of our case and their central arguments to the judge before first witnesses were called, I caught Madeleine's eye a couple of times. She seemed focused on keeping her expression neutral, as I'm sure her solicitor coached her to do. Tom Cooper seemed to pointedly avoid looking anywhere in my direction.

I didn't know him at all before this fiasco, but I remembered hearing from Christine that he was arrogant, and I wondered if he was worried about his ability to keep his temper if he locked eyes with me.

I was shocked when I saw Clara and Jake Cooper in the courtroom with them though. Both kids looked exhausted and beyond bored.

Seemingly reading my thoughts, Alison whispered, 'Can you get much lower than that?'

Declan hushed her. 'For the record, Kate, I would not have, nor will I ever, suggest you bring Rosie to court.'

I thought of Rosie at home with her rehab nurse, Hazel. I

couldn't even express how glad I still was to have my little girl back with me – if not back to normal.

After all that time in the hospital, at least now she was in a familiar place surrounded by her own things, helping to make her feel more comfortable. My heart dropped ever so slightly when I thought of how much assistance she needed all the time now, and how everything was so much harder due to the fact that we couldn't have our rented house retrofitted with the kind of features that would make things so much easier. For the first couple of months, because she couldn't walk – the brain injury robbing her of so many of her physical faculties – she had to sleep downstairs. But wanting her to feel more normal, now I carried her up and, even though she tired easily, she was able to get around herself well enough on the ground floor using a wheelchair. Thankfully, all those long months of rehab had helped her regain some of her upper body strength and thus the use of her arms, but her legs were still very weak.

On the plus side she was also, little by little, becoming more responsive verbally. She worked her hardest to speak to me, even though I knew she couldn't remember some words and had major problems with pronunciation – another direct result of the damage to her brain caused by the hypoxia.

But, despite it all, she was still my Rosie. She still loved to be hugged and kissed and, while I would do anything to take her frustration away, at least I was able to take some joy in the fact that she was OK.

What I didn't take joy in was applying to the state for welfare assistance to help pay for some of her needs. Not that it covered much. But at least there was *some* support, given that there was no question of my going back to work now. I had also been granted Carer's Allowance, which made my unemployment status official, and added a little more to our barely-above-water household income, albeit a pittance.

But now that our day in court was finally here, I was forced to consider the soaring cost of Declan's legal fees, which, if we lost, would be completely unsurmountable.

I couldn't even contemplate that prospect now.

*

Declan flipped through his notes, took a glance at the defendants' table to gauge their attention, and listened as their barrister, Patrick Nevin, called Dr Frank Barrett from Knockroe as the plaintiff's first witness. He knew Kate had been dubious about someone other than him presenting the case in court, but that was how the Irish legal system worked. 'The words might be coming out of someone else's mouth but it's still my case, still me and how I want to play it,' he assured her.

Now, recalling his first encounter with the Coopers' GP many months ago, Declan figured him to be an individual who played by the book, no matter how damaging it might be for people he considered his friends.

'Dr Barrett, thank you very much for being here today,' the barrister began graciously.

The older man nodded and Declan concluded that the Coopers' GP wasn't having the best of days. While he presented a gruff exterior, it was obvious that he was in the middle of a professional and personal conflict. Clearly fond of Madeleine and Tom Cooper and their children, he had nevertheless always been uneasy with their anti-vaccination stance.

And the discomfort that he was feeling right then was very visible.

'Dr Barrett, how long have you been treating Tom and Madeleine Cooper's children, Clara and Jake?' asked Patrick Nevin.

The older man answered, 'Since they were born.'

'How did you originally meet the Coopers?'

The doctor folded his arms across his chest – a defensive posture. 'I was Mrs Cooper's GP when she was a child, and remained friendly with her late parents.'

'So you have known the family for quite some time?'

'Yes,' said Dr Barrett. Declan waited a beat to see if the man would add anything to that. Either the doctor was a man of few words or this wasn't his first court appearance. He was guessing the latter was true.

'Did you encourage Tom and Madeleine Cooper to vaccinate Jake and Clara Cooper when they were babies?' The barrister looked up from his list of questions and met Dr Barrett's eyes. The physician didn't physically blanch, but it was apparent the wheels were turning in his head. There was only the slightest pause.

'I did.'

'I see. And did they take your advice?' Nevin enquired. Of course, he already knew the answer, but still he had to ask.

'No, they did not.'

The barrister nodded. 'I see. And did you treat Clara Cooper in March of last year when she became ill with measles?'

Another nod from Dr Barrett. 'Yes, I did.'

'Can you tell us about your experience treating Clara?'

Dr Barrett remained quiet, he looked at the floor, pondering the question. Finally, he returned his eyes to meet the barrister's and answered.

'I attended the child at her own house. She did not need to be admitted to the hospital.'

'Couldn't she have come to your office for treatment, Dr Barrett?'

'I did not want her to visit the surgery in person,' replied the doctor.

'And why is that, Doctor?'

The frown on the doctor's face deepened and Declan was sure there was a great inner conflict going on within his heart and mind right then. He also knew that his next answer was going to be bad for the Coopers' defence.

'Because Clara was highly contagious. And I didn't want any other children to get sick.'

'Do you make a habit of treating many unvaccinated children, Dr Barrett?'

'No, I don't.'

'And why is that?' the barrister pressed.

Barrett's face reddened, and he grimaced. But he knew he had to answer the question. 'Because it's a huge liability.'

'Why do you continue to treat the Coopers' then?' Nevin raised his eyebrows as he presented the question.

The doctor sighed. 'Because, as I said, I have known them for a long time. That's why. And I care about the children.'

'Of course you do, of course,' the barrister commented. 'And when Clara Cooper got sick, did any other cases of measles present in your office, amongst your patient population?'

'None in my office. I believe Rosie O'Hara was the only other case in Knockroe at the time, and I do not treat her as a patient.'

'Yes, we are aware of that, indeed,' replied Nevin. 'Dr Barrett, what is your experience pertaining to a situation when an unvaccinated child comes down with a highly infectious disease, and spreads it to other children who are not protected – for instance, children like Rosie O'Hara, who through no fault of her own could not be vaccinated as a baby because of a medical condition.'

'I can't speak about Rosie O'Hara,' replied the doctor shortly. 'As I said before, I don't treat her.'

'Of course, I'm well aware of that. However, my question pertains to how contagious a disease like measles would be amongst unvaccinated populations.'

'Well,' said the doctor, thoughtfully. 'Measles is indeed very contagious. Highly contagious. Of course, the belief is that there is a herd immunity of sorts, and that the disease might not spread as easily among the unvaccinated while widespread immunity is present.'

Nevin nodded thoughtfully and walked closer to where Dr Barrett sat in the witness stand. He placed a hand on the wooden ledge that separated them. 'And what about in the case of Rosie O'Hara and Clara Cooper; they were in the same classroom. They interacted every day.'

'As both were unvaccinated, I think it's very likely that the disease would easily pass from one to another. However, there is no way of knowing who was infected first – not when both presented symptoms so close together. Incubation time is not absolute and can vary.'

'Agreed,' said Nevin, wanting to move on and Declan realised Dr Barrett was saying more than he had in his original preparation. And now he was introducing some doubt based on incubation time, which was obviously better for the defence side.

'Do you believe that this situation might have been prevented if Clara Cooper had been vaccinated?'

Dr Barrett smirked, he wasn't going to give such an easy answer. 'I think it would have been prevented entirely if *both* girls were vaccinated.' Then he shrugged. 'Again, I cannot speak of Rosie

O'Hara's situation as I am not her physician. However, it's my understanding that both girls showed symptoms within days of each other, which would be expected with a highly infectious illness amongst the unvaccinated population. And the mere fact that the girls were in such close proximity – namely sharing the same school classroom – points to the obvious.'

'Objection. Speculation,' Michael McGuinness, the defence's barrister intoned.

'Sustained,' said the judge quickly.

'How does measles spread, Doctor?' enquired Nevin, moving swiftly on.

'Well, the short version of it is that measles is a virus, and it lives in the mucus of the nose and throat of one who is infected. It is spread through physical contact, coughing and sneezing etc. But it's important to note that infected droplets of mucus can remain active and be passed on by touching for about two hours *after* a cough or a sneeze, for instance.'

'Thank you for that, Doctor,' Nevin replied. 'I'm curious to know, is Mrs Cooper vaccinated? Did you vaccinate her when she was a child?'

The doctor nodded and relaxed just a little. 'Yes, with whatever vaccines were available here at the time. Vaccination protection for measles was not introduced in Ireland until the mid to late eighties.'

'But Mrs Cooper was vaccinated as per then current Health Service guidelines?'

'Correct.'

'And why is that, Doctor?'

This earned Nevin a smile from the older man. 'Because her parents listened to my advice as a medical professional.'

'But isn't it correct that Madeleine Cooper and her husband

didn't do that, when the time came to vaccinate their own children?'

'I believe I already said that was the case,' snapped the doctor.

The barrister held up his hands. 'I apologise, it's not my intent
to be repetitious.'

'Then don't *be* repetitious,' put in the judge, shortly.

'Again, my apologies,' said Nevin. 'Moving on. Are you aware
of any reason why the Coopers decided not to vaccinate their
children?'

'Yes,' said the doctor.

Declan had to smile. The man had *definitely* acted as a witness
at a trial or two in his career. He seemed loyal to the approach
of 'mum's the word'.

'And what are those reasons exactly?' the barrister probed.
There was no way that Dr Barrett was going to be allowed not
to elaborate.

The doctor briefly looked at opposing counsel and shook his
head. He appeared pained to have to say the words. 'The Coopers
have some concerns about the MMR vaccine and its connection
to autism.'

Declan heard the implied quotation marks around the word
'concerns'.

'But you don't share these concerns?'

It was a simple question, but Declan knew that a truthful
answer here from the doctor would discredit the Coopers enor-
mously.

'No. I do not.'

'And your reasoning is based on?'

The doctor sighed. 'Science,' he said. 'My reasoning is based on
science. Studies have repeatedly proven that there is absolutely no
connection between the MMR vaccine and autism.' Barrett paused

ever so briefly and then his instinct as a medical professional seemed to overpower his focus on providing direct, to-the-point answers. 'Or any other condition for that matter.'

Pursing his lips, Declan allowed himself a brief glance across to Matt Townsend. The defence's solicitor looked as if he wanted to throw up. He appreciated the doctor for his honesty, even though the man knew his answers were not benefiting his long-time friends.

Patrick Nevin then decided to enter into a new line of questioning.

'And while you were treating Clara Cooper, were both of her parents in attendance at her bedside?'

Dr Barrett's brow furrowed. It was apparent that he was trying to figure out Nevin's angle here. Slightly shaking his head, he said, 'It was primarily Mrs Cooper who was in attendance. Mr Cooper works full-time. Although I do know, based on a conversation with Mrs Cooper, that her husband did take some time off from work in the early days of Clara's illness.'

'As any good father would,' Nevin commented. 'Doctor, did either of Clara's parents at this point express any concern about how this situation with their daughter impacted their day-to-day life?'

Dr Barrett squinted his eyes, trying to comprehend what the barrister was getting at. 'I don't know what you mean. Of course they were concerned. What parent wouldn't be?'

Nevin held up his hands. 'Sure, sorry, let me clarify. Yes, the Coopers were concerned, but what negative repercussions did they themselves experience because of Clara's sickness? If any.'

Sitting back further in his chair, Dr Barrett considered this question carefully. 'Well, of course, Mrs Cooper experienced considerable fallout with her blog or her website or whatever it is that she does online, because of the publicity surrounding this issue. But I can't comment about what goes on in their home, I don't live there. So I can only go on what I have observed.'

'Correct, Doctor. And pertaining to what you observed at the time; was there any immediate change in the Coopers' lifestyle following Clara's sickness; perhaps the cost of medical bills, loss of income...?'

Declan frowned a little. He himself wasn't sure what Nevin was hoping to achieve through this line of questioning, unless their barrister was purposely trying to paint the Coopers as having gotten on with their lives unscathed, while Kate's present and future had been changed – extraordinarily in lieu of their negligence. Which was fine by him.

The doctor sighed, but raised a hand to his chin, as if calling upon the recesses of his brain to provide an answer to the question. 'To be honest, I don't believe there were many pertinent issues created from Clara being sick.' He shook his head ruefully. 'Possibly some short-term problems like used-up holiday leave entitlements, things like that.'

'What do you mean by that exactly?'

Dr Barrett shrugged and allowed his shoulders to droop ever so slightly. 'It was just an offhand comment that Mrs Cooper made at the time. She mentioned that Mr Cooper had used up annual leave time by staying home while Clara was sick, and that he needed to make it back up if they were to go on holiday this year.'

Across the way, Declan heard Tom Cooper elicit what could only be described as a hiss, and clearly Dr Barrett had heard it too. He realised too late that he had said too much, and there was no way to take the insinuation back.

Though this clearly inspired Nevin to pounce, as he worked to discover more.

'I see. And did Mrs Cooper know the status of Rosie O'Hara's condition at this time?'

The doctor looked over at the defence table, with tired eyes. He seemed eager to get rid of his next words – apparently he understood that he had already dug a pretty deep hole. 'Yes. By then we knew that Rosie O'Hara had been admitted to hospital. For what it's worth, please let the record show that I advised Madeleine that such a comment was in bad taste and she agreed.'

A low hush enveloped the room then. Looking then at Kate, Declan saw her face harden as she understood the gravity of what had been said, and he saw fresh anger blossoming on her face as she looked at Madeleine across the aisle.

The other woman stared straight ahead, unblinking.

And Declan realised that even the judge wore a look of distaste as he considered the callousness of what Dr Barrett had just relayed about his long-standing friends, the Coopers.

'Thank you, Dr Barrett, no further questions.'

Chapter 38

Madeleine could barely contain her frustration, hurt and, most of all, embarrassment.

Michael McGuinness hadn't been able to rescue much in his short cross-examination of Frank Barrett, and if the judge hadn't adjourned for the day when he did, she was pretty sure that she would have walked out of the room in mortification. As it was, as soon as he announced that today's session had ended, she grabbed both of her children's hands and, with as much decorum as she could muster given how she was feeling just then, ushered them outside to the hallway, leaving her husband and legal team following in her wake.

She couldn't even hazard a glance in Kate's direction. She just couldn't. Nor could she allow herself to look at any of the journalists or even members of the public present. She was almost certain Gemma Moore was amongst them but even if her nemesis wasn't Madeleine knew that all she would get was more judgement, scorn and ridicule. It was a lot to bear – and while she'd tried her utmost to prepare herself for the fresh onslaught the trial would bring, and had already had lots of practice in trying to save face, still she couldn't help but let it get to her.

However, if Madeleine thought that she would find any amount of solace outside the building she was wrong. The moment she exited out onto the street, she and the kids were bombarded on all sides. The sheer number of media and people clambering to get a piece of them was beyond overwhelming, and she felt Jake and Clara both move closer to her, clinging frightened to her hand, or the skirt of her conservative navy blue suit.

Feeling a growing sense of panic, Madeleine turned to look for Tom. Thankfully, her husband was right behind them ready to help and he put an arm around her shoulders and tried to lead his family through the throng of humanity to the car Townsend had arranged for them out front. From behind, she heard their solicitor shouting into the waiting microphones.

'No comment. We have nothing to say. No comment.'

But then, Madeleine was taken even further by surprise as the veritable mob around them began to shout hostilities.

'Not only irresponsible but callous and selfish too!' screamed a woman with wild blue eyes. She held up a sign that said, *Coopers = Criminals. Lock them up now and throw away the key.*

Another man yelled, 'Mad Mum really *is* mental. Hey, Tom, take your head out of your ass, idiot!'

The taunts and the jeers went on – getting louder and louder with each passing step.

Clara started to whimper. 'Mama, what's going on? Why do they all hate us?'

Madeleine pulled her daughter close and at once felt relief when she finally spotted the car pull up to the kerb. 'It's OK, honey. Just cover your ears. No one hates you. Your dad and I won't let anything happen to you. Just ignore them.'

Finally, the group burst free from the crowd and Tom hustled his family into the car. Seconds later, Matt Townsend crawled in after them. The moment the door was closed and the car pulled away, Madeleine brushed back her sweaty hair and exploded. She hated to have such an outburst in front of the kids, but what she had to say couldn't wait another second.

'That's it, Clara and Jake are not going back in there,' she stormed to Matt. 'No child should be exposed to that.'

Beside her Clara sat openly crying into her mother's sleeve and Jake appeared stricken. His face was pale as a sheet and his jaw slack; his shock and distress palpable.

'It's OK, guys,' Madeleine cooed, trying to lower her voice, pulling both children closer to her and kissing the tops of their heads. Then, she returned a laser focus onto their solicitor. 'I mean it. I'm *not* using them as pawns. And there is no way I'm going to expose them to that kind of insanity every day. Did you hear what some of those people were saying? And do you also think it's right that they hear the character assassinations that will be going on in that courtroom? This is only day one – and already it's nasty.'

She thought back to the picture that had been painted of them – of *her* – thus far by a family friend no less. Regardless of how embarrassed she had felt, in hindsight, she was also sick about the things she had said to Frank Barrett. Had she really been that worried about not being able to take a holiday last year? How could she have been so vapid and shallow? And while it felt like a betrayal on the GP's behalf, Madeleine understood that he had been required to answer the questions posed to him.

Then there was Kate. Madeleine hadn't been brave enough to look in her direction or face her. But still she could feel Kate's gaze on her at the end of Barrett's testimony, one of blatant loathing and distaste. Yet, hadn't she deserved it?

'Mama, why were all of those people yelling at us?' Clara asked, her voice thick with tears.

She stroked her daughter's head. 'They are just angry, sweet-heart. That's all. None of that stuff they were saying is true. And you don't have to hear it ever again.'

'Madeleine,' Matt soothed, 'if you would just calm down for a second...'

Her eyes growing wide, she shot daggers in her solicitor's direction. 'Don't even say it. I mean it, Jake and Clara are *not* going back there. So you'd better try and find a way to fight this without parading my kids around in front of an angry mob. I can take it, Tom can take it and we'll do what we have to do. But my kids are off limits, OK?' Suddenly, Madeleine realised that the one person who should also be speaking up and agreeing with her remained completely silent. 'Tom, have you nothing to say? Last time I checked these are your kids, too. Or are you going to say this is yet another of my bad decisions?'

Tom, who had been looking out the window, apparently deep in thought, turned to face his wife. He took in the appearance of both of his children and seemed to be weighing the pros and cons of both sides of the argument. Finally, sitting forward and running a hand through his hair, he looked pleadingly at Madeleine.

'I do think they're tougher than you think,' he said quietly. But then, as his wife's eyes filled with anger and she opened her mouth to unleash her thoughts once again, he put his hands up. 'But Matt, she's right. We shouldn't have the kids there.' He put a comforting hand on Madeleine's leg. 'I suppose I just didn't realise it would all be so... toxic.'

Chapter 39

I was already seated at the plaintiffs' table when the Coopers walked in the next morning. Compared to how she had left yesterday afternoon – visibly suffering a wide range of emotions – today, Madeleine had her chin raised high and she carried herself like a queen. She wore an expensively tailored dark suit and had a pink scarf artfully tied around her neck, expertly accessorising it. However, a couple of accessories she'd sported the day before were now conspicuously absent: her children.

I glanced at Declan, who was deep in dialogue with Patrick Nevin. Rosie's paediatrician Dr Ryan was scheduled to go on the stand first thing this morning and I knew that Declan wanted to make sure Nevin was adequately prepared to guide her.

He had confessed to me previously that while she was an obviously talented physician, she had not presented well in her preparation for trial. Declan was intent on making sure she came across comfortable and secure in the witness stand – he didn't want any medical doubt to be introduced this time round.

'Looks like Jake and Clara stayed at home today. I'm betting that isn't a coincidence,' Alison whispered. 'I wonder if it was Madeleine who put her foot down? There is no way any mother would like having her kids listen to this stuff,' she muttered, turning back to me.

But unwilling to be drawn, I simply raised my eyebrows and sat back in my chair, thinking back on what had gone down in the courtroom yesterday. It hadn't been pretty. In fact, it had been downright upsetting. Worried about losing out on a holiday…

And, if anything, it had only escalated interest in the trial and added even more fuel to the media fire.

'Dr Ryan is here,' Alison said turning back in her seat. 'She looks good, Kate. She seems calm.'

Shifting a bit in my own seat so I could look behind me, I waved a small hello to Dr Ryan at the same moment the bailiff asked that we all rise. The judge was entering, and court was starting.

Patrick Nevin wasted no time calling Dr Ryan to the stand. I was happy to see that Rosie's doctor did indeed look poised and confident. The nervousness she had apparently shown in preparation was gone, and the barrister artfully led her through a series of questions about my daughter's health, what she was facing currently, as well as her ongoing prognosis.

Dr Ryan outlined in stark detail the very serious side-effects of the measles virus Rosie had suffered, and how encephalitis was essentially an acute inflammation of her brain directly resulting from the infection.

'The brain becomes inflamed as a result of the body's attempt to fight the virus. In Rosie's case this was particularly severe, as her brain suffered repeat convulsions. And when the anti-convulsant drugs we administered did not work, we needed to medically induce a coma so as to essentially give her brain a rest from the seizures. However, throughout the course of those seizures, Rosie suffered hypoxia, a temporary loss of oxygen to her brain,' the doctor continued. 'The prognosis for such an occurrence depends on the duration of the episode and, unfortunately in Rosie's case, the oxygen loss was prolonged. Though thankfully,' she added, glancing encouragingly towards me, 'the resulting damage to the brain was not irreversible. What all this meant for Rosie was that she basically needed to relearn and regain many of her day-to-day physical abilities – such as using her limbs – but thankfully, retained much of her neurological faculties.

'She continues to receive physical and occupational therapy both at the hospital and at home, and while her prognosis is good from a medical point of view, as you can imagine, her life and that of her family, has been changed utterly.'

While it was unsettling to hear my Rosie's medical history and the injuries she'd sustained painted in such blunt and bleak terms, I knew that the judge needed to hear all this from the horse's mouth. I thought of the innocent little girl who was currently at home under the watchful eye of her nurse and wondered if life would ever be the same again. There was no point in sugar-coating the truth – this was our new reality.

Once Nevin concluded his questioning, he gave up the floor to opposing counsel.

It was their turn to cross-examine Rosie's doctor. And, as expected, Michael McGuinness did not wait to introduce the doubt re transmission of the virus that Dr Barrett had hinted upon the day before. He brought it out front and centre, and even while I cringed inwardly, I encouraged myself to get used to it.

'Now, Dr Ryan,' stated McGuinness, 'let's talk about the timeline for when each little girl got sick. Would you agree that Rosie O'Hara might well have been the first to contract the disease, even if we can all agree that it was Clara Cooper who presented first?'

Dr Ryan paused. She had her game face on. 'I cannot comment on Clara Cooper. I'm not her attending physician nor am I familiar with any of her medical records.'

McGuinness raised his hands apologetically. 'Of course, I understand. I was simply asking your opinion in that regard, that it's quite possible Rosie O'Hara could have been the one to contract measles first?'

Nevin jumped to attention. 'Objection. Speculation.'

'Sustained,' said the judge automatically.

Shrugging ever so slightly, the defence barrister was quiet for a moment as he looked to rephrase his question.

'Dr Ryan, in your expert opinion, is it possible in general terms to trace the course of a disease such as measles backward? Possible to trace it back to a "patient zero", so to speak.'

Shifting in her chair, Dr Ryan considered the question. Finally, she answered. 'I think the question is a bit simplistic. And let me explain why. Yes, at its most basic level, with a disease like measles, it would of course be possible in some instances to trace it back to Patient Zero. In large scale epidemics this might be the case. For instance, there was a widespread outbreak in the USA a couple of years back that was said to originate in California. The epidemic spread to almost two hundred cases in eighteen different states. Yet US health officials couldn't pinpoint the exact origin of the outbreak, even with those large numbers. When the CDC got involved, I believe they were able to match the strain of that virus to one that initially started in the Philippines – it had the same fingerprint, so to speak. However, it was not possible to determine with whom that outbreak started, and a Patient Zero was never identified.' The doctor paused for a moment, and then continued.

'On the flipside of that, there was another situation, also

involving the Philippines. A couple of US missionaries had gone there and this was linked one of the largest measles outbreak in decades. The disease was localised in Ohio, amongst the Amish community in which childhood immunisation is uncommon. Ultimately, it could be determined that members of the missionary group who had contracted this in the Philippines returned to the US. So investigators could determine exactly who brought the disease back.

'I mention these two cases simply because I want you to understand that the scope of an outbreak matters most in determining its origin. The mere fact that there wasn't a larger measles outbreak in this area at the time Rosie and Clara contracted the disease makes it nigh on impossible to determine who the primary carrier could be. But Clara had just returned from the US whereupon a smaller-scale outbreak had occurred, so it is reasonable to suspect, as an unvaccinated child, she picked it up while there.'

The barrister didn't look at all pleased with this answer, but he pressed on.

'But what if it could be determined?' he asked and I felt myself staring so hard at the back of his head it was as if I wanted to open up his skull and read his thoughts. Was he aware of some other point of origin, other than the Florida one?

Dr Ryan shrugged. 'I can't see how. This outbreak wasn't a blip on the HSE's radar – in fact with only two patients involved technically it's not even an outbreak. And it wouldn't have been at all, save for this court case. This involves two little girls, Clara and Rosie, attending the same school. To my knowledge, no one else at the school or any other person in the area was infected thereafter.'

I was glad that Dr Ryan was taking Declan's advice to always use the girls' names when referring to them together, instead of the defence barrister who'd so far spoken of them in more formal terms.

McGuinness nodded, as if he was carefully considering this. 'Indeed. And, of course, no national health agencies have been deployed in this regard. I agree with you. But surely it's not too hard to walk backwards in the lives of two five-year-old girls?'

Nevin jumped up once again to object, but Dr Ryan was already answering. 'That isn't a medical question I can answer. I would suggest you refer that to the girls' parents.'

'Thank you, Dr Ryan. We truly appreciate your time this morning,' replied McGuinness, who immediately turned on his heel and walked back to where the Coopers sat with their solicitor.

Matt Townsend had a small smirk on his face, and my mind immediately began to race as I wondered what ace card the defendant's solicitor evidently believed he had up his sleeve.

Chapter 40

Following the very damning testimony from Rosie O'Hara's doctor, Madeleine heard the plaintiff's side then call Dr Sebastian Goring, a university professor of some sort who was apparently an expert on infectious disease.

She sighed, settling in once again to having her authority as a parent crushed like a beetle under the heel of a shoe.

'Dr Goring, what is your experience in handling measles cases and the disease's effect on the community at large?' Patrick Nevin asked.

The older bespectacled gentleman crossed one leg over another. 'I was a family GP for twenty-five years before becoming a clinical professor in University College Dublin. I have spent considerable time studying and treating infectious diseases, and also served as a member of an infectious diseases symposium at the School of Public Health at Johns Hopkins University, Maryland.'

'Thank you for that. Very fine credentials you have, Doctor.' Goring nodded in response, waiting for the next question. 'Can you comment on the impact that the MMR vaccination has made to children and indeed adults in this country?'

'Of course,' said Dr Goring. 'Before the measles vaccine was introduced in 1985, the death rate was close to twice what it was from polio. The measles vaccine changed all that. Statistics show that for every one thousand children who get the disease, approximately one will die from it. Among some children who don't die from the disease, there is a chance of suffering lifelong, debilitating injury.' He paused for a moment, just as he had been coached to do. They wanted to make sure that the judge made the correlation between what had been said and Rosie's situation. 'Yet, there is currently no legal requirement in Ireland stating that you must vaccinate your children, even though results show the MMR vaccine is very effective. The HSE, as well as disease control authorities internationally – such as the CDC in the US – have determined that the vaccine is more than 97 per cent effective. Those who are vaccinated have only a small chance of contracting a mild form of measles, mumps or rubella,' said Dr Goring.

'Pretty conclusive,' Nevin agreed. 'But about this belief widely held by anti-vaccination proponents like the Coopers, that the MMR vaccine causes autism?'

At this question Dr Goring looked annoyed. 'This "movement" of sorts gained credibility in 1998 when a British gastroenterologist, Andrew Wakefield, published a paper in the medical journal *The Lancet*. In his paper, this... individual supported a belief based on entirely anecdotal research, that the MMR vaccine caused autism. Very quickly, Britain's General Medical Council revoked the doctor's medical licence, and in 2010 the journal retracted the study. They announced that it was utterly clear that the statements in the paper were completely false. It was all nonsense. However, the damage was done and, even now, you still have the conspiracy theorists and anti-government tinfoil hat wearers who promote this false line of thinking. And also, quite frankly, this line of thinking also persists because idiot Hollywood celebrities continue to propagate this nonsense and spread it to a gullible, starry-eyed public.'

Across the courtroom, Madeleine visibly flinched. It was as if she had been slapped. How dare he? Celebrities had *nothing* to do with her decision, nothing at all! She had to stop herself from standing up and telling this blustering ignoramus so.

'So you have all these celebrities practising armchair medicine – armchair *science* – and passing this faulty and highly illogical information on to members of the community who are inclined to believe the tabloid reporting so prevalent in today's media. I can tell you straight, when people choose not to vaccinate their children because of personal, religious, political, or any non-medical viewpoints, they put their own children and other people's children at risk.'

'Thank you, Doctor,' said Nevin, clearly worried that the doctor was laying it on a bit thick. 'You said choosing not to vaccinate based on non-medical viewpoints. What do you mean by that?'

Dr Goring considered the barrister and uncrossed and re-crossed his legs. 'I mean in situations where if a vaccine was administered to someone that a medical complication would occur. The proteins most often implicated in vaccine allergies are egg and gelatin, with perhaps rare reactions to yeast or latex. The number of people who experience this type of hypersensitivity is relatively low, but when it is experienced, it is quite serious.'

'I see. Like in the situation of Kate O'Hara and her late husband – who were faced with a child who experienced a severe medical reaction when the first round of vaccinations was given. In your view, was the decision not to vaccinate their daughter justified?'

Dr Goring nodded. 'Yes. From my viewpoint as a medical professional, this was completely justified. The allergic reaction that Rosie O'Hara experienced as a baby was quite rare, but it could have been fatal if it hadn't been recognised and addressed for what it was. Rosie is fortunate that her mother, Ms O'Hara, is a licensed medical professional who had the scientific and clinical knowledge and abilities to address it promptly, as well as seek proper care and counsel.'

Listening to the exchange, Madeleine closed her eyes. Not only were she and Tom being painted as 'gullible, empty-headed people' readily influenced by celebrity, but now Kate was being compared to Florence Nightingale.

Honestly, could things get any worse?

Chapter 41

That same afternoon, Madeleine had to face the ignominy of seeing one of her oldest and dearest friends testify against her.

She had no idea how Lucy's testimony was going to go down, but based on how everything had gone so far, she wasn't optimistic. Kate's legal team needed to persuade the judge that Madeleine had knowingly acted in a negligent manner by sending an infectious Clara to school.

Lucy was the smoking gun, the proof they needed that she had done so.

Her friend spoke clearly and confidently as the plaintiff's barrister asked her to outline their personal history. 'I've known Madeleine pretty much all my life,' she began, with little trace of nerves. 'We're both from the same town obviously and have always been friendly, but I suppose we really only became close friends about nine years ago when we were both on maternity leave around the same time. Me with my daughter, Stephanie, and Madeleine with Jake.'

'I see. And how did this aspect of your relationship develop?' Patrick Nevin asked.

'We used to meet up at a local mum and toddler group, but I

have to say from day one that I admired Madeleine's approach to motherhood.'

'How so?'

'Well, she seemed very relaxed with Jake, and considerably less inclined to fuss and stress like the rest of us did. She didn't obsess about feeding routines or complain about sleepless nights – things like that. I guess you could say she took things in her stride. When the rest of us worried about whether or not we should use soothers, or when we should start weaning, Madeleine took a much more practical approach and urged us all not to take things so seriously—'

'But taking care of a baby is a serious business, surely?'

'Of course, and I'm not suggesting she didn't take it seriously at all. I merely meant that she would have preferred the group to be less intense and judgemental and a little more fun. She used to say that we should all enjoy our babies more, instead of overthinking motherhood or treating it like this deeply stressful situation. She was right, of course, but I know some of the other mums were a bit annoyed by that. They *enjoyed* stressing and fussing. I did too, but that's not to say that I didn't see Madeleine's point. I just knew it wasn't me. However, we remained friends even when she stopped going to the group—'

'She didn't continue meeting with you and the other mums?'

'No. I think she found the gatherings a bit counterproductive. She's a doer at heart and didn't believe in sitting around navel-gazing. She much preferred to just get on with things instead of discussing them ad nauseam. And I know she hated the competitive, judgemental nature of it all. But some mums, myself included, we enjoyed playing the martyr that way – it was a sort of... bonding exercise, I suppose?'

'OK. So despite opposing parenting views, you and Madeleine

Cooper remained close and maintained your friendship as your children got older and began attending the same school, correct?'

'That's right.'

'And it became routine for you both to help each other out with pick-ups and drop-offs etc.'

'Yes, just like most busy parents – we were always happy to do each other a turn.'

'Can you tell us about the morning of March twentieth last year – when Madeleine Cooper asked you for a very specific favour?'

'Sure.' At this, I noticed a slight waver in Lucy's voice and her demeanour changed a little. Her hand shook as she picked up a glass of water and drank from it. 'Madeleine phoned me at around eight that morning. She mentioned that Clara hadn't been feeling the best, and that she was likely coming down with something. A note had gone round the school that week about—'

'Thank you,' Nevin interjected smoothly, cutting off what was surely Lucy's qualifier about the school note concerning chicken pox. 'Mrs Cooper said those exact words "she was likely coming down with something"?'

'To the best of my recollection, yes. But I'm almost certain she thought it was chicken pox; she had no idea—'

Thank you, Lucy, Madeleine thought, feeling heartened. As she'd assured, her friend wasn't here to hang her – while she was testifying on Kate's side, she was also trying her utmost to tell it like it was.

Despite herself, she felt tears prick at the corners of her eyes. It felt like the first time *anyone* had stood up for her throughout this whole nightmare.

'But why did Mrs Cooper put you on such an alert? Why was she not available to collect her own daughter herself?'

'Madeleine had a prior work commitment that she couldn't cancel.'

'And what was the nature of this work commitment...' Nevin said the last word with obvious distaste' '...so important that Mrs Cooper could not make herself available for her daughter?'

'Objection! Judge, this is prejudicial in the extreme.'

'Sustained. Mr Nevin, please abstain from personal commentary and focus solely on the facts,' said the judge. Then he addressed Lucy. 'The witness should answer the question.'

'It was a TV appearance on a Channel 2 chat show,' she replied. 'The show went out at eleven-thirty that morning and was too late to cancel—'

'So Mrs Cooper needed you to be on call in case her daughter was sent home early from school so she could attend a TV show. Certainly seems as though she was pretty certain this would happen, does it not?'

'Objection!' McGuinness shouted, sounding livid. 'Leading testimony and again prejudicial; plaintiff's counsel cannot possibly know what Mrs Cooper was or wasn't certain of.'

'Sustained. Mr Nevin...'

'My apologies. Mrs Murphy, what time did you pick up Clara Cooper from school that day?'

'I believe it was around 11.30, not long after morning break.'

'And how did Clara Cooper seem to you when you met her at the school?'

'Objection, calls for speculation.'

The judge looked irritated. 'Overruled, Mr McGuinness. It's already been established that the child was ill enough for the school to send her home, and the witness's opinion will be helpful in further illustrating the reality of Ms Cooper's condition.'

'Well… she did seem a little feverish yes, but I wouldn't have said—'

Nevin began walking away. 'Thank you, Mrs Murphy. No further questions.'

Lucy looked a little perturbed at not being allowed to fully have her say, but was somewhat relieved of another chance to do so when the defence barrister approached the witness stand to cross-examine.

'Mrs Murphy, you mentioned that you and Mrs Cooper had been friends throughout early motherhood and beyond. During this time did Madeleine Cooper ever discuss with you her decision not to vaccinate her children?'

'Yes. And while I didn't share her opinion, I could perhaps understand it all the same. Madeleine, or indeed Tom, don't make decisions lightly. They would have thought through all of the options and discussed the pros and cons at length. And, in fairness, when Jake came down with measles at eighteen months and came through it OK, it became less of an issue.'

'How so? Do you mean that Jake Cooper contracting the illness and recovering from it without incident justified the Coopers' decision?'

'Well, perhaps not justified it, but it certainly suggested, to me at least, that it was less of a big deal than it might have been before that.'

'I understand. And when Jake Cooper was diagnosed with measles as a baby, did Ms Cooper make you aware that her son might be contagious?'

Lucy thought about it. 'Yes, she did. We'd met up with the kids the previous week and Madeleine phoned to check if Stephanie was OK, or had any signs of infection. But Stephanie had been vaccinated with MMR so I didn't have too many concerns on that front.'

'You're saying that Madeleine went out of her way to check? She was not – as is suggested by the plaintiffs – cavalier about other children's safety?'

'Objection. Witness cannot speak for the defendant's actions in any scenario other than the one in question.'

But Lucy answered anyway. 'Of course she did,' she said, shaking her head. Then she took a deep breath. 'Look, Madeleine is a good person and a wonderful mother, despite the fact that this trial, and certainly the accompanying publicity, is trying to suggest otherwise. I know it in my bones that she would *never* harm anyone intentionally or otherwise. Yes, she might have made a mistake that morning, but any working parent could very easily have done the same. And while her approach might come across to some as unconventional, she's always done things on her own terms. She's never wrapped her kids in cotton wool, never mourned or fretted over every little scratch or lump and bump. And unlike my own two, who I'll admit were perhaps a little too indulged as babies and now still require much cosseting, Jake and Clara are confident, happy and well-adjusted children. Say what you will about Madeleine and Tom's style, but no one can deny that their children are all the better for it.'

'Thank you, no further questions.'

Oh Lucy... Now the tears had begun to fall freely from Madeleine's eyes. After all this time, being at the brunt of such horrible accusations and having to rethink (not to mention defend) every parenting decision she'd ever made, she really needed to hear that. The judge and the media needed to too. But, most of all, she thought, glancing across to the other table, Kate needed to hear it.

She wasn't a bad person or a terrible mother. She was just…
human.

Thank you.

But Patrick Nevin stood up immediately to redirect.

'And what of Rosie O'Hara?' he asked. 'Mrs Murphy, would you
also say that *she* is the better for Madeleine Cooper's approach?'

Lucy's mouth dropped open, and McGuinness jumped up to
object, while just as quickly Madeleine's heart plunged into her
stomach.

'Mrs Murphy, answer the question, please,' urged the judge.

Lucy exhaled loudly. 'I feel terrible about what happened to
little Rosie, of course I do. But if you're asking me if I think
Madeleine set out to harm her or is to blame for what happened
to her, then the answer is absolutely not.' She looked down at
Kate, her eyes full of sorrow and regret. 'No one is to blame for
this. It's a horrible situation – of course it is – but sometimes, bad
things just happen.'

Chapter 42

At home later that evening, my mind was troubled following events of the day.

It appeared that things had for the most part gone well for us with Lucy's testimony confirming Madeleine Cooper's intent, and following that another convincing expert from the Health Service Executive, who outlined the government's current recommendations on childhood vaccinations, and produced proven studies discrediting any link between the MMR vaccine and autism, or indeed any other disorder.

Following her own appearance that afternoon, I'd invited Lucy back to the house for catch-up and a bite to eat as a thank you for agreeing to take the stand. I'd always known that today would be very hard for her, and understood that while she'd given us the necessary 'proof' we needed to show negligence, she'd also mitigated a lot of the damage our side had caused to the defence.

I guess I'd hoped that she wouldn't come across so overtly sympathetic towards Madeleine on the day, but deep down I'd always known that she'd try her utmost to do right by both of us.

And I couldn't help but admire her for that.

Now she stood at my sink, insistent on washing pots and

pans as I sat at my kitchen table – Rosie parked beside me in her wheelchair.

'Are you hungry, sweetheart?' I asked my daughter. She gave a small nod and raised her hand just a bit. She had been wanting to try to feed herself lately, and more often than not it resulted in a huge mess and major frustration on her part.

It was like she was completely aware of what she wanted to do and what she was capable of, but she just couldn't get her body to comply. There was a disconnect somewhere, one that she was trying her hardest to re-learn – but I didn't discourage her progress. I placed the spoon in her hand and pushed a bowl of mashed potatoes closer to her.

'So when is Declan coming?' asked Lucy, turning her attention to me. Quickly, she reached for some paper towels and brought them over, placing the roll stealthily on the table. While many people had expressed shock and discomfort at Rosie's condition over the past year, Lucy had not.

She continued to be the great friend she'd always been and I really didn't know what I'd do without her.

'He said he was going to change out of his suit.' I don't know why, but I felt myself flushing and I hoped Lucy didn't notice.

'Hmm,' she replied pointedly. Damn. So she had seen that blush. At the same moment a quiet knock came from the front as Declan entered the room and gave us all a smile.

'And speak of the devil.'

'Who's calling me a devil?' he joked, leaning over to ruffle Rosie's hair – which earned him a sparkling smile from my daughter – before sitting down on the other side of her wheelchair.

Though he was initially a little uncomfortable about my on-going friendship with Lucy given her relationship with Madeleine, Declan had since got to know her well enough to realise that, unlike his cousin, she was doing her best to remain partisan in the situation.

Tucking in to our food, we chatted easily, Declan all the while including Rosie in the conversation, even though she could hardly contribute. He'd been the same way with her ever since she'd come home, and I couldn't deny that it melted my heart a little.

We'd never spoken again about the embrace that had led to that photograph in the *Daily Record* last year, and had been extra careful to keep our distance ever since. These days we had a nice easy friendship, which was exactly how I liked it.

'I didn't get to talk to you after you left with Alison,' I said, deciding to broach a concern I had about today. 'I wasn't altogether sure what McGuinness was suggesting during Dr Ryan's testimony about the timeline of Rosie's infection. Am I reading too much into it?'

Declan accepted the glass of wine that Lucy had poured, took a sip and then nodded.

'He was pressing on that a bit, all right. And remember we had a few misgivings ourselves about how in-depth we wanted to get with that. In case something came back to bite us.'

'Like what though?' Lucy asked. 'Madeleine and Tom admitted from the start that Clara must have picked it up in Florida.'

I nodded. 'And Dr Ryan said today that tracing it back to one source, when only two people were affected, is practically impossible.'

'Maybe, but it's the defence's job to pick holes and introduce doubt,' said Declan, in between mouthfuls of mashed potato. 'They're merely trying to introduce the idea that it's impossible to prove where the infection was picked up.'

Lucy wiped her hands on a dishtowel. 'So they're just trying to make it look inconclusive? Like, yes, maybe the girls were at school together, but really either one could have passed it to the other?'

'Exactly. If so, then how can the judge categorically rule that the Coopers are to blame.'

'But they must be – Clara got sick three days before Rosie,' I protested, getting anxious now, even though I wasn't comfortable discussing this topic in front of Rosie when she couldn't participate in the conversation. But Hazel, her rehab nurse, insisted that she shouldn't be sheltered or made to feel isolated, because we had no real idea of what she did or didn't understand. And the more we included her, the easier – psychologically at least – her recovery would be.

I also knew Declan wasn't too keen on discussing the case in front of Lucy – friend or not.

'That may be so,' he said, his easy-going manner reassuring me somewhat, 'but in court, if the defence can find and pinpoint any weakness in our case then they will. And, Kate, I told you from the start that this was always going to come up. Remember the counterclaim?'

I nodded, remembering. But I still didn't like the idea of the defence trying to suggest that there was no way to prove that Clara had introduced the infection to Rosie. It made it too easy for the judge to let them off.

That couldn't happen – we couldn't lose – not after all the time and effort we'd spent getting this far. *Not to mention money* – the thought came unbidden and I swallowed hard.

My body felt exhausted, but my brain continued to feel on high alert and my mind wouldn't stop working.

'Is there anything else you need, Kate?' asked Lucy, evidently picking up on my concern. 'A cup of tea maybe?' She wouldn't stop pottering around the kitchen and I waved her over.

'Yes, come and sit down with us; you're making Declan nervous,' I joked. While I was used to her need to constantly be doing something, he wasn't and I could tell by the look on his face that it did make him uncomfortable.

'You'll get used to it.' I smiled, only realising a beat later how weird that sounded. This was a temporary situation; when I was no longer his client, I wouldn't see him any more so he wouldn't be getting used to anything. That thought left me a little confounded, not to mention wistful. This last year, I had got so used to having him around as a confidant and friend.

'Lucy knows my life better than I do sometimes,' I said looking at my friend, feeling thankful she was there. 'I don't know what I would do without her.' I reached out then and grasped her hand, giving it a squeeze. 'Thanks for being at court today and for the moral support – I know it's hard... with everything. But I do appreciate it.' I reached for my daughter's hand too. 'And Rosie appreciates all you've done for us too.'

Lucy smiled at the compliment. She never asked for thanks – even after Greg passed away – and she seemed to never tire of helping me. But I know she did appreciate basking a little in the attention – especially after the strain of today.

I was also glad to have moved away from my idiotic overfamiliar comment to Declan. However, if he was in the least bit fazed by what I'd said, he didn't show it.

Lucy, however, shot me a knowing look. She had of course in the meantime pumped me for information about our unusually close client/solicitor relationship as well as about that infamous picture in the newspaper. But I'd insisted repeatedly that there was nothing to tell.

Nothing at all.

Chapter 43

Madeleine tapped her fingers impatiently on the wooden table before her. It was only the third day of the trial, but yet it felt like the third year.

Her nerves were absolutely shot, and while she understood that it was standard to get through all of the plaintiff's witnesses first, it was beginning to feel like each and every person going on the stand had it in for her.

In particular, that Health Services representative yesterday, who seemed to be holding her personally responsible for the recent decline in MMR vaccination uptake that had the Health Board concerned about the herd immunity threshold. Which had even resulted in government pressure to bring this very trial date forward 'in the interest of public safety'.

That was all they needed, to be held responsible for a public health epidemic as well as Rosie O'Hara's plight. The judge really needed to hear from someone who would paint her and Tom in a more impartial and sympathetic light.

Because Madeleine had realised a long time ago that it wasn't just her and Tom's decision on vaccination that was on trial here – it was their parenting.

She stole a sidelong look at her husband and Matt Townsend. As per the norm, they had their heads pressed together with Michael McGuinness discussing strategy, and only rarely did they include her. This made her mad as well. The case was affecting her life... she was heavily involved... and she had lots of opinions – shouldn't she be included in these discussions too?

Not for the first time, Madeleine started to doubt that the team were taking the right direction. Every once in a while she thought that their barrister might display a flash of brilliance from a legal standpoint, but all too often she felt that they freely allowed the plaintiff's side to make everything too personal, so as to make circumstances more real and heart-breaking to the judge.

And their side was missing that.

This was a very personal thing too, and her and Tom's decision to not vaccinate the kids was not something they took lightly. They had to be able to convey that and put an end to the conspiracy theory nonsense that had been endlessly sprouted by the media and everyone else who disagreed with their stance.

Of course, she had said as much many times, but Matt and the barrister had said just 'wait until the plaintiff rests and then we'll have our say'. She guessed that she would have to trust them and believe Tom that his family's testimony would do the necessary in that regard. However, Madeleine suspected that no one was going to be able to hit that point home more than her.

Then again, she'd tried that last year with the blog post, hadn't she? Tried speaking from the heart and explaining her position – only for Tom and Matt to insist she take the piece down before it had made barely a ripple.

Hardly anyone had viewed it, and she was almost certain Kate hadn't, which was a shame. Because, more than anything,

Madeleine had wanted to get through to Kate and let her know
that she was so sorry for what had happened.

But she had never truly been allowed to have her say.

*

The plaintiff side duly confirmed that their case had rested,
and Matt Townsend was ready to start presenting the Coopers'
defence.

The last few days had been character assassinations of his
clients at best, and while Michael McGuinness had experienced
a few wins during cross-examination of the plaintiff's witnesses,
he felt Madeleine and Tom's frustration growing – not to mention
his own.

Of course, it wasn't uncommon for clients to get upset during
the trial, but he really needed to regain some lost footing here –
especially since the other side couldn't actually *prove* that it was
the Coopers' kid who spread the disease. Their very own witnesses
had confirmed that.

Looking down at his notes, he heard the defence barrister
announce to Judge Dowling that the first witness they would like
to call was Dr Terrence Pitt.

Matt had of course vetted this guy thoroughly in preparation,
but it was Tom who had found him initially. It seemed that Pitt
was used to appearing in courtrooms all over the world, and he
seemed very legit.

Hopefully his viewpoint would go a long way towards undoing
some of the damage that Roe & Co. had caused, and help present
his clients in a more rational, level-headed light.

Dr Pitt stood up from where he sat and regally made his way
forward, almost as if he expected to be saluted for his stature

within the medical community. After taking his spot on the witness stand, he was sworn in and then placed an expectant look on his face, awaiting the first question.

'Dr Pitt, for the benefit of the court, could you give us an overview of your professional biography?'

The man nodded and Matt assessed that the guy couldn't be more than forty-five – compared to the plaintiff's expert witnesses, he looked baby-faced.

'Of course, and I am happy to be here today, thank you,' stated Dr Pitt with some significant bluster, as if he was about to accept an Academy Award. 'I graduated with my medical degree from the University of California in Los Angeles in 2002. I am a ranking member of the California Medical Review Board and ran a lab as an Assistant Professor of Neurology at Cal Tech.'

'And can you tell us why you came to Dublin to testify today?'

Pitt nodded. 'Well, for the majority of my career I confess I believed in the power of vaccines, and I never questioned any of it until I met my wife. She is a chiropractor, and her experience truly opened my eyes to the world of holistic medicine and natural therapies.'

'And can you explain what you mean by that?' McGuinness asked.

'Of course,' Dr Pitt replied easily. 'Diseases like chicken pox, measles, mumps, rubella and the like are all part of the natural world. It is actually vaccines that are unnatural and man-made. The human body, for thousands of years, has had the capability and the biological ability to counter these viruses, to attack these attackers, essentially. And our bodies still do. Vaccines, in essence, are a manufactured solution to a problem that doesn't exist.'

'And where do you believe the danger lies with vaccines?' enquired the defence barrister.

'Vaccination requires unnatural chemicals and components to be applied to an otherwise healthy individual. Think about it: virtually all other invasive medical interventions occur only once someone has actually fallen ill. And this is where the risk lies – and I suspect that the plaintiff herself would agree with me on this—'

Patrick Nevin jumped up from where he sat. 'Objection. Speculation.'

'Sustained,' replied the judge a moment later.

'Yes, well, without bringing the plaintiff's opinion into the equation, can you please continue?' pressed McGuinness.

'Certainly,' replied Dr Pitt, continuing with his testimony. 'In my studies, I've found that the dangers of vaccines are just as real as the diseases they profess to fight; the effects of the ingredients used in some can themselves be substantial, lifelong and, for some people, life ending. For instance, vaccines have not been subject to intensive toxicity studies for many ingredients, such as aluminium and mercury, which are known as neurotoxins. Vaccines have also not been studied for adverse effects in the combinations in which they're given – for example, when multiple shots are given in a single day to infants and children. Furthermore, and perhaps most important of all, most vaccines are not even guaranteed to provide the benefit of immunity for which they are given.'

Matt was heartened to see the judge raise his eyebrows at this. 'Explain further please, Doctor,' he interjected. 'Do you have statistics to back that up?'

'I do, but the plaintiff's own expert agrees with me. I believe Dr Goring proclaimed that the MMR vaccine has a ninety-seven per cent effective rate in preventing measles. That means we can vaccinate a child but there is still a three per cent chance they will contract the virus at some point in their lives. And I have to stress that point – some people can still contract the illness, even if they have been vaccinated.'

'And you are quoting which study?' McGuinness coaxed.

'One conducted by the Centre for Disease Control and Prevention as a follow up to the California measles outbreak in 2014, again already mentioned in this court,' stated Dr Pitt matter-of-factly. 'Some people who have both recommended doses of the MMR vaccine are considered non-responders, meaning they can still get sick from the virus. So if you think about it, you cannot say that vaccines alone prevent a virus from spreading, as so many in the pro-vaccination community like to claim. To illustrate this: if there were one million people infected in an outbreak, ten thousand of the people who received vaccinations would still get sick. In the scheme of things, that's something worth thinking about. It completely undermines this so-called herd immunity, and the fact that disease is going to spread, regardless. The mere fact that more people don't get sick is a testament to nature alone.'

'Objection,' said Nevin, again. 'Speculation.'

'Overruled,' answered the judge just as quickly as before, and Townsend couldn't help but smirk. Pitt's testimony about vaccination effectiveness really was having an impact on the judge.

Looks like they were getting somewhere.

'Go on, Doctor,' encouraged Judge Dowling.

'I was about to say, this is nature at its best. Children *should* be contracting various infections. It strengthens humanity's immune system as a whole. This is survival of the fittest at its best. However, it's impossible to place blame on who spread what and who caught it, or when, because no one is at fault when nature is doing what it is supposed to do. Nature needs to thin the herd.'

Across the way, Matt heard Kate O'Hara gasp, realising that Pitt was implying that if her daughter had died, it would have been nature simply 'taking its course'.

Damn. Too harsh.

A rustle duly came from the media gallery and Matt Townsend winced, worried that Pitt might have taken things too far. Hopefully, McGuinness would steer him back on track.

'But, Dr Pitt, surely you are compassionate to the plight of the families in this courtroom – to the plight of all children who might be affected by this terrible disease—' The barrister was about to move on to another line of questioning, but Dr Pitt cut him off.

'I don't think you understand my point, sir. Children should be getting these infections,' he said, his voice raising. 'We do not need to inject chemicals into ourselves and our children in order to boost our immune system. I personally am a big fan of paleo-nutrition. My children eat foods that our ancestors have been eating for millions of years. This is the best way to protect. And then, you don't play into the hands of Big Pharma either. I completely support the Coopers' belief that governments, pharmaceutical companies and multinational corporations are not helping our children, but profiting from them.'

Shit… Matt Townsend's eyes opened wider as Dr Pitt became more inflamed and passionate in his speech. McGuinness held up a hand to quiet the man, but to no avail.

'You know, I have been watching the media coverage of this trial since the defendant sought out my help, and I have to say that that is one of the reasons I agreed to be here today,' the doctor continued. 'There is so much misguided anger at anti-vaccination proponents like the Coopers – and this needs to be redirected – not at ordinary parents but at the authorities who herd us all like sheep, and force us to needlessly consume chemicals and toxins so as to line their own pockets.'

'Dr Pitt, if you would allow me to redirect our conversation,' pleaded McGuinness, his words falling on deaf ears, Matt realised, worried.

'We need to be angry at big corporations. Sugary cereals, cookies and cupcakes lead to millions of deaths worldwide every year. At its worst, chicken pox, for instance, kills one hundred people annually. Only one hundred! We should be calling up Nestlé and Coca-Cola and complaining, *they* are the real killers. Why aren't we protesting their products, sending them hate mail? And that's before we even consider the fast food restaurants: tortured meat burgers, fries dipped in pesticide, milkshakes pumped full of hormones. Honestly, measles is a mere drop in the ocean of our kids' problems.'

Townsend could feel a murmur go through the courtroom. At this point, Pitt looked almost ready to spring up and start pounding on his chest. And alongside him, Matt saw his clients shoot him horrified glares. He didn't even want to look in Declan Roe's direction; it was likely the guy was tap dancing in his seat. Why didn't McGuinness get this guy to shut up?

'Dr Pitt, if you would be so kind…'

'And we should also be angry with the corporations for spewing pollution into the environment while they make our toxic laundry detergent to make our clothes smell nice while simultaneously poisoning us. It's *these* chemicals that cause autism, heart disease and cancer.'

'Dr Pitt,' admonished the judge, now looking less than impressed, 'I'll advise you to lower your voice and sit down, or I'll hold you in contempt.'

'And we should also be angry at our parents, the mothers who didn't breastfeed us or co-sleep with us. Instead, they stuffed our faces with pizza! And washed our clothes with fancy detergent that will likely cause us to have brain cancer—'

At that moment, a court bailiff, along with another security guard, approached Dr Pitt and, without further ado, escorted him from the stand. They led him out of the room while he continued to insist that vaccines weren't the problem, but that capitalism and the government were hell-bent on controlling everyone via chemical injections and Starbucks lattes.

Matt Townsend stood with an open mouth, looking at the back of the courtroom, unable to believe just what had happened. He couldn't believe that Pitt had been their first defence witness, or that the erudite man who'd presented so well over the phone in preparation for this trial was in fact certifiably unhinged.

So much for not painting the Coopers as conspiracy theorists – their very first witness was the personification of one.

As Judge Dowling demanded order in the court, and silence eventually reigned, Patrick Nevin stood up and humbly smoothed his tie.

'Your Honour, I believe it's fortunate that I have no questions.'

Chapter 44

Later that evening, Madeleine and Tom sat across from their solicitor at their dining room table in Knockroe.

The couple looked tired and dejected, and Matt Townsend equally so. They had been conducting a post-mortem on the day's events, Matt continuing to insist that they could rebound from the Pitt disaster.

For her part, Madeleine stayed silent and Tom was visibly sheepish.

'I can't believe I'm the one who found him,' he moaned. 'I just… he spoke so well when I first contacted him. And his credentials were so impressive. He seemed so spot on – I trusted him.'

'Well,' she said, pointedly, 'maybe you shouldn't believe everything you read online.'

Tom, who had had his head in his hands, looked up at her and nodded tiredly. He had no colour in his face and Madeleine noticed some new lines on his forehead.

'I really think that tomorrow we can regain some lost ground,' Matt insisted.

Just then, Clara entered the room and climbed into her mother's lap. Madeleine encircled her daughter in her arms and breathed in her smell. She had just taken a bath and smelled like strawberries.

In the background somewhere, Tom and Matt carried on and she struggled to pay attention. She was thoroughly exhausted. Regardless of what their solicitor said, she had begun to consider the reality – face up to the fact they were going to lose once the judge ruled against them.

The scope of it was truly mind boggling.

She had no idea what kind of damages amount Judge Dowling would award, and whether or not, when it all came down to it, they would lose their house. She thought about their pension funds, their investments and savings and also about their kids' college funds, wondering if they might be protected.

She could just about stomach the idea that her and Tom's future would be irreparably damaged, but her kids were innocent in all of this – they shouldn't be party to the damages, surely? Jake and Clara were still entitled to their own futures, weren't they?

Maybe not. She was no longer so sure. It was hard enough to digest that if anyone felt wronged by another person, or was judgemental of their personal choices, they could simply take what didn't belong to them.

Although, maybe it was better if she and Tom did lose everything – their house included. The last year had been bad enough and she didn't know how she was going to go on living in Knockroe after this was all over with anyway. Madeleine couldn't fathom the idea of bumping into Kate at the supermarket, or outside the school afterwards.

She suddenly tuned back into what Matt was saying. 'So, if we focus the testimony of Dr James—'

She cut him off. 'No, Matt, I think we're finished with experts. In fact, we are finished – full stop,' she said resolutely.

Tom and Matt both looked at her with confused expressions and her husband spoke first. 'What do you mean, hon? We've only just got started.'

She pulled Clara closer, and rested her cheek on her little girl's head. 'I mean, that up until this point, I have gone along with the strategy you two have laid out. I have exposed my children to ugliness, I have suffered through personal character assassinations, I have had it up to my ears listening to "experts" who turned out to be complete crackpots and, frankly, I've had enough.

'Matt, with all due respect, I believe you are approaching this wrong and have been from the very start. You've approached it all on a legal and not a personal level. And, Tom, the last time I checked, you aren't a solicitor. Neither am I. But, if there is one thing I do know and have always believed, that it's the personal – not the legal or medical – approach that is going to convince the judge, if we even still have a shot, that is. We need to show him – *everyone* – who Tom and I truly are, where we are coming from and why we've made the decisions we've made. And, to my mind, all of that talk about asking the other side to prove that Rosie picked it up from Clara feels wrong and is making us look even more unsympathetic.'

She paused for a moment and considered her next words carefully. 'I felt it myself when that doctor explained what Rosie's suffered, and what she could be facing for the rest of her life. I physically felt the fear that Kate as a mother must have felt all the way through this and now. Right then, *I* would have ruled against us.'

The two men remained silent for a moment as her words sank in.

'What do you want to do then?' Tom asked, his voice soft.

'I want to testify,' she said, her voice certain. 'I know we hoped that Fiona would be enough, but I want to talk directly about our decision-making process – much like I tried to in that blog post you were so adamant I take down. I know you're not keen on the idea, Matt, but I think I deserve a shot at explaining why painting us as monsters is just too simplistic, and that we are not the villains everyone thinks. I want to explain that yes, we made certain choices for our kids, but there are so many factors involved here. Each day, the more damaging testimony I listen to, the more I myself think that maybe I *am* a terrible mother. But I know I'm not. And, as it stands, this is not justice. This is nothing more than a spectacle – which I never wanted, and quite frankly I don't think Kate does either.'

Madeleine kissed Clara's head and whispered, 'Time for bed, sweetheart.'

Then she rose, holding her daughter's hand. 'So that's the way I feel, and that's what we are going to do. I've stood by long enough being told by you two that we need to do things this way, and that such and such is the best way forward. For me, it's time to face the music. And I won't take no for an answer.'

With that, Madeleine exited the room with Clara in tow.

As far as she was concerned, her long ago imposed vow of silence was officially over.

Chapter 45

The following morning, Fiona Marsh felt her hands shake as she was called to the stand.

Not normally a nervous or anxious person, she supposed she was just taken aback by the enormity of what was going on. She was well aware that all this was not going well for her brother and sister-in-law – and she was truly worried about them, their welfare, as well as the futures of her niece and nephew. Therefore, when last year they had asked her to appear as a witness at this trial, there was no way she could say no.

Yet, she still felt her stomach churn when she realised some of the questions she would be asked. Fiona cringed at the lens of scrutiny that her brother's family had already been under, not to mention the criticism they had received from the media and the general public.

She worried about opening herself and her own family up to the same type of hateful vitriol.

'Thank you for taking the time to attend court today, Mrs Marsh,' greeted Michael McGuinness, a pleasant smile on his face. Fiona still couldn't get over the fact that they really did wear those gowns and funny wigs in the courtroom. It was like something out of an episode of *Downton Abbey*.

'Thanks, and no problem.'

'I also know your own family members greatly appreciate you sharing your personal story with the court.'

Fiona nodded and glanced over to the defendant's table where Madeleine and Tom sat. They both offered her small, encouraging smiles.

'So, Mrs Marsh, you have two sons I believe?'

Trying to quell her nervousness, Fiona sat on her hands and said, 'Yes, Cameron is nine and Bryan, my youngest, is seven.'

'Tricky ages for boys, I believe,' commented McGuinness smiling.

Fiona shrugged and offered a genuine grin. 'They have their days but are good boys. I'm very lucky.'

'That's wonderful,' said the barrister. 'So, on to more… sensitive topics. It's my understanding that your eldest, Cameron—'

'Cam – he goes by Cam.'

'Sure. It's my understanding that Cam is vaccinated but Bryan is not?'

Fiona nodded. 'That's correct. When Cam was a baby, we followed HSE recommendations and had him vaccinated according to the usual childhood immunisation programme. MMR, meningitis… all of that. For Bryan, though, we decided to take a different route with the MMR.'

Michael McGuinness placed his hands on the waist-high wooden barrier that surrounded the witness stand. 'And can you explain why you and your husband decided upon such different courses of action?'

'Of course,' answered Fiona, some of her nervousness leaving her body. She felt herself regaining her confidence. She had no problem at all explaining her position with this. 'When Cam was a baby, he was just the… loveliest… little boy. So affectionate, so caring, so…' she seemed to search for the word, '… engaged. He was handsy.' She smiled. 'That's what we nicknamed him, Handsy. He was always touching you, asking for hugs, wanting to be held. We felt so incredibly lucky. I know I'm his mother, and all mothers think their kids are the best in the world, but he was so wonderful. He had these lovely little chubby cheeks, and just…' She gave a small laugh and blushed. 'I'm sorry, that's probably irrelevant. Anyway, he was just a joy. Such a lovely pleasant baby – everyone said the same. Madeleine's Jake is the same age, just a couple of months younger, but more of a handful at the time, and I remember her saying, "Why can't he be like Cam?"'

She looked over at Madeleine, tears forming in her eyes at the memory.

Then she cleared her throat. 'Now, I should reiterate that my son is *still* wonderful and I love him just as much and just the same. It's just that… he changed. When he was thirteen months old, we took him for the MMR vaccination as scheduled. And within a day or so – my husband John and I saw this happening with our very own eyes this… almost… transformation of sorts occurred. That's the best way to describe it. He became withdrawn… aloof, even. He stopped talking. Up until then, he was jabbering and chattering all the time, learning how to talk and communicate. And then he just… wasn't. What's more it was like a light went out behind his eyes, almost like someone had pulled a plug somewhere. He wasn't expressive. Suddenly, in no time at all, he was a different child.'

'And how did you and your husband react to this?'

Fiona shook her head at the memory. 'Well, to put it bluntly, we freaked out. This obvious and sudden change in his demeanour terrified us. At first we thought maybe he bumped his head or perhaps swallowed something poisonous, got into something he shouldn't have. We took him to the GP and they ran all kinds of tests. And, eventually, we found out what was wrong.'

McGuinness waited expectantly. 'What did the doctors say?'

'That my son was on the spectrum, the autism spectrum.' Fiona's eyes welled with tears then, and she hastily wiped away one that had escaped her left eye. 'It completely threw us for a loop. But you know, it's not like we loved him any less after. Never anything like that. It just… caught us unprepared. You never expect to wake up one day and realise your entire life has changed. No parent wants to face that. Ever.'

Fiona looked at Kate with sad eyes then and the exchange did not go unnoticed by the judge.

Glancing at the media gallery, Matt Townsend was glad to see they were all paying rapt attention. Fiona's story was affecting them. Touching them emotionally. This was a good thing.

Finally.

'So what did you do then?' asked the barrister, continuing on.

'Well, we were really trying to figure out how this happened. What might have triggered it. Of course, we were first-time parents, but still we felt like we were doing the right things with his development. And then my husband started doing some other research, and we kept coming back to the vaccine issue.' She paused. 'Now, I don't want it to sound like I'm anti-science. I'm not. That's not the case at all. But something wasn't adding up to us the more that we read, the more we learned. And yes, I am well aware that this sort of thing has been debated at length much like we are doing now. But I was facing this in real life – my everyday life. One day my child was fine, the next he wasn't – and the only thing outside of the norm that had happened in between was the MMR vaccination. My GP assured us that this wasn't the case and that vaccines couldn't possibly cause this sort of condition. He quoted from medical journals and gave me all of these explanations. Yet I felt like I was being fed an official line.' She swallowed hard. 'Don't get me wrong, my husband and I weren't looking to blame or sue anyone. That's not our style. Wanting to hit back because we're angry.'

Brilliant... Matt thought, as an almost perfectly timed pause allowed that idea to sink in.

'In any case, we listened to what the doctors said, but when Bryan was born, we went a different route, and to a different GP actually. Someone who wouldn't force us or try to guilt us into vaccinating again.'

'And has Bryan suffered any adverse effects from not being vaccinated?' enquired McGuinness.

Fiona shook her head. 'No. He's a healthy, vibrant little boy who loves his brother, his cousins, everyone. He's a great child. But Cam is too. It's just Cam, well, like I said, he's a little bit different. But he's still a fantastic boy, and we were lucky to find him a really good school. We deal with it. We encourage him. We let him know just how loved he is.'

'How did your family members, specifically the defendants, react to the situation within your family?'

Fiona looked at her brother and sister-in-law and smiled sadly. 'Obviously I can't speak for Tom and Madeleine personally. But I do know that Cam's situation hugely affected their own approach.' She directed her attention back to the barrister. 'Like I said, there's only a couple of months between Jake and Cameron, and we were going through lots of the emotional stuff, trying to come to grips with what had happened, right when Jake was due his first MMR shot. So who could blame them for thinking twice?'

At this, Patrick Nevin jumped up. 'Objection… speculation.'

'Fine, Mr Nevin. Sustained. Mrs Marsh, please continue without speculating on the defendant's position.'

'Sure, I'm sorry. I didn't mean… Look, all I know is, something happened to Cam, and Tom and Madeleine saw it happen – they were right next to me, supporting me. And when the time came for them to make a choice with their own children, they had to take it into account. And so they made a choice not to vaccinate. Just as my husband and I did with our youngest.'

McGuinness nodded solemnly. 'Indeed. Every parent hopes to do what they feel is right for their kids. Absolutely.'

'And it's not as if they – or we – broke the law either,' Fiona continued, impassioned. 'That's why I think all of this is so unfair. There is no law in Ireland that says you have to vaccinate your kids. It's a personal choice. And I fully support that choice – as well as Tom and Madeleine's right as parents to make it.'

'Thank you, Mrs Marsh. No further questions.'

'Mr Nevin?' asked the judge.

Matt Townsend held his breath.

'Thank you, but we have no questions for the witness at this time.'

Chapter 46

'*Today, Tom Cooper's sister, Fiona Marsh, took the stand in defence of her in-laws' decision to not vaccinate their son Jake and daughter, Clara.*

'*Ms Marsh gave a stirring and heartfelt account of her own son's autism diagnosis, and its possible connection to his receipt of the MMR vaccine when he was a mere thirteen months old. Her testimony cut through early beliefs that the Cooper family's decision was borne of conspiracy theories and governmental cover-ups, and for the first time put a very human face on the real life issues the family has faced.*

'*I believe, madam, that you have been supporting Kate O'Hara's cause, and following this situation closely? Can you share your thoughts on the trial so far with RTE News viewers?*'

'*Oh yes, from day one, I've been paying attention. And I've been standing here since the trial started. This is a major story and it's happening right in our backyard. It's a big deal.*'

'*Indeed it is. And I'm assuming from your placard that you in are in support of Kate O'Hara?*'

'*Yes. I have supported Kate from the very beginning. I feel so terrible for her and her little girl.*'

'*And what do you think of today's information? That the Coopers may have some sound reasoning for not vaccinating their children?*'

'*Well, I mean, it's tough. You can't help but feel bad for them too. After all, every parent just wants to protect their kids. And if they had firsthand experience with their nephew developing autism because of vaccines... well, I'm a mother – that might give me pause too.*'

'*Yet medical professionals have stated, repeatedly, that there is no correlation between vaccinations and the chance of developing autism or any other condition. Are you saying that those medical professionals – doctors and experts all of them – are wrong?*'

'*I'm not saying they are necessarily wrong, but they might not be right either. I mean, if I saw my child change from one day to the next, I might start to think that the vaccine caused it too. I think as parents we have to trust our instincts. And I think there is a lot of stuff that the general public isn't told, lots of cover-ups. This could be one of them.*'

'*It sounds as if you might be changing your stance on this? Is that correct?*'

'*Well, I don't know if I would say I'm changing it, but everything certainly doesn't feel so black and white. I guess there are two sides to every story.*'

'*Interesting commentary from a bystander in the crowd here outside High Court buildings. Begging the question: what does this mean for Kate O'Hara's case? Is the tide of public opinion shifting in favour of the defendants? And most important of all, how is all of this playing to the judge? Hannah Slattery, RTE News.*'

Declan and I watched the evening news reports from my kitchen table, Rosie between us in her wheelchair.

Whatever about public opinion, truth be told, Fiona Marsh's testimony had made a huge impact on me. I also thought that the judge seemed relieved to finally hear something positive about Madeleine and her family, and for once I was starting to understand why the vaccination issue hadn't been so clear cut for them.

Of course, I didn't say anything like that to Declan. He had optimism in spades and kept telling me that everything was going great.

While I was working very hard to take his advice, I was also trying to envision my and Rosie's future once this case was over.

Regardless of what happened, I had started to think about the idea that we would probably have to move. Outside of the obvious discomfort of living in a community where I could possibly run into the family I'd sued, I knew we couldn't continue living in this house, which being on two floors was wholly inappropriate for Rosie's incapacitation.

There must have been something distant in my expression, because Declan abruptly stopped talking.

'Hey,' he said gently. 'Are you there? You seem a million miles away this evening.'

I offered him a tired smile. 'Sorry.' I pulled the bowl of chicken soup I'd been helping Rosie with closer to me and glanced around, trying to organise my thoughts.

Seemingly reading my mind, Declan jumped up. 'I'll get a napkin,' he offered and grabbed the kitchen roll.

He returned to me a moment later and put the napkin in front of Rosie. I was about to mutter an automatic thanks but was startled when she in a somewhat mumbled and garbled way got in before me. 'Thank you.'

My mouth dropped open and my heart lifted as I looked

from Rosie to Declan in delight. 'Good girl, sweetheart, that was amazing!'

Whenever she initiated communication or worked to say something – which she tried really hard to do – I felt hope spring from within me. She was getting there and that meant so much.

'You are so welcome, Rosie,' replied Declan with a grin, placing a gentle hand on her shoulder. 'Any time.'

I would be lying if I said I didn't like having him around and sharing these little moments of positivity with him. There was something so comforting about his presence – the way he seemed to fill a room. Thankfully, Rosie seemed to feel the same way.

Interrupting my thoughts, he asked, 'Are you hungry, Kate? Can I get you anything?'

He seemed to always be aware of what and how often I was eating. I knew I could stand to put on a few pounds – it's just sometimes I didn't have the time or the appetite to eat three square meals a day. Regardless, I was touched by his concern.

'I will after I put her to bed,' I said quietly. 'And... thank you.'

For the next few minutes the three of us sat in companionable silence as Rosie finished her soup. While Hazel was looking after her during the trial, I was determined to use her only when I wasn't around – not just because I was hoping to achieve a new normal, but also to try control the scarily expensive medical care bills appearing on a monthly basis.

I picked up the bowl and stood to take it to the sink at the same moment that Rosie offered up a pretty large yawn. She got tired much earlier these days, another side effect of the trauma her brain had suffered.

'Ready for bed, sweetheart?' I asked.

Declan took the bowl out of my hands without asking and, smiling gratefully, I grasped the handles of her wheelchair and pushed her across the wooden floor to the base of the stairs. Unclipping the strap, I put my arms around her in an effort to lift her up (my daughter wasn't heavy, but she was no longer as easy to carry as she used to be).

Declan's touch on my back caused me to pause and I turned around to face him.

'I can carry her up, if you're OK with that?'

Glancing at his broad shoulders and strong arms, I welcomed the help. 'If you're sure you don't mind? I hate to…'

'Not in the least.' He got close to Rosie and smiled. 'As long as you don't either, Rosie?' Her eyes brightened immediately and I knew she was fine with it too. 'I'm going to help you up to your room, OK?'

Seconds later, she was cradled easily in his arms and I was following them up the stairs. I couldn't deny that it was lovely having someone ready to take on some of the load that had been piling on my shoulders.

Knowing the layout of my house, Declan carried Rosie into the bathroom and placed her in a special chair so I could help her brush her teeth and ready her for bed. He then retreated to the hallway, and I entered the room and stood next to my daughter, going through her usual bedtime ritual. Then when we were ready, Declan re-entered the bathroom and picked Rosie up, taking her to her room where he laid her gently on her bed, amongst all her dinosaur posters.

He stood in the doorway as I kissed her goodnight and sang her favourite night-time lullaby. I'd stopped doing that shortly after her fifth birthday, when she'd joked that she was 'too cool' for that kind of thing, but had resumed last year when she came home from the hospital. I wasn't entirely sure if it was more soothing for her or me.

Soon her eyelids grew heavy, but she managed to raise a small hand and place it on my cheek. My throat closed over with emotion. 'Goodnight, sweetheart,' I said, trying to fight back tears. 'Sleep tight.'

By the time I returned to the hallway, I could already hear Rosie's quiet snores. She was out for the count.

Declan was waiting at the top of the stairs. 'She OK?' he whispered, as we headed back down together.

'She's fine. Whacked. You're really good with kids,' I commented.

'I'm happy to help, Kate. Rosie's a great child. She deserves... so much.' He paused then on the step below me and met my gaze. 'So do you.'

Suddenly, all of the air seemed to be sucked out of the room, and I felt my breath catch in my throat as Declan looked up at me with gentle eyes.

'Thanks, I...'

Just then, the doorbell rang and I jumped, my mind flooded with confusion and embarrassment. With a bright red face – I felt like I was on fire – I sputtered out the words, 'Someone's at the door.'

Thanks for that, Captain Obvious...

I stole a glance at his face, trying to determine what I saw. Was that embarrassment? Or concern in the form of worry and confusion...

Not wanting to examine it too closely, I marched down the steps past him and went to the door.

Out front, under the soft glow of the porch light, stood Alison. Stealing a glance at my watch, I realised that it was a bit late for her to be making house calls, or indeed for her brother to be at a client's house.

'Alison, hi.' I stood back to let her inside and the moment she did so her eyebrows raised at the appearance of Declan, walking slowly down the stairs. His hair looked a little mussed after his efforts in carrying Rosie and a single dark lock spilled over his forehead.

Like Superman.

I worked to arrange my expression and control it, but regardless, I felt Alison's curious gaze on us both.

'Sorry – we were just putting Rosie to bed. I mean, Declan helped carry her up the stairs.'

His sister smiled, a knowing twinkle in her eye.

'What's going on, Alison?' Declan asked evenly, all business.

She looked at us both and unfurled a piece of paper. 'I just dropped by the office. The defence has issued an addition to the witness roster for tomorrow. Madeleine Cooper is going to testify.'

Chapter 47

On Friday morning, Madeleine held her head high as she walked to the witness stand. She knew that this was a risky move, but it was one that she had to take.

The judge, the media and, most of all, Kate needed to hear from her.

Her sister-in-law had already been brave and done an incredible job, and her great friend Lucy had done her utmost to paint her in a decent light. Now, she had to top their performances and make the case for why she, and especially her family, were not guilty of negligence, and while they might be considered indirectly responsible for this, their decision not to vaccinate Jake and Clara did not make them monsters.

Eschewing the conservative suits she'd worn to court so far, today she wore a flowing floral skirt and light pink cashmere polo neck sweater that was much more her usual day-to-day style. She smoothed the skirt carefully as she took her seat.

Looking around the courtroom, she adjusted to the change in landscape of the room from this point of view, and decided that this was how a pet goldfish must feel like in a fish tank.

'Mrs Cooper – Madeleine – thank you for taking the stand

today and for your willingness to share your testimony with the court.'

Nodding at Michael McGuinness, she clasped her hands in her lap and tried to remain calm.

But her palms were sweating.

'Madeleine, I would like to begin by recounting your own experience of March twentieth last year when Clara fell ill,' the barrister said. 'Can you talk us through the events of that day?'

'Yes. Clara had been a little sniffly the night before, and my husband commented that she might be coming down with chicken pox. The school had sent a note home – another girl in my daughter's class had come down with it that week – so we knew that it was going round and I was prepared for the fact that Clara might well catch it. She'd never had the disease before but Jake, my eldest, had.'

'Indeed. And how did you feel about that?'

Madeleine decided to be circumspect. She'd agonised over how she should play it today, especially knowing that she and Tom had always been considered unconventional, or even cavalier, in their approach. And as that same approach had been criticised long and hard well before this whole thing started, she felt there was no point in trying to paint things any differently to how she saw them. The judge, and indeed the media, would see right through that. 'No parent likes to see their child ill,' she said, 'but these diseases, particularly amongst school-going children, are almost a rite of passage.'

'I see. So the idea of Clara contracting such a disease didn't bother you.'

'Not at all. Chicken pox in particular is an uncomfortable, but relatively harmless illness. In fact, many parents hold chicken pox parties so they can control when their children fall ill with it, and thus can make work arrangements around this.'

'Just for clarification, you're saying that some parents arrange to actually infect their children on purpose?'

'Correct. In my experience, this occurs often when there are a few siblings involved so that all children in the house can be cared for at the same time, and particularly in the case of working parents, so that no further time off is needed to deal with the same illness subsequently. But I am lucky in the sense that I work from home, so I don't need to plan around these things as much as most.'

'But you did have a work commitment on the morning of March twentieth, did you not?'

Madeleine took a deep breath. 'On that particular morning, yes I did. The nature of my work sometimes necessitates media appearances, which by their nature are often time sensitive and last minute.'

'But you were aware of this prior commitment on Monday evening were you not?' McGuinness probed.

'I was, yes. But chicken pox usually takes a couple of days to develop and I'd hoped, as did my husband, that Clara's sniffles were the result of her immune system trying to fight off the numerous bugs and infections all school-going kids are exposed to. As I'm sure most parents know, if you worried about every little cough and sneeze, you'd never be able to sleep a wink.'

She winced a little, realising that last remark had come out a little more glibly than she'd intended, and she hoped it hadn't made her come across as uncaring. But she got the sense that the judge was a bit of a no-nonsense sort who wouldn't be inclined to mollycoddle every child with a runny nose, and she needed him to view her as a competent, sensible parent and not the feckless irresponsible monster the media, and indeed Kate's solicitors, had painted her thus far.

And Madeleine also felt it was especially important to get a mention of Tom in there too, so everyone could see that both parents were equally unconcerned about Clara's prognosis, so much so that they both intended to carry on the following day as planned.

'OK, so you assumed, although you couldn't yet be sure, that Clara might be coming down with chicken pox?'

'Based on the school note we'd received, I thought this was a reasonable assumption, though of course I couldn't be sure. Like I said, there are always various bugs going round at all times. She could just as easily have been coming down with a common cold. Or nothing at all.' She paused then. 'But, as we know now, it wasn't quite that simple and, of course, with the benefit of hindsight—'

'Objection. The witness is illustrating hindsight bias.'

'Agreed, Counsel,' said the judge, before turning to address her. 'Mrs Cooper, if you can, try to continue your testimony without referring to the outcome, so as not to distort your recollection of events.'

Madeleine swallowed hard. Damn. Matt Townsend had warned her about this, that hindsight bias was a cognitive phenomenon that could be especially damaging in a defence situation. She needed to focus her testimony on how things actually happened rather than try to alter them based on her knowledge of the outcome.

She cleared her throat. 'Sure. I'm sorry.'

The defence barrister helped her along. 'So on the morning of March twentieth, your family got ready for the day as normal. Was there any further development or deterioration in Clara's condition – perhaps a difficult night or any sickness?'

'No, nothing at all. We went to her grandmother's house after dinner, and she even seemed to brighten a little as the evening went on. I gave her some paracetamol as a precaution before bedtime, and had her eat an orange and some blackberries to boost up her levels of vitamin C...'

This earned a titter from the media gallery and Madeleine flushed despite herself. What, were they laughing at her naivety in attempting to, God forbid, use a natural means of boosting her child's immune system? Talk about hindsight bias...

'OK, so Clara showed no sign of further deterioration. Talk us through what happened the following morning.'

'She woke up, again a little sniffly but, for the most part, she seemed OK. She refused breakfast, but can be a fussy eater at the best of times, so this didn't ring any alarm bells.'

'So, to your mind, there was still no outward reason to keep her home from school?'

Madeleine paused. 'That's correct. So I made a call. Just like every parent up and down the country would do in a situation like this. I can't deny that she was a bit off but seemed OK, and I honestly didn't see any reason to keep her home. And my husband and I already had other commitments, responsibilities that couldn't be cancelled last minute for something that we both felt was your typical childhood sniffles situation. And you have to understand that more often than not, kids are troopers – they can be at death's door one minute and then bounce back the next as if nothing had happened.' Again, she grimaced inside, wishing for Kate's sake, that she'd phrased that a little better. But the room was so quiet when she was speaking, and everyone clearly playing close attention, that she felt she was coming across OK.

'Yet you still decided to engage your friend Lucy as backup, just in case, did you not?'

'That's correct; of course I wasn't going to head off that morning without a care in the world. And because on that particular morning I would be away, I needed to ensure that someone would be there for Clara just in case she did happen to get worse.'

Madeleine was very careful this time not to evoke hindsight but it was nigh on impossible. If she'd known then what she knew now, obviously things would have been very different...

'Where were you and how did you feel when the school phoned to let you know Clara had indeed got worse?'

'I was at the Channel 2 studio about to go live. I was upset naturally, and felt guilty for not being there the one time she needed me. But I also knew she was in good hands with Lucy and, in fairness to Clara, she's not needy or clingy, neither of my kids are.'

'Because, as Mrs Murphy herself testified just a few days ago, you raised them to be confident, independent—'

'Objection. Irrelevant and shamelessly misleading!'

'Sustained. Counsel, you're on dangerous ground with that nonsense. I won't tolerate it.'

'My apologies, Judge. I was merely trying to help illustrate that Mrs Cooper was acting in accordance with her daughter's behaviour and personality.' He turned back to Madeleine.

'So, let's continue. Far from being negligent or wilfully irresponsible, you took the necessary steps to ensure your daughter was taken care of should she become ill.'

'Counsel...' the judge warned, but for her part Madeleine was buoyed by the defence barrister's bravery. It made the whole thing come across so much more reasonable.

'Duly noted, Judge, and again my apologies. Mrs Cooper, tell us what happened afterwards when you returned from your work commitment in Dublin?'

Feeling heartened by how things were going so far, Madeleine continued, her voice becoming more confident. 'Lucy was good enough to stay with Clara at my house for the hour or so it took me to get home, and after that I kept her in bed, gave her some more Paracetamol and kept a close eye on her to see how things would develop. Obviously I kept her home from school from thereon in. I began operating under the assumption that it must in fact be chicken pox – after all, it was going around. But then her temperature spiked and I became concerned, though not enough to take her to the doctor or anything. My feeling was that these things had to take their course.'

'And when did you discover the true nature of Clara's illness?'

'It was a few days later. I was tending to Clara at home when I received a call from Lucy. She called to tell me that Rosie O'Hara had gotten sick too and I told her that I wasn't too surprised, especially when chicken pox is so contagious. But then she mentioned that Rosie had already had it a couple of years before. At the same time, I didn't think that was particularly odd either; I believe some kids can get different variants of a disease more than once. But Lucy told me that wasn't the case, and urged me to check Clara's chest for spots. It seemed Rosie's mum had very quickly recognised her own daughter's symptoms as measles. She's a nurse, of course, so she would know.'

McGuinness considered this information. 'And how did you feel then?'

'Well, I was taken aback. And worried obviously, as well as annoyed at myself too for missing it. It had been some time since I'd come across measles before though, a good six years previous when Jake was a baby, so it wasn't foremost in my mind. And I immediately thought about the holiday we'd taken to Florida over Easter, where there'd been news of a small measles outbreak, and wondered if she could have picked it up there, or on the flight back even.' Despite Matt's, and indeed Tom's, advice, she thought it best to own up to the idea that Clara was likely the source of the infection, because she felt the alternative was just too damaging.

'So I immediately pulled my son out of school too. Even though Jake had already had the disease he could still be carrying it, and I didn't want to put other kids at risk.' Her voice was earnest, and Madeleine didn't think there could be anyone in the courtroom who believed she wasn't telling the truth.

'Responsible move,' commented McGuinness, while Madeleine waited for the other side's barrister to object.

But Patrick Nevin didn't, because what was there to object about? She had acted responsibly, based on her knowledge of events at the time.

Hindsight.

Michael McGuinness looked at Madeleine thoughtfully. 'So you did wonder if Clara might have picked it up in Florida, but how could you know for sure? As previous witnesses already mentioned it is not easy to locate Patient Zero.' The defence barrister still wasn't quite willing to give up the proof angle.

'That is correct, but from what I understand, our time there did coincide with the incubation period for the disease.'

Nevin stood up. 'I object. Speculation. Mrs Cooper is not a medical professional.'

She rolled her eyes inwardly, wondering how she was supposed to win when just then she was effectively playing devil's advocate for the other side.

'Sustained,' replied the judge.

'But, looking at the timeline, it seems a bit of a reach to automatically assume Clara infected Rosie, doesn't it? Couldn't it just as easily have been the other way round?'

'Objection! Speculation!' shouted Nevin.

'Sustained,' replied the judge. 'May I remind you, Counsel, that the source or origin of the infection is not under discussion here, rather the question of whether or not Mrs Cooper was negligent in sending her daughter to school given the risk her unvaccinated status posed. Please refrain from commenting or alluding to the source.'

'Apologies, Judge. It won't happen again.' He turned back to the witness. 'Mrs Cooper... Madeleine, this last year has been tough on your family, hasn't it?'

Grimacing, Madeleine shook her head sadly. 'It's not just about my family. I know this hasn't been easy for Kate O'Hara or Rosie either. And maybe I can understand how frustrated and out of control all of this must feel – she lost her husband a few years back, and now this terrible situation with her daughter. I also suspect that she's had some people in her ear, giving her bad advice. But I know all of us could have handled this whole situation better, myself included. When it was evident that both Clara and Rosie were sick, I should have made more of an effort to help Kate – we could have helped each other. I know I'm not supposed to talk about hindsight, but there's no denying that if I could go back to that morning and change things I would. But, well, all I can say now is that it's been a trying and scary time for both of us, but we can't change the past.'

Finally, she'd had the chance to say this to Kate, to speak directly to her. Madeleine tried to meet the other woman's gaze as she did so, but Kate kept her eyes fixed on a spot somewhere else in the room, away from the witness stand. She would give anything to be able to read what was in her mind just then. Couldn't she see that Madeleine had never meant for any of this to happen, had done nothing wrong and was desperately sorry about the outcome?

'Speaking of moving forward, remind us of the timeline of

Clara's illness and when you became aware that she had measles?'
McGuinness went on, swiftly changing the subject and she guessed
the barrister was concerned she was being almost too sympathetic
to the plaintiff's position. Time to get back on track.

'Clara started showing symptoms of… something on Monday
evening, and she came home from school Tuesday morning. It was
Friday by the time I actually realised she had measles.'

The implication was clear. There was no way Madeleine had
sent Clara to school knowing she was measles infectious.

'Thank you very much, Mrs Cooper,' said the defence barrister.
'No further questions.'

Chapter 48

She was good, Declan thought. Likeable even.

But, of course, this lady had lots of experience in playing to the cameras, hadn't she? And like any shamed media personality tasked with preserving their reputation, Madeleine Cooper had performed well and played her part to perfection as the sympathetic, reasonable parent who had made quick decisions while at the same time openly admitting she hadn't done everything right.

A stark contrast to the woman who'd issued a counterclaim accusing Kate of slander and defamation.

Declan couldn't wait for Nevin to start in their side's cross-examination, although he also hoped the barrister did not come across as overly aggressive. The media had been dancing gleefully on this woman's grave for the past year, and he knew everyone, including the judge, had been very eager to hear her side of the story.

'Mrs Cooper,' Patrick Nevin began smoothly. 'Good afternoon.'

'Please, call me Madeleine,' she replied, evidently feeling a lot more comfortable.

'Madeleine, of course,' said the barrister with a smile. 'So, Madeleine, you stated previously that as soon as you realised your daughter had contracted measles, you took your son out of Applewood primary school right away.'

'Yes, that's correct. I kept Jake at home as soon as I knew for sure that Clara had the disease.'

'Despite the fact that Jake had contracted the disease previously?'

'Yes, but he could still transmit the infection, I knew that. But no other children from the school came down with it, thank goodness.'

'Thank goodness indeed,' said Nevin carefully. 'Now, you also said that, as a parent, you wouldn't want to put other children at risk.'

Madeleine nodded in agreement. 'Of course. It goes without saying that no parent wants to see a child get sick – no matter if it's theirs or someone else's.'

'Indeed. But, Mrs Cooper, you are surely aware that you put other children at risk of this every day because of your decision to not vaccinate yours?'

'Objection!' called out Michael McGuinness. 'Argumentative.'

'Overruled,' said the judge. 'Answer the question please, Mrs Cooper.'

'I don't believe so actually,' answered Madeleine, lifting her chin a little. 'That also depends on parental decisions for the child in question.'

'Such as?'

'Such as whether that parent decides to vaccinate their own child. Either way, it is none of my business, nor is it up to me to interfere. There is no law against not vaccinating children in Ireland.'

'I am not looking to discuss other parents' decisions regarding vaccination as a point of law, or otherwise, but rather the facts,' replied Nevin. 'Based on previous testimony of medical professionals in this court, do you or do you not understand the concept of herd immunity, and how in not vaccinating your children, you compromise this and put other – particularly more vulnerable – members of the public at risk?'

'Mr Nevin, I believe the same question could be asked of your own client. After all, her daughter is not vaccinated either.' Declan noticed the irritation in Madeleine's voice here as she shot a glance in Kate's direction.

'But my client is not on the stand, Mrs Cooper. Please, answer the question.'

Visibly stiffening, Madeleine rearranged her features carefully.

'Mrs Cooper?' Judge Dowling said. 'Your response?'

'My choices as a parent are my choices, and indeed my husband's,' stated Madeleine crisply. 'Just as Ms O'Hara and her late husband chose not to vaccinate their daughter based on evidence that doing so could impact their child's health, so too, did my husband and I. Which is our right. No laws were broken.'

Nevin seemed to consider the witness as he formulated his next question.

'Yet isn't it true, Mrs Cooper – Madeleine – that you have somewhat of a reputation, even publicly, for being cavalier about not just your own children's safety, but others' too?'

'I'm not sure what you're referring to,' she answered quickly, but Declan was pretty sure that she knew *exactly* what was coming. Cue *Mad Mum* and the litany of damaging articles that so readily painted her as a self-confessed laissez-faire parent.

'While I have much to draw on, I'm referring in particular to one appearance on the very same TV show that necessitated your absence on the morning of your daughter's illness,' Nevin went on, 'whereby you proclaimed live on the show that "children don't need to be mollycoddled, they *should* get scraped and cut up now and again… it helps with their development". Are these not your own words, Mrs Cooper?'

'They are, but they were uttered in the context of an article I'd written about playgrounds and how parents can sometimes be too overprotective.'

'And do you still stand by those words today?' Nevin asked.

She nodded. 'In the context in which they were uttered, yes I do.'

'So you admit that you are an advocate of leaving children unprotected, and left at the whims of—'

'Objection. Mrs Cooper has already stated that her words refer to a specific context, not the issue at hand.'

The judge sighed. 'Where are you going with this, Counsel?' he asked.

'Judge, I am trying to establish a pattern in Mrs Cooper's attitude and behaviour towards risk, specifically pertaining to children. She appears to have a history of advocating dangerous parenting and an irresponsible attitude to child protection—'

'That is absolutely not true!' Madeleine cut in, becoming somewhat rattled now. 'For goodness' sake, that article related to one thing and one thing only. Children's welfare is *always* a parent's priority, every minute of the day. We lose sleep over it, we worry and we fret because we are constantly trying to live up to what's best. Endless so-called "rules" laid down by doctors, health experts, well-meaning strangers, or other parents, who love to tell us what we're doing wrong, or how our kids *should* be behaving at that age. And then, just in case that's not enough, continuous judgement on top of it all! So how can you honestly stand there and tell me that a little bit of leeway once in a while is a bad thing for either a child or a parent?'

Declan saw how Madeleine now commanded every pair of
eyes in the room. It was a stirring speech and she did make some
good points, but he got the sense that she was only managing to
dig herself in deeper where Nevin was concerned.

'Quite the diatribe, Mrs Cooper, thank you. However, I believe
my point still stands that your decisions as a parent aren't always
in the interests of protecting other children, and this is personified
by your approach to the vaccination issue, is it not?'

Madeleine was stony faced. 'I believe I've already explained
myself at length in that regard.'

'Let's move on. So, in relation to the same vaccination issue,
you said earlier that you felt other parents' decisions in this regard
were equally important. Yet isn't also true that you immediately
took some level of responsibility for Rosie O'Hara's measles
infection – specifically while she was in the hospital?'

Madeleine wore a neutral expression. 'Obviously I felt terrible
for what Kate and Rosie were going through. I was very worried
and hugely sympathetic – I still am.'

The barrister nodded at her response. 'Of course, but I asked
you if you felt responsible.'

Quickly, Madeleine replied, 'It wasn't that I felt directly responsible... I just felt bad that Clara had got over her own illness
so well and Rosie didn't. But it wasn't anyone's fault. It just...
happened.'

At this, Nevin seemed to smirk ever so slightly as he motioned
to Alison. He looked to the judge. 'I would like to submit the following evidence for the court's consideration, namely a blog post
that Mrs Cooper published for public consumption shortly after
Ms O'Hara issued legal proceedings.' Declan studied Madeleine's
face when a written transcript of the blog was produced. He
couldn't be sure but he thought he spotted a flash of panic in her

eyes. 'Mrs Cooper, would you like to read these words as written by you?'

She looked to Townsend then, as if for guidance, and he seemed to shake his head no. Declan was flabbergasted. Surely he'd prepared his client for this possibility, and must have known that their side would have the errant blog post in their arsenal, ready to use at just the right moment? Why else had they been so quick to take it down?

But maybe they'd been foolish enough to believe they'd done so in the nick of time, before anyone had seen it. Luckily for him, Alison had added herself to the ranks of *Mad Mum*'s devoted followers the day after Kate agreed to proceed with the case.

And his little sister missed nothing.

'Very well. Do you then, or indeed the court, have any objection to it being read out loud by a third party?'

'Judge, how is this relevant? Mrs Cooper's missive to her social media followers is hardly of interest to the court.'

'Oh, it is indeed of interest, Mr McGuinness, and also very pertinent to the witness's current line of testimony, as we shall soon discover. Mrs Cooper?'

Madeleine nodded almost imperceptibly and the judge waved a hand.

'Proceed, Counsel.'

At this, Alison stood up and cleared her throat. If, as it turned out, Madeleine did not want to read out her blog post, Declan felt it better and more impactful to have her words be read by another female, so as to closely associate them in the judge's mind with the defendant.

Or to be more specific, her plea.

'"I know there are a lot of opinions out there on what is happening at the moment with my daughter, my family, and the

O'Hara family. Yes, I openly admit that my husband and I did not vaccinate our children against MMR – we have never hidden that. We have our reasons – they are multifaceted and very personal – and I don't wish to discuss them on a public forum. But, in short, and following extensive research and much soul-searching, we are not completely convinced of the MMR vaccine's safety. The risk involved in participating with the vaccine programme is one my husband and I could not, in good faith, take with our own children. The worry of bringing them to harm by doing so, taken against the risks borne from contracting a disease, were just too great. Additionally, my eldest son Jake had measles when he was eighteen months old, and, like my daughter Clara, recovered well with no ill effects. For us, that risk of not vaccinating paid off, in that our children both contracted the disease yet remain healthy and unharmed.

'"Kate O'Hara chose to take the same risk in not vaccinating, but for health rather than personal reasons. And while my daughter recovered well, her little girl Rosie is now fighting for her life in the hospital.

'"I feel so sorry for Kate and would honestly do anything for her so that she could experience the same thing as I did: a happy healthy child who has made a complete recovery. But since I can't do that, all I can say is that I am sorry – from the bottom of my heart, I am sorry that this has happened, and for my part in it. If I could somehow go back in time to change things, I would. But I can't.

'"I cannot imagine how scared Kate must be at the moment, or how helpless she feels. And to the people who don't know me, who are criticising me and calling me a terrible parent, I want to say that I never claimed to be Mother of the Year, nor do I want to.

'"Most of us parents are just trying to do the best we can, one day at a time. I will try to do better in the future, but, for what it's worth, I'm truly, deeply sorry for any harm my actions might have caused."'

At those words, a loud hush enveloped the courtroom and, having said her piece, Alison sat down.

'Quite the apology, for someone who says they don't believe they are at fault,' Nevin commented, a quizzical expression on his face.

Declan felt elated. It was fairly categoric; in her own words, Madeleine Cooper outright admitted she was to blame for what had happened.

'When you wrote this piece, what were you sorry for, Mrs Cooper?' pressed Nevin. 'What did you mean when apologising "for your part in it"?'

'That post was written in the heat of the moment,' she replied shortly, and Declan was pleased to note that finally she seemed to be losing her cool.

There it was: the chink in her armour. Her profile.

Nevin didn't say anything; he was waiting for a continued explanation. 'Mrs Cooper?'

'Look,' she went on, a noticeable quiver now in her voice, 'at the time I wrote that piece I was receiving a lot of flack. People were sending me hate emails and posting insulting things online, telling me what a bad mother I was. Complete strangers were lambasting my parenting skills and calling me names. One journalist in particular was buzzing around, asking questions and stirring things up – all because of some personal beef she had against me. There was so much anger and pushback about the vaccination thing from people I don't even know. And it just kept on coming and getting worse. I did feel sorry for Rosie and bad for Kate – I still do – and, of course, I felt guilty that my daughter was the one who'd emerged unscathed. I hadn't been able to contact Kate or get through to her, and I wanted to get the word out that, yes, maybe I made some bad choices, but I wasn't the villain people were making me out to be.'

'You mean you wanted to try and save face?'

'Objection!' shouted Michael McGuinness. 'Judge, he's badgering the witness.'

'Sustained. Mr Nevin, please watch your tone.'

'Understood,' the barrister replied and Declan realised that it really didn't matter if that last comment had been disallowed. They'd needed to paint Madeleine as self-serving – someone who perhaps even spoke out of both sides of her mouth – and it had worked.

'My apologies, Mrs Cooper. Let me rephrase that question; did you write the blog post because you felt personally responsible for Rosie O'Hara's condition, or for some other reason?'

Now they had just presented Madeleine Cooper with a complete Catch-22. If she answered yes, then it was an admission of guilt. If she said that it was for another reason, she came across as insincere; someone who would say anything in order to make herself look good.

Her truthful answer here would either win this case or at least show her true character to the judge, which might help them win it anyway. He thought for sure that McGuinness would offer a further objection – even though doing so might look like he too was trying to prevent an admission of guilt, which wouldn't play well with the judge. But when the defence barrister's silence continued, Declan knew that Madeleine was going to have to show her hand, and answer the question truthfully.

'Mrs Cooper?' Nevin pressed. 'Did you hear my question? Did you write that post because you felt personally responsible for Rosie O'Hara's condition?'

Madeleine took a deep breath. 'No, I did not,' she said with resignation.

Nevin nodded and crossed his arms. 'Then why did you write it?' he asked simply.

'Because I was upset by people harassing me online. And, on top of that, I'd just been offered a publishing deal for my blog, and I suppose I didn't want to mess that up,' she added defeatedly. Now, she appeared resigned, as if there was no choice other than to come clean.

Pursing his lips and narrowing his eyes, the barrister continued, 'Yes, I'm sure that is quite upsetting and hard to deal with.' Then, as quickly as he could, he added, 'Being harassed online and potentially losing a publishing deal must be very upsetting indeed, compared to the stress, worry and fear associated with having a child seriously ill in hospital.'

Madeleine's face looked drawn and it was clear she was finding this line of questioning a lot more harrowing now. While this morning, she came across as reasonable and rational, now she was being painted as selfish and insincere.

Nevin was moving on. 'So while you don't accept responsibility for what has happened to Rosie directly, you do admit that by choosing not to vaccinate your daughter against serious disease, you increased the risk of her not only contracting such a disease, but passing infection on to others, do you not?'

She nodded uncertainly, but didn't reply, clearly unsure as to what she should say.

'In which case,' Nevin continued, 'it would be reasonable to assume you would be more inclined to evaluate such a risk when either of your children showed any signs of illness, would it not?'

'It's not that simple. I had no idea measles could get that serious.'

'But it did, didn't it? Certainly in Rosie O'Hara's case. Honestly, Mrs Cooper, can you not appreciate how your and your husband's actions, or should I say inaction in this situation – in not vaccinating your children – potentially made it far more dangerous for the general population should they fall ill? And in your blog post, by wishing you could go back and change things, you openly admit neglecting to take that fact into account when you sent your already sick daughter to school. You said it yourself this morning, Madeleine; you made a call. Turns out it was the wrong one.'

Madeleine sat forward, her expression pained as she realised the trap Nevin was laying for her. 'But... I never meant for *any* of this to happen, of course I didn't!'

'Don't get me wrong, Mrs Cooper, I do sympathise. We see such situations in this court all the time, the driver who didn't mean to cause a fatal accident by sending a text while behind the wheel, the hospital staff member who made the wrong call during a routine procedure. The point is, these actions all have consequences, some of them devastating, and, in Rosie O'Hara's case, life changing. Just because you didn't *mean* to do something doesn't make those consequences go away. And in choosing not to vaccinate your child, Mrs Cooper, and going against proven HSE-approved immunity recommendations, your inaction created a default duty to protect other children in your daughter's immediate environment – an onus to be mindful of other, more vulnerable children such as Rosie. A duty of care you chose to ignore.'

There was complete silence in the court as Patrick Nevin's words were driven home not just to the entire court, but Madeleine Cooper too.

'I was just trying to keep them safe!' she argued, tears in her eyes. 'I couldn't do it... not after what I'd seen with Cameron, not when I'd seen a perfect little boy change before my eyes. All the medical assurances in the world can't make you discount what you've seen with your own two eyes. I just *couldn't* run that risk with my children and, yes, you're right, I didn't consider the effect this might have on others, or on the greater good. But for crying out loud, who the hell *does*?'

At this, an awed gasp cut across the courtroom from the media gallery.

Oh wow, Declan thought. Here we go. After being made to stay silent for so long, now they were really seeing *Mad Mum* in all her glory.

She wiped at her eyes furiously, as if offended that tears should dare make an appearance in the court, but then she stared defiantly back at Nevin, evidently deciding to own what she had just said.

'If somebody told you to throw your child under a bus for the sake of the greater good, would you do it? Of course not! But that's how the MMR vaccination felt to me. Why should making the best decision for *my* child somehow make me responsible for someone else's? Any mother – if she truly felt her child was in danger – would do the very same thing. And, Kate, when it came down to it,' she pleaded, looking over at the plaintiff's table, her blue eyes now boring directly into the other woman's as she addressed her directly, 'didn't you make the very same call?'

Chapter 49

'Kate, Kate! What is your response to Madeleine Cooper's testimony this afternoon, particularly her assertion that you are just as much to blame for Rosie's illness? Kate? Kate, do you think that Madeleine Cooper has a point? Did your own decision regarding Rosie's vaccination—'

'Please; I just want to go home now. My daughter is waiting…'

'Let us past, please! It's been a long enough week.'

'Kate, like Madeleine said in court, if you could go back in time and change things, would you alter any of the choices you made?'

'The very idea is nonsense, of course. But if I could go back in time, it would be to the dinosaur expo Rosie and I visited over the school holidays in the RDS, the last time I saw my daughter truly healthy and happy.'

'But, Kate…'

'Thank you. Please… we need to go. As Kate's representative, I'll be more than happy to make a full statement when all of this is over.'

*

A complete and utter disaster.

Madeleine still couldn't get over just how badly her performance on the witness stand had turned out to be. How had she *ever* thought it would be a good idea?

She had known deep down that the damning blog post had been out there somewhere, but still she'd been rattled by it. And then if that cocky barrister hadn't done enough in getting her worked up by throwing her words back in her face, he'd also succeeded in making her angry enough to try to defend herself by basically suggesting that Kate was just as much at fault for Rosie's troubles.

She could only imagine what the judge, let alone the public, thought of that.

Case closed.

Far from coming across as rational and sympathetic, now she looked like the world's most heartless woman. Her head ached with the reality of it all and she felt like throwing up. She couldn't bring herself to watch any news coverage of the trial, or listen to what the talking heads on TV were saying; Madeleine already knew that they were going to lose, and that when the trial resumed next week, the judge was sure to rule against them.

Their lives as they knew it were over. She and Tom were going to have to completely remake themselves – her especially. Now, there was no going back to blogging, would definitely be no more radio or TV segments. All of that was over, for good. All her good work undone. Publishing deal withdrawn, advertising pulled.

Nothing left of *Mad Mum* but a collection of blog posts that now, in hindsight, seemed trite and naive.

And when she considered the bigger problems they were about to have financially, as well as personally – after today Tom hadn't known what to say to her – her head swam with anxiety.

Looking around her already scrupulously clean kitchen, Madeleine needed something to do. The kids were in bed and Tom had been holed up in his office since they got back from court. He said he had some work to catch up on, but Madeleine knew better. Likely her husband was examining their bank statements, checking their insurance limits and protections. Thanks to his wife's performance that afternoon, Tom had no choice but to concede that however spurious Kate O'Hara's claims might have been, it wouldn't be long before the judge cleaned them out and handed their life savings over to her.

How were they going to survive this? Madeleine wondered, as she made her way upstairs to her office. Frankly, she had no idea, but she knew what she could do. In fact, it was something that had been on her mind for a while now. She had been putting it off over the last year in case things miraculously turned in their favour.

Tonight though seemed like a fitting time to check this last task off her to-do list.

It was time to delete her website and all of her social media pages.

Mad Mum was dead in the water.

Sitting down at her desk with a heavy heart, Madeleine recounted all the happy times she had spent chronicling her life as a parent, from the early days of Jake and Clara's babyhood to the trials of the toddler years, and now their school going exploits. It was a montage of sorts, all this detailing of her children's comings and goings through her eyes, and logging their adventures as a family. She had the sudden thought then that maybe she should just unpublish it, rather than delete everything in its entirety.

After all, weren't these a big part of her family memories?

No, she thought, no sense in looking back. Already Madeleine knew that going forward, her life would be divided into two parts: Before the Trial and After the Trial.

And, in truth, it would probably do her sanity some good if she did just delete all of this stuff. She would then also be spared the temptation to go online and read all the angry judgemental opinions complete strangers seemed so dedicated in making known to her. The hate mail was something that she wouldn't miss.

Not in the least.

Logging on to her website, she pulled up the email platform that held all communications coming through the *Mad Mum* contact form. As expected, there were endless messages from angry people who felt it necessary to offer commentary on her testimony that day. And, as always, her parenting choices.

She didn't read any of them. Madeleine simply clicked 'delete' as she made her way down the list, emptying the inbox as quickly as she could.

But all of a sudden, one email in particular caught her eye. It had been flagged as of 'high importance' and a little red flag sat next to the sender's name. The email address didn't ring any bells, but the subject line was enough to stop her in her tracks: *Rosie O'Hara not your fault and I can prove it*.

Curious, but wary that this blatantly intriguing subject line was simply another tactic to get her to open the message before bawling her out or worse, Madeleine prepared herself for a verbal – albeit virtual – assault.

Instead, she found a simple message from a City College student called Scott Ferguson.

Furrowing her brow, she felt like her synapses weren't connecting fast enough. Was it just some Medicine student who thought they had something interesting to say about the spread of infectious disease? Or perhaps another one of those flag-waving social justice warriors so eager to attach themselves to their anti-vaccination stance, considering it a fashionable 'cause'. Students seemed to be all over that kind of thing.

But, for some reason, and she truly couldn't say why, Madeleine was intrigued. And there was no denying that their defence of this case was at rock bottom, so why not? If this kid had something to offer, be it 'proof' or otherwise, how was it going to hurt at this stage?

Hitting reply to his email, she wrote, 'Thanks for your message. Intrigued by subject line.' Pressing send, Madeleine found herself shocked when a message popped back up in her email inbox not ten seconds later. Scott, whoever he was, was obviously online at that very moment.

At the end of the message, Scott offered his phone number for her to call. And within seconds of reading his message, Madeleine had him on the line.

I'm sorry I didn't get in touch sooner, but I've had my head down studying and haven't really been keeping up with current news events. But I'm pretty certain that your daughter didn't infect that little girl with measles, and I think I can prove it.

Chapter 50

Striding toward the courthouse the following Monday morning, Declan had a strong feeling that the judge would adjourn for deliberations first thing.

And if not, this afternoon at the latest.

Before Madeleine's... performance on Friday, I would have definitely been worried about this. Indeed, there was still a considerable amount of angst sloshing around in my stomach about how all of this was going to go, but, at the same time, Declan's confidence was contagious. The realisation that this could all be over soon buoyed my spirits.

What did *not* help my spirits was the memory of Madeleine's words, now seared into my consciousness that I had made the same decision, and that by choosing not to vaccinate Rosie, I was equally responsible for what had happened to her.

It wasn't as if I hadn't already had that thought myself, but the fact that Madeleine felt much the same way about the MMR autism risk, gave me food for thought.

If she was truly worried for her children's safety, was genuinely terrified that the vaccine would cause harm to Jake or

Clara, in the same way I'd worried about Rosie's allergy, then how could I realistically castigate that decision?

And despite all the denials and studies debunking the autism link, it would indeed be very difficult to take a chance and simply trust that everything would be OK, when you'd seen another child change utterly in front of your own eyes.

Anecdotal yes, but weren't most parenting decisions borne from personal experience? Yes, Madeleine had made a mistake in not recognising the additional risks posed any time one of her children contracted an infection, but again, like any parent, she couldn't realistically be on alert twenty-four hours a day.

But most of all, seeing and listening to her on the stand that day, I'd finally got what I'd always wanted, the one thing from Madeleine I'd always felt was missing right from the very beginning – genuine contrition. That wasn't a simple rehash of her face-saving blog post or a half-hearted attempt to smooth things over by sending gifts; it was a genuine apology and what I could see was huge remorse on her side.

The woman had been suffering too, possibly more than I knew, and in more ways than one too, when I thought about how she'd been vilified and ridiculed, not only by the general public, but amongst our own community.

While, all along, everyone had my back.

And I had to admit that after all that, taking the stand and facing down her detractors took courage, even if she'd likely blown it all in the end. Much to Declan and the legal team's delight. But now, I couldn't help but feel that if Madeleine Cooper was guilty of anything, it was of being her own worst enemy.

Still, we'd all come way too far to back out now, and while I might have done things differently if I'd had the opportunity to hear Madeleine's side way back, now I needed to push on and let this play out, for Rosie's sake at least.

The state only covered so much of her rehabilitation expenses and equipment, and I needed to do the best for my daughter if I wanted to give her the best chance of a full recovery. I owed it to her.

Approaching the entrance to the building, and the sea of media that seemed to live outside, I remembered that out-of-the-blue comment I'd made after the trial broke up for the weekend to that journalist Gemma Moore when she'd stuck a microphone in my face outside the courtroom. About how that dinosaur expo had been the last time I'd seen my daughter truly happy and carefree.

It was true and I would give my right arm to see Rosie back playing with her dinosaurs and creating havoc in her bedroom as she faced down one plastic herd of carnivores against another of its herbivore rivals.

I hoped against hope that day would come soon.

'Well, if everything is coming to an end shortly,' I said to Declan, 'I certainly won't miss all this.' I waved my hand in the media's direction.

He stole a glance at me and smiled. 'Not keen on the spotlight, eh? I must say though, you were pretty good with that journalist on Friday afternoon, really spoke from the heart. Which was great, as we needed the focus to remain on Rosie and not on what Madeleine Cooper said.'

But today, just as we had in previous days, we walked through the mass of cameras, keeping our eyes focused on the doors in front of us. I said nothing and Declan kept up his usual script of 'No comment' to their litany of questions.

I'm still not quite sure what it was that had made me stop

and say something to them the other day. Possibly because Madeleine's words had made more of an impression on me than was comfortable. In any case, it hardly mattered, but it did have the effect of making them even more insistent than usual, and now they crowded around, blocking our entrance, hoping for a fresh insight.

Making our way purposefully into the building we headed towards the bank of lifts and waited to be taken up to the fifth floor. I straightened my shoulders. Come to think of it, I wouldn't miss this building either when all of this was over. I had better not get called for jury duty any time soon, I thought ruefully to myself.

Then again, I did have a very good reason for being excused.

A moment later, we were exiting onto our floor. Some errant reporters had made their way in and now waited outside the courtroom. That had been happening more frequently, hence my broken silence the other day. I spied Gemma Moore amongst their numbers and, acknowledging her from before, I made brief eye contact, but that was it. Her relentless pursuit of Madeleine over the last year or so had in fact scared the living bejeezus out of me, and now I didn't want to do anything else to ignite her interest in me.

Declan held the door to the courtroom open for me and I entered. The room was just then only about half full, and we took our usual seats without hesitation.

Madeleine, Tom and their solicitor weren't there yet. Glancing at my watch, I realised it was only about ten minutes or so until our Monday morning session was scheduled to start. Weird. They had been here bright and early all last week and I wondered if they were held up in traffic. Or had perhaps just given up?

But if they had, surely we would know about it?

Saying as much to Declan as we got settled, he shrugged and said basically what I'd been thinking, when suddenly the court bailiff approached us.

'Mr Roe?' the man said. 'Judge Dowling requests to see you and your client in his chambers this morning.'

Declan wore a confused expression. 'What's this about?'

The bailiff shrugged. 'I don't know, sir. If you could follow me, please.'

After gathering the papers that he had been arranging on the table, Declan shoved the lot back into his briefcase and nodded to me. I grabbed my things and followed unquestioningly.

'What's going on?' I whispered to him.

'I really don't know,' he replied, looking concerned.

In my mind, I started going through all of the possible scenarios that could have happened in the previous weekend that we needed to have a private audience with the judge. Had Madeleine and Tom been in an accident, and were waylaid at the hospital? Maybe after her testimony they had decided they wanted to settle? Or perhaps they'd skipped the country and were currently headed to Timbuktu? Idea after idea floated through my head – all of them wrong.

Nothing – *nothing* – could have prepared me for what happened next.

The bailiff opened the door to the judge's chambers and upon our entry we discovered that Madeleine and Tom weren't running late, nor had escaped the country. They were already there, as was their solicitor, Townsend. There were also two other people in the room: one a younger man I didn't recognise, aged around nineteen or twenty I surmised, as well as an older gentleman who had the look of another solicitor or legal representative of some kind.

The younger of the two looked as if he had just rolled out of bed a half an hour ago and found a crumpled and ill-fitting suit balled up in the back of his wardrobe. He wore a pair of glasses that seemed far too big for his face, but held himself in such a way that it was evident he was confident about himself – appearances aside. He met my gaze with a knowing look that conveyed he felt he was the smartest person in the room just then.

The look chilled me.

The other man looked to be somewhere in his mid-sixties and was carrying on a quiet discourse with Judge Dowling – it was clear that they knew each other. How, I wasn't sure. The man wore a carefully tailored navy blue suit and his hands were manicured and buffed. Well turned out and put together. I was curious to know who these two strangers were and what their sudden involvement in our case could be.

'Ah, Mr Roe and Ms O'Hara,' said Judge Dowling. 'Good morning.'

Declan seemed to be studying the room. 'Good morning, Judge.' He paused. 'Forgive me for being so blunt, but I'm hoping someone can tell us what is going on.'

'Yes, yes, of course. Not our plan to catch you unawares, but something important has developed over the weekend,' replied the judge. 'Mrs Cooper, I believe you wanted to say something.'

I turned my attention to Madeleine, who had been sitting quietly next to her husband. She wore an expression on her face that I was unable to read, but I noticed in that moment that her hands were shaking. She was nervous about something. I wondered if she was about to say they were ready to mediate a settlement.

Turning to face me, she said, 'Kate, an interesting piece of information emerged on Friday evening. Something important. And, even in light of all that has happened, I didn't feel it appropriate to present this in court and catch you off guard – I didn't want you to feel like you had been blindsided.' I listened carefully to her words, realising that this was the first time we'd conversed with one another outside of that terrible day in the grocery store. 'I know that this has been a difficult experience. For all of us.' She glanced around the room and rested her eyes briefly on the young man who had not yet been introduced – to us at least. 'But I think that this new information could change what happens next.'

I felt completely confused. Honestly, was anyone going to tell us what the hell was going on? Glancing at the solicitors, and then returning my gaze to Madeleine, I said, 'OK, seriously, what's going on? Who are these people?'

Madeleine continued. 'Kate, this is Scott Ferguson, he's a biology student at City College. Scott contacted me on Friday via my website about some information that he thought might be important to me – to both of us really.' Looking at the older man, Madeleine said, 'And this man is his solicitor, John Fleming.'

I still didn't know how these two people fitted into our case and, while I waited for someone to offer a further explanation, the student spoke up.

'Ms O'Hara, I contacted Mrs Cooper after something you said in the six o'clock news report on Friday caught my attention. It isn't because I am interested in your case or the controversy surrounding it. It was because of what you said, about your daughter and the dinosaur expo.'

I frowned, taken aback. 'What has that got to do with anything…'

'Well, it caught my attention because I was a guide at that exhibition. I work on a part-time basis in the RDS during the school holidays. Mostly, I'm responsible for talking people through the various exhibits and answering questions about the displays. Regardless, the news report followed up with a mention that you had attended the Dinosaur Live expo, followed by a picture of your daughter on screen. I remember her.'

The student's solicitor obviously read my confused expression, because he held up a hand to Scott.

'Ms O'Hara, I have been fully briefed on the details of your case and the nature of the legal proceedings currently before the court. I understand that your and Mrs Cooper's children contracted measles largely at the same time, and that the thrust of this case has been focused on appropriating blame for the infection. Well, we are here to tell you that you can no longer blame the Cooper family for your daughter's illness. It was almost certainly Scott who exposed her at the exhibition, because he was deeply infectious with the disease at that time.'

Chapter 51

My mouth dropped open. 'I'm sorry – what? I don't understand!' I exclaimed and Declan moved to put a comforting hand on my arm.

'I remember your daughter; she was talking about Mosasaurus and how the latest *Jurassic Park* movie got the details all wrong,' Scott continued. He smiled a little. 'And I agreed with her, but it was only the other day, when I saw her picture on the news report, that I put two and two together. Over the weekend, I contacted a buddy at the RDS who was able to pull the security footage for the dates in question, and we brought that here this morning for you all to see. I figured that would be necessary to prove my involvement.' He motioned to a laptop situated on a table next to the judge. On the screen a black and white video was paused – it showed the inside of the expo location and a mass of people congregated in groups around the various dinosaur exhibits.

'In any case, I probably wouldn't have made the connection at all and wouldn't have shown any interest, if that journalist hadn't talked to you. Like I said, I remember the day you and your daughter were there, and it was the following day that I ended up going home early from my shift because I was feeling so off. I couldn't get out of bed after that and was out of commission for almost two weeks.'

I was shaking my head, still in disbelief when Declan spoke up. 'You were diagnosed with measles at the time? I assume you reported your infection to the RDS?'

Scott continued, 'Well, firstly, I didn't actually realise until now that what I had actually *was* measles, because I am vaccinated. So I suppose it's very possible that I'm a non-responder. I only compared my symptoms with what was standard for the virus when I thought there might be a connection between myself and your case. I did phone Care Doc at the time last year, and they said it was likely a viral infection – and I wasn't going to spend more money going to a GP or the hospital, when I know that viruses cannot be treated. As you know, Ms O'Hara, since you are a nurse, antibiotics don't do anything for viruses and, as I had no further complications – my symptoms were mild and nowhere near what either of your daughters experienced – my only option was to sit at home and wait the thing out. Mrs Cooper, I understand that your daughter did much the same.'

Madeleine nodded solemnly. 'That's right. We just kept Clara at home until she was feeling better.'

'Measles is one of those diseases that is very manageable, if it's not too serious,' stated Scott knowledgeably. 'So I managed it. Recounting my experience with the benefit of hindsight, yes, I had a slight rash, as well as the coughing, sneezing, sore throat, fever, all of those things. I loaded myself up on vitamin A, vitamin C, zinc, Paracetamol and what have you, drank plenty of fluids and I got rest. However, I now realise I was also contagious. Dangerously so.'

Hindsight…

John Fleming pulled the laptop closer to him. 'Ms O'Hara, Mr Roe, it's probably best if you watch the security footage.'

Declan and I both approached the laptop like it was a ticking time bomb. As Fleming pressed play and pointed to where Scott was on the screen, I immediately spied Rosie on the day we attended the expo. She was chatting to Scott beside a Triceratops display, nodding attentively while also touching and inspecting the various elements that Scott – who all the while kept sneezing and coughing into his hand – indicated.

It was something of an otherworldly experience – as I watched this strange man visibly infect my child with an invisible virus that would fester within her for the next few days, waiting to rear its ugly head and change our lives for ever.

I watched the tape back a few times until I was clear of one thing – the most important thing – which in itself led to a terrifying realisation: Clara didn't infect Rosie with measles.

In fact, it was the other way round…

I turned to Madeleine Cooper, my eyes full of remorse and mortification. 'I… I'm not sure what to say.'

To her credit, she, and indeed her husband, didn't appear superior or dismissive towards me. As I struggled to find more words, Declan asked a question. 'Where would you have been exposed, Scott?'

'Well, I started trying to figure this out once I realised it was measles that I actually had. My best guess is that I picked it up in the lab at some point. I had a molecular biology module earlier this year that paid great attention to the spread of infectious diseases. Measles is a member of the Paramyxoviridae family, and we worked with some strains of this disease in the lab – family members I mean, not necessarily a live measles virus. I'm thinking that perhaps whatever strain we worked with actually morphed and changed, which is possible with viral structures such as this. Like they say in that old dinosaur movie, nature always finds its own way – nothing anyone can do to prevent it. And coupled with the fact that your immunity becomes reduced as you get older, which would be impactful for me if I did happen to be a non-responder, it's completely possible that my blood contains fewer igG antibodies…'

John Fleming held up a hand as his client grew more and more animated.

'Scott, I really don't think it's necessary to go into that much scientific detail,' admonished his solicitor.

'Right,' the young man said, realising that the majority of his audience did not hold scientific backgrounds in molecular biology, and therefore were unimpressed by such an explanation. 'In any case, I think I'm going to write a paper on it. Maybe I can get it published.'

The solicitor cleared his throat. 'I hope it goes without saying, Ms O'Hara, that Scott deeply regrets the distress caused to you and your daughter as a result of further complications from the virus transmitted. But I am here today primarily to protect his interests, given the seriousness of the current court proceedings despite the fact that there is no issue of negligence on Scott's part nor the university's —'

I put my hand up, stopping him from saying any more. 'That won't be necessary. Of course I don't intend to hold Scott liable,' I assured, feeling sick to my stomach that people saw me as 'that person', someone who would sue everyone in sight for the slightest wrongdoing.

But, like it or not, I had become that person, I realised, looking askance at Madeleine and Tom Cooper who were both watching me closely, relief written all over their faces.

And who could blame them?

When, in the end, I had got it all so terribly wrong.

'Obviously my client and I will need some time to discuss this new development.' I felt Declan's hand at my elbow, as he addressed the Coopers and the judge.

But, as far as I was concerned, there was nothing to discuss. I'd made a huge mistake, had cast aspersions and made serious accusations towards people – my own neighbours – that had proven utterly false. Because I was aware of the Coopers' vaccination stance, I'd made a huge assumption, automatically blaming their daughter for visiting misfortune on mine when it had been the other way round.

The other way round.

Oh God, did this mean that the Coopers were now going to come back and countersue me, not only for infecting Clara, but for the unbelievable suffering and disruption they'd endured over the last year and more?

The very idea made me feel dizzy.

'Kate, are you OK?' Declan asked, as he led me into another side room off the judge's chambers no bigger than a broom closet, and I wondered idly if the room existed for this very purpose – to house people who took frivolous cases before the court and needed to reflect on their idiocy.

'Of course I'm not OK. Didn't you hear what was just said, see that guy on screen *actually* infect Rosie?'

'Well, from a medical point of view, and certainly from a legal one, that's not conclusive…'

'Oh come on, Declan, we both know this is a mess, a complete disaster! The judge has no choice but to dismiss the case now. In fairness, I wouldn't blame him if after all this, he wanted to put me in jail.'

'I can assure you', Kate, there's no way something like that will happen—' he began, but I knew he was unable to truly grasp the extent of my despair. How could anyone?

'What am I going to do?' I whispered, my voice sounding frail even to myself.

How would I get over this? Not only had I made a monumental mistake, which had already cost me a huge amount emotion-ally – to say nothing of financially – caused needless hassle and heartbreak to another perfectly innocent family, but, in the end, it had all been for nothing.

'It's a shock I know,' Declan replied, his tone reassuring as always. I looked at him then, thinking about what a wonderful man he was, and how incredible he'd been throughout all of this in so many ways: the case, keeping my spirits up while Rosie was still in the hospital, being a shoulder to cry on, as well as helping us tackle many day-to-day domestic concerns since she came home.

In short, he'd got me through everything.

And I could only imagine how much my problems had cost him personally and professionally; how he'd given up so much of the legal practice's resources, as well as forgone so many regular paid cases, and indeed his own personal time and energy, to help me out.

How would I ever repay him?

'I don't know what to say to you except sorry,' I began. 'I'm so sorry for dragging you into all this. It never crossed my mind for a second that Clara might not have been the source of infection. I was so dogged about it…'

He waved my apologies away. 'Try not to think about that now, Kate, there's no point going down that road. We could only work with the information we had to hand.'

'But we can't pretend that this isn't a huge disaster in every way. When I think of your fees… and all the bills for Rosie's care…'

The world was starting to swim before my eyes. I had no idea what I was going to do to make things right. An apology to all parties concerned would be a start, of course, but after that? I had no idea.

All along I'd believed (prayed) that this trial would be the light at the end of the tunnel, and that if I just kept working towards it, everything would work out for the better.

I could never have imagined that the light would turn out to be the headlights of a fast-approaching train.

Chapter 52

'In what has presented itself as a startling turn of events on week two of *O'Hara* v. *Cooper*, I am standing outside High Court Buildings this Monday lunchtime amongst a crowd that is still in shock over this morning's abrupt dismissal of the case – a lawsuit that has divided the nation and given rise to strong opinions from all sides in the controversial vaccination debate.

'It is being reported that some new information came to light over the weekend that effectively invalidated all claims in the legal proceedings against Tom and Madeleine Cooper issued last year by Kate O'Hara on behalf of her daughter Rosie.

'With us now to illuminate these new findings are City College biology student, Scott Ferguson, and his solicitor, John Fleming. Gentlemen, thank you both for agreeing to talk to *Sky News*…'

*

Judge Dowling was gracious enough to allow the group of former plaintiffs and defendants to leave the court building through a service entrance out back. Dealing with the media frenzy out front would have been way too much, especially as all parties were still managing their shock and trying to absorb what had just happened.

Madeleine was reeling all weekend from Scott's revelations, and had been so eager for the judge to learn the glorious truth that would get her and Tom off the hook on Monday morning, that she hadn't properly considered how Kate would react.

But, she warned her husband and Matt Townsend, there would be no triumphant courtroom posturing over Kate's mistake; hence her insistence that the legal team introduce Scott in private.

In this situation, Madeleine realised sadly, nobody won.

For her part, Kate had informed the judge that she wanted to drop the case and wasn't going to drag it out any longer. Yes, she had suffered a loss of income and other hardships, and she and Rosie would continue to live in an altered reality, but what had happened was no one's fault, it was just nature doing what it did.

Viruses evolved and people got sick.

'I'm so sorry,' she kept saying to Madeleine, clearly distraught. 'I was so certain…'

'You weren't to know. Try not to think too much about that now, and just go home to Rosie,' she soothed, while behind her she felt the weight of Tom's incredulous stare.

'She's bloody lucky we're not going to take her goddamn lawsuit and throw the very same charges back in her face,' her husband fumed, as all parties quietly made their way outside to the waiting car.

But it was not the time for remonstration or gloating.

Up ahead, Declan opened the door of their car so Kate could climb in. However, just as she was about to enter, she turned back to look at the vehicle that had pulled up behind it, where she and Tom waited for their lift home.

Madeleine paused then to meet Kate's eyes. The two women

held each other's gaze for just a moment, and something passed between them. All at once it seemed to communicate a mixture of regret, forgiveness but not quite acceptance, Madeleine realised. It might have been resignation that, yes, this whole ordeal might be over, but there were still other struggles that needed to be addressed within their small community and within each of their respective families.

There were still issues that both she and Kate had to face.

The time for placing blame was over. Now it was time to address a new reality.

Chapter 53

A week later, Madeleine was standing in her kitchen, loading the dishwasher, and reflecting on her life – and her family's life – over the course of the past year and a half.

Everything felt so… odd.

The case had been so abruptly dismissed that she was still trying to process what had happened. It had only been days since that meeting in the judge's chambers, yet it felt like an eternity.

However, at least life seemed to be returning to normal.

The press coverage had subsided, thank goodness, or finally they had decided that Kate and Madeleine's feud was yesterday's news. Yes, a few journalists were still calling, looking for a comment, but the majority now seemed to be focusing on just how 'at risk' the general public was for transmitting highly communicable diseases, and just how dangerous places like the RDS, the various museums or other so-called 'child-friendly' places happened to be.

In the wake of the dismissal, Matt had broached the possibility with Tom about potentially issuing counter proceedings against Kate or indeed the university authorities, but Madeleine had very quickly shut that idea right down. She'd had enough legalities and so had their family; their lives had been upended in the worst way and they needed to get back to normal. Thankfully, Tom had agreed with her, joking that maybe now would be an ideal time to buy stock in a company that produced highly effective hand sanitisers. Madeleine had appreciated his attempt at humour – it was a step towards returning to normality.

Yes, they had bills to pay, and challenges to face and definitely fences to mend as they tried to get family life back on track, but she was confident that they had withstood the storm. She and her Tom had faced without doubt the most challenging time of their married life together, but they would prevail.

However, she also knew that in order for that to become a reality she needed to reassess some priorities. So she decided that from now on, she wanted to remain focused on being a mum privately, and forget all about the public side.

There was no point in worrying about her public image if her private life was a disaster. Madeleine was just going to focus on her family, and be happy. She was well aware of how close she had come to losing everything.

As she pressed 'start' on the dishwasher, her ears perked up at the sound of a car pulling into the driveway outside. Leaning forward to peer out the window, she thought it interesting that she didn't feel in the least bit surprised when she saw Kate O'Hara getting out of a battered-looking car.

Wiping her hands on a dishtowel, Madeleine headed to the front door, not waiting for the other woman to ring the doorbell. She stepped out into the cool autumn air.

Kate, who had been walking up the front path, stopped in her tracks and eyed her warily, like an animal who had just been spotted by a predator.

But Madeleine offered a small smile. 'It's OK,' she said, easily plopping down on the leaf-covered front steps. Regardless of how she felt, she knew Tom wasn't quite at the stage where he'd want Kate O'Hara comfortably ensconced in their front room. This would have to do for now. 'I won't bite.'

Kate approached the steps and sat down next to her. Neither of them spoke for a beat, but then Madeleine did. 'I was wondering when you would come.'

'How did you know I would?' Kate asked, glancing at her out of the corner of her eye.

'I just did.'

Another beat of silence passed.

'Is your husband here?' asked Kate.

Madeleine shook her head. 'No, he's back at work. It's weird how quickly life picks up where it left off, isn't it?' Then she winced, suddenly realising that Kate and Rosie's lives were still far from being back to normal. 'Sorry about that,' she said quietly.

'No worries,' said Kate. 'We're managing. We will manage.'

Turning to Madeleine, she ran her hands through her hair. 'I knew I needed to come over here. I knew I needed to tell you again I'm truly sorry – for all of this. I was so, so wrong. And I was too embarrassed to face you until now.'

But Madeleine was already shaking her head. 'But you didn't know that you were wrong. No one could have predicted how this would turn out. I certainly couldn't have.' She offered a small laugh. 'You know, I was thinking I really have Gemma Moore to thank, in light of everything. If it hadn't been for her issue with me, she might never have stuck that microphone in your face, and Scott would never have made the connection or had anything to do with us. Life is weird sometimes.'

Kate nodded, looking downcast. 'It's a bit overwhelming to think about, actually. And when I think that I was blaming you for something that wasn't even your fault, and dragging your family over the coals…' She stopped, her voice choking. 'Madeleine, I can't even begin to tell you how sorry I am for what I put you and your family through. There are… no words.'

Placing a comforting hand on her arm, Madeleine leaned in to her. 'I know it wasn't all you either. And yes, I was angry about it, especially when I really didn't believe I'd done anything wrong. But I'm pretty certain that you had other people in your ear.' She didn't say Christine's name, but she didn't need to. 'I also know that many people in Knockroe have very strong opinions about me and my family, and our parenting decisions over the years. You've been through the wringer over the last while yourself, and I can't even begin to put myself in your place. But, you and me, we've only done the things we did because we both love our kids, and it's our job to keep them safe. How is Rosie now?'

Kate smiled. 'She's still Rosie, and yes, she still has a lot of work ahead of her, we both do. She's showing great progress though. We have a brilliant carer who helps out, but well, we probably are going to make some changes with that now. I need to find a way to get back to work, and I also have to consider moving.'

Madeleine nodded sympathetically. 'Will you stay in Knockroe?'

Shrugging, Kate admitted, 'I don't honestly know. There are a lot of uncertainties at the moment.'

'And your solicitor?' she enquired with raised eyebrows. It was clear what she was implying, but Kate only shrugged, deferring the question.

Accepting this, Madeleine said, 'If there is anything I can do to help, I hope you will let me know.'

Shaking her head incredulously, Kate said, 'Actually, I think that's my job to say that, and offer the same to you.'

'What on earth are you talking about?'

Kate continued on, 'Well, it's all because of me that you and your husband ran up what I am sure is a sizeable legal bill. And I wanted to tell you that maybe I can't pay everything all at once, but I plan to take full responsibility for that.'

Madeleine looked at Kate with an open mouth. 'You must be joking. Please, while I appreciate your attempt to make amends, I have to say that we certainly don't expect this of you. You have other things to worry about.'

'But you can't be expected to pay out all that money for…' Kate insisted, but Madeleine shook her head.

'It'll be fine, honestly. Believe it or not, I've had offers to write a book about all this.' She smiled at the irony. Her *Mad Mum* tome might have been put on the back burner, but since the trial ended, there'd been a slew of newspapers and publishers lining up for Madeleine's take on her treatment by the media and the public, in the wake of what turned out to be false allegations. 'You don't mind, do you? Obviously I'll consult with you on all aspects concerning Rosie and—'

'Lucy was right,' Kate laughed through her tears. 'You are a good person. And I'm so sorry I didn't believe her, or take the time to call you back all those times you tried to talk to me before… everything. I wish I hadn't been so stubborn.'

At this, Madeleine could only nod sadly. 'Me too.'

Chapter 54

As I left Madeleine's house, I had to admit that the weight I had been carrying around like an anvil for the past week had been lifted off of my shoulders.

Of course, I had been totally genuine in my offer of paying the Coopers' legal bill, but it was also a huge relief to know that the offer was declined. I knew I would be struggling to climb out of my own debt hole for quite some time and I really hadn't had a notion how I would pay their bills too. But I knew I had to offer.

Driving the couple of miles across Knockroe that separated the Cooper house from my own, I realised something else was nagging me now though.

Declan. He was on my mind constantly, and while he and I had communicated a little since the trial ended, we hadn't talked face to face since he'd dropped me home from the courthouse that Monday morning.

If I was being honest, I missed him – I had grown so used to having him around that the sudden absence stung on some level. I knew he and Alison were working on getting the practice back in order after the mayhem of *O'Hara* v. *Cooper*, just as I was trying to establish a new normal in my home, but that didn't erase him from my thoughts.

Yes, I was attracted to him, I might as well admit that. And given the few... awkward moments we'd shared, especially in recent weeks, I was pretty confident that the feeling was mutual. But was I ready for a relationship if the prospect of one was even in the offing?

I had become so used to being on my own – and with all the upheavals Rosie and I had experienced – would it even be fair to Declan, if he did want to be with me? Was it right for him to be involved with, or more correctly shackled to, someone with as much baggage as I had? Did I even *remember* how to share my life with someone?

As I turned onto my road, a million different thoughts danced around my head – and none of them made clear or concrete sense. But all of them came to a grinding halt when I realised that regardless of if I was ready or not to face those realisations, I would have to.

A car was parked in my driveway – Declan's Volvo. And the man himself sat on the front step. He smiled broadly as he watched me approach, and my heart did a little flip.

After pulling my car up next to his, I got out of the driver's side and shut the door behind me. 'Well, this is unexpected,' I said lightly. 'I figured that I wouldn't be seeing you much, since I'm no longer a client. Although, let me guess – you have my bill, which is obviously so huge it needs to be delivered physically.'

He got up from where he sat and grinned at me. It was odd to see him so casual. I was so used him in suits – all buttoned up, pressed and proper. Today though, he was wearing a pair of jeans, suede boots and a dark blue sweatshirt that brought out the colour of his eyes. 'Well, technically, I *am* still your solicitor,' he said. Then his voice grew serious. 'And there is another pressing legal matter we need to talk to about.'

From his back pocket he extracted a brown envelope. The outside of the envelope was addressed to me, but care of Declan's office. The seal was broken and it was clear that Declan or Alison had opened the communication. He handed it to me and my heart sank.

What now?

'This arrived at the office yesterday. I wanted to make sure it was kosher before I gave it to you.' He paused for a moment as he took in my questioning expression. 'You probably should sit down.'

Furrowing my brow, I continued standing and opened the envelope, extracting a letter. 'Oh God. What?' I asked, an all too familiar dread seeping through me. Had the Coopers decided to sue me after all? Maybe the judge had, in fact, decided to punish me for wasting the court's time? Either way I was sure it wasn't going to be good.

'Just read it,' Declan said. 'And then we should talk.'

Unfolding the letter, I was caught off guard when a piece of paper that looked like a cheque fluttered out. I caught it in mid-air and looked at what it said. My eyes grew wide when I read the figure inscribed.

'What on earth!' I exclaimed as I looked to the accompanying letter for explanation. What I found was a simple note. It read:

Dear Ms. O'Hara: It is our hope that you will accept this sum (strictly without prejudice) on behalf of the City College Biology Department. The situation that you faced is unfortunate, and we feel our laboratory is on some small level culpable for the misfortunate events that led to your daughter's sickness, and ultimately her current challenges.

With a clear understanding that this sum doesn't provide all the answers – nor is any admission of liability – we do hope that it might go some way towards alleviating the burden of what you and your daughter have faced. Very best wishes for the future and we hope that medicine, science and innovation help your daughter regain her independence in the near future.

My mouth dropped open. This cheque wasn't massive by any means but at least enough to allow me to pay some of Rosie's recent care bills while I was in court, help me make a start on Declan's legal bill and, most importantly, allow me the breather I needed to pick up the pieces while I figured out what do next.

It was an absolute gift and I knew I certainly didn't deserve it.

But perhaps Rosie did?

'This can't be real…' I was in a state of shock. My hands were shaking and my heart was hammering in my chest.

Declan chuckled. 'It's real, Kate. Someone from the biology department are apparently very eager to make sure their lab doesn't receive bad press or get shut down. That, or they are just really good Samaritans.'

'This is more than just a nice gesture though,' I said, still unable to believe it. This was the best thing, perhaps the *only* good thing, that had happened to me in an age. 'And I already said I wasn't taking any further action – this is just too much.' Then a thought struck me. 'Declan, you can't possibly think I should take this. Can you?'

I looked back down at the letter. No way was this really happening to me. It was just too good to be true.

'Well, it's up to you what you do with it,' he said slowly standing up, and I noticed his voice had changed. He shoved his hands in his pockets and looked at the ground. 'However, I should tell you that I'm now no longer in a position to offer you legal advice.'

Turning my attention from the documents in my hand to the man in front of me, I met his eyes, confusion rushing through me. Was there some sort of hidden liability here that I wasn't considering? I wondered, frowning.

'What do you mean? I trust you, Declan. I need you to tell me what you think.' He hadn't guided me wrong since I first met him, and now I trusted him more than I'd trusted anyone in a long time – since Greg in fact.

'Well,' he continued, meeting my gaze, his eyes twinkling now, 'there is another reason for my visit – outside of this.' He motioned to the envelope. 'Delivering it was officially my last professional duty to you. Kate, I can't be your solicitor any more.'

He took the documents out of my hands and placed them on the front step. Then, without further hesitation, he reached for me, encircling my waist in his strong arms. He pulled me close so that our bodies were touching, and my breath caught.

'I'm officially ending our professional engagement,' he said huskily when, finally, the meaning of his words hit me.

I felt an all too familiar blush creeping up my neck. But, this time, I didn't fight it. 'But what if I'm feeling litigious again?' I teased.

'You're out of luck. And, for the record, I think you have experienced enough courtroom action for one lifetime.' He smiled, pulling me yet closer.

'Counsel, I thought you said we should talk.' I grinned up at him, feeling so giddy my head was spinning. 'This doesn't look like talking. And it doesn't feel like—'

'To hell with talking,' Declan interrupted, his voice thick with emotion.

And then he kissed me.

EPILOGUE

Rosie sat next to the Christmas tree in the living room of their house. She had overheard her mum and Declan talking a while back about the possibility of them moving to a smaller house – somewhere easier for her to move around in her wheelchair – but then nothing came of it.

Declan had told her mum that she shouldn't be too hasty, and to try to take one day at a time.

Rosie thought he was right. Of course, it had helped a lot when Declan moved in with them just after Halloween. He was lovely – she really liked him and he seemed to really love her mum. And Rosie was happy when she saw her mum happy, too.

Which was a lot these days.

Of course, Rosie knew that she and her mum had gone through some terrible problems when she got sick, and that she was still dealing with the effects of all that. She also knew that she wasn't exactly the same as how she was before, but her mum and Declan were helping her get better, and were always cheering her on.

So she knew everything would be OK.

Yes, there were times when she got really frustrated because she felt like her brain knew what she wanted to do, but couldn't make her body do it. And she pronounced words a little weird.

But the doctors – physical and speech therapists, her mum called them, kind ones that really helped her – said she was making great progress. Rosie didn't even really need to use her wheelchair much any more, which was great. She hated that thing and only used it when she was really tired. She had her walker most of the time now, and she felt herself getting stronger all the time.

Because she really, really wanted to go back to school to see her friends and learn to be a palaeontologist.

'OK, Rosie, who's next for a present?' Declan said, sitting on the other side of the tree next to her mum. He wore a huge smile – in fact, he couldn't stop smiling – probably because her mum had said 'yes' earlier, and was now wearing a pretty diamond ring on her left hand.

'I don't know,' said her mum, crawling closer to the tree to get a better view. 'These all look like they are for Rosie from Santa. Somebody was obviously very good this year. You keep on opening them, sweetheart.' She and Declan then settled back on the couch across from the tree, enjoying watching her open her presents.

While her movements were still a bit awkward, Rosie leaned forward and moved some of the remaining presents around, checking the labels. Yes, they all had her name on them. She smiled happily at the realisation, but then remembered that gift for her mum Declan had helped her with.

'Mum,' she said, pronouncing the words determinedly. 'Here's one for you.' She was proud that she had got so much better at talking recently and she had practised this a lot. She scooted around to right herself as she reached over to her walker, and hoisted herself to a standing position.

'Oh don't worry. I can come over there and get it,' said her mum with concern in her voice. Declan nudged her arm – silently encouraging her to give Rosie the space to do her own thing. He did that a lot and she appreciated it. She wanted to do things on her own more than anything else.

'It's OK,' she said, moving the walker across the wooden floor ever so slowly.

Something dawned on her as she started to move, her steps heavy and stomping, and the notion that she must look a bit like a T. Rex made Rosie giggle.

But she felt good. And, most importantly, her legs felt good, too. Slowly, as she gained confidence, she pushed the walker to one side.

And much to the astonishment of her mum who cried out with amazement and tears, Rosie walked towards her mother all on her own.

Just like she and Declan had planned.

Acknowledgements

Lots of love and thanks to Kevin and Carrie, and to my family and friends for their continued support as always.

Impossible to put into words just how important Sheila Crowley – my incredible agent and wonderful friend – is to me. I truly don't know what I would do without you, S, thank you. This one's for you.

To Katie, Abbie, Rebecca, Luke, Anne and all the team at Curtis Brown for championing my work so well in translation and film; I really appreciate it.

To my amazing editor Anna Baggaley who made this story infinitely better for having worked her magic on it – and to the wonderful Lisa Milton for championing the book from the outset; working with you both has been such a joy, thank you.

To the brilliant UK HarperCollins team in London – and also Annemarie, Tony and the gang for such a warm welcome to the HC family in Dublin. Big thanks too to Margaret Marbury O'Neill and the Mira team in the US.

Huge gratitude to the fantastic booksellers all over the world who continuously give my books such amazing support, and a special thanks to Irish booksellers for being so generous with their time whenever I pop in for signings.

Thank you Janice Philp Davidson for helping with a small, but very crucial part of my research; I'm so grateful, and am sure it's only a matter of time before one of Jason's stories hits the bookshelves.

As always, huge, huge, thanks to readers everywhere who buy and read my books. I'm so very grateful and I really love hearing from you.

Please do get in touch via my website **www.melissahill.info** or Facebook, Twitter and Instagram.

Keep You Safe is very special to me and I really hope you enjoy it.

HQ
One Place. Many Stories

The home of bold, innovative
and empowering publishing.

Follow us online

@HQStories

@HQStories

HQStories

YouTube HQ Stories

HQMusic